ELIZABETH VILLARS

Wars of the Heart

DOUBLEDAY & COMPANY, INC.
GARDEN CITY, NEW YORK
1987

YOU CAN'T SAY NO TO A SOLDIER by Harry Warren & Mack Gordon
Copyright 1942 by TWENTIETH CENTURY MUSIC CORPORATION
Copyright Renewed in 1970 by TWENTIETH CENTURY MUSIC CORPORA-
TION
All Rights Throughout the World Controlled by MORLEY MUSIC CO.
International Copyright Secured All Rights Reserved
Used by Permission

SAY IT by Frank Loesser & Jimmy McHugh
Copyright 1940 by Famous Music Corporation
Copyright Renewed in 1967 by Famous Music Corporation
Used by Permission of Publisher

Library of Congress Cataloging-in-Publication Data
Villars, Elizabeth.
Wars of the heart.
I. Title.
PS3572.I38W3   1987   813'.54   86–13529

ISBN: 0-385-19569-9
Copyright © 1987 by Elizabeth Villars
All Rights Reserved
Printed in the United States of America
First Edition

For Nina

A GREAT MANY PEOPLE helped me find my way back to the war years. I would like to thank for time, help, and materials so generously given: Margie Dyer, Pearl Hanig, Anna Jane Hayes, Meredith Kay, Saul Lapidus, Jerome Link, James Morrow, Josh Reibel, Judith Schwartz, Nick Tobier, and Brooke Wayne. I am also grateful to Lewis Kay for his research of the battle of Bougainville; to Mark Piel and the staff of the New York Society Library; to Jack and Barbara Noone for aid and inspiration; to my editor, Susan Schwartz; and especially to my agent, Amanda Urban, for her faith; to E. Russell Snyder for his vivid and moving memories of the war; and to Stephen Reibel for uncommon valor in the field.

WARS OF THE HEART

1

EAST SIXTY-SEVENTH STREET
NEW YORK CITY

"NOTHING," Isabel Childs said, staring at the Sunday paper that was black with bad news, "separates men from women like war."

From behind her own paper Grace Childs glanced at her daughter. "And nothing drives them together as recklessly."

Isabel looked up from the bold letters that scurried across the front page like insects. ROOSEVELT APPEALS TO HIROHITO AFTER NEW THREAT IN INDO-CHINA; GERMANS TRAPPED AT TAGANROG. "I was talking about danger, courage, that sort of thing. You're worried about sex."

Grace put down the paper and looked at her daughter. There was no point in arguing. In sex as in everything else young people thought they'd cornered the market. She went on staring at her daughter. Isabel's face was angular, like the sails of the old square riggers that had made her ancestors rich, her nose straight and a little too proud, her eyes wide and intelligent. She wore her silky copper-colored hair in the pageboy style of the day that made every girl look beautiful from behind. Isabel was not beautiful, though she attracted men as if she were. She had good bones, a lean, well-disciplined body, and a simmering restlessness that was evident in the way she moved, the way she sat, even the way she spoke. Isabel's voice, low, throaty, and unbearably promising, had been known to conquer men over the telephone. And Isabel had been known to respond in kind. She went through men the way she did books, at a fast and heady clip. Isabel Childs was looking for something, and the times and world she inhabited dictated that she look for it in a man rather than herself.

For the past few months she'd been looking for it in Jack Livingston, but that was beginning to fade. Only last night, tangled together in the backseat of a taxi, she'd felt the first quietings of passion. Like the first stirrings, they filled her with a terrible unrest. She stood, stretched, and held the paper out to her mother.

"Leave it on the table for your father, dear."

"Aren't you even interested in the war news?"

"Your father and I have an agreement. I don't try to run the world, and he doesn't interfere in the house. Besides, I'm reading about the war. There's an article here in the *Tribune* about our military base in Pearl Harbor."

"Pearl Harbor?"

Somewhere on the chill December streets of the city a siren sounded. The noise shattered the Sunday afternoon quiet. It might have been an ambulance or fire engine racing with disaster or merely a civilian defense team rehearsing for it. Whichever, the sound barely penetrated the thick draperies of the second-floor sitting room.

"It's in Hawaii." Grace handed the paper to her daughter, and Isabel glanced at the photographs. Men in helmets, khaki, and military leggings marched beneath arching palms while fighter planes flew in neat formation over Diamond Head. It was a travel piece. War was as distant from that tropical Eden as from her own life.

Then her father entered the room, followed by her brother Spencer dragging his own little piece of the war in his wake. "You talk to him, Grace," Eliot said. "Maybe he'll listen to you. God knows he won't to me."

Spence slumped in a chair and ran a hand through his sandy hair. His father stood behind him and smoothed his own that was only a little grayer. They were both slender men of moderate height and faintly overbred appearance. The veins at the temples of their long, lean faces throbbed blue and tense. A stranger would know them for father and son. Both of them would have been surprised by the fact.

"He has six months till graduation. Six months!" Eliot repeated. "There'll be plenty of time to enlist then. We're going to get into this war, and it's going to go on for a long time. I promise you that." There was a hard certainty to his voice, as if he were capable of promising such things. "Graduate from Yale." His voice softened slightly. "Join the Navy. Then with a little luck—and a little cooperation from you for once—I'll get you assigned to Admiral Stark's staff."

Spencer flung a gray flannel leg over the arm of the chair. On a tennis court, a yacht deck, or a horse he had an uncanny agility. He was good, he liked to say, at all the things that didn't matter. "I don't want to be assigned to the admiral's staff."

"You'd rather get your ass shot off somewhere over Europe." Eliot's eyes darted to his wife and daughter. In his anger he'd forgot himself. Eliot had his standards where women were concerned. There were a variety of things he'd do with them that he wouldn't mention in front of them.

"Other guys are."

"Other guys are damn fools. Also dead heroes. Other guys are not—"

"I know, I know. Your son."

"There are worse things to be."

"I didn't mean—"

"I know what you meant." Eliot turned and started out of the room. "You talk to him, Grace. Maybe he'll listen to you."

"Of course, your father's right," Grace said after she'd heard the heavy doors to the library across the hall slide closed. "It's only six months."

Spence looked at his mother across the gulf of years that turned six months into a lifetime. "And after that a nice cushy job on the admiral's staff where I'll be known as old Eliot Childs's boy."

"You ought to be proud to be—"

"For God's sake!" Isabel interrupted. "Do it! If you're so hot to fly, stop arguing and sulking and trying to convince everyone, and just go out and do it."

Spencer's eyes met hers. They were the same size and shape and

shade of hazel. They were eyes seen in a mirror, except that gold
lights were going off in Isabel's.

"I'm sorry," she said.

"No, you're right."

"He's right. You might as well finish school. It's just that then
you'll be able to enlist. And I'll still be stuck here, collecting bundles for Britain and raising money for the Free French, and"—she
stopped and caught her breath—"and damn it, still feeling sorry for
myself." Her long upper lip grew longer with disapproval. "Forget
it. Forget everything I said." She left the room quickly, but after
she was gone, the air still had a charged feeling, as it often does
after a storm that has threatened rather than occurred.

Isabel climbed past the third floor, past her mother's room and
her father's. No battles raged here. Her mother was the Neville
Chamberlain of marital relations. She'd settled for peace in her
time.

On the fourth floor Isabel went into her own room and turned on
the radio. Glenn Miller filled the air. Ray Eberle promised he'd be
seeing her. A suitcase filled with the few things she'd brought home
from school for the weekend stood open on the luggage stand. She
tossed in a copy of *Coming of Age in Samoa* and some history notes
she'd never got around to looking at and was just closing it when
Spence appeared in the door. "I guess we know who has the balls in
this family."

"Talk, to coin a perfectly new cliché, is cheap. Anyway, it was a
stupid thing to say. I don't want you getting your ass shot off any
more than they do. I—"

"Forget it." He flung himself into a chair. "I'm sick of the whole
business."

"Consider it closed. Tell me about last night. What happened?
One minute you were with us, the next you were gone."

"Sally wanted to go back to the Stork."

"And the fatal Sally always gets what she wants."

Spence turned away and began to fiddle with the radio dial.

"I'm sorry," Isabel said, "but I just don't see what you see in
her."

"I wouldn't expect you to."

"In other words, sex."

"Don't ever let anyone accuse you of being a romantic, kiddo."

"No one ever has."

"Not even Jack Livingston?"

"Unlike you, he *is* only interested in sex."

"I don't think so."

"You weren't in the backseat of that taxi last night."

"Men who are only interested in sex don't go around talking about marriage."

Isabel looked across the room at her brother and grinned. Her mouth was thin and wide, her smile knowing.

"Okay. You have a point," he said. "But I still think Livingston's serious."

"Jack may be, but I'm not."

"You're going to have to marry someone eventually. You can't spend the rest of your life falling in and out of love. There's a name for people like that."

"Actually there are two. Women are called tramps. Men are bachelors."

"What do you have against marriage, anyway? They can't all be like theirs."

Isabel would have known whom he meant even if he hadn't nodded toward the door. "They're not all unfaithful, if that's what you mean, but they're all unbalanced."

"Unbalanced?"

"I know a girl at school who goes through two packs of Camels a day. She's engaged to a man who says he has no intention of allowing his wife to smoke. Another girl I know campaigned for Roosevelt in the last election. Her fiancé thought it was 'cute' she was doing something, but he said that no wife of his was going to vote for 'that man' let alone work for him."

She walked around the bed and sat on the edge facing him. They remained that way for a moment, their knees, like their sensibilities, not quite touching. "Tell me, Spence. Why are you so eager to fly?"

His eyes slid away from hers. "You know. To do something. To prove something, I guess. To get away from him. To get free."

"Exactly," she said. "To get free. It's the one thing you and I aren't. With all our advantages—God, how I hate that word—and all our money, we aren't free. And I don't think marriage to Jack Livingston or anyone else is going to make me that way."

2

CENTRAL PARK WEST
NEW YORK CITY

ELIZA KRAMER lay in bed not so much listening to Michael's breathing as feeling the warmth of it against her shoulder. He slept on his side, one hand curled childlike beneath his cheek, the other arm thrown across her body. She debated getting up—there were a million things to do before everyone arrived—but she didn't want to wake him. Michael could sleep through Teddy's crying and the neighbors' parties and the noise of the street four floors below, but Eliza's slightest attempt to escape from under his arm set off an alarm.

She wished she could go back to sleep, but the worries had already begun to take form in her consciousness like figures emerging from a fog. Would she be able to get the ends of the roast well done enough for her father and keep the center rare enough for Michael? She hoped he and her brother-in-law Harold wouldn't get into another argument about the Hitler-Stalin Pact or who was doing more for the Jews of Europe. She prayed the maid would keep her word. Dolly had sworn she'd be in this morning, but Dolly's complicated love life, which took place mainly on Saturday nights, made her unreliable for Sunday dinners. Eliza rarely invited anyone on Sunday, but today was an exception. Today was a magical date, more important than her birthday. Today was her wedding anniversary. She'd been Mrs. Michael Kramer for five years.

Michael coughed and shifted position. His trim dark mustache tickled her shoulder. His arm still pinned her to the bed. Another worry marched across the horizon of her mind. She hoped he liked his present. He had to like his present. She'd been saving money from her grocery allowance for months. When her mother had told her father about her plan to pay for Michael's gift that way, her father had thought the idea so cute that he'd called and offered to give her the money. But Eliza had been determined to save it herself, even if it meant cutting corners on lunches for her and Dolly. She wouldn't skimp on Teddy's meals and couldn't on Michael's. He'd notice if he didn't have his steak on Thursday night and his roast beef on Sunday. Of course, she could have asked him for a bigger allowance. He would have given it to her in a minute and made some sweet corny joke about how it was lucky she was pretty because she certainly wasn't smart with money, but it didn't seem fair to ask Michael for a bigger allowance to buy him a present, any more than it did to take the money from her father. She had to save it herself. That way the golf bag was really from her.

She looked at the clock on the night table. It was almost ten o'clock. She was glad her mother had taken Teddy for the night. Still, she had to get started. She twisted slightly beneath Michael's arm, not enough to wake him, not really. His lashes fluttered. He sighed. He opened one eye. A brown globe, soft as mink, focused on her. "I'm sorry," she whispered. "I didn't mean to wake you."

"What time?" he groaned.

"Almost ten."

"Teddy?"

"He's at my parents. Remember?"

He remembered. He opened both eyes. "Happy Anniversary." He kissed her shoulder. "Happy Anniversary, Mrs. Kramer." His arm tightened around her. "How many years is it again? Ten? Eleven?"

She put her arm around him. His skin beneath the pajamas was warm and smooth. She traced the long line of vertebrae that she'd learned to massage whenever his back went out. "You know it's five."

He kissed her. "You getting tired of me, Mrs. Kramer?"

She shook her head. Her nose grazed his cheek. He smelled of Yardley shaving soap and cigarettes. He smelled exactly as a husband ought to. "Never."

He kissed her again, a sweet, lingering, not exactly morning kiss. Then he seemed to change his mind and rolled away from her. "I want to give you your present."

He got out of bed and walked to his dresser, a wiry, compact man, dapper even in pajamas. He moved lightly on the balls of his feet, alert, aggressive, a middleweight champion. His dark hair was neatly clipped, his mustache trim. Only the early-morning stubble on his cheeks detracted from the air of perfection.

He returned to bed with a small box. Eliza recognized the Tiffany wrapping. Both their families were scandalized that Michael bought retail. She was the only girl she knew who had an engagement ring from Tiffany. Her mother had said that if Michael had gone to her jeweler he could have gotten something twice as nice for half the price. "Twice as big," Michael had answered, "but not twice as nice."

"Wait, I want to get yours," Eliza said, and slid out of bed.

He watched her cross the room to the closet, her body small and trim beneath the clinging satin nightgown he'd bought for her last birthday. There wasn't an ounce of fat on her except for a beautifully rounded bottom that made Michael's hands curl every time he looked at it. She emerged from the closet dragging a big, obviously heavy box.

He laughed as she lugged it back to the bed. "You bought me a new watch."

"A wallet. Open it."

"No, you open yours first."

"Please," she said, and her delicate features took on the wistfulness of a child's, but he shook his head and handed her the small box again.

She untied the ribbon and took the paper off carefully. He always laughed at her for that, because she never used paper again, but she always removed it carefully. Inside the cardboard box was another velvet one. She snapped it open. She gasped. Two tiny diamonds blinked up at her from the white satin.

"Now you'll have to pierce your ears," he said.

"Oh, Michael!"

He stopped smiling. "Do you like them? Really?"

"I love them. How could I not love them? They're magnificent."

"Really?" he asked again.

She leaned across the small pile of wrapping paper and kissed him. "Really. Thank you." She kissed him again. "Thank you, thank you, thank you. Now open yours."

He tore the paper off in two strokes. "The salesman said it's the best one they make. Abercrombie's. But he said you can exchange it if you'd rather have something else. I mean, if this is wrong, you can choose another one. Whatever you want."

"This is right. Absolutely perfect."

"Do you really like it?"

"I love it."

"And you don't mind having to wait till spring to use it?"

"I told you, you sweet little dummy, it's perfect." He got out of bed and slung the bag over his shoulder. "Wait till they get a load of this at the club. All the boys are going to be begging to caddy for me."

He slid the strap from his shoulder and climbed back into bed.

"I'd better get started," she said. "I've got a million things to do, and my parents are always early."

He was stretched out on his back, and he pulled her down on top of him and kissed her again. "Not so fast, Mrs. Kramer. It's your anniversary." He took her hand and held it against him. "And there's one more thing I want to give you."

"What about Dolly?" she murmured as she untied the string of his pajamas.

"Dolly," he said sliding the strap of her nightgown from her shoulder with his teeth, "has never been on time in her life." He slid the satin fabric down her body. "Bless her soul."

Eliza couldn't stop smiling. As she hurried around the apartment, showering, dressing, tidying up, she thought she was more completely happy than she'd ever been. It was her fifth anniversary. They were in love. They'd made wonderful love. Even the timing was perfect. With any luck, and luck was one thing she and Michael had, she'd conceived.

Dolly was late, as Michael had predicted, but so was everyone else. Michael's parents arrived carrying his mother's trinity of culinary specialties—chopped liver, noodle pudding, and apple pie—and Eliza's parents followed with more food and Teddy. Then her sister Pam and her husband Harold turned up, and they all settled in the big living room overlooking Central Park. Dolly brought in the chopped liver with some Ritz crackers, and Michael's father said he wouldn't mind a little *schnapps,* and Michael poured a finger of scotch for his father and Eliza's and highballs for Harold and himself.

Then, just when Eliza was sure everything was going to be all right, Harold started in on Michael. She tried to ignore him, because everyone knew Harold was just envious. Michael had a college and a law degree, and not from CCNY but from Cornell, a real *goyishe* Ivy League University upstate, and a job with Mayor LaGuardia, and a brilliant future in politics, and poor Harold had no degree at all just a lot of angry opinions he called communism, and a job in his father-in-law's wholesale paper business. But pretty soon Eliza couldn't ignore Harold's cracks and had to say something about all the European refugees her husband was sponsoring. Michael shot her a warning look, but it was too late.

"It's easy to play the Messiah," Harold said, "when you've got money. Besides, think how good saving all those refugees is going to make Mike look when he runs for office."

Eliza's father intervened then. He crossed the room to the big RCA console radio and asked everyone to be quiet so he could hear the score of the Giant-Dodger football game. Then her mother said he must have a bet on it, and Michael's father asked to see the new golf bag. Michael went into the bedroom to get it, and Eliza followed him there.

"Don't pay any attention to him," she said.

"I don't, but you do."

"He makes me so mad. I still don't understand what Pam ever saw in him."

Michael picked up the golf bag. "Harold's all right. He's just angry. He should have stayed with his old job. He was making less money, but he was his own man."

"I don't know how you can be so good."

"I'm not good, Eliza, I'm realistic. That's why I didn't want you to say anything about sponsoring those refugees. I knew the meaning Harold would put on it."

"But you don't do it for political reasons."

He shrugged. "Who knows why anyone does anything."

"I know why you do that. Because you're good."

"Eliza," he said, and there was the slightest edge of exasperation in his voice. He dropped the golf bag, crossed the room, and put his arms around her. "Little Eliza." She hated to be called little. Petite was all right, but not little. "I love you. You're a wonderful wife and a terrific mother, but when it comes to politics you aren't exactly Dorothy Thompson. So do me a favor, will you? Let me fight my own battles from now on."

"I was just trying to help."

He ran his hands down her back and let them come to rest on her bottom. "I know you were, sweetheart, and I appreciate it. But don't." His palms traced a lazy pattern. "Okay?"

"Okay," she murmured.

3

LILY HARTARSKI knelt in the last pew, listening to the bell tolling for communion. It echoed through the silent high-vaulted gloom calling her to the body of Christ.

Domine, non sum dignus; ut intres sub tectum meum; sed tantum dic verbo, et sanabitur anima mea. . . .

People were flowing out of the pews, and Lily longed to let the tide carry her along. She loved the sacrament of communion, the solemn march down the aisle, the smooth waxy taste of the host, the light-headed feeling of purity and peace that followed. She loved all that, but she loved Tom Lund too. If it weren't for Tom, she'd be able to take communion this morning.

She'd gone to confession yesterday afternoon, and she'd been scrupulous. She'd been lucky as well because Father Wade had been in the confessional. Father Wade was younger and almost handsome, and he never asked the really awful questions Father Feary did. When she'd told Father Wade what she and Tom had done, he'd asked only one question. Had they gone all the way? That was the way he'd said it, as if he were one of the kids. Father Feary talked about carnal knowledge and demanded details. Did he put his hand here? Did you touch him there? But Father Wade had just asked if they'd gone all the way, and when she'd said they hadn't, he'd told her to say ten Hail Marys. She had, right then, kneeling in the back of the church. Then she'd gone out into the winter twilight feeling as clean as the pale moon suspended overhead. The wind was cold and fresh on her face, and the church spire rose like an icicle into the December dusk.

The sensation of purity and exhilaration had carried her all the way home, and she'd sworn she wasn't going to sin again, not by fighting with her sisters or talking back to her mother or with Tom. She knew that God could see into her heart and know that she meant it, and the knowledge made her run and skip along the uneven sidewalks. Then she opened the door to the smell of boiling laundry and last night's cabbage and saw that her sister Rose was wearing the pink sweater she'd planned to wear with Tom that night. Lily had said, quietly, nicely really, that it was her sweater, and Rose had answered she was only borrowing it, and it had gone on from there with Rose screaming that Lily got all the nice things and Lily shouting that she worked damn hard for the few nice things she had. Then her mother, looking as faded and wrinkled as the shirt she was ironing, had snapped at her to watch her tongue.

The house was quiet for a while then since her father wasn't home yet, and finally Lily had heated up the *kapusta* because there was no telling when her mother was going to get around to it. After supper she'd gone into the room she shared with Rose and Iris, taken her best bra and newest girdle from the drawer, put on her good blue skirt, pulled the white angora sweater over her head, and turned to her makeup. Someday, she swore, peering into the cracked shard of mirror with silver showing through, she'd have a house with a room of her own and dozens of mirrors, full length and three-way and little lighted ones in the bathroom to make sure she always looked right.

She peered more closely now. Lily never forgot to give thanks to the Blessed Virgin that she had the equipment. Not like poor Rose. When they weren't fighting, Lily felt sorry for Rose. With her football shoulders and piano legs and spotty skin, Rose would never get out. They all knew it, even Rose, and that was probably what made her mean. Iris was another story. At twelve, with scarecrow straw hair and arms and legs falling over each other like blades of a windmill, Iris was anybody's guess. Lily hoped Iris would turn out to be the kind of girl who attracts the kind of man who gets you out, but she couldn't even hope for Rose anymore. She couldn't hope, but she could pray, and sometimes when Lily was through thanking the Blessed Virgin for violet eyes and the thick dark lashes that were so startling against that blond hair and not having to stuff her bra with socks, she threw in a prayer for Rose. The nuns said the Blessed Virgin didn't care about such things, but Lily wasn't so sure.

Rose came into the room just as Lily was applying a second coat of Revlon's All Clear Red. "The lips he loves to kiss," she said, and Lily pressed her lips together as much to keep from saying anything as to blot them.

But the silence egged on Rose more than any words would have. She grabbed a faded, torn stuffed rabbit that had been given to Iris too many Easters ago and began kissing it. "Oh, Tom," she crooned. "Oh, Tommy, how I love you." Lily went on pretending to examine her image in the mirror. "I love your three school letters, and your family's big house up on the bluff, and your long shiny Buick convertible. Especially your long shiny Buick convertible. So much more comfortable than going out to the cemetery with Eddie Sadowski."

"I never did anything with Eddie Sadowski," Lily said.

"I mean, Eddie was okay," Rose went on to the rabbit. "Of course, he wasn't rich like you, but that cemetery. You can't imagine, Tommy darling, how cold those tomb stones were under my fanny—"

"Stop it!" Lily screamed.

"My little white fanny that matches your big cream-colored Buick. Oh, Tommy—"

The bell tolled a second time for the blood of Christ. *Corpus Domini nostri Jesu Christi custodiat animam tuam in vitam aeternam.* Lily tore herself away from the memory of Rose's taunts. She longed to heed the call of the communion bell.

Had she sinned last night? They still hadn't gone all the way, but they'd come close, closer than they ever had before. Last night, when she'd pushed Tom away and said no, she hadn't meant it. She didn't suppose she ever did, but last night she'd had not only no

1

will to stop Tom but no breath. His hands did that to her, and his mouth, and everything about him. A hair's breadth away, she'd gasped a hot, lying no, and if Tom hadn't stopped then, she wouldn't have said no again.

At the altar rail the communicants knelt, heads drooping like wilted flowers. It was her last chance. She stood and began edging out of the pew. It wasn't that God didn't know about last night. He knew everything. The Blessed Virgin did too, but Lily had the feeling She forgave, or at least understood more. A part of Lily's mind wasn't exactly private from Them, but it was negotiable territory. There she reasoned with Them. How, she asked, could something that made two people feel so good be bad? But Father Feary and Father Wade and the nuns and her mother insisted that what she and Tom had done in the car last night was filthy, evil, a sin that would send you to hell. And if they were right and she was wrong, if she took communion in a state of sin . . . The enormity of the idea stopped her. She fell to her knees and began to pray.

Lily came out of the dim church into the unforgiving light of the winter morning. And there among all those good parishioners in states of grace, the cream-colored Buick sat parked at the bottom of the steps, smooth and shiny and round as the apple of temptation. From behind the wheel Tom smiled an easy lapsed-Lutheran smile at her. Beneath close-cropped fair hair his broad face was shadowless. On Sunday mornings while Lily wrestled with her conscience, Tom slept late. Somewhere in his background was a hellfire-and-brimstone minister, but the preacher had lost standing as Tom's grandfather and father had made money. Lily started down the steps.

Tom got out of the car. "Hi," he said, and tugged at her kerchief. Cornsilk hair spilled over her shoulders. Several dozen parishioners turned to stare.

He held the door open for her, she slid across the leather upholstery that smelled as rich and mysterious as incense, and he got in after her. "Mom said I could bring you for lunch." That was the way Tom talked. On the rare occasions Lily mentioned her parents, she always said my mother or my father, but Tom just said mom and dad as if his were the only ones in the world.

"Your mother invited me to Sunday dinner!" Lily had never

been to the Lunds for dinner. This must mean things were changing. The Blessed Virgin was watching over her. Maybe she'd gone
too far last night, but she hadn't gone all the way, and the Blessed
Virgin knew it. So now she was invited to Tom's for Sunday dinner.
And if she went on being good, if she didn't give in to Tom or her
own impure desires, if she didn't go all the way, someday she'd be
married to Tom, and then no one in the church or in all of Duquel
could forbid her to do the things she wanted to.

He turned on the ignition, switched on the radio, and inched the
car out into traffic. Lily looked so damn happy, he was glad he
hadn't backed down. His mother had put up a battle, but in the end
she'd given in. What Tom didn't know was that his mother had
given in for a reason. Matilda Lund read books on child and adoles-
cent psychology. They told her that the surest way to drive Tom to
Lily was to try to keep him from her. So Mrs. Lund was careful. She
walked a narrow line, yielding when she wanted to argue, acquiesc-
ing when she wanted to forbid. Matilda Lund had no intention of
allowing her only son to ruin his life because of overactive glands
and an underdeveloped sense of social priorities.

4

EAST SIXTY-SEVENTH STREET

We interrupt this program . . . the voice on the radio said, and Spencer stopped fiddling with the dial.

CENTRAL PARK WEST

President Roosevelt has announced that at one-twenty P.M. *Washington time . . .*

"What happened to the game?" Eliza's father asked.

"Shhh," Michael said.

DUQUEL, IOWA

. . . Japanese planes attacked Pearl Harbor.

"Where's Pearl Harbor?" Lily asked.

Tom didn't know, and he didn't care. He let out a war whoop and pulled her to him.

It's finally come, Isabel thought. Her father had predicted it and her brother had wished for it, but she'd never believed it would really happen. She looked at Spence. He was sitting across from her, one hand on the radio dial as if he were trying to hang on to the news, his body hunched forward, ready to spring into action. She glanced around the room at the bed that her mother and grandmother had slept in as girls, at the silver-backed comb and brush and mirror set engraved with her initials, at the silver-framed snapshots of her and her friends on boats and tennis courts and dance floors. The war had come, but she had a feeling not to her.

"It can't be," Eliza whispered.

"It was only a matter of time," Michael said.

She looked across the living room crowded with the people she loved to the one adult whom she loved more than any other in the world. Michael wasn't looking back at her. His eyes were focused on the carpet as he listened to the newscaster's staccato words. He stroked his mustache with thumb and forefinger as he did when he was concentrating. He wouldn't be drafted, Eliza thought. He was a husband and a father, and he had a bad back. He wouldn't be drafted, but he might be able to enlist. At that moment Eliza would have given a great deal to know what Michael was thinking.

At first, Lily was frightened. She'd seen pictures of war in *Life*. People wounded and crying and looking as if it were the end of the world. Was all that going to happen in Duquel? Then she remembered something else, a movie she'd seen about the last war, the one before she was born. It was about a boy and a girl who'd wanted to get married but hadn't for a lot of reasons that Lily thought were just plain silly. Then the war had come, and the boy had married the girl even though all the silly reasons were still there, and by the time he'd come home from Europe, she'd had a baby, and they'd lived happily ever after. As Tom listened to the news broadcast, Lily kept thinking about the movie, and she wasn't so frightened after all.

5

ALL THAT SUNDAY America stayed beside the radio. The first reaction was one of disbelief, especially since announcements were spotty. Newscasters interrupted the football game and some local broadcasts with bulletins, but neither CBS nor NBC broke into their music programs. Finally at two-thirty both stations announced the attack on their regular newscasts. After that there was little news, only repetition of the confusion. The Japanese had bombed Pearl Harbor. Pearl Harbor was a military base on Hawaii. Early reports indicated little damage had been sustained. People sat in their living rooms, and stood in drug stores and movie lobbies and restaurants, and listened to the bulletins in disbelief. They shook their heads and clicked their tongues and wondered what it meant.

In the house on Sixty-seventh Street it meant that Spence was finally and irrevocably in it.

In the apartment on Central Park West it meant that Michael left his family to celebrate his wedding anniversary without him while he raced downtown to cover City Hall until the mayor could return from Washington, where he'd gone to confer about civilian defense.

In Duquel it meant that Tom Lund exceeded the speed limit all the way back to his house. And on the way, he made two decisions. He was going to be the first one in line at the recruiting office the next morning. And he was going to marry Lily.

The Childses were still in the library. The butler had brought the tray in, and Eliot had mixed the martinis. Now he and his wife were about to do something unprecedented. They were about to listen to Mrs. Roosevelt's weekly radio talk. When, as a young man, Eliot had been forced to dance with Eleanor the wallflower, her voice had grated on his senses. As Eliot frequently observed to his wife, her voice had not improved with the years and her ideas had grown a damn sight sillier. He usually refused to allow the voice or the ideas to enter his home, but this evening he was making an exception.

After her own family and Michael's had left and Teddy had gone in whimpering exhaustion to an early bed, Eliza went into the kitchen, poured herself another cup of coffee, and carried it into the living room. Across the park the lights of the Upper East Side glittered as brilliantly as her new earrings. She wondered where Michael was now. He'd managed a quick call late in the afternoon. The mayor had rushed back from Washington to spend the day racing around in a police car, sirens screaming and Michael in tow, shouting, "Calm! Calm!" Then he'd held a press conference on WNYC to warn New Yorkers against a false sense of security because they lived on the East Coast. Eliza had pictured Michael standing in the background as the mayor talked. She wished he were home now. She looked around the apartment at the furnishings, not old but lovingly familiar. The beige velvet sofa and the long Chinese coffee table were from the small apartment on West Eighty-first Street that she and Michael had moved into when they'd returned from their honeymoon in Europe. She'd bought the imitation Queen Ann chairs and various end tables, ordered the wall-to-wall carpeting and draperies two years ago when they'd taken this apartment overlooking the park. Eliza had said at the time that it was too large for them, and too grand. She'd grown up in Brooklyn, Michael in the Bronx. She didn't know how they'd got to West Eighty-first Street. She wasn't sure they belonged on Central Park West. But Michael had told her to stop worrying. "Leave that to me," he said. "Just trust me," he added, and of course she did.

She kicked off her shoes, turned on the radio, and curled up on the sofa. She'd spent dozens of nights this way, reading or starting poems or short stories she rarely finished, killing time while Michael worked in his office or followed the mayor around the city, killing time while Michael made the money and the decisions and did the worrying.

The Lunds' house was far above the city. From it you could see the wide ribbon of river and, Lily supposed though she'd never looked, her own roof among the greasy jumble of buildings below. The house was midwestern Georgian with a big center entrance hall. There was a large dining room on one side and a huge living room leading into a spacious sun porch on the other. "Big" was the operative word, or so it seemed to Lily. She also noticed that the carpeting and upholstery were thick and soft, the surfaces were polished, and there were lots of pictures on the walls. In the sun porch where they gathered after dinner, which Lily noticed all the Lunds called lunch, there was a darling little spinning wheel. It was, simply, the most splendid house Lily had ever seen, though dinner didn't go as splendidly as Lily had hoped. Nothing was really wrong. Lily watched Mrs. Lund out of the corner of her eye, so she knew to pick up the big fork for her chicken and save the smaller one for the pie. And she didn't have to say anything, not with Tom announcing as soon as they sat down that he was going to enlist and they were going to be married.

Mrs. Lund's foot lingered a little too long on the bell beneath the table then, and Lily heard the demanding sound of a buzzer somewhere behind the closed door to the pantry. Finally, Mrs. Lund caught herself, and the noise stopped. "I understand how you feel," she said. "Oh, I know you both think I'm an old lady, but I'm not too old to understand. Of course, you want to be married right away. And we want you to. But I don't see how it's possible."

"All we have to do—" Tom began, but his mother cut him off.

"If you're serious about enlisting—"

"Of course, I'm serious."

"Then you'll be going off to basic training immediately." Mrs. Lund hesitated. It wasn't a question of the lesser of two evils. She'd do anything to keep her son out of this war, even more than she'd do to keep him out of this marriage, but she knew she was no match for the United States government. Lily Hartarski was another story. "So there won't be time to post the banns and make all the other arrangements." She looked at Lily with an air of complicity. "All the arrangements for a proper church wedding."

"Forget the church. We don't need—"

"Tom!" Mrs. Lund said. "The church is important to Lily even if it isn't to you. You must learn to respect other people's feelings. Marriage is based on mutual respect." She smiled at Mr. Lund. "But if we start making plans now, you can be married when you come home on leave after your basic training. Then you can have a real wedding, the kind every girl dreams of."

Mrs. Lund patted her mouth with the linen napkin, tucked it into the silver napkin holder, and stood. "I hope you'll stay and listen to Mrs. Roosevelt's speech with us, Lily. It's time we got to know each other."

"Thank you." Lily spoke for the first time since they'd sat down. "I'd like that very much." It was one of the phrases she sometimes practiced in front of the mirror.

They all went into the sun porch, where there was a big console radio, and Mrs. Lund motioned to Lily to sit beside her on the chintz-covered sofa. Lily felt bad then for suspecting Mrs. Lund of making all that fuss about a church wedding just to keep them from getting married at all.

Mr. Lund fiddled with the tuning knob of the big console until he got rid of the static. Then he turned up the volume and told Tom's two younger sisters to stop fidgeting. Mrs. Lund folded her hands in her lap and looked serious, and Lily tried to do the same.

I am speaking to you tonight at a very serious moment in our history. The cabinet is convening. . . .

In the second-floor library of the house on Sixty-seventh Street, Isabel crossed and recrossed her legs. She felt as if she'd been sitting in this chair, listening to news of the outside world all her life.

In the living room overlooking Central Park, Eliza looked at her watch. It wasn't even seven o'clock. Michael wouldn't be home before midnight.

In the sun porch of the house high on the bluffs of Duquel, Tom perched on the side of the couch and put an arm around Lily's shoulders. And sitting there in Tom's house beside Tom's mother with Tom's arm securely around her, Lily felt happier than she ever had in her life.

. . . to the young people of the nation. You are going to have a great opportunity; there will be high moments in which your strength and your ability will be tested.

When, Isabel wondered. How.

Outside in the bleak December night a civilian defense siren screamed, and Eliza wondered where Michael was now.

Lily's mind was wandering. She was trying to figure out if the six dollars she'd saved would buy enough white satin for a wedding dress.

I have a boy at sea on a destroyer—for all I know he may be on his way to the Pacific; two of my children are in coast cities in the Pacific. Many of you all over the country have boys in the service who will now be called upon to go into action; you have friends and families in what has become a danger zone. You cannot escape anxiety, you cannot escape the clutch of fear at your heart and yet I hope that the certainty of what we have to meet will make you rise above those fears.

I feel as though I were standing upon a rock and that rock is my faith in my fellow citizens.

Isabel thought of Mrs. Miniver and the brave British she was always reading about these days. She tried to imagine her father patrolling a beach guarding against saboteurs, her mother huddling all night in an underground, herself ministering to maimed and frightened victims of a bombing. She couldn't quite focus the picture.

Eliza was trying to concentrate on the First Lady's words but her mind kept going back to a conversation they'd had over dinner. "Don't worry," her father had said after one look at her face when she'd come back from saying goodbye to Michael. "They're not going to draft him. He's too old."

"He's only twenty-nine," Michael's mother said.

"In civilian life twenty-nine is young. In war twenty-nine is old. Besides, he's married. And there's Teddy. So everyone can just stop worrying about it."

"Unless," Harold said. "Mike decides to enlist."

"Don't talk crazy," her father snapped. "We've got enough trouble just being Jews. We don't have to go looking for more. Mike knows that."

"Mike also knows," Harold went on, "that when this thing is over, every politician worth his salt is going to be running on his war record. Am I right or am I rig' t?" he'd asked the other two men.

And now sitting in her living room listening to Mrs. Roosevelt talk about courage and sacrifice, Eliza remembered that neither of them had answered.

Maybe white lace, Lily thought. Of course, lace would be more expensive.

6

ON DECEMBER 8TH, America's first full day of war, men swung into action and women began to wait. By eight-thirty in the morning, Spencer Childs was in line at 39 Whitehall Street. By five o'clock he'd taken the physical and mental exams, been sworn in as an aviation cadet, and managed to get uptown to Brooks Brothers to be measured for his uniforms.

Isabel spent the day waiting in train stations and on railway sidings. She reached Northampton just before the ten o'clock week-night curfew. The taxi let her out in front of Northrup House. A fresh dusting of snow had fallen over the weekend. The dorm loomed warm and safe across the carpet of white, its windows glowing amber invitation. The scene was Christmas card perfect. It proclaimed peace on earth and goodwill toward man. It denied the very existence of war.

Inside, a telegram from Jack Livingston was waiting. He'd enlisted in the Navy.

She went up to her room. As she unpacked she listened to the familiar post-quiet-hours sounds of the dorm. Bedroom slippers slap-slapped up and down the hall. Doors opened to let out bursts of Beethoven and Benny Goodman, then slammed closed. Voices rose and fell. Radiators hissed. Security emanated like the heat.

She finished unpacking and wandered down the hall. In Sally Sayre's room a group of girls in identical wool bathrobes with satin piping argued the pros and cons of marrying before the boys, who would soon be called men by their drill instructors, shipped out. Sally maintained it was a risky if not foolhardy undertaking. "What's the point of being married, if your husband isn't around?" She caught Isabel's eye. They both knew Spence would be begging Sally to marry him before he left.

Another girl insisted they ought to send the boys off happy. No one mentioned what everyone knew. You didn't have to marry a man to send him off happy. They were nice girls, or at least proper girls, and the boys were nice too. They wanted to sleep with the girls, but in most cases they wanted to marry them as well.

Isabel wandered on down the hall. In another room a civilian defense committee was organizing. One girl had already fashioned a makeshift armband. They solicited her support. "For what?" Isabel asked.

"Patrolling, policing, checking fire equipment, making sure everyone follows the rules."

"Right," Isabel said. "Smith College, the strategic center of the country. No doubt the Japanese and Germans are zeroing in on us this minute."

She went back to her room. The heat was suffocating. She walked to the window and opened it. Icy air stung her face. She stood there until the goosebumps came out on her skin and she began to shiver. Then she slammed the window shut. There was a picture of Jack Livingston on her desk, large if temporary, and a smaller more permanent one of Spencer on her bookcase. You couldn't shut out the cold in the cockpit of an airplane or on the deck of a ship. Jack and Spence were risking life while she sat wrapped in a cocoon of comfort and safety watching it race by.

She thought of the arguments raging up and down the hall. Marriage bands and armbands. Such pathetic puny sacrifices. Isabel swore she'd find a way to do better.

7

ELIZA WAS AWAKENED that morning by the noise of Michael opening and closing drawers. It sounded as if an entire battalion were on the move.

"I think she does it on purpose," he muttered.

"What?" Eliza asked sleepily.

"Dolly. She purposely irons the shirts that are missing buttons. Do you think you could teach her to sew them on first? Do you think that's asking too much?"

Eliza got out of bed, slipped into her scuffs, and padded across the room to Michael's dresser. She took another shirt from the drawer, checked the buttons, and handed it to him. "I'm sorry. I keep telling her to check and sew them on before she irons, but she forgets, and then by the time she notices that one's missing, the shirt's ironed and she doesn't want to wrinkle it."

Michael turned his back as he pulled on the crisp white shirt. "I'm sure it's all very complicated, but unfortunately I don't have time for your servant problems this morning, Eliza."

She sat on the side of the bed and looked at the clock on the night table. "What are you doing up so early? It isn't even six o'clock."

"I should have been at the office hours ago. I never should have come home. Last night the police and the FBI rounded up two hundred Japanese and placed them in detention on Ellis Island. They closed all the Japanese restaurants. Someone's got to take care of the legal side of all that. Not to mention Civilian Defense. There'll be questions about preparedness. Prepared! Hell, I'm not even prepared for the office. You think she could sew on a lousy button."

Eliza rubbed her eyes. "All right. I'm sorry. But don't take it out on me."

That was usually his cue to apologize—he was an animal, a short-tempered beast who didn't deserve a wife like Eliza—but not this morning. This morning Michael had the weight of a city at war on his shoulders and no time to humor a wife.

8

THE LINE outside the Duquel recruiting office formed at six forty-five that morning. Tom Lund was at the head of it. The office was bedlam and processing slow, but the examining physicians were heartened by Tom Lund. They'd spent the last several months rejecting young men whose physical development had been as stunted as the nation's economy. A decade of depression had taken its toll in rickets and scurvy, poor eyesight and pellagra. Tom Lund was six feet one and a half inches tall, weighed in at a hundred and eighty-three muscular pounds, had twenty-twenty vision, quick reflexes, and an ability to pump adrenaline at will on a football field and other appropriate places. By four o'clock Tom was a marine, or rather had been accepted into the Marine Corps. Becoming a marine, he knew, was another ordeal entirely.

Everything began to move quickly then. Tom had a hundred things to do before he left, and Mrs. Lund had a million to do for the going-away party she was determined to give him, and Lily had school and her job at the five-and-ten and the dress she had to make for the party. She'd never been to the country club, and the dress had to be special. No one had time to think about what was really happening, which, in view of what was happening, was just as well.

On Thursday, the day of the party, the day before Tom was to leave the town in which he'd spent his life for the place he was to begin the war, he found himself driving the streets of Duquel aimlessly. At least he thought his wanderings were aimless. He drove along the bluffs, past the empty lot where he'd first discovered that his fast ball was faster than other boys'. He stopped in front of Penny Stickney's house, where he'd learned behind the Stickney garage that little girls liked to kiss him more than they liked to kiss other boys. He cruised through town, down White, up Central, across Twelfth, down Main, past the bank and the various shops where he'd come to realize that adults treated Tom Lund III differently from the way they treated other kids. He went to the high school and listened to the echo of his footsteps in the halls, quiet now during class hours, as he made his way to the gym, where the juniors and seniors on the basketball court gazed at him enviously and the coach slapped him on the back and told him man to man to give those little yellow Nips hell. He drove down to the five-and-ten, even though Lily was still in school and didn't have to work today anyway because Mr. Beezeley, like everyone else in town, knew that Tom was going off to war tomorrow and had given her the day off.

Tom slid onto a red leatherette stool, ordered a cherry Coke from skinny old Mrs. Kick, who worked behind the counter during the day, and sat sipping the sweet thick liquid through a straw and remembering the first time he'd seen Lily. Her hair had been imprisoned by a net and a stiff cardboard crown, and she'd kept her eyes hidden beneath downcast lashes as she'd served him. She'd refused to look at Tom, but he hadn't been able to stop looking at her. The ugly pink uniform, starched and ironed to a wooden stiffness, hadn't been able to camouflage the soft richness of her body. He'd stared and stared until finally Penny Stickney had said something mean about cheap girls in tight clothes, and Tom had finished his Coke quickly and driven Penny home.

"Guess you won't get no cherry Cokes where you're going," Mrs. Kick said. "You know what them Japs eat. Babies. White Christian babies."

"That's just a story, Mrs. Kick." Tom knew all about the Japanese. Last summer he'd read a long article in a magazine. It had a lot of scientific stuff about their eyesight. "Besides, I'm not afraid of the Nips. They can't even see straight."

"It's them funny eyes, I guess."

"So they say," Tom answered and finished his Coke because it was almost three o'clock and he wanted to be waiting in front of school when Lily came out.

As soon as she saw him, she broke away from a group of girls and came running down the steps toward the car. Tom watched her coming, her windblown hair like a streak of sunlight in the winter-gray afternoon, her skin glowing like fire, her long legs bare from skirt hem to bobby socks. He watched her coming toward him and never guessed that he'd carry that picture with him for a long time.

The afternoon was falling into place for Tom. He was beginning to understand what he'd been doing. Now he had one more pilgrimage. He brought the car to a stop at their place on the bluff overlooking the river. Tom had taken other girls there before he'd known Lily, but never since, and never, he'd sworn, again.

He turned off the ignition. The engine died. His arm went around her shoulders. She lifted her face to his. And then it began, the tenderly urgent dance they'd performed so many times in the past. She savored the sweet Coke-spearmint-Tom taste of his tongue. His hand found the buttons of her coat, the crisp blouse beneath, the stiff cotton bra. It moved to her back. His fingers undid the hooks on the first try. There were jokes about that, Lily knew, among the boys and among some of the girls. Once she'd heard Tom called a one-handed bandit. But Lily could never joke about this.

His hands were explorers on the soft terrain of her body. His mouth followed, kindling fires as it went. She closed her eyes and saw tiny flames dancing on the inside of her lids. She opened them and saw the soft fair hair on the back of Tom's neck, the reflection of their bodies in the icy chrome of the dashboard, the bleak, unforgiving winter dusk. She felt him hard and urgent against her and closed her eyes again. The flames were still there, but now they were the flames of hell, rising around a woman's body. She felt them, licking at her, hot and irresistible as Tom's tongue, consuming her legs, creeping up her belly and over her breasts, leaping to her hair. The burning image howled in pain and cried out for forgiveness. Lily's mouth opened. "Stop," she said and wrenched away.

Tom was poised above her, his face set in hard unrecognizable lines, his eyes covered with a thin film like the frost on the windows. His legs still pinned her to the seat. She could feel the icy door handle digging into her bare shoulder. A moment went by. Neither of them moved. No emotion crossed his face. Then he groaned and collapsed onto her. "Lily," he said, but the word was muffled by the soft flesh of her shoulder, and her hand traced patterns of solace on his back.

They drove home in silence. When Tom pulled up in front of the house with its peeling paint and two broken shutters, he didn't bother to get out of the car. Lily sat there with her hand on the cold door handle. "What time will you come back for me?" she asked.

He didn't say anything. He didn't even look at her.

"Tom," she said. "Your party. What time should I be ready?"

His big hands opened and closed on the steering wheel, his eyes stared down the sooty street. "Six-thirty." He raced the engine. "I'll pick you up at six-thirty," he repeated, but he still wouldn't look at her.

Tom was late, late enough for Lily's stomach to begin to ache. Finally, through the cracked front window she saw him coming up the dirt path to the house. She opened the door for him. He stood there almost filling the frame, just looking at her in the new dress with the thin silver straps. Then his face cracked in a smile that revealed his big white teeth and made his eyes almost disappear, and Lily knew that everything was all right.

A broad gravel path, white in the winter moonlight, curled off the main road toward a long low clubhouse. From every window, gold light poured out into the icy night. The sound of dance music and laughter floated on the air like snow.

In the wide entrance hall the air was warm and thick with the aroma of evergreen and burning wood and expensive perfume. A huge tree, cut and decorated early because Mrs. Lund had wanted Tom to have a Christmas tree before he went away, shimmered with light and color. As Tom helped Lily off with her coat, the dress rustled like a million whispered compliments.

Tom took off his own coat. He was wearing a black tuxedo with a starched white shirt that made him look as if he'd just stepped off the screen down at the RKO Palace, and Lily thought she'd die with loving him.

They went into the ballroom and everyone clustered around Tom, but he kept her beside him, his big hand tight around hers. Finally they broke away to dance. Lily moved into Tom's arms and her forehead came to rest in its customary place against his jaw as they circled the floor. Soon other boys tried to cut in, but Tom told them not tonight. This was his last night, and on his last night his girl danced only with him. But then Mrs. Lund came over and said she'd like to dance once with Tom and that he ought to have a last dance with his sisters and some of his old friends. Lily danced with a lot of different boys then, and a few gave her a line, but not many because they were all Tom's friends who were either going off themselves in a few days or weeks or wishing they were. Finally Lily broke away for a few minutes to go to the ladies' room and that was where she found Mrs. Lund sitting alone at the dressing table. Her face was as crumpled as the handkerchief she clutched in one hand and her rouge smeared.

She sat facing her own image as if it were a truth she'd just discovered. Tomorrow, her firstborn, her only son, the child she'd been in labor with for twenty-seven hours, the little boy who used to tell her that when he grew up he was going to marry her, the favorite for whom she saved the juicy dark meat of the chicken or the biggest slice of the cake, was going off to war. He was going off, and he might never come back. Matilda Lund thought of all the meaningless phrases she'd mouthed over the years. No country, no cause, nothing was worth her son.

Lily stood staring at Mrs. Lund. She wished she could pretend she hadn't seen her, but it was too late for that. Was she supposed to do something, say something? She couldn't very well walk up to Mrs. Lund and put an arm around her shoulders the way she would to a friend. She opened her mouth to ask if there was something she could do.

"What do you know?" Mrs. Lund cut her off. She sounded angry, as if Lily had done something wrong. "You say you love him. Love him! You don't even know him."

Lily was too surprised to answer.

Mrs. Lund went on staring at Lily as if it were all her fault. "You don't know the first thing about him. Not his favorite foods or the stories I used to tell him or how frightened he was of thunderstorms."

"He's not frightened of thunderstorms anymore, Mrs. Lund."

Matilda Lund's face collapsed. "You think you're smart, don't you? Well, we'll see how smart you are. Tom's a baby." She started to cry again. "An eighteen-year-old baby who doesn't know his own mind." She was sobbing so violently now, she'd begun to hiccup. "So after he goes away," she screamed, "we'll see how smart you are. We'll see!" Then she went into one of the stalls and locked the door behind her.

Lily stood staring after her, feeling her own tears welling up. She went to the mirror and blotted them. Then she combed her hair and put on lipstick quickly before Mrs. Lund could come out. When she went back to the party, she didn't say a word to Tom about what had happened in the ladies' room. She didn't want to ruin his last night home. And she didn't want to go to battle against his mother.

It was after midnight by the time the last guests finally spilled out into the chill night. They stood around on the wide front porch saying good night and good luck and thank you and good night again, and Lily had the feeling none of them wanted to let Tom go. The women kept kissing him goodbye so that by the time he and Lily broke away his cheeks were streaked with red as if he'd been cut.

He drove quickly now along the familiar roads, shifting gears smoothly at the curves, reaching an arm around Lily's shoulders for the long straight stretches. He brought the car to a stop at their place on the bluff, turned off the ignition, and drew her to him just as he had that afternoon, and she lifted her face to him just as she had that afternoon, but neither of them mentioned or even thought of the afternoon because that had happened dozens of times before, and because this was always new.

With his mouth on hers he whispered that it was fewer than three months, and she breathed the magical date they'd decided on into his ear, and as his hands found their way beneath the white tulle dress, he murmured they'd have his two-week leave as a honeymoon. Then they stopped talking entirely and in the dark steamy car there was only the sound of Tom's short rasping breath and Lily's little gasps. After a while he whispered "Lily" and "love" and "please," and she felt him rising against her and herself falling beneath him and knew this time she would not stop. She clung to him, devouring his mouth with hers, moving against him hungrily. When he tasted the demand in her mouth and felt it in the arch of her back, he stopped. "I have something," he whispered, searching with one hand through the tangle of disgarded clothing.

"No," she said, still holding him to her. "That's a sin." His hand left the tangle of clothing and found its way back to her. He forced himself to move slowly, gently, to bank the terrible fire within him, and she tried not to be afraid. Then all thought and fear and even the small moment of pain faded before the overwhelming, astonishing immediacy of the two of them finally and irrevocably together.

Much later, after they'd made love and talked and kissed and made love again because they were young and had no time at all, Tom said there was nothing to worry about because they'd be married soon anyway. Lily agreed but she was really thinking of a different sacrament. At least they hadn't used anything. Now she'd have to confess only one sin.

9

EARLY BULLETINS on Pearl Harbor had lied, or at least erred. Damage proved to be not only extensive but devastating. The war news grew worse. Wake Island fell. Hong Kong surrendered to the Japanese. The Germans destroyed more tanks in Libya. People read the papers, listened to the radio, and shook their heads in disbelief. This couldn't be happening. Not to America. In fact, it wasn't. The only changes at home during those last days of 1941 were a certain bluing and khakiing of the streets and a desperate intensification of holiday feeling. There was a run on expensive toys, liquor, and bridal dresses. Coming-out parties were transformed into wedding receptions. Isabel served as a bridesmaid six times in ten days. All that romance and champagne conspired to breath new life into her passion for Jack Livingston. She still refused to marry him, but she was determined to send him off to war a happy man. Unfortunately, by the time she made her decision, Jack had given up hope. They'd attended two weddings in one day, and all those bottles of Dom Perignon and Veuve Cliquot had taken their toll. Jack passed out in the backseat of a taxi. The next morning he had to return to New-port.

Spence didn't fare much better. Sally wouldn't marry him, and if she wasn't going to marry him, she certainly wasn't going to go to bed with him, though after a particularly bitter argument when Spence swore, convincingly, that this time he was finished, she did permit him a handful of naked breast, which she'd never done before. Perhaps the war was beginning to change things after all.

A few days after New Year's, Eliot Childs came home to the house on Sixty-seventh Street, mixed a pitcher of martinis on the tray the butler had left in the library, and dropped a bombshell.

"I've volunteered," he announced to his wife and daughter.

Grace put down her glass. A few drops spilled over onto the table. It was the only indication that she was upset.

"In the military?" Isabel said.

Eliot smiled, condescending, perhaps even a little impatient. "In the government. Someone has to show those do-gooders how to get things done. They know how to tax—they know a million ways to do that—but do they know how to turn out planes and ships and guns? Not on your life. Some pretty good men are going down there to show them how, and I've decided to go along."

"You're going to work for Roosevelt!" Isabel said.

"I'm going to work for the country in this war." Eliot turned to his wife. "It won't inconvenience you, Grace. I'll camp out down there in a hotel and get back to town as often as possible."

Isabel wondered if the woman on Seventy-ninth Street would be camping out in the hotel too, but her mother didn't even seem aware of the possibility.

Grace pieced together her expression until it resembled a smile. Of course, he'd be taking that woman to Washington. Perhaps that was better. Perhaps the illicit would become less attractive when it was more accessible.

"I've been thinking about it too," Isabel said.

Her parents turned to her. "Thinking about what?" Grace asked.

"A job."

Eliot smiled, again condescending and a touch impatient. "What kind of job?"

"I don't know, but I'm going to find out."

"What can you do?" Eliot asked.

"There must be something."

"Can you type?"

"Not really. . . ."

"Bookkeeping perhaps?"

"You know I can't, and I wish you'd stop making fun of me."

"I'm not making fun of you. I'm trying to find out what sort of work you plan to do."

"I can learn something."

"Why would you want to?" Grace asked.

"Because I feel so useless, sitting in Northampton reading Shakespeare and studying Renaissance art while the rest of the world is doing something. Spencer's learning to fly a plane. Jack's in the Navy." She turned to her father. "Now you're going to Washington to run things."

"Exactly," her father said. "We're all doing what we're suited to do. And you're suited to stay at school and write to your brother and Jack and keep all our spirits up."

"I agree, dear." There was, Grace believed, a certain lopsided justice to the world. If women were betrayed, they were also sheltered. "What do you think the boys are fighting for?"

"I don't want them to fight for me. If I can't do anything else, I'll get a job in a factory."

Grace's beautifully cared for skin blanched. Eliot's face darkened as if he'd sapped the blood from his wife. "I didn't raise my daughter to work in a factory."

"But—"

"You don't have to go back to school if you don't want to," he went on as if Isabel hadn't spoken. "I never have seen the point of it for a girl. I'm perfectly willing to have you stay home with your mother. You can help her with her volunteer work. I believe she rolls bandages at the Red Cross on Tuesday afternoons and wraps Bundles for Britain on Thursday."

"No, Eliot, I work for the Free French on Thursday. Wednesday is Bundles for Britain."

"There you are," he said, flashing a silvery smile. "You can stay here and help your mother in the war effort or you can go back to school." He paused and took the last sip of his martini. "But no daughter of mine is going to work for money."

"Nice girls really don't, dear."

"That's absurd."

"That," Eliot said, "is my final word on the subject. Of course, I can't force you to do anything, Isabel, but I do think you'll have a hard time supporting yourself and finding a place to live on what you're likely to make—in the unlikely event you find a job."

The fantasy was enticing, but the reality, Isabel knew, was something else again. The life of a typist or manicurist—and she didn't know how to type, as her father had pointed out, and had her nails done at Elizabeth Arden—was romantic only when played by Carole Lombard in a zany Hollywood comedy. After dinner Isabel went to her room to pack for school.

10

THAT CHRISTMAS Eliza's life took on the start-stop quality of blinking tree lights. Wait for Michael, life on hold, Michael's home, life begins. There was no telling when he might turn up or for how long. Sometimes he came home at 2 A.M., slept for three hours, showered, changed clothes, and returned to his office. Occasionally he showed up at nine with an assistant or colleague announcing they hadn't eaten a thing all day. On the first night of Chanukah he called at seven to say there was an emergency, another emergency, and he wouldn't be home till well after midnight.

Eliza looked at her hands. They were raw and cut from grating the potatoes for the traditional pancakes, a job Dolly always botched. "Why should this night be different from all others?" she asked.

"Wrong holiday," Michael said. "Kiss Teddy for me."

He made it home for Christmas Eve. Teddy was already asleep, and Eliza had spread out the last-minute wrapping on the dining room table. Michael looked over the presents. "Did you get that remote-control bomber I mentioned?"

"Teddy's too young for remote control bombers."

Michael walked across the central hallway into the living room to the chrome and glass cocktail wagon Sam Wicker had sent as a wedding gift and poured himself a scotch on the rocks. "Don't be ridiculous. He'll love it."

"The war's bad enough. Do we have to give him toys about it?"

Michael came back to the dining room. "What do you want to give him, dolls?"

Actually, just the other day Eliza had stood in F.A.O. Schwarz for several minutes admiring the most lifelike Madame Alexander baby doll and dreaming about the time she'd have a daughter to buy it for. Despite her optimism on her anniversary, she still wasn't pregnant, but she was still hopeful. "I just don't think a four-year-old needs a remote control bomber."

"He doesn't need it, sweetheart. You didn't need those diamond earrings I gave you for our anniversary—or the little surprise I have for you for Christmas. But I bet he'll get a hell of a kick out of it." Michael put his drink on the table and looked at his watch. "The stores are open late tonight. I bet I can still find one."

"But you just got home."

He was halfway down the hall toward the coat closet. "I'll be back in less than an hour." He returned to the dining room, his coat half on, his hat in hand. "Then we'll have a quiet dinner. Just the two of us. And then"—he shrugged into the other arm of his coat and walked around the table until he was standing behind her —"I'll give you your present." His free hand circled her body and came to rest on her breast. Eliza didn't exactly mind. She loved Michael, and she loved the physical part of loving him. It wasn't her duty, as some of the books and magazine articles she read implied. And it wasn't just a means to an end. It was her pleasure. Sometimes she worried that it was too much her pleasure. Sometimes she found herself thinking about going to bed with Michael, wanting to go to bed with Michael at the strangest times. But then there were other times, like this, when she wasn't interested at all. It was awfully hard to feel romantic when you were standing at the sink up to your elbows in soapy water or bending over the bed to tuck in a hospital corner, but Michael didn't seem to understand that. There was something about the sight of Eliza with her mind on something else that worked on Michael like an aphrodisiac. Now his hand went on toying with her breast. "All your presents," he whispered, and his mustache tickled the back of her neck where her hair began its smooth upsweep. "Be back in a flash," he said, and was gone.

Michael was right about the plane. Teddy adored it. He renounced all other toys except the bear Teddytoo, which was, in fact, less a toy than a sleeping companion. Eliza had thought she knew her son, but Michael had spotted the warrior in her sweet-smelling, soft-cheeked boy.

Sometimes life with Michael was just a little daunting. He was right so much of the time. When they drove anywhere, his sense of direction was unerring. He never made a mistake in balancing the checkbook. He knew the most arcane facts about history and politics. And the things he didn't know like which heroine belonged in which Jane Austen novel and how to choose a ripe melon and the difference between Teddy's sincere cry and his fake one weren't what you'd call important things to know.

Eliza had never stopped marveling at her good fortune in finding Michael. These days she thought about it more and more. It was hard not to with women all around her suddenly finding themselves alone. Every morning her sister Pam called to say someone else had enlisted. Then one morning in January she called and didn't mention a single friend who'd signed up. Instead she asked if Eliza and Michael wanted to go to a show that Saturday night. A customer had given Harold four tickets to *Lady in the Dark*. Eliza asked Michael, and he swore he'd get away. When Eliza called her sister back, Pam said she and Harold wanted to make a night of it. "Dinner at Sardi's first and a nightclub after." Eliza should have suspected something then.

Eliza was the first one to arrive at the restaurant. Michael, who'd been held up at the office, had said he'd meet her there, and Pam and Harold were late. The headwaiter directed her to a bench in the foyer to wait. She huddled there, enveloped in her Persian lamb coat and her self-consciousness, as groups of twos and fours arrived and were seated. She took off her left glove, adjusted her hat, let her hand lie strategically in her lap. The diamond wedding and engagement rings caught the light and reflected the message. She was not alone in the world. She had a husband, a respectable successful provider who would arrive at any moment to claim her.

Finally Michael did arrive. Pam and Harold turned up a few

minutes later. Eliza watched in disbelief as they threaded their way across the room to their table. Harold was wearing a Coast Guard uniform.

Michael stood as they reached the table. "At ease, at ease," Harold said.

"So you did it," Michael answered, and Eliza had to look at him, because the voice didn't sound like Michael's at all.

"Figured I had to," Harold said, and signaled for the waiter. "This is our war. As Jews and as Americans. Hell, German U-boats are shelling Aruba and Curaçao. That's practically next door."

That was the end of the political talk for the night. They went on to the theater, where they discussed Kurt Weill and Ira Gershwin during the intermission, and then to the Copacabana, where they roared at Jimmy Durante, and they danced and drank, and Michael laughed and danced and drank harder than any of them. They toasted Harold and made jokes about the idea of him in the military and grew maudlin about his leaving. Then Eliza and Michael were alone in the cab going home.

"It was a good play, don't you think?" she asked.

He didn't answer.

"I love Gertrude Lawrence."

Silence.

"And I didn't think the psychoanalytic part was too serious for a musical, did you?"

Michael wasn't saying what he thought.

Finally Eliza decided to face the subject head on. "It's kind of funny, don't you think, Harold's enlisting that way."

"Funny?"

"Remember all those fights you two had about the war when they signed the Hitler-Stalin Pact?"

"Harold was just being true to his ideals then. I may not agree, but he was being true to them."

"Maybe, but I still think it's funny. I can't picture him in the military. Of course, the Coast Guard isn't exactly the military."

"It's close enough."

"I didn't mean to belittle him," she said quickly.

"At least he enlisted."

"That's what I'm talking about."

"Which is a hell of a lot more than I've done!"

Eliza wasn't surprised at the outburst. She'd been waiting for it ever since the Sunday afternoon of their anniversary. It had only been a matter of time.

The next morning Michael was up at six again. He might not be in the military, but he was no slacker. Eliza heard the sound of the shower, the opening and closing of the medicine cabinet, but not the slightly off-key humming that usually accompanied his shave. He padded back into the bedroom, a towel wound around his waist. Dark hair fanned out across his chest like wings, then narrowed to a neat line down his stomach. Eliza turned and stretched and watched her husband through half-closed eyes. He took the ironed boxer shorts and undershirt from a drawer and dropped the towel to the floor. He was precise in his dress and grooming but not his habits. He drew a starched white shirt from another drawer, pulled it on, began buttoning. His hand traveled down his chest, then to his left cuff. His left hand moved to his right wrist. "Goddammit!"

Eliza's eyes opened wide.

He tore off the shirt, managing to pop another button, and flung it across the room. It hit the wall and fell to the floor.

Eliza sat up in bed, her back pushed against the headboard. "I spoke to her, Michael. Honestly I did."

"Apparently she didn't hear."

"I'll talk to her again. From now on I'll check all the buttons myself."

He yanked another shirt from the drawer, examined the buttons, pulled it on. "You shouldn't have to check the buttons. You wouldn't have to if you knew how to handle servants." He tugged on his trousers, snapped the suspenders over his shoulders. "I don't care what you do, Eliza, but for Christ's sake, do something!"

"I will," she promised, and slipped out of bed. "Coffee will be ready in a minute."

"I don't have time for coffee." He jerked his tie into place. "Besides, you'd probably let it boil over.

"I'm sorry," he said when he called from his office later that day. "I shouldn't take it out on you. And you make wonderful coffee."

"I make terrible coffee, and you know it. It's either too weak or too bitter."

Michael was late getting home again that night. He'd known the stores would be closed by the time he left the office so he'd sent his secretary to a florist that afternoon. A dozen long-stemmed red roses bobbed their heads in apology.

11

FATHER WADE had failed Lily. The Church had failed her. Even the Blessed Virgin had failed her. She'd done her penance but found no absolution.

The day after Tom's party Lily had thought she would literally die before she got to confession. Behind the lunch counter in the five-and-ten the big clock with the smiling Coca-Cola girl seemed to stand still. No prayers, no tricks, no forcing herself not to look at it made the recalcitrant arms move. Finally they lined up to mark six o'clock, and Lily tore off her cardboard crown and hairnet, grabbed her coat, and raced out the door. By the time she got to the church her breath was coming in short dry gasps that hurt her chest and perspiration had soaked through her uniform.

A handful of people, mostly women with a scattering of children, sat or knelt in the pews waiting for their turns in the confessional. Lily made the sign of the cross, pressing the wet uniform against her hot skin, slid into the pew, and knelt. She bent her head to the back of the bench in front of her and closed her eyes, but she couldn't shut out the sound of the voices rising and falling in the gloom. Father Wade was hearing confession, thank heaven.

A woman came out of the confessional. A boy inched toward it as if his legs were bound. Lily watched him and longed for the innocent confessions of childhood, unkind thoughts, impure if imperfectly understood words, neglected duties.

Minutes later the boy emerged from behind the curtain and raced down the aisle. The heavy wooden door banged closed behind him. A pregnant woman, her coat pulling over the high sphere of belly, heaved herself up out of the pew using both hands. The gold band on the third finger of her left hand glowed dully in the thick half-darkness. She fitted herself into the confessional, and Lily shut her eyes again and tried to pray, but her mind kept wandering to the expectant mother. What could she have to confess? From under the heavy fringe of lashes, Lily glanced around her. What could any of these people have done to compare with her sin?

The pregnant woman struggled out of the coffinlike box. Beside Lily another woman, old and smelling of dishsoap and perspiration, stood and shuffled away. The aroma lingered behind. Lily heard her begin to speak and pulled the scarf tighter over her ears. She didn't want to hear anyone else's sins. She didn't want anyone else to know hers. She could turn now and flee. And live in mortal sin and die to an eternity of blood and fire and endless torture.

Lily began to pray. The priest's voice droned in the quiet dusk; the woman's whispered excitedly. She reminded Lily of her mother, relishing each transgression for the absolution it would bring.

Lily didn't want to think about her mother. She especially didn't want to think about her father. He'd kill her if he knew. The phrase had been going around in Lily's head all day. *He'd kill me.* Once when he'd come home late from Charlie's Grill and seen Tom kissing her in the car, he'd wrenched open the door and pulled her out. At least he hadn't slapped her until they were inside the house. And then he hadn't hit her hard.

Her father hadn't always been like that. There'd been a time when he'd laughed a lot, not the mean little snorting sound he made now, but a deep rolling laugh that sounded as if it came from a man twice the size of Joseph Hartarski. And there'd been a time when he'd been crazy about Lily. She remembered the day he'd left her mother home with baby Rose and taken Lily to the state fair, where he'd shot at things and hammered on things and won Lily a Kewpie doll because she was, he said, his girl. And then there were those summer nights after Iris had come along when he and Lily, her hand like a small bird resting in the strong nest of his, used to walk to the drugstore to buy ice cream. Sometimes he'd let her have a cone of strawberry or peach right there in the store even though he knew she'd get her share when they got home. Lily had known that wasn't fair, but justice, unlike ice cream, is an acquired adult taste. The best memory, though, was of the time he'd taken her up to Kelly's Bluff and told her about old Tom Kelly, who'd mined the hill a long time ago and buried his fortune back in the soil. Over the years people had found thousands of dollars, and someday, her father had promised, he and Lily would find their own fortune there. Then they'd get on a boat, just the two of them, and go around the world. It was a big promise, but her father had seemed so big then, the hand that held hers, the arms that lifted her above the crowds, the feet she stood on as he moved around the living room–kitchen pretending ...ey were dancing. Then two things happened. Joseph Hartarski lost his job in the packing plant. And Lily got her period. Her mother always said that her father had changed after he'd lost his job, and Lily knew that was true. But he'd changed even more toward Lily after she'd come home from school and told her mother about the terrible thing that had happened that day.

The woman emerged from the confessional. Lily stood. Her feet felt as if someone had attached weights. She dragged them to the confessional, stepped in, pulled the dusty curtain closed. The bench was hard beneath her knees. She clasped her hands until the nails made indentations in the flesh, and heard the sound of the slide lifting. The dark outline of Father Wade's head hovered behind the screen.

"Bless me, Father, for I have sinned. . . . I confess to Almighty God and to you, Father that I have sinned. . . ." Lily searched the backwaters of her conscience for minor transgressions. "I've been mean to my sisters."

"How, my child?"

Lily described a handful of domestic squabbles. The shadow behind the screen changed configuration, as if in a yawn. "Go on, my child."

"I've sinned against my mother and father."

"How, my child?" he asked again.

"By wishing I was not their daughter."

"You think you're better than your parents?"

"Not better," Lily started, then remembered she was in the confessional. Still she equivocated. "Different, Father."

"What else, my child?"

Lily was silent. The shadow behind the screen didn't move. "I have impure thoughts and desires, Father."

Father Feary would have asked her to describe them. Father Wade just asked how often she had these thoughts and desires.

"I don't know. Often."

"Once a week. Once a day."

"More than once a day." Lily's voice was the faintest breath against the screen.

"Have you yielded to these desires?" The question curled serpentine through the screen.

Lily swallowed. Her saliva had turned to sawdust. She opened her mouth. No sound came out. She nodded her head. On the other side of the screen Father Wade bowed his and waited. And waited.

"Yes." It was not a word, only a sibilant sound. She saw Father Wade's head turn toward the screen, then away from it.

"Have you gone with a man?"

She repeated the sound.

"You went all the way?"

Even that primitive noise died in her throat.

"You had carnal knowledge of a man?" he insisted.

Again a sibilant whisper crept through the screen.

"How many times?"

She didn't know how to answer that. Did it count as more than once if it was the same night? He'd never asked how many times they'd kissed or how often Tom had touched her, only if he had. "One night," she whispered.

"And not again since then?"

"No."

"Did you take an unnatural precaution, my child? Did you use anything?"

"No, Father." She could almost hear Father Wade's sigh of relief mingling with her own.

Then it was over. She had her penance. For close to an hour she knelt in the back of the church and said Hail Mary's. When she left the sweet-smelling dusk of the church, she felt as clean and white as the snow that had begun to fall. Each flake, she knew, was unlike every other, and the miracle astounded her all over again.

That night she went to the Illinois Central Station to see Tom off on the Hawkeye that left Duquel at ten fifty-four for Omaha. There he would join other mothers' sons, tall and short, thin and husky, street smart and book smart, stupidly brave and secretly frightened, from the small towns of America's patriotically thumping heart to head west for California and the war. The train was made up of old wooden cars brought back into service for the emergency, and the boys jostled and joked their way aboard, hats slouched at debonair angles, luggage ranging from Tom's soft cowhide gladstone with the brass fittings to cardboard suitcases tied with rope. On the station platform mothers cried and fathers clenched their jaws, sisters and brothers regretted things they'd done and girlfriends regretted things they hadn't.

The whistle sounded, the smoke curled through the thin winter air, and the train began to move. Tom managed to fight his way to a window. He was waving wildly, and all the Lunds and Lily were waving back, and the last she saw of him was the gray herringbone arm of the topcoat they'd sometimes used as a blanket in the cream Buick on the bluff overlooking the river.

But the penance hadn't worked. Her soul had been scrubbed clean, but her body still carried its mark, Tom's mark. By New Years she was five days late. By the Thursday afternoon she passed Mrs. Lund sitting in front of school in her Packard waiting for Eloise and Marion and Mrs. Lund didn't even see her, she was ten.

Lily was never late. She'd heard from other girls that she was lucky. When you were regular, you could time things the way the Church told you to, and sometimes it worked. But she hadn't timed things, and it hadn't worked. By the middle of January she was sure.

She was lying on her bed, reading about Gene Tierney in *Silver*

Screen and counting months—months till the wedding, months till the baby—when her mother came into the bedroom and told Rose to leave. Anna Hartarski remained standing at the foot of the bed. Her eyes were hard little coals in her worn white face. Her fingers, gnarled by arthritis and other people's laundry, clutched the cross that hung around her neck. "You didn't get the curse this month."

"Sure I did."

"Don't lie to me. I see the box of napkins in your room. I see the garbage. You didn't get the curse."

"I'm a little late."

"You're not late. Rose is late. You're like a clock."

Lily turned a page of the magazine and pretended to study a picture of Tyrone Power. "Well, this month I'm late."

Her mother's fingers clung to the crucifix between her flat, tired breasts. "I know what you been doing, you and that boy. Now I want to know what he's going to do about it."

Lily closed the magazine and sat up. "He's going to marry me. As soon as he finishes his basic training."

"Sure, he tells you that. You tell me. You tell Father Feary and Father Wade. But he's off there in California, and you're here. You and that baby."

"Tom'll marry me."

"Why would he marry a tramp like you when he could have any nice girl in town?"

"I'm not a tramp!"

"You go in a car. You do what tramps do. You're a tramp."

Lily was on her knees on the bed now, facing her mother. "You don't know! You don't know anything!"

"I know what I see. Tramp!"

"I'm not!"

"Whore!" Anna's voice climbed to drown out her daughter's. "Whore with a whore's baby!"

The door burst open and Joseph Hartarski stood staring at his wife and daughter. His slight frame radiated menace, acrid as a smell. "Shut up! You close your mouths, both of you."

Still clutching her cross, Anna took a step closer to her daughter. They were on the same side now, bound together in fear and weakness and biological guilt. The mother could be no better than the daughter.

"Who's calling who a whore?"

Neither of them spoke.

"I ask you something, you answer."

"It's nothing," Anna mumbled.

The slap to her face was so quick and glancing she barely had time to wince. "I ask you a question, you don't answer me 'nothing.'"

"We were just—"

The back of his hand silenced Lily. "I ask your mother." He turned to his wife. "I hear you. You call her whore. Whore and whore's baby. Right?"

Anna clutched the cross so tightly her reddened knuckles turned white. His hand slapped her silent face again. "You tell me." Still she said nothing, and this time the back of his hand caught the side of her head. She staggered sideways from the blow.

"Stop it!" Lily screamed.

He whirled on her, and his hand followed, leaving a red imprint on her white cheek. "You don't tell me to stop it." His hand came back across her face. "You don't give me orders. I don't take no orders from a whore." His open hand hit the side of her head. A thousand lights shattered in her consciousness. "You got a baby, right?" He pushed her, and she fell back on the bed. He swung his leg over and put a knee on her stomach. "You got a baby in there. Right? You got that rich boy's baby." His knee pressed harder.

"Stop," Anna screamed, and grabbed his shoulders from behind, but he pried her fingers off.

His hands pinned Lily to the bed, his knee dug into her belly. "You tell me, whore, you tell me the truth."

"Yes!" Her scream exploded like the pain in her head. "Yes. I went with Tom and I have his baby and I'm glad. I'm glad I have something better than you and your drunken—" His open hand went back and forth across her face. Lily tasted blood in her mouth.

He grabbed her hair, pulled her head up, and held her that way, his sharp face only inches from hers. His fingers made a knot of her hair. Lily felt as if it was being ripped from her head. He twisted harder. She screamed and felt the blood dribble down her chin. "Whore," he shouted, and spit into her face. "I don't want no whores in my house." Then he dropped her head, slapped her once more across the face, and walked out of the room.

Lily left Duquel on the Hawkeye, the same train Tom had taken. The station was crowded again—train stations were always crowded these days—but no one stood on the platform waving to her. Iris had clung to her for a moment and Rose had cried noisy sick-sounding sobs in their shared bedroom. Her father hadn't even looked up from the *Catholic Daily Tribune* as she crossed the living room-kitchen, but her mother had followed her out the door. They stood there in the chill moonless night, Anna clutching her faded cotton housedress, Lily holding the cardboard suitcase her mother had carried out of her own past.

"I hope he marries you," Anna said.

Lily was silent.

Anna reached into the pocket of her dress and took out a packet of neatly folded bills. "It's seventeen dollars." She held it out to Lily. "Take it."

"It's all you have."

"Take it."

Lily put the money in her handbag and stood waiting, but her mother was finished. She didn't kiss Lily goodbye, didn't even touch her. Lily turned and started off, her shoes crunching savagely on the frozen dirt path.

At the station she bought her ticket and went out onto the platform. The wind was as cruel on her face as her father's hands, but the waiting room was full of people. She was less alone on the platform.

The train wailed into the station. The crowd surged toward it. As Lily struggled to heave her suitcase up the three stairs to the coach, a boy she knew from school grabbed it from behind and carried it aboard. She was afraid he'd want to sit beside her, but he just put it in the overhead rack and found an open window to lean out of. Lily slipped into a seat on the side of the train facing away from the station. Most of the boys were hanging out the windows on the other side, shouting, waving, promising to write, to clean up that mess, to come home soon. The whistle sounded again. Words stretched between window and platform like ribbons trying to hold the train in place. The wheels began to move. The ribbons snapped. The train picked up speed and left the station behind.

At each stop the coach grew more crowded. Men sat on suitcases.

One boy climbed into the overhead luggage rack and went to sleep. There were few women. The air grew hot and fetid. Even through her skirt the stiff plush chafed the back of Lily's thighs. She had to go to the bathroom, but she was afraid to leave her seat and climb over all those men and all that luggage. She began to perspire. Between her legs her underpants felt warm and wet. Maybe she'd got her period. Maybe she wasn't pregnant after all. She slid her hand beneath her to feel her skirt. Inconclusive dampness. Hot with embarrassment, she made her way to the ladies' room. Masculine legs made way for her, masculine arms steadied her as the train lurched, masculine voices asked where she was going and invited her to stay and said hi, how-are-you, how-ya-doin?

Lily slammed the door behind her, lifted her skirt, took down her pants. They were pristine. She sat on the toilet and stared at the sign. *Passengers will please refrain . . .* She began to cry.

She went back to her seat and tried to sleep, but it was no good. Men stared, snored, bet on cards, told their life stories. The train started and stopped. The horizon turned pink as flesh.

The train pulled into Omaha a little after nine. The boy from school carried her suitcase down the stairs, then hurried away. Lily followed the crowd. A man held the door to the waiting room open for her. She passed through it into bedlam. Beneath the high-vaulted ceiling hundreds of men in uniform and twice as many in civilian clothes stood, sat, paced, and milled. Everyone rushed to wait, waited to rush.

She found the ladies' room. In front of the mirror two girls stood applying rouge and talking about factory jobs in California. A young woman had spread a blanket on the floor and was diapering a baby. He squirmed and wailed in misery.

There was a restaurant in the station, but it looked too grand and expensive. She found the drug store. Men waited three deep at the counter. A disembodied voice announced that the Challenger to Los Angeles was now boarding passengers. She picked up her suitcase. Her shoulder ached from lugging it around. Again she refused to ask directions. By the time she found the proper track every seat and inch of aisle space was taken. She wedged herself and her suitcase into a corner of the open vestibule.

She rode with the wind stinging her sore face and her woolen mitten frozen to the icy hand rail. The two girls she'd seen in the ladies' room came out onto the open platform with two soldiers. One of them, a tall, skinny boy with orange hair, passed around a pack of Chesterfields. The taller of the two girls, who would have been pretty if her skin beneath heavy pancake makeup was not so cruelly ravaged, cupped the boy's hand with her own as he lit the cigarette, then picked an imaginary shred of tobacco off her tongue with her thumb and forefinger. The train lurched and she fell against the orange-haired soldier. He put an arm around her waist to steady her. She went on leaning against him. His hand slid to her hip. The other soldier put his arm around the other girl.

Two men in civilian clothes came out onto the platform. The orange-haired boy began kissing the girl with the bad skin. One hand steadied them against the bouncing train while the other kneaded her breast. The two men looked at them, then at Lily, and laughed. She glanced past them through the window to the coach. There was space in the aisle. She picked up her suitcase and went into the car.

The warmth assaulted her. She didn't even mind the smell of breath and sweat and humanity. She climbed over several pairs of legs, some in khaki, some in wool or denim or corduroy, found a few inches for her suitcase, and sat on it. The train bounced and lurched along the uneven roadbed, and she clutched the armrest of the nearest seat to steady herself. The soldier smiled at her. His smile was a little like Tom's, not so handsome or warm, but big and easy. "Rough trip," he said. Lily smiled back. His buddy in the window seat took a package of gum from his blouse pocket and held it out to Lily. She took a piece. The mint tasted fresh in her stale mouth.

The soldier with Tom's smile stood. "Why don't you take this for a while." Lily said she was all right. "Come on," he insisted. "I've been sitting since Omaha." He maneuvered her around to the seat. The rough upholstery felt almost soft after the sharp edges of her suitcase. The soldier perched on her armrest.

She unbuttoned her coat and before she could stop him the soldier was helping her off with it. He stared at the white angora sweater for a long minute.

They asked her where she'd come from and where she was going. They said Tom was a lucky guy. Every now and then one of them said something to the other that she didn't entirely understand and they laughed. The soldier with Tom's smile reached across her to take another stick of gum from his buddy. His arm brushed her breast. Lily crossed her arms in front of her and shrank back against the seat. The roadbed turned rough again. The soldier on her armrest put his hand on her knee to steady himself. His face was close to hers. Beneath the spearmint his breath was sour. "Listen, blondie," he said, "how about you and me go get something to eat in the dining car. I got a uniform that entitles me to get in, and I got a five spot that can get me in fast."

She stood. The soldier stood too and put an arm around her waist. Her stomach contracted. Her girdle was killing her. She had to go to the bathroom again. This time she was sure she'd got her period.

"No. No, I have to go."

"Wait a minute, blondie," he began, but she picked up her suitcase and began fighting her way to the end of the car. He didn't follow her, and she heard his laugh, loud and raucous and not like Tom's at all, behind her.

By the time she reached the end of the car her thighs felt wet. This couldn't be her imagination. She pushed through a group of men into the ladies' room. She lifted her skirt and yanked down the white cotton underpants. They were stained crimson. She sat on the toilet seat and stared at the same sign asking her to please refrain. Then she began to cry again.

When she came out of the ladies' room some time later, the boy she knew from school was sitting on his suitcase a little way down the aisle. He held out a sandwich wrapped in waxed paper. "I bought an extra one in the station," he said. "You look as if you could use it. I hope you like ham."

The bread was stale and the butter a little rancid, but Lily had never tasted anything so good in her life.

12

BY LATE WINTER of 1942 the war was beginning to come home to America. On the East Coast people watched the glare over the Atlantic almost every night as Nazi subs sank one merchant ship after another. On the West Coast the Japanese shelled an oil field near Santa Barbara, and Americans agreed that citizens of Japanese descent belonged in concentration camps. Joe Louis knocked out Buddy Baer in fewer than three minutes, turned the purse over to the Navy Relief Society, and joined an Army that still drew a straight and wide color line. Sugar and gas shortages loomed. There was talk of forming a woman's branch of the Army. America was mobilizing.

Smith College introduced a course in auto mechanics. Isabel signed up for it. She learned to change spark plugs and check oil for various faculty members whose cars were used as guinea pigs. On the last Saturday in March, one of those premature spring mornings in Massachusetts that begin to melt the snow and make the young women of Northampton ache with unidentified longing, she was delivering an old Ford to Professor Boissevain, who'd taught her

everything she knew about Zola. The only hint of war in the softening air was her throaty voice singing "You Can't Say No to a Soldier." Then the recently checked engine slowed to a stop right in
the middle of the road, and Isabel's song came to an abrupt end.
She turned the ignition. Nothing happened. She pumped the gas,
then tried the ignition again. Still nothing.

A car came up behind her, honked, swerved, and continued on
down the road. She got out, walked around to the front, opened
the hood, and looked at the tangle of machinery. After weeks of
classes she still felt more at home with Zola. Maybe there was
something wrong with the fuel pump. They'd had a lesson on the
fuel pump just the other day. Whatever it was, she had to get the
car off the road.

She closed the hood, released the brake, put the car in drive, and
began to push. It was, literally, an uphill battle. The car had stopped
at the foot of an incline, and Isabel couldn't budge it.

Another car came up behind her and pulled over to the side of
the road. The man didn't so much get out of as unfold from it. For
the first time that morning Isabel was aware of her grease-stained
overalls. His air cadet's uniform was starched and pressed to within
an inch of its life, but the body beneath it moved with a long, lean
laziness. He ambled over to the car. Beneath the brim of his cap his
eyes were a clear and startling blue, like Caribbean water or, on
second thought, glaciers glistening in the sunlight. The wide thin
mouth smiled at her, but the eyes didn't. They ran a quick tally of
the overalls and came to rest again on her face.

"Engine trouble?"

"I think it's the fuel pump." She hadn't meant to make it sound
like an argument, but the eyes unnerved her.

He walked to the front of the car, opened the hood, and pushed
his cap back on his head. The sandy hair looked a little too long for
regulation. He bent over the engine. The starched military blouse
pulled across the width of his shoulders. "It just stopped?" he asked
without looking at her.

"Dead."

"Did you try to start it again?"

"Of course. It won't."

"Try again."

"I told you, it won't start."

He looked at her for a minute before he spoke. "Sounds like something wrong with the fuel pump."

"I just told you that."

He closed the hood and tugged his cap back in place. "Then you don't need me," he said, and started back to his car. He had the walk of a cowboy rather than a soldier, hands in pockets, legs moving easy and loose from narrow hips. As he pulled away he gave her a mock salute.

She stood there cursing him for several seconds before turning back to the car. The sensible thing would be to push from the front, but without anyone in the driver's seat, she was afraid the car would gain momentum and get away from her. She stood staring at it, greasy hands on greasy hips.

The sound of an engine grew louder behind her. She turned. He was backing up slowly, one elbow resting on the open window, the other hand guiding the wheel with a lazy finger. He parked the car, got out again, and stood looking down at her. His face was long and lean with beautiful hollows beneath the cheekbones. "You may be a hell of a mechanic—you've even got the overalls to prove it— but you might as well admit you haven't got the muscle. Get behind the wheel."

"I can push too."

"Do you want help or not?" He stood staring down at her. He seemed to have plenty of time.

"Yes." She hesitated. "Thank you."

"Then get behind the wheel and steer."

"It'll be easier if you push from the front. I can use the brake if it starts to roll too fast."

The eyes measured her again, not the body beneath the overalls, but her. "Okay, whiz kid, now get in."

He pushed and she steered and they got the car off the road. "You'll have to get a tow," he said. "Do you want a ride into town or are you so independent you want to walk?"

She said she'd take a ride.

"I suppose you're a Smithy," he said when they'd started toward town. "Winning the war through Automechanics 101."

"Not everyone can be a flyboy."

He just laughed, impervious and a little proud. "I drove over from the air base with my buddy. The kid's crazy about some girl here. Sally Sayre. You know her?"

Isabel said she did.

"Yeah, it figures. Someone like you would know someone like her."

"What's that supposed to mean?"

"Those overalls don't provide much camouflage. I can spot the type. You might as well be wearing pearls. The accent too. It gives you away. Not the voice—that's a different story—but the accent."

"Do you always judge people so quickly?"

He laughed again. "Read the handbook. A good officer is a good judge of men—and women. And the Army says I'm an officer, not to mention a gentleman."

"The Army's made mistakes before. Look at Pearl Harbor," she said, and directed him to Northrup House.

He pulled up in front of the dorm and turned to her. "Listen, my buddy wants me to meet his sister, but, to tell you the truth, I'm not much on guys' sisters. Have dinner with me tonight. I can tell you the story of my life, and you can tell me all about fuel pumps."

She said she'd love to in a tone that clearly implied she wouldn't, but that she had another date. The easy smile didn't change. "Another time," he lied, and drove off with another mock salute.

"You're going to adore him," Sally said when she came to Isabel's room that evening. "Tall with the most heavenly blue eyes. From Harvard. Of course, he's not quite Porcellian, but Spence says he's all right. In fact, according to Spence he's just about perfect, not to mention being the best flyer in the whole air cadet program. I don't know about that—I don't even care about that—but those eyes just go right through you. I felt as if I wasn't wearing anything at all."

It occurred to Isabel that Spence might be in big trouble.

Spence and the tall flyer with the heavenly or tropical or glacial eyes—it depended on your point of view, or perhaps his mood—were waiting in the hall at the bottom of the big open staircase. Spence took a few steps up the stairs as if he couldn't wait to get to Sally, though he'd left her only an hour earlier. Leaning against the newel post, his hands in his pockets, his cap crushed beneath his arm, the tall flyer stood looking up at Isabel. She waited for the

shock of recognition followed by the aftershock of embarrassment.
All she saw was a glint of amusement.

She took the last few steps. Spence introduced them. Andy
Barnes smiled down at her. He wasn't embarrassed. He didn't even
seem surprised.

They went to Wiggans Tavern for dinner. Spence and Andy
talked about altitudes and angles of approach and throttling down
and bringing the old stick back just a little before the old wheels
touch down. They talked about chandelles and contrails and the
CO and chow and ops. The one thing they did not talk about was
who would get to be a pilot and who would be relegated to the
minor leagues of navigator and bombardier. Then Sally reminded
them that she was along and wanted to go dancing, and they drove
to a roadhouse where the drinks were watered and the band tried
hard but ineffectually to sound like one of the Dorsey Brothers.

Andy Barnes danced the way he walked and drove, loose, easy,
overly confident. Neither of them had mentioned this afternoon's
meeting yet. Isabel dropped her head back and looked up at him.
His face looked chiseled.

"At least you could have the good grace to be embarrassed," she
said.

"For what?"

"For offering to stand me up."

He smiled. She wished he hadn't. The smile was almost as bad as
the eyes. "For offering to stand you up for you. Isabel," he said,
and the sound of her name made her shiver, "Spence has a picture
of you on his desk. I've been opening my eyes to you every morning for the last month."

His hand moved down her spine, eliminating the inch of space
between their bodies. "That's better," he said, and she felt a few
strands of her hair dance in the breeze of his words.

The band swung into a jitterbug, and they returned to the table.
It was far enough from the dance floor to talk. He hadn't been
kidding, it turned out, about the story of his life.

Andy Barnes had been born in Alabama and raised in Connecticut. His mother was a beautiful Southern belle who'd been sought
after by the scores of officers who'd come to the nearby army camp
to train in the last war. His father, a flyer of those early wood, wire,
and prayer contraptions, had been the officer who'd won her. After

the war, he'd taken his fragile belle and their son—"That's me"—
back to Connecticut and the family insurance business. "Nice irony,
don't you think. There was nothing crazier than those planes, and
nothing safer than insurance. But my mother wanted security—
women seem to—and by the time my father realized what had
happened it was too late."

"Too late for him but not for you."

He moved his shoulders beneath the starched uniform as if it
chafed, and managed to ambush a passing waiter to order another
round of drinks. He hadn't even asked if she wanted one. "You, of
course, see her side of things, the woman's side. I bet you've got it
all mapped out. Even down to your kids' names."

"You bet wrong."

"What about the blue-chip navy guy?"

"What about him?"

"According to the plan, you're supposed to marry him and settle
down to raise a bunch of blue-chip kids."

"That's what they tell me," she said. "Only maybe I won't."

He tipped his chair back on two legs and stared at her. "Oh, you
will, eventually, but you'll put up a fight first. This war's going to
be good for you, Isabel."

"What do you mean?"

"It's going to give you a chance to sow some wild oats. Slum with
guys like me. Maybe even see a little of the way the rest of the
world lives. The ones who aren't born with gold spoons in their
mouths and million-dollar trust funds. Then you'll settle down with
that nice upright navy officer who has a million-dollar trust fund of
his own and raise a passel of upright brats who will grow into their
own trust funds."

"You sound bitter about it," she said.

He laughed. "The funny thing is so do you."

"You still haven't told me about fuel pumps," he said in the
backseat of the car, and reached an arm around her shoulders.

"The fuel pump is a hose. . . ." Her voice was mock didactic,
but she didn't move out from the circle of his arm.

He leaned closer until his mouth was beside her ear. "You have
the damnedest voice."

She'd been told that before, and she knew the rest of it too from dates with other boys who were well read but not quite family approved. "You're going to tell me it's full of money."

"I was going to tell you," he said, his breath warm against her ear, "that it was full of sex."

Spence brought the car to a stop in front of the dorm, let Isabel and Andy out, and drove off. They had half an hour till curfew, and Spence obviously planned to spend it alone with Sally. On the long porch connecting the twin dorms, couples clung and writhed in the shadows. Isabel stood looking after the disappearing car. The closeness of the evening had evaporated. They'd reached the awkward time of night.

Andy started walking. "Young love," he said, and his voice wasn't entirely kind.

She tried to keep step but his legs were too long for her. "Why do you patronize him?"

He stopped walking and leaned against a tree. Isabel was left standing in front of him, awkward as a wallflower on a ballroom floor. She jammed her hands into the pockets of her coat.

"You mean Spence?"

She nodded.

"Hell, I'm not patronizing him. I'm trying to protect him. And me."

"I should have known you'd come into it somewhere."

"Look, someday I might end up in a plane with Spence. If I do, I want his mind on his job, not on Little Miss Tease."

"You think Sally's a tease?"

His smile was conspiratorial. "Don't you?"

She did, of course—she had for some time—but it wasn't the sort of thing you said about an old friend, even an old friend you didn't particularly like, especially to a man.

"Well, you do, but you're not going to admit it to me. The point is she's got him going in circles, and that's not a safe navigational course. If he had any sense, he'd take her to bed and forget her."

"Is that the way you work?"

He laughed. "Are you worried?"

"Merely curious."

He took her hand from her pocket and drew her closer. "That's a shame. I was hoping you were worried." He traced the contour of her cheek with his thumb. "I don't forget, but I don't get tied up. On the ground I don't worry about flying." He did, of course, but she wasn't going to argue with him now. "In the air I don't worry about women." His hand moved from her cheek to her mouth. The pressure of his thumb made her lower lip tremble. "Do I make myself clear."

"You're a model of lucidity."

"Good," he murmured, and drew her to him.

Isabel noticed that he kissed the way he did everything else, with enviable ease and confidence. She also noticed that without touching any other part of her body, he managed to set off a series of sensations that Jack Livingston had never even stirred.

They stopped kissing and looked at each other for a long, hard minute. Then Isabel put her arms around his neck and lifted her face to his again. His mouth set off another extraordinary chain reaction. Finally they stopped kissing but didn't let go of each other. "You know," he said, and traced the line of her body with his hands, "I was right about your voice, but maybe I was wrong about you. Maybe you won't settle for that nice safe life of navy guys and trust funds after all."

13

IN APRIL the Office of Price Administration announced that sugar would be rationed. Eliza asked Dolly to make Michael's favorite chocolate layer cake as a farewell tribute. In May gas was rationed on the East Coast. The Sunday before the ruling went into effect Michael took an unusual day off and drove Eliza and Teddy to the country. By June German subs had sunk so much shipping in coastal waters and New York had remained so recalcitrantly bright that the city was dimmed out by military decree. Times Square went black. Theatergoers groped their way to darkened theaters, hoping they'd found the right one. Eliza went to Altman's and bought blackout curtains for all the windows. She and Dolly were in the process of hanging them when the phone rang. Eliza went to answer it. Dolly continued working. Mrs. Kramer had promised her the night off as soon as they finished the curtains. Now that Mr. Kramer rarely came home for dinner and Mrs. Kramer usually settled for scrambled eggs or a sandwich with the New York Philharmonic or Orson Welles and the ABC Playhouse, Dolly had lots of nights off. Her love life was growing more complicated. Tonight she had a date with a navy mess steward.

"Hi, Mrs. Kramer," Michael said. "Remember me. I'm the guy you married five and a half years ago. The one who used to come home occasionally." Eliza said she had vague recollections of a dark man with a mustache. "Sounds like Gable. Or Hitler. Listen, sweetheart, I'm going to make it home for dinner. Central Park West or bust. And I'm bringing Sam." From the phone table in the hall Eliza watched as Dolly finished hanging the last curtain and started for her room. Eliza didn't have the heart to stop her. She'd been talking about that mess steward all afternoon. "He's with me now," Michael went on. "We'll be home by seven." Eliza was too pleased to have Michael home to mind having Sam with him.

Michael and Sam had roomed together in college. That was when Sam Wicker was still Sammy Wischansky. It wasn't the name change that Eliza held against Sam, though she didn't much like Jews who tried to pass. Michael insisted Sam wasn't trying to pass, only get ahead. Sam was in the ad game, as he called it, and in the ad game you had to be able to pronounce the product name as well as spell it. Wischansky was out.

But it wasn't Sam Wicker's name that bothered Eliza. It was Sam Wicker. He was smart and successful and handsome in a too perfect way that Eliza didn't entirely trust. His hair was jet black, his lashes so long they cast spiky shadows over his cheeks, and there was even a cleft in his chin. Sam was always admiring their perfect marriage and their perfect baby and their perfect apartment full of new furniture and old values. He was always swearing that he wanted nothing more than to marry and settle down. If only, he'd add, he could find a girl like Eliza. But, as Eliza occasionally remarked to Michael, if Sam wanted to marry, especially if he wanted to marry someone like Eliza, he was going about it the wrong way. At Cornell he'd often fixed Michael up with gentile girls, and not one of the dozens of women he'd brought to Eliza's house over the years had been Jewish. All of them, however, had been blond, beautiful, and as far as Sam was concerned, short-lived. After each breakup, orchestrated invariably by Sam, he turned up for Sunday night supper sighing about gold diggers and good-time girls and swearing he'd learned his lesson. But in a week or two he'd be back with another tall, blond *shiksa* he'd discovered posing for a soap ad or singing on the radio in a toothpaste commercial.

And then there was the drinking. It wasn't that Sam drank a lot, only that he drank more than most of the people Eliza knew. Whenever the two men met for lunch, Michael had martinis to start and a headache by the time he got home at night.

Everyone said that Sam Wicker was a terrific catch, and Eliza always agreed. In fact, she was praying for the day that some girl, gentile or Jewish, blond or brunette, like Eliza or her exact opposite, would catch him.

As soon as Eliza opened the door for them she could tell they'd stopped for a martini on the way home, perhaps more than one. Michael's kiss was pure eighty proof. He picked up Teddy, whom she'd finally managed to calm down enough for sleep. Teddy turned his face away and scowled. "Daddy smells." Michael and Sam laughed. Sam took Teddy from his father. "Uncle Sam too," Teddy yelled. The men laughed again, and Eliza took her son from Sam.

"You've got to do something about that boy of yours," Sam said, and kissed Eliza on the cheek. "He can't even spot a perfect dry martini when he smells one." Sam put his smooth leather briefcase with the gold initials on the hall table and opened it. "But I bet I have something that'll win him over." He took a brightly wrapped package from the case and handed it to Teddy. The boy squirmed out of Eliza's arms and tore off the paper. Sam had added a miniature submarine to Teddy's arsenal for defense. Teddy howled with joy.

"Thank you," Eliza said to Sam. "It was very thoughtful of you." She heard her own voice, cool and insincere, and hoped Michael hadn't noticed it.

"You're the one who's thoughtful, Eliza." Sam's voice, unlike hers, sounded as genuine as his cowhide briefcase. "Taking a poor lonely bachelor in out of the cold. Giving him a good home-cooked meal."

"It's a warm evening," Eliza said. "And don't count your dinner until you've tasted it. I gave Dolly the night off, and you know what my cooking is like."

Michael put an arm around her shoulders. "She has a point, Sam. It's lucky she's beautiful, because she sure as hell can't cook."

Sam stood staring at them as if he were looking at a painting. Grant Wood, no doubt, Eliza thought. "If you two only knew how I envy you. You have each other. You've got Teddy."

"Whom you're not going to find so adorable in about five minutes," Eliza interrupted before he could go on with the catalogue of things he envied. She picked up Teddy. "Let me just put him to bed, and I'll start dinner."

Sam held out his arms to Teddy. "Let me. Please."

Teddy, who usually insisted on a bedtime story from his mother, wasn't one to look a gift horse, or a submarine, in the mouth. He went straight to Sam. "Will you read me a story?" he asked as they started down the hall.

"Better than that," Sam answered. "I'll tell you one. An original Sam Wicker story. It's all about a little boy named Teddy who lives in an apartment on Central Park West. Once upon a time Teddy . . ."

Michael headed for the living room to mix a pitcher of martinis, then pitcher and glasses in hand, followed Eliza to the kitchen.

"You okay?" he asked. She said she was fine. "You look a little pale."

"I got my period today."

He frowned. "No baby."

"No baby," she repeated.

He put the pitcher down on the table. "I hope you don't mind my bringing Sam home," he whispered, "but he was in my office and, frankly, I think he was waiting around for an invitation. That bachelor life—all those restaurants and nightclubs—isn't what it's cracked up to be."

Eliza patted Michael's cheek on her way from refrigerator to counter. "You just keep thinking that way, darling. Why was he in your office anyway?"

Michael pulled out a chair and sat at the table. "We were doing our part for the war effort—or at least the Office of Civilian Defense." His voice scratched like a bad needle on a record you didn't want to hear in the first place. "Mrs. Roosevelt and Fiorello are at it again. This time it's uniforms for the women volunteers. She's in favor of some blue denim suit that goes for about three dollars. He's got his heart set on some stylish, sexy number. So it's Michael Kramer to the rescue. A man of taste." He sipped his drink. "A man of discrimination." He took a longer swallow. "A veteran of the great uniform battle." He finished his drink and refilled the glass. "We needed models to show off Fiorello's uniforms, so I called Sam and told him to round some up. Half looked like Garbo, the other half like Dietrich, and none was under five feet ten."

"I see Mike's bringing you up to date on our latest contribution to the war effort." Sam took the chair across from Michael and poured himself a drink from the pitcher.

Eliza struggled to open the can of peas. Dolly had neglected to mention that she'd broken the handle of the can opener. "Michael's been working like a dog. It isn't all sexy uniforms and models. He's in Washington almost every week, doing the real OCD work while the mayor struts around in cabinet meetings. You have to admit civilian defense is important. And someone has to run the city. You don't have to wear a uniform to—"

"Eliza," Sam said, and held up his hands as if he were surrendering. "You don't have to convince me. I think Mike's doing a terrific job. Winning the goddamn war singlehanded. And even if he weren't, I wouldn't care. I told him he was crazy to enlist."

The can of peas slid from her hand. Tiny green spheres rolled in every direction. The clear liquid made a puddle around her pumps. Eliza stood there staring at it, her back to the two men. He didn't mean that. I'll turn and see them both laughing at me and know it was a joke.

She turned. The soft vegetables squished beneath her feet. Michael was staring at her. There was no smile on his face.

Sam looked from Eliza to Michael. "I guess I said something I wasn't supposed to."

"I haven't done anything yet," Michael said, his eyes holding Eliza's.

"But you're going to."

"I told him he's crazy," Sam repeated.

"You're going to enlist," Eliza said.

"Eliza." Michael pronounced her name as if it were a plea.

"You're going to leave Teddy and me and go off to play hero."

"I'm not going off to play hero. Hell, I'll probably never hear a shot fired in anger. If I get in at all, at my age, with my bad back, they'll probably put me in the Judge Advocate's office or stick me in PR writing speeches for some general."

"I just want to know one thing," Eliza said. "When were you planning to tell me? You told Sam. When were you planning to tell me?"

"I told you I haven't done anything yet."

"No, but you've made up your mind to. Without discussing it with me. Without even mentioning it to me. I had to hear it from Sam."

"Eliza," Sam began, but she cut him off.

"You stay out of this, Sam. The perfect husband and the perfect wife are having some perfect words, and you just stay out of it." She turned back to Michael. "Did you plan to come home from the office in uniform one day? Surprise! Surprise! As if you were bringing a piece of jewelry for me or a toy for Teddy. Or did you plan to write me from camp?"

"I was going to tell you tonight, Eliza. You know I've been thinking about it for months, but I didn't make up my mind till this afternoon. Rommel's on the move in Africa again, the Luftwaffe just bombed the hell out of Canterbury, and I'm sitting around designing ladies' uniforms. Worse than that, I'm sitting around worrying about buttons on my shirts while other guys are dying."

She moved to the table, her hands clutching the back of an empty chair, her knuckles as white as the painted wood. "All right, we'll talk about other guys. We'll talk about Sam. Our friend Sam. Sam doesn't think it's his war. He doesn't have a wife or a child. All he has is that black book full of beautiful blond *shiksas,* but you don't see him enlisting."

"Eliza!" Michael stopped her.

"Listen," Sam said. "I told him he was crazy."

Eliza looked at her husband's best friend. The handsome features were wavy through the stream of tears. "Tell him again," she shouted. "Maybe he'll listen to you."

"I have to go, Eliza. I can't live with myself if I don't." Michael's mouth was set in a firm line and his eyes were hard, but his voice was soft and patronizing. He sounded as if he were talking to Teddy, explaining some fact of adult life, laying down the law as he saw it. And she had about as much recourse as Teddy.

The army took Michael. They didn't think he was too old. They weren't bothered by a back that occasionally got a little stiff. They weren't worried about his wife and son if he wasn't. And they didn't care that a second child was not yet on the way. For the moment no mention was made of the Judge Advocate's office or that general in need of a speech writer. Michael was told to wind up his affairs and report to the Pennsylvania Station at oh eight hundred hours on June twenty-fourth.

The sun poured through the high windows like streams of honey, but the marble station remained cold in the early morning. Eliza listened to the sound of her pumps clicking down the long entrance way. The narrow skirt of her best suit forced her to take small steps. The feather of a new hat tickled her temple as she walked. She'd dressed carefully for the morning. Michael walked beside her, his single suitcase in his right hand, his left firm on her elbow. Crowds swirled around them. A month ago Eliza would have cataloged the differences between her and Michael and the strangers. One woman wore a cheap, ill-fitting suit, another too much makeup, a third a stunning Lily Dache hat. One's husband was fat, another's wore an expensive blazer jacket and air of success, a third's walked several steps ahead of her. Now she saw only the similarity. The men were leaving. The women were saying goodbye.

It was a little after seven. "How about some coffee?" Michael asked. Eliza nodded. She didn't trust her voice this morning.

They went into the Savarin coffee shop and found two seats at the counter. Across the way a woman sat staring into space, tears running down her carefully made up cheeks into an untouched cup of coffee. Two men, boys really, in uniform, were putting away eggs and bacon and potatoes and toast and milk and coffee. They stopped eating long enough to let their eyes follow a girl in a white dress with red and blue piping down the counter, then went back to their breakfasts.

Neither Eliza nor Michael drank the coffee. He paid for it, and they went down to the waiting room.

Over the loudspeaker a voice ran down a list of strange-sounding towns. Somewhere at the end of them, Eliza knew, would be a place called Camp Wheeler, Georgia, a place Michael would come to know as home and she'd never see. She'd wanted to follow him there, but the government pleaded with her not to and Michael put his foot down. "I can just see you and Teddy sitting up all night in a coach—you'll never get Pullman reservations or a bedroom on the train—then the two of you living in a single rented room in some broken-down rooming house—if you're lucky enough to find that. And half the time I won't be able to get off base to see you so you'll be alone anyway. You couldn't handle it, Eliza," he'd said, and she'd supposed he was right. But now with a voice calling strange destinations and an army sergeant shouting orders and a crowd of couples all around them, clinging, kissing, standing in silence, women crying, men with expressions carved of granite, she thought she could take it better than she could take saying goodbye.

"Now, remember everything I told you," Michael said, and his expression was rock hard too. "My father has the checkbook. He'll take care of the bills and see that you get your house money every week. If you need anything else, just give him a call. They'll probably call you every day anyway."

She could feel the tears starting in her eyes.

"I gave the super five dollars before I left, so if anything goes wrong in the apartment, call him. Don't try to fix it yourself. And don't let him give you the runaround. You tell him Mr. Kramer wants it fixed and wants it fixed now."

The line of his mouth was growing firmer, as if he were clenching his teeth.

"Don't be too proud to change your mind and go stay with your folks. At least you'll have someone to take care of you there."

"I'll be all right," she said, and her voice sounded as tight as the line of his mouth.

He put an arm around her shoulders. "Sure you will." He rubbed his eyes with thumb and forefinger. "Now, did I forget anything?"

She tried to think of practical things. She knew Michael wanted her to. "The car," she said. "I don't even know where the keys are."

He looked relieved. These were matters he could handle. "You don't have to worry about the car. I sold it."

"You sold the car! Without even telling me?"

"I knew you wouldn't want to be bothered with it. If you want to take Teddy to the beach, call my folks, or yours, or Sam. Sam would love to play daddy for a day."

"But—"

The distant voice was announcing that the train was ready for boarding and the sergeant was shouting and all around them people were hugging and kissing and trying to joke and crying. She looked up at Michael. The granite expression cracked. He put his other arm around her and pulled her to him. She buried her face in his neck. "I love you," he said, and she began to cry. "Just remember that I love you."

"I love you too." She squeezed out the words between sobs.

He kissed her. She tasted the salt of her tears on his mouth.

"I'll be home before you know it. And we'll get to work on that baby."

They kissed again. His mouth was hard on hers, as if he were imprinting something in memory.

The loudspeaker was still chanting towns and the sergeant was still shouting and all around them men were beginning to break away, picking up possessions, leaving women, starting down the long flight of stairs to the train.

"Take care of Teddy." Michael's voice sounded choked and funny. "And you." He kissed her again, quick and hard. "I love you." Then he was gone.

She watched his back moving down the stairs with the other men, but before he reached the first landing, he'd disappeared from her view, cut off by taller heads and broader shoulders and the jostling bodies of strangers.

As she crossed the waiting room her heels made the same click click sound. They echoed up the marble stairs to the street level. When she let herself into the empty apartment, the carpet finally killed the echo. There was only silence.

Teddy was at her mother's. It was Dolly's day off. She looked at her watch. It was a little before nine. She went into the bedroom to take off her hat and jacket. Michael's pajamas were flung over the back of a chair. She picked them up and hung them on the hook inside the closet. The aroma of Yardley lingered among the clothes like a ghost. She started to close the door, then remembered. She took the pajamas from the hook, carried them into the bathroom, and dropped them into the hamper. Back in the bedroom the closet door was still open. Michael's suits hung in a row, lifeless as scarecrows. His shoes, each one filled with a wooden tree, lined the floor. She remembered an afternoon in childhood. She was sitting on the big old four-poster bed in her grandparents' room. Only now it was only her grandmother's room because her grandfather had died and her mother and grandmother were going through the closet, sorting his clothes. This for a poor relative, that for the rag man. Eliza slammed the door to Michael's closet.

She went into the kitchen and turned on the flame under the coffee pot. She hated reheated coffee, but it was silly to make a fresh pot just for herself. She sat at the table and waited for it to warm. The white metal cabinets and appliances gleamed. The refrigerator hummed in the silence. She got up and took a piece of bread from the metal breadbox and put it in the toaster. Then she took the butter and jam from the refrigerator. She set the table carefully with a plate, cup and saucer, and silverware, and folded a paper napkin into a triangle. The toast popped up. She poured the coffee, buttered the bread, raised a piece to her mouth, then put it down again. She tasted the coffee. It was bitter. She poured out the coffee, threw the bread in the trash, washed, dried, and put away the dishes. From the wall over the refrigerator the clock, shaped like a teapot, stared down at her. The second hand dragged through one circle. The minute hand crept toward the twelve. Nine o'clock. Only three hours to go. Then she could pick up Teddy. She blocked out the afternoon. His lunch, nap, a walk in the park. Four o'clock. Then his supper. The baked potato would take an hour, the lamb chop twenty minutes. Dinner, bath, bedtime stories. Then the night stretched ahead. She looked from the clock to the calendar hanging on the wall. A girl in a flower print dress danced above the neat squares marking off the days. Eliza lifted the page to see July's picture. Another girl in a two-piece bathing suit held up a beachball. Beneath her lay thirty-one empty white squares.

14

BY JUNE Tom had shipped out, but Lily lingered on in San Diego. It had become a kind of home to her, and to thousands of others who'd flooded into the city in the wake of servicemen husbands and boyfriends or in search of war jobs. It was a kind of a home now, but four months earlier it had been an alien and terrifying place. That first afternoon, dizzy with exhaustion from the long ride west, Lily had staggered out of the station, lugging her cheap cardboard suitcase, and stood blinking in amazement at the blinding sunshine and towering palms. She'd never seen palm trees before, or women with bare midriffs and turbans, or bougainvillea and oleander rioting around orange-roofed adobe buildings. At least she'd never seen them outside a movie.

There'd been a line of cabs in front of the station, and some of the drivers had been women. She'd never seen that before either. It had been one of those lady taxi drivers who'd taken Lily to the warehouse some enterprising San Diegan had turned into a dormitory for military wives and war workers. Within hours Lily had found a place to sleep and wait for Sundays.

Tom had told her she could see him on Sundays. He hadn't mentioned that she could see and speak to him for only those two precious hours each Sunday. Every week they had one hundred and twenty minutes alone with each other and several thousand boots and their visitors. Wives and girls, parents and siblings arrived with overflowing picnic baskets and inflated hopes. Two hours later they filed off the base with depleted hampers and a few crumbs of memories. Lily left with them, carrying the empty picnic basket, the money Tom gave her to live on, and the paltry recollections that would have to get her through her empty life in that crowded room.

It was strange living so intimately with so many women—listening to their sighs in the night, waiting with them in interminable lines for showers and sinks in the morning, dressing and talking and borrowing and lending—and still feeling so alone. She was alone and at loose ends. While Tom arose at five to hike with full combat gear in blazing sun and bone-chilling downpours, smoked a full pack of cigarettes—though he wasn't a smoker—standing at attention with a bucket of sand on his head, and slept with his rifle under his buttocks because he'd neglected to clean a particle of dust from the barrel, Lily went to the movies. There were twenty movie theaters in San Diego and by the end of her first month there the women who sold tickets and signed up blood donors and recruited for the Red Cross in half of them knew Lily by sight. Their greetings and the casual words of the women who came and went in the beds around her in the dorm provided her only companionship from Sunday to Sunday. Then she met Carrie Snyder.

"Are you going to lie there reading movie magazines again today?" the young woman with a mop of curly brown hair and round saucer eyes stopped at the foot of Lily's cot and asked one morning. She looked so much like Little Orphan Annie that Lily wanted to laugh.

"Do you want to borrow some?"

"Listen, kid, I've got a husband away at sea and two kids back in Oklahoma with my mother. I've got to find an apartment so I can bring the kids west and make enough money to keep them here. I haven't got time for movie magazines. And neither do you."

"I don't have any kids. And my boyfriend's at Oceanside. I can only see him on Sundays. Time's about the only thing I do have."

Little Orphan Annie picked up a copy of *Silver Screen.* "It seems to me you could find better ways to spend it than reading these rags."

"Look," Lily said, "I wasn't bothering you. I'm not bothering anyone."

The woman sat on the end of Lily's cot. "I'm sorry. My husband Marty says I've got a big mouth. I guess that's why I don't have a lot of friends around here. But neither do you. Don't take that the wrong way. It's just that I've been watching you. You're not one of the good-time girls who came out here for the fast money in the factories and a little fun with the servicemen. And you're not one of the wives who spend all their time looking for apartments."

"You mean I don't fit in."

"I mean I think you're at loose ends. At least between Sundays. And if you'd read a newspaper instead of this junk—I'm sorry—but if you'd just look around, you'd realize there are a lot of jobs, war jobs, going begging. You'd be helping the war effort, and a job wouldn't do you any harm either." The woman stood. "You're a pretty girl, and you've got a great shape, but you're going to get fat lying around like this. Incidentally, my name's Carrie Snyder, and I'll be leaving for the swing shift around two."

Lily went to the factory with Carrie that afternoon. The interview was cursory. Manpower was draining away, and womanpower was in short supply. Lily had a job.

The following day she put on a pair of slacks, hid her hair beneath the regulation bandanna, and turned up at the factory at three in the afternoon as directed. She was terrified. Baby-sitting and working behind the counter in the five-and-ten were one thing, but doing a man's job in a man's world was something else. Carrie told her not to worry. "Some of the men on the line actually asked me to slow down. I was making them look bad." But that was Carrie.

The factory was a long gray building, or rather a jumble of gray buildings that stretched for acres. On the roof anti-aircraft guns formed menacing black shadows against the blue-white sky. The smell of oil hung in the air like a rugged after-shave lotion. Lily followed Carrie into the building. The noise was deafening. Machines clanked, screamed, and whined. People shouted. Piped-in music droned in a dull undertone.

Carrie pointed Lily in the right direction and went to her own job. Lily walked for what felt like miles, down narrow aisles, across open spaces, past workers who stared and some who scowled and others who didn't even glance up. She got lost several times before she found the right section.

A man with a square face that glistened like the oily machinery looked her up and down and told her she was going to be trained to file. Personally, he said, he didn't think she could do it. Management said women were good at precision work, and he had to listen to management, but just because she could file her nails didn't mean she could file the trailing edge of a plane to within one one-thousandth of an inch, which was what she damn well better learn to do if she wanted to work for him. By the time he handed Lily a tool, her hands were trembling so badly she dropped it. He stood there with his hands on his hips waiting for her to pick it up. When she straightened, she saw that he was smiling for the first time. "Hey, Joe," he called down the line, "they sent me another bimbo who thinks this is a beauty parlor."

Somehow Lily made it through the first week. Carrie was proud of her. Tom's reaction was less enthusiastic. "No wife of mine is going to work." He was standing with his feet, encased in heavy boots, wide apart, his hands behind him, his head high. That was the way he always stood these days, as if the drill instructor had just shouted "at ease."

Lily looked up at him. It never occurred to her to point out that they weren't married, though she thought about the fact constantly.

"Besides, it isn't as if you need the money. Between my pay and the checks from the folks, we've got more than we can spend." He sat beside her on the bench and put an arm around her shoulders. It was always better when he was sitting. "But that's not the real issue, honey. I know what women who work are like, especially women who work in factories. You'll start out dressing like a guy, then you'll be talking like a guy, and before I know it you'll be acting like a guy. I don't want you to go and get all tough and masculine on me. I love you the way you are."

That was the end of the discussion. At least Lily thought it was until she told Carrie she was going to quit.

"Don't you like the job?"

"I like having something to do, but Tom doesn't want me to work." Lily told Carrie about their conversation that afternoon.

"Doesn't he care about the war?"

"Of course he cares about the war! He's a marine."

"Then you're going to have to explain to him that for you the job is like being a marine. No, forget that. There's nothing like being a marine to those guys. Just tell him you want to do your part in the war effort, your part in backing him up. He'll like that. And tell him about the other women in the factory. Tell him the only guys left are old men and 4-Fs. Because that's what he's really worried about. Other guys."

Tom still didn't like the idea, but he said he guessed it was okay for a while. Besides, he had more serious matters on his mind that Sunday. A boot had disappeared from camp the previous week. The rumor was that he'd hung himself in the latrine. Just couldn't take it, men muttered to each other. Then why the hell did he join the marines, they argued and toughened their own resolve.

In February Tom graduated, Lily quit her job—"I knew you wouldn't make it," the foreman with the greasy face smirked—and they took their two-week honeymoon in Laguna Beach. At least they called it a honeymoon. They still weren't married. Lily would be eighteen in August. Until that time the state of California left all marital decisions to the superior wisdom and profound concern of her parents. Lily had written them for the required permission, though it had taken Tom several weeks to convince her to.

"I don't want to have anything to do with them," she'd insisted.

Tom was surprised. He'd never thought of Lily as stubborn.

"There must be a way we can get married without their permission."

"Only if we wait till August, and I might not be here in August," he said.

Lily wrote the letter.

Confident that good manners and a little charm would do the trick as they always had with his parents, Tom wrote one of his own. Joseph Hartarski threw out his daughter's letter without opening it. He didn't read Tom's, but he did check the envelope to make sure no money had been enclosed. After all, Tom was a rich man's son. He could afford to pay for what he wanted.

Tom said it didn't matter. In the wide bed in the hotel overlooking the sea, he insisted they were as married as any church or government could make them. He pulled Lily down on top of him.

His dog tags, cushioned with rubber so no clinking sound would give him away to the enemy, were the only thing between them. "Right?" he asked.

"Right," she agreed, and almost believed it. After all, the man at the desk called her Mrs. Lund, and the maids who made up the room and asked if she wanted this laundered or that pressed called her ma'am, and a woman in the next chair in the hotel beauty parlor had confided that Lily and her husband made such a handsome couple.

Handsome and blissfully happy. Swimming in the pool because the beach was covered with barbed wire and anti-aircraft guns, basking in the liquid sun, dancing every night, making love in the wide old-fashioned bed with the massive carved posts whenever they wanted, as often as they wanted, they were happy. Lily was so happy that she barely thought about the fact that she'd stopped going to church.

Someday she'd go back and confess. She'd tell the priest that she and Tom had made love and, what was worse, used something.

They'd had an argument about that, or at least the closest thing to an argument they had during those two weeks. She was horrified that first night when he turned away from her in bed and opened the drawer of the night table. It was filled with little packets. She hadn't seen him put them there. FOR PREVENTION OF DISEASE ONLY ran across each one in bold black letters. "No," she whispered as she had that first night in his car, but this time Tom paid no attention. He took one of the packets from the drawer and tore it open. She sat up in bed. "It's awful."

"It's not awful, Lily. It's practical."

"It's a sin."

"For Christ sake—" he started, then stopped abruptly, and she knew he'd been about to say something against the Church. "Look, Lily, it will be more of a sin to bring some poor kid into this world as a bastard. Is that what you want?"

"Of course not."

"That makes two of us. If we were married, I wouldn't care. Christ, if we were married, I'd love a kid, but we're not married, and the chances of our getting married before I ship out are getting slimmer all the time, so we've got to be practical."

"But they're so ugly."

He kissed her. "Then close your eyes."

"And they're a sin," she repeated.

He pulled her down beside him. "They'll be my sin." He kissed her again. "Tell the priest I forced you."

"But—"

He licked away the word. "Be quiet, Lily," he whispered against her mouth. "Be quiet because we don't have any time at all."

And that was what convinced her. She hated the sin, and she hated the ugly romance-killing things, but she loved Tom and she had so little time left to love him.

At the end of their two weeks Tom reported to his combat unit, and Lily returned to the dorm. Carrie Snyder was gone. Someone said she'd left Lily a note but no one seemed to know what had happened to it. That was wartime, someone else said. Ships that pass in the night.

Tom's unit prepared to move out. He didn't know where and he didn't know when, but he knew it would be soon. Occasionally he got an overnight pass, and they went to a hotel. At the beginning of May, the week Corregidor finally fell, he got a weekend pass. That was the tipoff. After that he telephoned Lily every day to say goodbye.

"When are you leaving?" she asked the first time he called.

"I don't know."

"Then why are you saying goodbye?"

Tom turned his back to the crowd of men on the other side of the telephone booth window. A sign above his head caught his eye.

> When calling Anne or Louise
> Don't dally by shooting the breeze
> Make your talk short and sweet
> Then beat a retreat
> So your buddies can call if they please

"Because there's a war on, honey. Once we get orders, they don't give us a chance to make phone calls. It's all hush-hush."

"Then how will I know you're shipping out?"

"When I don't call anymore."

"Can't I see you to say goodbye?"

"Not unless I get another pass, and there isn't much chance of that. Though you never know. The brass is always screwing up.

We're ready to leave tonight so they'll probably keep us here for another six months."

Lily went back to her cot, lay down, and stared at the ceiling. Gradually the tears began to run down her temples into her hair. Tom was only a few miles away, but he might as well have been halfway around the world.

They didn't keep Tom there for another six months. He and thousands of other American boys were needed in the East, where Burma had followed Corregidor into Japanese hands.

He called for the next three days. Then the shouts of Lily's name summoning her to the pay phone at the end of the dorm stopped.

The following day she went to the Spanish style church she'd been passing ever since she'd arrived in San Diego. The aroma of incense brought her home. The adobe arches might have been the soaring gothic spaces of St. Peter's. The bell of the confessional tinkled familiarly. Her fingers recognized the dusty plush curtain. The shadowy outline of the priest's face was the same.

The words still came with difficulty. This time the priest didn't ask how many times but how many men.

"One." Her voice struck a chord of indignation. "We're going to be married."

The priest gave her a light penance. The war was revaluing sin.

That Sunday Lily took communion. The host tasted exactly as it had six months earlier halfway across the country, but the peace and joy were gone. Tom had taken them with him.

She returned to the movies, although she was careful about which theaters she chose. She gave Broadway, especially Broadway from Twelfth to Sixteenth, a wide berth. If you stood anywhere in that area and looked down to the harbor, you'd see a sea of white hats. The navy had landed, and the navy could be raucous and drunk and dangerous, especially to a girl alone, especially to a girl alone who looked like Lily. She went to out-of-the-way theaters. There she sat in the darkness day after day, night after night, and tried not to think. Sometimes she sat through a movie two or three times because when the image on the screen faded and the lights came up, she had neither the strength nor the courage to get up and go out into the world.

Then one night fear, instead of keeping her in her seat, drove her from the theater. As the voice of Movietone News droned through the darkness, she fought her way out the row of seats. The announcer's words mingled with her own of apology and her neighbors' of protest. *The Battle of Midway,* the voice intoned. "Sorry," Lily murmured. "Watch it, lady." The soundtrack shrieked and hissed and popped. On the screen planes exploded, water erupted in geysers, and flames consumed everything. *One hundred and forty-seven American planes lost compared to the devastating Japanese total of three hundred thirty-two.* "Excuse me." "Down in front." Lily struggled out the row of seats and up the center aisle but the sound of gunfire and explosions and death continued to thunder in her ears.

In the lobby she stopped and leaned against a pillar. One of the ushers who knew her by sight asked if she was okay. From the dark reaches beyond the curtain the Voice of Movietone News turned to the homefront. The deep sonorous tones asked several women workers in a shipyard how they liked their jobs. They said they liked them just fine.

Lily dragged herself out of the theater. Across the street a diner was still open. She went in, sat at the counter, and ordered coffee. The waitress was young and wore a starched dress and cap that reminded Lily of the uniform she'd worn in the five-and-ten. That was when she realized what Carrie had meant months earlier. Lily had always had a job because she'd always needed the money, but there were other reasons to work.

The following morning she went back to the aircraft factory. The man in the hiring office sighed and said that was the trouble with gals. They had no sense of responsibility. They thought work was a party you could show up for if you felt like it. Still, he was short-handed on the graveyard shift, eleven to seven, he added with a smirk.

Lily hesitated. She couldn't imagine going to work in the middle of the night, going to sleep when everyone else was starting the day. "Take it or leave it," the man said. She said she'd take it.

After a week on the graveyard shift Lily went back to the hiring office. She delivered a practiced smile to the man behind the desk. "I thought something might have opened up on another shift."

"You got something against the graveyard shift, honey?"

"I've been there every night. On time. I just thought there might be something else."

He sat staring at her for a while, then shuffled through some papers on his desk. "You interested in a training program? Wanna be a grinder?"

Lily had no idea what a grinder was. "On what shift?"

"You'll train days. Then maybe I can get you on the swing shift."

"How much does it pay?"

"More than you're making now."

She said she'd take it.

For eight hours a day, six days a week, she studied calipers and micrometers and various testing devices. Then she was assigned to the engine division on the swing shift.

This time as she put on her trousers and wound a bandanna around her hair for her first day on the new job she was more excited than nervous. There was something she could do, and the training supervisor had said she did it okay—for a girl.

She reached the factory well before three that afternoon. Hundreds of workers were pouring in. Hundreds more began flowing out. Gulls swooped and shrieked over the anti-aircraft guns. The smell of machinery and oil floated on the soft afternoon breeze. Lily tucked an errant strand of hair in..o her bandanna, showed her badge, and passed through the gate. She was an old pro.

She walked and walked, past miles of machinery and workers. Trucks drove up and down the aisles. A mini-firewagon came wailing toward her, then swerved away. She kept going, through the noise and dirt and confusion. It was like walking through a purposeful madhouse.

Finally she reached the engine division. Carrie had lied about the feminization of the factory. This was still a male domain. Fifty pairs of eyes turned to stare. "Well, what do we have here?" The foreman's eyes roved up and down Lily measuring every millimeter. He reminded her of her father, though she couldn't figure out why. There was no physical resemblance. The foreman was huge, as tall as Tom, with wide shoulders and thick arms and legs that looked as if they were going to burst the fabric of his shirt and trousers. It wasn't his facial features. They were as fleshy as her father's were sharp. Then it came to her. He reeked with the foul smell of abused power.

He told the men to get back to work and took Lily to her machine. He didn't tell her she'd never be able to do the job, but he didn't act as if he thought she could either. He just stood watching her. He watched her all that first day. Even when she left her machine and crossed the work area for supper and her two ladies' room breaks, he went on staring at her.

The second day was better. One of the men actually said hello to her when they came on shift. Smitty—that was what the men called the foreman; he called them by their last names—was still watching her, but just before supper, he told her she'd be okay. "You're going to make it, honey," he said. And on her second day she found Carrie Snyder again.

Carrie was sitting at one of the long cluttered tables in the cafeteria with a coffee cup in one hand and a newspaper in the other. She didn't look up from the war news when Lily sat across from her.

"Are you memorizing that paper?" Lily asked.

Carrie glanced up, her face tired and worn as the dog-eared newspaper. Then she recognized Lily and all the anger and exhaustion disappeared into the tiny lines that gathered at the corners of her big round eyes when she smiled.

They had a lot of catching up to do. Carrie had found an apartment and brought her kids west. "Not a real apartment, of course. My landlady has an eye for a fast buck. She put a sink and toilet in her garage and calls it an efficiency. But now she wants to evict me. She doesn't like kids. No one does. Have you seen the signs? 'No pets and children.' I want to know what we're fighting for." Carrie stood as the whistle blew. "A country that has no room for kids?"

By the end of the second week Lily had fallen into a routine. If she got up an hour earlier, she had to wait only ten or fifteen minutes for a shower. She learned to put on her makeup and comb her hair in the mirror of her compact rather than wait for a turn in the bathroom. At work the pressure was unrelenting, but she managed to keep up. Most of the men greeted her now, a few even talked to her on the way to or from the machines. Smitty said she was doing fine. "A-okay, honey," he added, and patted her bottom. Lily twisted away quickly, but he'd already moved on to the knot of men who'd gathered for their break to trade war news and sports scores and wisecracks Lily wasn't supposed to hear. In his back pocket Smitty carried a fat wallet bound by a rubber band, and he liked to take it out and pass around pictures of his wife and children.

There was no doubt about it, by the end of the second week Lily was an old pro, and a full-fledged member of the union. She would have joined even if they'd given her a choice—Joseph Hartarski used to say the union was the only friend a working man had, at least he used to say it when he was a working man—but they hadn't given her a choice. They'd just told her it was a union shop, and if she wanted to work in it, she had to join. The initiation fee was high, but then so were Lily's wages.

"I can't believe it," she said to Carrie one day in the cafeteria. "With time and a half for Saturdays, I'm making almost forty dollars a week."

"You're making seventy-eight cents an hour, right?" Carrie asked, her eyes growing rounder with anger. "The men who're doing that job are making a dollar twenty-five."

Lily looked up from the bathing suit ads she'd been studying. She'd already bought three new suits which were about two too many since she could wear them only on Sundays, but she didn't think she'd be able to resist these cute knotted handkerchief numbers. "They've been doing it for longer."

Carrie put down her cup. "What difference does that make? You're doing the same job."

"But they have families to support."

"*I* have a family to support. You don't think you can take care of two kids on a chief petty officer's pay, do you?"

Lily was glad when the whistle sounded. Carrie did have a family to support, but Lily still thought it was, well, right that men got paid more. After all, they were men.

Carrie wasn't in the cafeteria for the next few days. At first Lily thought she was angry and avoiding her, then she found out from the bucker Carrie worked with—riveters always worked in pairs—that Carrie hadn't been to work at all. The following day she was back with black smudges beneath her eyes and a new sharpness to her chin. Three nights ago she'd returned home to find six-year-old Tricia and four-year-old Martin alone in the house. The high school girl who cared for them from three to eleven had put their dinner on the table and gone off with a sailor. Carrie had spent the past three days hunting for a replacement, but who wanted to earn thirty-five cents an hour taking care of children when she could make twice that working in a factory?

"I lock my little one in the car," a woman halfway down the table said.

Carrie's round eyes bulged in horror. "I wouldn't lock a dog in a car. Even if I had a car."

"I send mine to the movies," another riveter added. "They're open twenty-four hours now, and there're always plenty of other kids around."

Carrie stood though the whistle hadn't blown. "In England they have nurseries to care for the children."

"In England," the woman who locked her child in the car said, "they got the Blitz. Give me the good old U.S. of A. every time."

Carrie began missing work more often. Tricia had a cold. Martin caught it. The new baby-sitter didn't show up. Management accused her of taking time off to go joyriding and on shopping sprees.

"I don't know how much longer I can take it," she confided to Lily one night in a corner of the garage. The children were asleep behind a curtain, and Carrie had broken out two bottles of beer. "I worry about the kids, and there's never enough time to market and cook and clean, and I'm so—" She put her beer down on the white metal table and put her head in her hands. "I'm so damn lonely. You don't know. You can't know. You and Tom weren't together for that long." Lily peeled away the label on her beer. "But I've lived with Marty for nine years. For nine years I could turn over in the middle of the night, and he'd be there." She took a long swallow of her beer. "And now there's no one. I'm alone. I'm mother and father and breadwinner, and I'm so damn tired of being alone."

Lily knew what she meant, even if she hadn't been married to Tom for nine years, even if she wasn't married to Tom at all. A world without men was as gray and bleak as the factory walls that framed her days.

"You're good, honey. Real good," Smitty said the morning after Carrie had broken down about her loneliness, and this time his hand rested on Lily's bottom as if he thought it belonged there. She pushed it away. He grinned. He had a disreputable smile that he knew women liked. Any number of them had told him so. "How 'bout a beer after work?" he asked.

"No thanks," Lily said.

"Come on, honey, just a beer." He was still smiling.

"I have to write to my boyfriend."

"You finish that letter to your boyfriend yet?" he asked the next afternoon.

"I write every day."

"What do you do after you write?"

"I go to bed."

His tongue darted over his lips. "What do you do for a good time?"

"I'm not looking for a good time."

He moved closer. The smile was frozen on his big face now. "Listen, honey, maybe you don't understand. I can do you a lot of good." His stomach grazed her arm. "I can do you a lot of harm too. Every couple of months you get reviewed. It's me who says whether you get upgraded." He pressed closer. His breath rasped like a machine that needed oiling. Over his shoulder she saw the other men watching. One or two looked sorry, most merely curious. "And it's up to me to say whether you get fired."

Fired. Like her father. Like so many of the men she'd known when she was growing up. Then Lily remembered the pile of bathing suits on her shelf, the line of dresses hanging on the rack beside her bed, the money Tom had left her. She didn't need the job. But the job needed her. Suddenly there were thousands of jobs that needed her. She took both her hands and pushed against him. His chest felt like stone. He didn't budge. She moved her leg threateningly. He stepped back. "Then fire me," she said, and pushed past him to the ladies' room, the only place in the factory he couldn't follow her.

Smitty didn't fire her, but he didn't give up either. He was all hands and smiles and veiled threats.

"You don't have to take that," Carrie said.

"Take what?" Lily asked.

"His harassment."

Lily looked across the table in surprise. Carrie was smarter than she and older, but sometimes she just didn't know very much. "That's the way men are. Like the deacon in my church and Mr. Bannion when I used to baby-sit. They don't mean anything by it."

"Of course, they mean something by it!" Carrie's voice rose above the din of the cafeteria.

Lily put her sandwich down. "All right, I suppose they do, but a girl just has to know how to take care of herself. Don't worry, Carrie. I can handle Smitty." She laughed. "He isn't half as quick as Mr. Bannion."

That week Lily got her first batch of letters from Tom. Carrie had warned her it would be that way, weeks of silence, then a feast of mail. Tom wrote that he'd received eighteen of Lily's letters in one delivery.

Between the dense black patches left by the censor, Lily read about Tom's friends. He said he couldn't tell her where he was, and it wouldn't matter if he could, because no one had ever heard of the godforsaken hole to begin with and no one would miss it if it were blown off the face of the earth. But his buddies, his buddies were something else. The funniest, smartest, toughest guys you were ever likely to run across. Tom wrote that he missed Lily and loved her, but it sounded from those letters as if he didn't love her nearly so much as he loved those buddies.

15

BY JUNE of 1942 the war being fought in the name of democracy was, in fact, turning into a democratic war. The sons of the rich were dying alongside the sons of the poor; a custom-tailored uniform was no more bulletproof than government issue; a college education less an advantage on the front lines than practical experience. Even on the homefront the war knew neither social nor economic lines. If the poor suddenly had money in their pockets thanks to the demands of war production and the small businessman was getting rich quick on the government's cost-plus contracts, old money was making new sacrifices. The people Isabel had grown up among who were accustomed to savoring the simple pleasures of life on Long Island's eastern tip faced bleak prospects that first summer of the war. The ban on weather reports on the radio and in the newspaper made it impossible to plan anything. The oil slick from sunken shipping covering the beach inconvenienced those who'd neglected to put pools on their estates. And there was a shortage of golf balls.

"War is hell," Andy said to her one night in the club bar as they listened to the group at the next table complaining. He and Spence had got a weekend pass and managed to catch a flight down. "What's going to happen to your handicap, Isabel?"

"I don't have a handicap. And don't be so smug. Not everyone can be a flyboy." She found herself repeating the phrase often these days. The closer Andy and Spence got to going overseas, the more inadequate she felt.

They left the dance early, though back at the sleeping house they found a portable radio that they took out to the patio so they could go on dancing. Glenn Miller's band was playing and Ray Eberle was singing about "Imagination" and pretty soon they stopped dancing and ended up in one of the chaises, a tangle of arms and legs and mouths and surplus clothing. He kept waiting for her to say stop and sit up and straighten her clothing the way girls like her did, and then when it had gone so far that he'd stopped expecting her to, she did. Actually, she didn't so much say stop as breath it into his ear. He knew the lie of that sound and probably wouldn't have stopped at all if the radio announcer hadn't broken into the music at that point with a bulletin. Isabel's unsteady hands were trying to make some order of her clothing, and Andy was lying there looking up at her with the most god-awful ache, and the announcer was telling them that the FBI had seized eight saboteurs who'd been landed by German U-boats off Long Island and Florida.

"Amagansett," she said, and stopped worrying about her clothing. "That's practically next door."

"Scared?" His hand began to toy with those buttons again.

She looked down at him. In the darkness his grin was as white and hard as the crescent of moon suspended over the house. "How could I be scared? The Army Air Corp's here. Besides, it happened days ago. The radio says they've been caught."

The music returned and Ray Eberle pleaded with them to "say it over and over again" and Andy pulled her down beside him on the chaise, but for the first time in her life Isabel resisted her own inclinations. Some instinct of self-preservation warned her that with Andy Barnes she had to.

He lay there looking up at her, and there was no particular kindness in his face. "I suppose it would be all right if I told you I loved you."

"It would be all right," she said, and went and sat on another chaise, "if I thought *I* loved *you.*"

He laughed then, but the sound was off-key.

The next afternoon she drove him and Spence to the airfield to catch a flight back to the base. The sun was a garish balloon sinking toward the horizon and she shielded her eyes with her hand as she watched them slouch across the tarmac, their caps set at raffish angles, their duffles slung over their shoulders. Unlike army and navy officers, flyers, Isabel had noticed, made a point of honor of their lack of military bearing. Spence climbed into the plane. Andy grabbed the hatch and swung his long body up in a single smooth motion. The sheer grace of his movement made her catch her breath.

On the way back to the house, she stopped for gas. Her father's position in Washington had its bright side. He'd managed to get them an x-card.

A man standing beside a Chevy coupe was asking directions, but old Hap who ran the station was pretending not to hear. The only thing Hap hated more than summer people was strangers.

The man pushed a battered straw hat back on his head and looked at Isabel. "I'm trying to find Amagansett," he said without taking the cigarette from his mouth.

She gave him directions. Hap glowered at both of them and screwed the cap back on Isabel's car.

"You from around here?" the man asked.

"Summer people," Isabel said, and Hap glowered again.

"Know your way around the back roads and beaches?"

"More or less." Isabel couldn't figure out what he was getting at.

The man took out his wallet and showed Isabel a card. "Lew Packer. I'm with CBS news. I suppose you heard about those spies the Nazis dropped off from one of their U-boats."

Hap stopped glowering and moved a step closer.

"I thought they'd already caught them," Isabel said.

"They did. They were landed on June thirteenth, but the FBI didn't dare break the news until they'd rounded them up. Can you imagine the panic if word got out that a bunch of Nazi spies were running around Long Island?"

"Then, it's not much of a story anymore, is it?"

"Are you kidding? Now that the public doesn't have to be scared, they want all the gory details. Which beach they were dropped on. How they buried their stuff in the dead of night. Their devious path to New York. Their nefarious contacts here."

"I thought you said you were a newsman. No vivid writing, please."

Lew Packer smiled at her. "A smart girl, eh? That's even better. Listen, how would you like to help? Time is, as they say, of the essence. The papers can run pictures. All I've got on my side is speed. So if you show me around, I won't have to waste time asking directions from local yokels or getting lost. What do you say?"

She said sure.

It wasn't much of a story. Isabel didn't fool herself that she was helping the war effort or even keeping the public informed. There was little enough to see. The police had cordoned off the beach. Inhabitants of the area had only vague or obviously fabricated recollections of that foggy night two weeks earlier. No, Isabel didn't fool herself that she was doing something important, but she was doing something.

"Normally, I'd offer to pay you," Packer said as they stood beside their cars later that evening. The sun had disappeared in the direction of the city and he was obviously eager to follow it. "But" —he looked from Isabel, her long arms and legs tan against the white linen dress, to the LaSalle and back—"you don't look as if you need it. So if there's ever anything—"

"There is," Isabel said.

Packer looked surprised.

"A job. Are there any jobs at CBS? I might as well tell you right now that I can't type."

He took the cigarette out of his mouth and laughed. "Are you kidding? There's nothing but jobs. Don't you know there's a war on?"

Isabel debated how to ask the next question. She'd been brought up never to talk about money. "How much would I get paid? I mean, could I make enough to support myself?"

Packer ground his half-smoked cigarette out in the sandy shoulder of the road, took a fresh one from the pack in his pocket, and lit it. He looked at Isabel closely. Even in the quick flare of a match she spelled money. "Look, kid, it's none of my business, but are you running away from some guy?"

Isabel laughed. "You've been reading—or writing—too many spy stories. I just want to know if I'll be able to find a place to live and support myself."

"Support yourself, yes. Find a place to live, not likely. These days you can barely find an empty hotel room. But listen, my girl's roommate just joined the WAC. You could probably move in with her." It was growing darker, but Isabel's silky polish glowed in the moonlight. He didn't want some society kid screwing up his personal life. "I have to warn you though. I'm around at all hours. And I mean all hours."

Isabel said she didn't care if he slept there, which, of course, was exactly what he'd meant.

"Okay, kid, you've got a job. Show up here tomorrow morning." He leaned on the hood of the car, scribbled on a scrap of paper, and handed it to her. "I promise they'll have a job for you."

The following morning Isabel turned up at 485 Madison Avenue. She felt as if she'd come home. The clatter of the teletype machines and the jangling bells that signaled a bulletin or flash were more seductive to her than any music. The constant pressure as news surged in from correspondents and stringers all over the world and reports flowed in from the short-wave-listening staff that monitored foreign broadcasts quickened her pulse. A week earlier, hours had dragged; now units of time had no meaning. Life in the newsroom was that exciting.

As things turned out, she didn't interfere in Lew Packer's personal life. For the first time anyone could remember, Eliot Childs backed down. He said he supposed it was all right for his daughter to work in the CBS newsroom—as long as there was a war on. The house in town was partially closed, the furniture protected by dust covers, the old family portraits shrouded in green baize, the rugs rolled up, but old Cora had stayed on to keep an eye on things. Isabel, Eliot announced, might as well camp out there as with some stranger.

In the newsroom she was assigned to cover the UP service. For hours on end she sat hunched over the ticker picking up stories that might be news and rewriting them for the air. The job wasn't likely to win any Pulitzers, but Isabel wasn't complaining. She knew she was a beginner. More important, she was convinced this was only the beginning for her.

That was the important part. Her. Suddenly she wasn't the daughter of Eliot Childs, the financier, or Grace Childs, the social arbiter. She wasn't even the deb who'd had half the Yale crew in love with her in one season or the girl who could have married Jack Livingston but decided not to. She was just an untested amalgam of intelligence and ability and determination that had to prove itself.

Of course, the amalgam came packaged. It wasn't entirely true that no one cared who she was or where she'd come from. Some of the men recognized her father's name. Most of the women noticed her clothes that were too simple not to be expensive. But when the bell jangled signaling a bulletin and the minute hand moved inexorably toward the hourly news broadcast, all they wanted to know was if she could get the job done.

Sam Wicker had no doubts. That first day he saw her in the newsroom, where he'd turned up because one of his accounts had decided to sponsor the three o'clock broadcast, he made up his mind. He stood watching her at the ticker, her fine cheekbone resting on one fist, her copper hair hanging forward to half hide her face, the concentration that made her chew the end of her pencil childishly, and knew. His eyes followed her as she crossed the room, delivering stories, picking up assignments, trading quips, and he knew this was no lightweight glamour girl who sang about toothpaste or posed for soap.

If she had been, he would have asked her out then and there. Instead he waited more than a week. By that time Isabel was nodding to him, albeit absentmindedly, when they passed in the halls of 485 Madison. They were alone in the elevator when he asked her to lunch. Isabel looked up from the typescript she was studying and took the pencil she'd been chewing from her mouth. "Thanks, but I don't go out for lunch. I share a sandwich with the ticker."

"Then how about dinner? Or a drink? I understand the ticker's a teetotaler."

She looked up from the script again, and he could tell that she was seeing him for the first time.

He was handsome, Isabel thought. There was no doubt about that. The lashes would have been unfair even on a girl. And that cleft in his chin was too good to be true. But that was the trouble. All of him looked too good to be true. His pin-striped suit was meticulously tailored, his shirt and tie carefully chosen, his collar pin too shiny. Try as she might to shed them, Isabel still carried the prejudices of her background. "We don't buy clothes," her mother used to say. "We have clothes." Everything about Sam Wicker looked too new and perfect. He wasn't her type. An image of Andy Barnes as he'd looked swinging up into the plane flashed through her mind. "Thanks, but I usually work late."

"Look," Sam said, and followed her off the elevator. "Think of it as working late. You don't plan to spend the rest of your life rewriting stories off the wires, do you?"

She stopped walking and turned to him. "What do you mean?"

"I mean you want to get ahead in radio, and I know a lot about radio. At least, the commercial end of it. Pick my brain."

By August when the American Eighth Air Force had launched their first independent raids on the continent, she was picking his brain regularly over lunch and dinner, before the theater and after the movies. He taught her about Crossley and Hooper Ratings, about sponsors who were willing to pay $22,000 a week to a comedian to plug a cigarette no one could get anyway because of the shortages, and about sustaining programs that carried the name of no sponsor but a lot of cachet. She learned who had the power and all about network politics and the importance of being in the right place at the right time. Though the last, he warned one night, was not enough. When things didn't fall into your lap, you had to make them happen. They were having dinner at 21. Sam had been coming there since he'd first had an expense account. On the day Isabel was born, Eliot had laid down a bottle of Chateau Lafitte in the cellar to be drunk on her twenty-first birthday.

"The way you do?" she asked. Over the past few months Isabel had learned quite a bit about Sam Wicker. He didn't flaunt his past, but as they got to know each other, he didn't hide it either. Isabel knew that a lot of men in his position would.

His laugh was deep and quiet, one of the few things about him that wasn't brash. "I had to. No one comes along and offers little Jewish boys from the Bronx scholarships to Cornell. I had to fight tooth and nail—not to mention study round the clock and sweat my guts out on the basketball court—for it. And when I got out, the agency didn't come knocking on Sammy Wischansky's door offering me a job. I've brought in more new clients than any other account executive, and I've had to scramble for every one of them. Just the way I had to for you." He put his hand over hers on the table. She didn't take hers away, but she didn't respond either. She liked Sam, but not that way. There was no passion to their relationship, at least on her part—except when they discussed the war.

Sam was quick to admit he wasn't 4-F, merely smart. He had a desire, absurd, he supposed, but heartfelt, to be alive to see the end of this war. So he contributed enough of his advertising expertise to publicizing scrap metal collections, promoting observance of OPA restrictions, and organizing war bond drives to make him indispensable to the war effort. Isabel didn't argue with his position—if you weren't risking your own life, you didn't have the right to suggest that someone else ought to—but she was no good at hiding her feelings. "I know you think I'm a coward, Isabel—hell, maybe I am —but until the generals decide they can't win the war without me, I'm going to stay right here and do what I know how to do best. I'm not interested in being a hero—not even for you."

Sam's other lessons, however, were not lost on her. She began making opportunities for herself. When a newscaster needed background on some unpronounceable place where all hell had just broken loose, Isabel, who followed the war maps with a vengeance, just happened to have the information. When one of the reporters returned from lunch drunk, she found an empty office for him to sleep it off and covered the daily OPA briefing for him. Luck was with her—again. It happened to be an important news conference. Coffee rationing was announced.

"Well done," Sam said when he toasted her coffee coup that night with scotch that wasn't rationed but was becoming harder to find. "Well done, but not good enough."

"What do you mean?"

"I'm not going to be happy until you're broadcasting the news as well as writing it. What's more important, neither are you."

"Don't be silly," she said, but Sam could tell from the throaty excitement in her voice that she didn't think he was in the least silly. "There are no women newscasters."

"That's right, Isabel, and before the war there were no women steelworkers or cabdrivers or members of the military. Now there are Rosie the Riveters and WACs and WAVEs and SPARs. Why not the news by Isabel Childs?"

Why not indeed? Her opportunity came ten days later. The broadcaster for the noon news had been felled by a vicious flu. The head of the newsroom was on the phone to every restaurant and bar in town trying to track down another announcer. "I can do it," Isabel said when she dropped a script on his desk.

"You can do what?"

"Broadcast the twelve o'clock news."

"What've you been putting in your coffee, Isabel?"

"I mean it. You need someone to read the news, and I'm qualified. And willing."

"You've been taking lessons from Murrow and Kaltenborn and Severeid, no doubt."

"All my life people have been telling me that my diction's good, and my voice, well, that that's pretty good too. I know how to read. I learned as a kid."

He looked her up and down. "There's only one small problem. You're a woman, and women can't read the news. Their voices aren't suited to it."

"What's that supposed to mean?"

He turned back to the phone. "It means I said no. Now get out of here and let me get back to work. I've got forty-five minutes to track down a man who can read the news."

The story of Isabel's offer traveled the network grapevine. Lew Packer said the kid had guts, another man and a few secretaries said she had her nerve, but most people just laughed. What if she had to announce a defeat, one reporter joked. She'd probably break down and cry. What if she got her period, a particular misogynist added. She probably wouldn't show up for the broadcast at all.

So much for the news by Isabel Childs, she reported to Sam over dinner a few nights later.

16

BY FALL Michael had almost completed his basic training and between them he and Eliza had more than a hundred and fifty letters to show for it. Every night after she put Teddy to bed, she went to Michael's desk and tried to make something of interest of her empty life. Michael wrote that he loved her letters. They were the high point of his days. His own letters were less carefully composed but always funny. He could tell about staggering off a train at three in the morning, being marched through rain and mud to a mess hall, and being fed lima beans and baloney—*That's the army's idea of* haute cuisine; *I'm working on getting the recipe for Dolly.*—and make it sound amusing. He could find humor in a week spent wandering around in various states of undress while doctors shot him full of antibodies for every disease known to man and a few still unknown and officers lectured him endlessly on how, when, and where to salute. He could turn the joke on himself and his former meticulousness when he wrote that the army had two size uniforms—too big and too small.

Then two weeks before the end of his thirteen-week training

period, he called to say he'd be home a week early but for less time than he'd expected. It was the army way of doing things. He was due in on Friday night.

"What time?" Eliza's mind was already racing ahead. What would she make for dinner? What would she wear? If his train didn't get in till late, should she keep Teddy up?

"Sometime between five and midnight. We do things by the clock in the army, sweetheart. See you then."

Her hand tightened on the phone. Don't hang up yet, she wanted to scream. Don't take your voice away yet. "Are you all right?" she asked.

"I'm fine. Listen, sweetheart, I have to go. There're about three thousand guys waiting for this phone."

A minute, she prayed. Just one minute. "Is it very hot down there?"

"As hell. Listen, sweetheart . . ."

She could hear the shouts in the background. Come-on-Kramer-hey-you-camping-out-in-there and other words, ruder words.

". . . I have to go. Otherwise, a couple of buddies are going to use me for target practice."

She hung up and sat staring at the small black machine that had attached them tenuously for a few minutes. She'd pleaded with him to stay on, but the men behind him, his "buddies"—a word he'd never used before—had told him to get off, and he'd listened to them.

She stood and started moving around the apartment. He'd be home Friday. Then they'd have five days. Saturday, Sunday, Monday, Tuesday, Wednesday. Five whole days. It sounded almost like a lifetime. She wouldn't waste a minute of it. She'd make everything count.

Or almost everything. The timing was a little off. The army didn't take ovulation cycles into consideration when scheduling leaves. There'd be no new baby this time around.

For the next two days she and Dolly cleaned and scrubbed. Dolly was exhausted, but Eliza was functioning on pure adrenaline. Thursday she put Teddy in his stroller and went to the florist, where she bought roses and lilies and daisies and freesias. The florist delivered them that afternoon, and she spent two hours arranging them in bowls and vases all over the apartment. Then she left Teddy with Dolly and took a taxi downtown. She went to Saks and Bergdorfs and Jay Thorpe before she found the right night-gown. It was creamy satin with coffee-colored lace and would have to be sent to a French cleaner rather than laundered. But that would be after the leave. *After the leave.* A time Eliza refused to think about.

That night after Teddy was asleep she ran a hot bath and sprinkled it with the Chanel No. 5 Michael had bought her last spring for no reason other than pleasure. It was her dress rehearsal bath. She lay in the tub, her hair curling in the gently rising steam, and counted the time until he'd be home. The anticipation was so delicious she could almost taste it.

At two the next afternoon she repeated the ritual, but found it harder to linger in the tub. Her expectancy had taken on a sharp edge.

She stood in front of her closet and began sliding hangers across the rod. An afternoon dress? A suit? An evening dress? What would he want her to wear? What would he expect her to wear? Would he rather go out? She'd paid a fortune for those steaks. She thought of the new nightgown, folded lovingly around a sachet in her lingerie drawer. Would he expect to go to bed right away? Eliza sat on the side of the bed and stared at her open closet. She felt as if she were going on a blind date.

By ten o'clock she was no longer shy, only desperate. The ice in the bucket had melted. She'd taken the steaks out to get them to room temperature and replaced them in the refrigerator twice. It had taken her more than an hour to get Teddy to sleep. She'd had the sense not to tell him Daddy was coming home, but Teddy was no fool. He knew something was up.

The bell rang at a little after ten. She was in the bedroom combing her hair, again. She ran for the door. On the other side of it was a stranger in uniform. His face was brown and boyishly thin. His upper lip was naked. The uniform was neat and starched, the crossed rifles on the lapel polished to a blinding brilliance. The stranger took off his service cap, stepped inside the apartment, and kissed her. Without the mustache he even felt different.

He stepped back and looked at her. She felt the shyness creeping up her throat, spreading over her cheeks. "You look wonderful," he said. Then he moved in and kissed her again.

"Are you all right?" he asked.

"Fine. Are you?"

"Never better."

She looked up at him. "Never better?" she repeated.

He laughed. "I meant I'm okay. Now that I'm back with you. And I'm fine otherwise."

He put his arm around her and they moved into the living room. "I want three things," he said. "I want to see Teddy. I want a perfect dry martini. And I want a hot bath. I'm filthy from the train. And I'm sick to death of showers. Crowded showers."

"So that's why you're home."

His arm tightened around her waist. "I should have said I want three things first. I have a major plan in mind, Mrs. Kramer. I'm talking strategy not tactics."

He went down the hall to Teddy's room and she refilled the ice bucket and made a martini the way she knew he liked it.

"He looks bigger," Michael said when he came back. "Even sleeping he looks bigger. If he can do that in a couple of months, I hate to think . . ." He let his voice trail off. She handed him the drink.

"I got steaks," she said. "And baked potatoes." Her voice sounded thin and nervous, the way it did when she was entertaining strangers for dinner. "But you said you wanted a bath. I'll run it for you." She brushed past him, and he didn't try to stop her.

By the time she came out of the bathroom he was naked. Except for a band of white his body was as brown as his face and as thin. She could count the ribs. And every muscle and tendon. She would have liked that, to run a tally with her hands and her mouth. She was sure he could read the thought on her face. She turned away and began picking up his clothes.

He started for the bathroom. "Come keep me company." He balanced the glass on the side of the tub and slid into the steaming water. She sat on the closed toilet seat.

"I like your dress," he said. "But you're going to get it wet."

"It doesn't matter."

"Silk stains."

He took a sip of his drink, then put it on the floor beside the tub. He glanced up at her. His eyes looked exactly like Teddy's when he was being introduced to a stranger. "Eliza," he said. "I'm trying to get you to take off that dress. I'm trying to get you into this tub."

She went into the bedroom, took off the dress, and kicked off her pumps. Then she went back to the bathroom. He barely gave her time to get out of the rest of her clothes.

They didn't get to the steaks till close to midnight. Michael was opening a bottle of wine as she carried them into the dining room. They'd decided to dress for dinner. He was wearing a silk foulard robe. She'd put on the new nightgown.

He told her about basic training—about learning to take steps that were precisely thirty inches straight to the front for drill and finding the stride best suited to his own build on route march; about oiling his rifle sling and pack carrier strap enough to keep it from drying out, but not so much that it stained his carefully washed uniforms; and about the lines, lines for showers and the writing desk in the company dayroom and the movies and a beer at the post exchange and a bus into town and, worst of all, the phones. And he told her about being no one. Suddenly he was no longer Michael Kramer, brilliant young attorney, the mayor's fair-haired boy, a man with a big future. These days his identity, like everything else about him was government issue, GI, indistinguishable from millions of other men's. "And it's even worse off the base. The only thing Southerners hate more than a soldier is a soldier with a Yankee accent. I've been refused service in a store and asked to pay for a meal before it was served. Women, at least nice women, cross the street to avoid passing me."

Eliza was shocked, then furious. She'd imagined the danger but not the indignity. "All that will change when you're an officer." Michael toyed with his wine glass and said nothing. "You are going to apply for Officer Candidate School, aren't you?"

"I don't think so." His eyes were still focused on the glass. "All my life I've been treated as someone special—"

"Because you deserve to be. Because you worked to be."

"Maybe, but I still think this is a good lesson for me. Besides," he went on before she could interrupt, "I'd probably end up a second lieutenant, and you wouldn't like that at all. He's the guy who says, 'All right, men, follow me.' In other words he's out there in front, and his life expectancy in war or what the sergeant insists on calling 'the greatest game of all' is measured in seconds."

Eliza didn't mention Officer Candidate School again.

After dinner she took the coffee into the living room, Michael poured himself a brandy, and they settled on the sofa. She fit snugly into the crook of his arm. He kissed her temple. "Your hair's still wet," he said.

"Whose fault is that?" She brushed her lips against the back of his hand. "We never made love in a tub before."

"I told you I have a strategy." His fingers toyed with the thin strap of her nightgown. "A furlough plan. I worked it out during all those interminable lectures on military etiquette." His hand moved down her arm taking the strap with it. "I plan to make love to you in every room in this apartment."

She twisted toward him. Beneath the silk robe his body was hard and taut.

"And when we run out of rooms," he murmured against her mouth, "we'll start over again."

It began Monday evening just before dinner. Michael was rough-housing on the floor with Teddy, and Eliza's mother and Michael's were worrying aloud about how thin Michael had grown, and her father and Michael's were asking about what life was like, for a Jew that is, in the army, when suddenly Eliza realized that they'd passed the halfway mark. "What's wrong?" her mother asked, and everyone turned to Eliza. She caught herself and smiled and said nothing was wrong. They all turned back to Michael then, and Eliza went on laughing and talking, touching Michael each time she passed him, trailing a hand across his back or brushing against his arm. Don't ruin it, she warned herself. Don't waste the minutes he's here thinking about the days and months he won't be. But she couldn't help it. The hour glass had been turned upside down, and Eliza couldn't take her eyes off the rapidly running sand.

On Wednesday night she went to the station to see him off again. The destination was different—Fort Bragg, North Carolina—but the scene played the same, maybe worse. He was no longer a raw recruit, but a trained soldier. He was that much closer to the job for which the army was preparing him.

Then two weeks after Michael's furlough, Dolly kicked the last supports out from under the fragile structure that was Eliza's life. She took a war job, if you could call cleaning the ladies' room in a factory that made buttons for military uniforms war work. She didn't like cleaning up after a bunch of women and she didn't like the supervisor who was a lot stricter than Mrs. Kramer, but she liked the hours and the freedom and the money.

Eliza sublet the apartment and took Teddy to live with her parents. There in the old rooms where she'd grown up she and Teddy could be children together. Her mother made her favorite dishes, and her father came home every night and brought toys for Teddy and books and magazines for her, and she had nothing to do but write to Michael and read the letters he wrote in return.

Her sister Pam was there too. She'd moved back when Harold had been assigned to a troopship, the *S.S. Wakefield,* which had been in an earlier incarnation the luxury liner *Manhattan,* on which Michael and Eliza had sailed for their European honeymoon.

"Just like old times," her father said, glancing around the dining room table from his wife to his daughters. "I've got all my girls with me again. And my little boy." Jake Stern beamed at his grandson. Teddy took advantage of his time in the spotlight to spill his milk. Three women sprang into action to clean up the mess and replace it with a fresh glass. Grandpa Stern made funny faces to entertain him while they did.

For Eliza, at least, it wasn't like old times. The bedroom she shared with Pam, the closet, even the space that separated their twin beds had diminished over the years, while the Victorian furniture had grown heavier and darker, the surfaces more cluttered with china figures and cut glass candy dishes, the atmosphere more suffocating. Teddy slept in the alcove that was Sarah Stern's sewing room. If he got up during the night, Sarah reached him before Eliza did. Gradually Eliza's hearing grew less sensitive. She didn't wake to every whimper. Sarah was pleased. "You need your rest," she said.

It was a tribute to the three women that there were few quarrels in the apartment where they all spent their days. Every now and then loneliness and frustration made Eliza and Pam snap at each other, but Sarah always spread cheer, thick as butter in that household, over the wounds. "Just like when you were children," she'd cluck, and both girls, confronted with their regression, would back away.

Besides, they had more to worry about than lingering rivalries and imagined slights. Someday historians would report that during those last months of 1942 the allies had begun to turn the tide of the Battle of the Atlantic, sinking more U-boats and losing less tonnage every month. But that knowledge lay in the future, and in any event, statistics would have offered little consolation to the wife of a man stationed on a troop transport. Pam lay awake night after night thinking that all it took was one torpedo. And a foot away from her, Eliza turned and twisted with her own fears. Michael was still at Fort Bragg, but training bases could be as dangerous as battlefields. Everyone knew someone who knew someone who'd been accidentally and mysteriously killed during maneuvers, had succumbed to scarlet fever in a military hospital, or given the miseries of military life and the few escapes from it, had died in a car crash on the way back to the base. The newspapers and radio reported battle news—inches of North Africa and Guadalcanal won or lost, ships sunk, bombing raids completed—but Eliza and Pam and millions of American women measured the war in more intimate and terrifying terms.

17

IN OCTOBER Lily moved out of the dormitory. Carrie had found a place at the Buena Vista Arms, a complex of garden apartments converted from an old beach club, and one of her new neighbors had an extra room to rent. It was small and sparsely furnished, but the single window opened onto the sea. For the first time in her life Lily had a room of her own. At night she lay in bed listening to the waves on the beach below her window. Sometimes she got out of bed and went to the window. Beyond the barbed wire, ribbons of white foam came rolling in, growing wider and wider until they crashed on the shore, then retreated into the sea. She thought about oceans and tides and the same water crashing on a beach thousands of miles away, on Tom's beach. Then she'd go back to bed and think what a crazy world it was. She now had so many of the things she'd dreamed of back in Duquel, but she didn't have any of them in the way she'd dreamed.

What she had, of course, were material things. Her wardrobe grew. Her dresser top overflowed with makeup and nail polish and perfumes and creams. Signs and radio slogans kept telling her to save more and buy less, but it was hard to save money when you'd never had it to spend before. That morning a few weeks after she'd moved in, she was trying to find a lipstick to go with a sweater she'd bought the day before. It was a deep and subtle blue, the exact color of her eyes, the salesgirl had insisted.

The sweater must have been flattering because later that day as she walked the now-familiar distances to her factory niche, both men and women turned to stare. In her own division every machine stopped and all eyes fastened on Lily as they had that first day. This time Smitty didn't tell them to go back to work. Only later did Lily realize he wanted an audience. "Jesus," he said, playing to every man within hearing distance. "These girls." He took a step toward Lily. "Don't you know the rules, honey."

"I'm not late," she protested.

"You're gonna be by the time you go home and take off that sweater."

"I don't understand."

"I asked you if you knew the ru' ·s, honey. No sweaters in the plant."

Lily put one hand on her machine. She was a good grinder. Everyone said so. "No one told me that."

"Well, I'm telling you now. No sweaters. Management says they ain't moral." He bared his teeth in the disreputable smile. "So you better go home and take it off." He glanced around at the men. "Or do you want me to take it off for you?"

She blinked several times. She was not going to cry, not with all these men staring at her. And she was not going to let Smitty make a fool of her. What was the word Carrie used? She was not going to let him harass her. "Then you'll dock me for being late."

"You should've thought of that when you put it on." His eyes moved from her face to her sweater. "Or were you too busy thinking about showing off them tits?"

She looked from Smitty to the other men. Some were grinning, others just staring. Behind her she heard one of the men say, "Lay off, Smitty," and another start his machine, but the rest of them just stood there, their faces split wide and leering as jack-o'-lanterns. Then she started to run. Down the long aisles, careening into wagons and walls and machinery, while people called after her to watch herself and warn her that she was going to get hurt and tell her to get the hell out of the way. She ran across the yard, out the gate, all the way to the bus stop.

Carrie came to her room that night. "I heard what happened. Everyone heard what happened. They're not going to get away with it."

Lily sat up on her bed. It was covered with Tom's letters. "I don't care what happens. I'm not going back."

"Of course, you're going back. And you're going back in a sweater. We're going to break that rule."

"I won't. You can't make me."

Carrie stood staring at her. Lily sounded exactly like Tricia, who, with her succession of baby-sitters and abundance of freedom, was becoming increasingly intractable. If she could reason with a six-year-old, she could reason with Lily. "Look," Carrie said, "I have to get back to my place. I haven't even checked on the kids yet. Come with me. I want to talk to you. And I want you to meet someone."

For a moment Lily forgot her own problems in the vicarious excitement. "Your husband's home!"

Carrie frowned. "If Marty were home, Lily, I wouldn't be standing here with you arguing about factory regulations. No, this is someone else."

Lily followed Carrie down the flagstone path connecting the apartments that had once been cabanas. No lights illuminated the moonless night, and the scent of bougainvillea and oleander hung in the thick darkness.

It took Lily a moment to grow accustomed to the bright light of Carrie's kitchen. A man sat at the table. His face would have been handsome if someone hadn't worked over his nose somewhere along the line and taken a piece out of one eyebrow. He had a sinewy body, dark curly hair, and the look of an altar boy gone wrong. "So this is the sweater girl," he said.

"Forget it," Lily said to Carrie, and turned to leave.

"I'm sorry." His smile was lopsided and strangely sweet in that roughed up face. "I was only kidding. I'm on your side."

"This is Jerry Crowley," Carrie said. "He works for the union. Talk to each other while I check on the kids."

"Want a beer?" Crowley walked to the refrigerator and opened it. He seemed to know his way around the house.

Carrie came back into the kitchen, and Crowley handed them each a bottle. Then he sat at the table again and pushed a chair toward Lily with his foot. "Tell me what happened today."

"Nothing."

Crowley looked from Lily to Carrie. The maimed eyebrow rose. He turned back to Lily. "Look, honey, we're sitting on a timebomb. This isn't just some foreman getting out of line with you. This is big labor-management trouble. We can't afford to back down on it. The story's all over the factory."

"If it's all over the factory you don't need me to tell you what happened."

Again Crowley's eyes slid to Carrie, then back. "All right, let's see if I have it straight. You turned up at work this afternoon on time. . . ."

It took Crowley and Carrie close to half an hour to get the whole story. Everything, that is, except Smitty's last words. Lily refused to repeat those. Finally Crowley had to repeat them for her. They'd got around the factory too. "Is that what he said?" Crowley asked.

Lily nodded.

"The man's a pig," Carrie said, but for once Crowley was silent. He'd been organizing factories long before women war workers had come on the scene. That was where he'd lost the fine line of his nose and a piece of his eyebrow. Talk was the least of the violences.

"Let me make sure I've got this right," Crowley said. "He told you sweaters were forbidden because they were immoral?"

Lily nodded. She wished they'd leave it alone. She wished they'd leave her alone.

Crowley leaned back until his chair was balanced on two legs. "Oh, those bastards. Those hypocritical bastards. Have you ever noticed how the girls in the office dress? How come sweaters are moral in the office and immoral on the assembly line?" Because, he thought but didn't say, those SOBs in the office like to look, but they don't think the poor slobs in the factory are entitled to the same pleasures. Crowley brought the chair forward with a bang. "Tomorrow you're going to put on that sweater and go to work, and I'm going to be right behind you."

"I won't. Not after what he did to me today."

"Don't you see," Carrie said, and leaned across the table, "this is more important than you or Smitty or any one person. This is about equal pay for equal work and sexual harassment and all the injustices."

"I don't know anything about any of that. All I know is I'm not going back. I'll get another job. I don't even need a job. I've got enough money."

"Lily!" Carrie said in the same tone she used when the kids had gone too far. "How can you be—"

Crowley put a hand on Carrie's. "Hold on. There's no point fighting among ourselves. Save it for the bosses." He turned to Lily. His eyes under sleepy lids were kind. She hadn't noticed until then just how kind. "Look, Lily, I know how you feel. Someone ought to take Smitty out and beat the pants off him. If your boyfriend—Tom, right?—were home, I bet that's just what he'd do. But Tom isn't home, so we've got to find another way to fight Smitty and guys like him. Carrie's right about that. It isn't just a question of you and Smitty. Because if you don't go back, they're going to put someone else in your place. Now, maybe she won't be as smart as you—"

"I'm not smart."

"You know how to take care of yourself. Carrie told me how Smitty's been riding you. She said she wanted you to complain a long time ago, but you said you could take care of yourself. Well, not every girl can. Now if you don't go in tomorrow, they're going to put some other girl on your machine, maybe some high school kid—" Crowley hesitated and looked across the table at Lily. She'd changed into an oversize shirt but it provided little camouflage. He tried to keep his eyes on her face. It didn't help. She was only a high school kid herself, his conscience warned, and there were rules about that, not to mention laws. He took a swig of his beer. "So they put some high school kid in your place," he repeated, "and Smitty starts putting the pressure on her. Now maybe she needs the job, or she's just plain scared, and before you know it Smitty's got her in the sack. All because you wouldn't stick up for your rights."

Crowley watched her carefully. Persuasion was his trade, and he knew when to stop and when to go on. "Think about it, Lily. Think about Smitty muscling in on some poor kid. Do you have a sister?" Lily nodded. Her lashes fluttered over downcast eyes. Crowley felt them somewhere in his gut. "Think about Smitty putting the make on your kid sister." He recognized the softening of her mouth. He swallowed. His throat felt dry. "You won't be alone," he said. "There was a meeting tonight. Half the assembly line's going to wear sweaters tomorrow. And I'll be right there with you. I'm going to drive you and Carrie to work, and I'm going into the factory and following you right to your machine. If Smitty wants trouble, he's going to get it from me and from the whole damn union. How's that for odds, honey? You won't be alone tomorrow. You'll have the union behind you. What do you say?" he asked, but before she could say anything, he stood and began inching her toward the door. "So you go home now, write to your marine, and get a good night's sleep because tomorrow's a big day."

After she left, he turned back to Carrie, but he could still feel the softness of Lily's shoulder in his hand.

The next afternoon Carrie and Crowley were waiting in his old Ford at the foot of the hill when Lily came down from her apartment. "Christ," he said, "now I know why every guy stopped working."

"Don't say that to her," Carrie warned. "She'll go right back to her room. I know Lily. This is agony for her."

Crowley turned away from the sight of Lily coming down the hill in the sweater and slacks that hugged her body as lovingly as any man ever had. It didn't seem fair to Carrie to keep watching. "You know something, Carrie, under that tough guy front, you're a nice girl."

"I don't feel like a nice girl this morning. I feel like a perfect bitch."

"Because we're making Lily do this?"

She looked at him, then off toward the ocean. "You know why."

He reached for her hand, but she pulled it away. "You're not a bitch, you're just lonely. You'd never have let me near you if your husband were around. You know it, and so do I. So don't waste your time feeling guilty. If you were a man, no one would think twice about it."

"That's what I keep telling myself. Now I've just got to start believing it," she said, and slid across the front seat to make room for Lily.

The day was a triumph for Crowley and the union. Everyone said it was a triumph for Lily too, but she didn't feel triumphant. When she walked the distances to her station that afternoon she felt frightened, despite the fact that Jerry Crowley was walking beside her. When she reached her machine and all the men stopped and turned to stare again, she felt ashamed. Crowley was still there, but they weren't staring at Crowley, they were staring at her in the blue sweater. They were staring at her breasts as if she weren't wearing any sweater at all.

Smitty told Lily and Crowley to get the hell out, but Crowley stood his ground and made Lily stand beside him. Then some men came down from the office and took them back upstairs. Lily didn't want to go because the men from the office stared at her the same way the men on the floor did, only with more malice, but Crowley insisted she come along. Lily hated being in the conference room with all those men. They talked and talked and every once in a while someone said "immoral" and they all turned and stared at her. They were the ones who'd come up with the word, but somehow it had become her fault.

Finally it was over, and they went out into the yard. A couple of hundred women, all in sweaters, began to cheer, and suddenly photographers were snapping her picture and people were coming up and shaking her hand and hugging her and telling her she was great. That was when she stopped feeling frightened and ashamed.

The next day the news services and papers, sick of a diet of death, destruction, and defeat, fell on the story hungrily. Lily was the Joan of Arc of the United Auto Workers.

In the CBS newsroom at 485 Madison Avenue, Isabel Childs picked the item up off the wire and wrote it into the three o'clock broadcast.

In the Lund house on the bluffs of Duquel, Marion and Eloise came shrieking into the sun porch with the *Telegraph Herald and Times Journal.* Proud of a hometown girl, the paper had printed a full-length picture and given it good space. Mrs. Lund examined the photograph briefly, then tossed it aside. "She's looking more common than ever."

In Charlie's Grill in a less well-manicured section of Duquel, Charlie handed Joseph Hartarski the paper folded open to Lily's picture. Joe studied it in the dim light of the bar. It was Lily, all right, and she wasn't pregnant, not in that outfit. "I told her when I sent her out there," he said, "you stick with the union. The union won't let you down." Then he gave the paper to Charlie, who wanted to clip the picture and paste it up behind the bar, and accepted a drink on the house in recognition of his achievement.

Closer to San Diego, Fred Wirtz, the only public relations executive at World Pictures who wasn't a yes man, handed the morning edition of the Los Angeles *Times* to Alec Zeal, né Avram Zelinsky, head of World, as he emerged from his pool. "Take a look at the blonde, A.Z."

Zeal studied the paper just long enough for the water dripping from his thick, hairy body to blur the photograph. "Blondes I don't need. I'm up to my *tuchis* in blondes. Find me a male lead. Find me another Gable who doesn't wanna kill Japs and Nazis. I don't care if he's a pansy. As long as he looks like a *mensch* and doesn't wanna be a hero."

The car was parked at the bottom of the hill when Lily came down from her apartment that morning. It was a long yellow roadster with wire wheels and a jump seat. Lily had never seen anything like it, or the man sitting inside it. He wasn't handsome, but he sat there in a camel's hair jacket that looked soft as butter and a silk ascot as if he were. His face was darkly tanned and crisscrossed with lines like the scarred surface of an old mahogany bar. "Miss Hartarski?" he asked in a voice that made Lily think he would have tipped his hat if he'd been wearing one.

She said she was, then began to tremble. She'd heard about officers coming to deliver bad news. But that was silly. Bad news, especially bad war news, didn't come from men in ascots and dark glasses driving yellow roadsters.

"My name is Fred Wirtz. World Pictures." He took a soft leather case from his pocket and handed her a card. Carrie came up behind her and read over her shoulder. She looked from the card to Wirtz.

"I saw your picture in the paper," he said. "The UAW's sweater girl."

"The UAW's Joan of Arc," Carrie corrected.

Wirtz smiled. "Whichever. I thought you might be interested in a screen test."

This didn't really happen. At least it didn't really happen to girls like her. To Joan Crawford, maybe, to Jane Wyman, but not to her.

"Come on," Carrie said, "you can do better than that. How about 'Stick with me, baby, and I'll get you in pictures'?"

Wirtz began to laugh. "I know. It's a lousy line. But it's on the level. I saw your picture, and I'd like to test you for World."

He sounded as if he meant it. Lily took a step back and examined the car. Still, just because he was rich, he wasn't necessarily in the movies.

"Look," Wirtz said, "you have my card. Why don't you two ladies go back up to your apartment and call that number? The switchboard will answer 'World Pictures' and connect you with my office. Then my secretary will tell you I'm not in, but she'd say that even if I were. You couldn't get through to me if you tried. But I'm trying to get through to you."

"Are you serious?" Lily asked.

"Go find out."

They went back up the hill to Carrie's apartment and called the number. The secretary practically hung up on them. Lily floated back down the hill. "You *are* from World Pictures."

"I'll set up the test for tomorrow morning. Is eleven all right? I'll send a limo for you at eight. That'll give you plenty of time for the drive up and all the rest," he said, and disappeared in a cloud of dust like the hero of one of World's B westerns.

Lily was up at six. She fixed her hair five different ways, tried a dozen different lipsticks, put on and took off half the dresses she owned. At least she had a good pair of stockings left. She wasn't going to World Pictures in leg makeup, war shortages or no war shortages. None of the hundreds of movie magazines she'd read over the years had told her she needn't have bothered. She was in the studio's hands now.

The limousine was black and long. Carrie came to the bottom of the hill to see her off. Behind them curtains in half a dozen windows swayed as the women of the Buena Vista Arms watched.

There was a panel of glass between the front seat and the back. Lily drove up the coast in silence. When they reached the studio gate, a group of girls on the sidewalk turned to stare. The guard passed the car through with a wave of his hand. The limousine crawled slowly along the narrow street, slowed by several Indians, a woman in a powdered wig and ball gown, an infantry platoon. It almost ran over George Washington.

Fred Wirtz was waiting outside an ugly gray building. He led her inside and turned her over to a makeup man. "Don't ruin her, Harry. I want her to look natural."

"Sure thing," Harry answered, and went to work. By the time he was finished, Lily's eyebrows were a fraction of an inch higher, her full lower lip half its former size, and her complexion the shade of an invalid's. Then the hairdresser took over. He pinned and laquered her hair into a mountain of upswept curls. Lily had never looked so glamorous, or so absurd.

In the wardrobe room a woman with an unlit cigarette dangling from her lips stuffed and laced Lily into a satin gown. She could barely breath. And she didn't dare bend over. The dress was that low-cut.

On the set the director looked her up and down. "Another babe who thinks she's going to make it on her chest," he said to no one in particular.

They shot her right profile, her left, her full face. A series of men walked up to her and put an arm around her waist, and she had to say, "Darling, it's been so long," to one after another of them. Then it was over.

Lily didn't hear from Fred Wirtz for several days. Once she called his office, but when the secretary answered she hung up.

"I knew it was too good to be true," she said that night in Carrie's kitchen.

"It's been less than a week," Carrie answered, but she secretly believed Lily was right. Things like this just didn't happen.

"What do you mean it was too good to be true?" Jerry asked. "You've got to stop thinking that way, Lily. These things do happen." His eyes moved from her full lower lip to her shoulders, bare and brown above the halter top. "Why shouldn't they happen to you?"

Lily went back to her room and stood staring at herself in the mirror over the dresser. Jerry was right. These things did happen. Why shouldn't they happen to her? She was as pretty as anyone else. And she was willing to work hard. The good people of Duquel crowded into her room. Lily Hartarski. They laughed and jeered at the name. Father's a rummy. Mother's a little strange, though she irons a good shirt. Smitty and his men elbowed in. Who was she trying to kid? A piece of ass, maybe, but no movie star. Lily was glad she hadn't written Tom about the test. Now she wouldn't have to write him about the results.

The darkened screening room was silent except for the sound of Alec Zeal's digestive system. Every time his stomach rumbled, half a dozen grown men leaned forward in their upholstered chairs as if waiting for orders.

"When are you going to get smart and give up the pastrami, A.Z.?" Fred Wirtz asked.

"As soon as you get smart and give up the booze. Don't nag me. I got a wife for that. Just show me the test."

Wirtz gestured to the projection room, and Lily's face lit up the screen. Zeal watched in silence, but his stomach protested. As the lights came up, he burped violently.

"Well?" Wirtz asked.

"She's got a little Harlow."

"Right," a man in the second row of viewers chimed in. "A little Harlow."

"Maybe a touch of Lombard," Zeal went on.

"Lombard," another voice behind them repeated.

"Forget Harlow and Lombard. This girl can make it on her own," Wirtz said.

"What makes you so sure?"

"You ought to see her."

"I just saw her. Another blonde. I told you, I got a stable full of blondes."

"Take another look." Wirtz gestured to the projection room again. The magic of celluloid put Lily through her paces a second time.

"Just another blonde," someone in the second row murmured.

Zeal shrugged. "She doesn't do anything to me."

"Listen, A.Z., she wore a sweater to work, and the local UAW threatened to go out on strike."

Zeal turned his thick body until he was facing Wirtz. He liked the fact that Fred wasn't afraid to express an opinion, but he didn't necessarily agree with Fred's opinions. "Why're you so hot on this kid, Freddy? You *shtuptting* her?"

"You know me better than that, A.Z. If I tested every girl I laid, you wouldn't have any film left over to make movies. I haven't put a hand on her. But I think she's got potential. Big potential."

"What do you think, Ira?" Zeal asked without turning around.

"Well, she does have that Lombard quality . . . a little. But, like you say, A.Z., you already got a lot of blondes."

"What about you, Dave? You got an opinion?"

"Well, Uncle Alec, I see more Harlow than Lombard. What're her legs like?"

"Like the rest of her," Wirtz said.

Zeal laughed, then burped. "You're probably wrong, Freddy, but at least you're not afraid to say what you think—like my brother Ira and his kid back there. You want the girl, you got her." He stood and rubbed his stomach. "For three months. No more. If I still don't like her then, we don't pick up the option."

By the following week Lily Hartarski was Jeanne Storey. She had a contract with World Pictures for a hundred and fifty dollars a week, not just a room of her own but an entire apartment on Beverly Green Drive, which was so close to Beverly Hills it might as well have been part of it, and a secondhand Ford or at least that part of it bought by the first downpayment. Her letters to Tom were filled with the news. She was on her way. Nothing could stop her now. Lily didn't know what an option was.

18

ANDY BARNES had to wait in line for close to an hour that night to reach the phones. When he finally got inside a booth, it smelled of cigarettes and chewing gum and the sweat of too many men calling too many women. He heard Isabel's voice on the other end of the line and closed his eyes. He wished she wouldn't sound that way. Her voice made him remember that night on the patio last summer. What was worse, it made him forget any number of girls he'd seen between, girls with prettier faces and better bodies and easier natures. He told himself he was crazy to be calling her. He had one weekend left, one lousy weekend. It would be different if he were in love, but he wasn't in love. He was leaving for England in four days, and he'd have to be crazy to be in love. All he wanted was to have a good time. All he wanted was to drink some real scotch, hear some good music, and get laid.

He told Isabel he'd be in town that weekend and asked if she felt like having a few drinks and hearing some good music. He didn't mention that he was leaving. She didn't ask why he'd be in town on a weekend pass. She just said she'd love to have some drinks and hear some music. It was all very off-hand, I-don't-give-a-damn. It was all very flyboy.

Spence called Isabel later that night. He admitted they were leaving. "Do me a favor, though. Don't tell them till I'm gone. He'd expect me to come down to Washington, and she'd feel bad that I didn't catch a flight down to Palm Beach, and, well . . ."

". . . and you'd rather spend the time with Sally?"

"Right."

That Friday for the first time since she'd started working in the newsroom Isabel left the office early. At Elizabeth Arden they greeted her like the prodigal daughter. She left two hours later feeling as newly minted as a coin and much more frivolous. The doorman offered to call her a cab, but she said she'd walk. Fifth Avenue hurried through the winter dusk as if there were no war. In the shop windows jewels and furs and expensive clothes denied wartime shortages. In one display a pair of evening pumps promised you could dance away your troubles. Isabel went into the store and spent thirty dollars, which had no meaning for her, and her last ration coupon, which did.

She walked home feeling extravagant. That was what the war did to people. It made them profligate. They squandered money, feelings, everything but time.

Andy arrived. He stood in the formal entrance hall of the townhouse staring down at her. "So Spence told you we're shipping out." She nodded. "Are you going to give me a big send-off, Isabel?" She laughed. The sound, he thought, was like a deep, secret spring.

The weekend was a kaleidoscope of too many restaurants and nightclubs and noisy, smoky rooms. Sally said there was a cocktail party on Sutton Place they couldn't miss, and Andy had heard of a better one in the Village, and Neddie, the little navigator Andy and Spence treated like a mascot because he was only eighteen, had to be taken to Jimmy Ryan's on Fifty-second Street because he'd never heard live jazz. They were always attaching men in uniform and girls in evening dresses or suits only to lose them somewhere along the way, then rediscover them in another uniform-crowded room. Galoshes were being continually slipped over or off evening sandals and suede pumps. The city was one constantly swirling party.

On Saturday night they ran into Sam Wicker at Café Society Downtown. He was wearing another impeccably tailored suit. The expensive fabric looked soft beside Andy's rough khaki. Isabel introduced them. Over Lee and Lester Young's music, the two men sized each other up.

"Is that the competition?" Andy asked half an hour later. They were, miraculously, alone in a cab going uptown. Somehow they'd managed to shed all the army and navy officers and their girls, Spence and Sally, even little Neddie and a tall redhead he'd acquired somewhere along the way.

"Just a friend."

Andy laughed. "That means he is the competition. Otherwise, you wouldn't try to pass him off as harmless." He reached an arm around her shoulders. "Still, I'm not worried."

The man was impossible. He'd seen Sam Wicker, who was, just for the record, the better-looking of the two. He'd seen that Sam Wicker was interested in her. He was going off for months if not years. And he said he wasn't worried.

She turned to say something, but his mouth on hers brushed away the words. They kissed from Thirty-fourth Street to Fifty-eighth. By then his mouth was tracing the line of her dress where it dipped low in front. His hand had found its way beneath the yards of silk skirt. His fingers were maddening on her thigh.

The cab drew up in front of the house on Sixty-seventh Street. They struggled apart. The driver had thrown the flag and the meter had stopped ticking. The only sounds in the dark privacy of the backseat were ragged rasps of breath.

Andy helped her out of the cab, then turned to pay the driver. Her mouth felt chafed and dry. Her skin burned from the roughness of his beard. She watched his hands as he took a wad of bills from his pocket and peeled one off. His fingers were long, gracefully arched, exciting. Strange about men. They were so busy noticing what aroused them in a woman they never bothered to think about what in them aroused a woman.

He stood staring down at her. He didn't speak. He didn't even smile. A muscle in his jaw moved. He put an arm around her. They started up the stairs to the empty house.

Inside the heavy grille outer door the vestibule was dark. As she bent over her handbag fumbling for the key, her hair fell forward exposing the long white line of her neck. He pressed his mouth against it. She shivered.

The only sound in the vestibule was the scraping of the key in the lock of the heavy inner door. He pushed it open. Light from the foyer flooded the vestibule. Voices and music came rushing down from the second floor. Sally had insisted on bringing the party home, and Spence had gone along with the idea.

Isabel and Andy climbed the stairs. The group was growing more international. There was an RAF officer they'd annexed earlier in the evening and a man in a Dutch naval uniform and the usual assortment of navy and khaki and satin and silk and taffeta. Neddie had replaced the tall redhead with a tall blonde. "Hey, Andy, look who's here," Neddie called across the room. "Remember Betty."

Betty remembered Andy. She crossed the room to him, put her arms around his neck, and kissed him on the mouth. Then she turned to Isabel and smiled. "We're old friends," she said. "Isn't that right?"

Andy agreed that it was right. She still had her arms around his neck and his hands were on her waist and their bodies fit together neatly as pieces of a puzzle.

"You said you'd call me when you got to town again." She pouted. "That was eight weeks ago."

Isabel tried not to run the calculations. Eight weeks ago Spence had come home for the weekend, but he hadn't brought Andy.

She went upstairs to comb her hair and put fresh lipstick on her bruised mouth. On the way down she stopped in front of the closed door to her father's room. He hadn't been home for close to a year. He remained in Washington with his work and his woman while her mother shuttled aimlessly between Southampton and Palm Beach waiting for a few crumbs of his time. Isabel turned away from her father's door and went back to the party, if that was what you could call it.

On Sunday morning Isabel opened the blackout curtains to a gray sky. It matched the atmosphere in the house. Spence and Andy had to report to Mitchell Field at five that afternoon. She felt as if every clock in the house were ticking out loud. She was sick to her stomach, and not from the aftermath of alcohol.

That afternoon she and Andy went for a walk in the park. The wind off the yacht basin was brutal. Snow threatened. The sky grew darker until it looked like the side of a battleship. They didn't exchange more than half a dozen words.

Back at the house the second-floor sitting room was cool. Even with half the house closed off, the heating fuel shortage was making itself felt. Andy built a fire. Isabel watched him kneeling at the hearth. He worked quickly and surely. "Where did you learn that? The Boy Scouts?"

"I was never a Boy Scout."

"I should have known."

He stretched out on the floor in front of the hearth. She remained on the sofa. Gradually they began to thaw. He took her hand and pulled her down until she was sitting beside him on the floor. He lay on his back looking up at her. "What happened last night?" he asked finally.

"What do you mean?"

"You know what I mean."

She turned from him to the flames. Mankind's eternal fascination with fire. "You mean in the cab you thought I was going to go to bed with you, and then I didn't."

"I mean in the cab *you* thought you were going to go to bed with me, and then you wouldn't."

She shrugged. "There was a party. The house was full of people."

"All the people left. We were alone again."

She went on staring at the fire in silence.

"The blonde, right? Neddie's blonde?"

Isabel thought but didn't say that the blonde wasn't exactly Neddie's property.

"I told you how I felt the first time I met you," he said.

Which of course, Isabel thought, made it all right.

"I spend half my life up in a plane. I don't need any strings to the ground."

She turned back to him. Her smile was wide and bright and, he thought, damn phony. "And now, thanks to Betty, you don't have any."

Isabel drove Andy and Spence out to Mitchell Field. Sally didn't come along. She said she hated goodbyes. As if other people didn't.

A new B-17 was waiting. Spence looked at his watch and said they were barely in time to warm it up. Isabel got out of the car with them. Spence held her for a minute, told her to stay out of trouble, and walked off across the field.

"He's right," Andy said. "Stay out of trouble."

"You too," she said, and there was a terrible catch in her voice. He kissed her then, hard and quickly. "See you," he said, and followed Spence across the field.

Andy felt her eyes on his back as he headed for the plane, but he didn't turn around. He wished she hadn't had that catch in her voice. He wished Betty hadn't turned up last night. He wished he'd never got mixed up with Betty. A good piece of tail, but not worth it. Not worth Isabel.

He swung himself up through the belly hatch of the plane. Neddie was at the navigator's table. Spence was already sitting in the copilot's seat. He said something about the big bird, their big bird. Andy could barely hear him above the roar of the engines. He slid into the pilot's seat and forgot everything but the panel of dials in front of him and the nine men behind him. Iceland lay ahead, then England. That was all he knew.

On the way back to town Isabel kept seeing Andy Barnes's shadow in the headlights of the oncoming cars. Again and again he slouched across the tarmac, pulled himself up in the hatch, and disappeared into the big ungainly bird. You had to be out of your mind to get mixed up with a flyer. Even Sally knew the statistics. Sally could be a royal pain, but for once she was right. The average life of a flyer in the Eighth Air Force was fifteen missions. The assigned tour of duty was twenty-five. Isabel switched on the radio for the evening news. You had to be out of your mind.

Isabel didn't see Sam Wicker for more than a week. Then one afternoon he turned up in the newsroom with theater tickets for an opening that night. He made only one reference to their meeting at Café Society. "You really do go for the glamour boys, don't you?" he asked during the intermission. She pretended not to hear him.

In the front vestibule of the house on East Sixty-seventh Street, Sam bent to kiss her good night as he always did. But that night, for the first time, Isabel kissed him back. And that night Sam Wicker, who'd bedded the Silk and Satin Soap girl, the Copley Tea voice, and Miss Brite and White of 1942, to mention only a few, went home like a kid who'd just kissed his first girl.

19

LILY HAD BEEN in the movies for three months, if that's what you called two bit parts in which she went entirely unnoticed, except by Fred Wirtz, who still thought she had something, and Alec Zeal, who still didn't see anything in her. But the studio managed to keep her busy. She posed for pinups. She gave interviews to fan magazines. She toured military camps. She spent an afternoon in a low-cut playsuit picking tomatoes with several other young women under contract to World Pictures. One of Fred Wirtz's underlings had got the idea after he'd read about the shortage of farm labor. What the paper didn't say was that there were plenty of migrant Mexican workers, and that day they stood by sullenly watching the girls smiling and posing and ruining their manicures on the tomato plants. When it was all over, the half-dozen starlets gave their pay to the Mexican workers. That was Lily's idea, but no one protested. The starlets were, for the most part, girls who'd worked hard to get where they were. They understood the value of a dollar.

The studio provided for her nights as well as her days. Fred Wirtz's department made sure she was seen at the right restaurants

and nightclubs with the most promising young actors. A few were
fresh, and one or two were mean, but most were just kids like her,
trying to make it in movies.

Two nights a week she wore out more shoes than rationing
would permit her to replace dancing with soldiers and sailors and
marines at the Hollywood Canteen. The girls weren't supposed to
date the servicemen they met at the canteen, but official rules were
no match for the appetites of youth and the loneliness of war. Many
of the girls continued their romances after hours and off limits, but
not Lily. She was usually careful not to mention Tom to the hundreds of boys she danced with, unless they tried to get either serious or fresh. Then she'd tell them about her fiancé—she'd picked
up the word at the studio—who was with the marines in the South
Pacific. Though the news was heavily censored, you didn't have to
be a military genius to figure out where he probably was. "Guadalcanal, I think," she'd tell the boys she was trying to discourage. The
name had not yet taken on the tragic resonance of history, but Lily
still felt sick at the sound of it.

Each morning she went to mass and prayed Tom would be all
right. And as she knelt beneath the statue of the Blessed Virgin, she
knew, with the certainty of religious faith and the confidence of
youth in its own immortality, that he had to be all right.

Her life wasn't exactly happy, but for the first time it was orderly
and secure. Then World tossed a grenade into it. They declined to
pick up her option.

Fred Wirtz was sorry but that was show biz, he told his valet.
Besides, he had other things on his mind. Alec Zeal still wanted
another Gable. "That's the trouble with this town. They're always
looking for what's hot today or yesterday. They're afraid to take a
chance on something new that'll be hot tomorrow."

He was less candid when he ran into Lily on her last day on the
lot. By midnight she'd be a has-been, an eighteen-and-a-half-year-
old has-been. "It's a shame, honey," he said, "but you keep a stiff
upper lip. Some other studio is bound to pick you up."

As Lily was always the first to say, she wasn't smart, but she did
know a little about men. At least, she knew when they were lying.
Still, Mr. Wirtz had been nice to her, and she was grateful to him.
"Sure," she said, and the thick dark lashes fluttered. She might as
well have batted them against his cheek.

Unlike most of his colleagues, Fred Wirtz stayed away from the studio's starlets. Full-fledged stars and girls without movie ambitions, or at least possibilities, were safer. Lily had just dropped into the second category. He asked her if she'd like to have dinner that night. Lily thought of the closet full of evening dresses she wasn't likely to get much of a chance to wear anymore, the glamorous nights of popping flashbulbs and naked admiration that were already a thing of the past, and Fred Wirtz's kindness. She said yes.

He took her to Lamaze for dinner and ordered filet mignon for both of them and champagne. He was a Seagrams man himself or, at worst, would have settled for a good burgundy, but he believed that girls liked champagne. Then they moved down Sunset Boulevard to the Trocadero. The headwaiter led Wirtz to "his" table in the first row ringside. Lily looked around. Loretta Young was there, and Lucille Ball, and Robert Taylor. She felt like crying.

Wirtz ordered another bottle of champagne. He wasn't trying to get Lily drunk. It was just the way he did things.

She was wearing a black satin dress that made her skin—and the dress showed a lot of skin—look like white marble, only warmer. Wirtz knew it was warm because he kept finding ways to touch it.

They were halfway through the second bottle of champagne before Lily realized what it was doing to her. But that was all right, because it made her stop hurting. She raised her glass to him. "This helps. Thanks."

He touched her glass with his own. "To hell with A.Z. The shortsighted bastard."

She giggled. "To hell with the shortsighted bastard." She emptied her glass. He refilled it, then took her hand. "In a couple of months, you'll laugh at this. You've got what it takes, honey. I've seen a lot of them come and go, and I know what I'm talking about."

She was beginning to believe him. "You really think so?"

"I'd put money on it." He turned her hand over and rubbed her palm with his thumb. "By the way, how're you fixed for money? You going to be okay until something else turns up?"

Lily said she was fixed fine. Even with all the new clothes she'd bought, she'd managed to save something during the last three months.

"Well, if you need anything," he went on, her hand in both of his now, "don't hesitate to ask. I'm always here for you, honey."

She knew what was coming, and for the first time in her life she didn't care. She didn't give a damn about damnation or sin or becoming one of those girls. She was miserable and lonely. Mr. Wirtz had been nice to her. He was still being nice to her. No one else had offered to help. Besides, everyone did it. The girls she'd met on the lot said you couldn't hope to get anywhere in movies if you didn't. And it wasn't just movie people. Look at Carrie. Carrie was older and smarter and even married, but that hadn't stopped her with Jerry Crowley. Jerry Crowley with his battered eyebrow and smart smooth mouth. Lily forced her mind back to Fred Wirtz. "Thanks, but I'm okay."

He signaled for the waiter. Lily was expecting another bottle of champagne, but Wirtz asked for the check. He wasn't old, but he was old enough to know when alcohol stopped enhancing his mood and threatened to affect his performance.

As they left the room filled with celebrities, a few of them known to the public, others famous only within the confines of the industry and even more powerful, several heads turned to follow Lily. Wirtz couldn't shake the feeling the studio he'd worked at for fifteen years and loved more faithfully than any woman was making a big mistake.

There were more celebrities downstairs in the bar. Wirtz said hello to two leading men, an agent who could have—and had—bought and sold them both, a producer, and Gustave Dressler. They all said hello back. Dressler suggested a drink. He was talking to Wirtz, but his eyes were on Lily. Hollywood gossip said that Dressler loved women, but Wirtz knew that wasn't exactly true. Dressler's camera loved the women Dressler created. Wirtz's mind snapped into sobriety. He introduced the director to Lily. With a wave of his hand, Dressler rearranged the others at the table so Lily could sit beside him.

As Lily took the chair Dressler held for her, she looked up to thank him. She'd never seen such eyes in her life. They were marbles, small and hard and black, with faint white and yellow lines running through them. In the dim light his face was thin and sharp and gray, like a steel knife. "Tell me about yourself, Miss Storey,"

he said in a strange accent that sounded to her like a cross between
Ronald Colman and her father when he was speaking Polish.

"Well," Lily began, "until today . . ."

"We've got big plans for Miss Storey," Wirtz interrupted. "Big
plans. Her career's just about to take off."

"Really, Freddy," Dressler said without taking his eyes from Lily,
"you must have me mixed up with those cretinous columnists of
yours."

Between the noise and the champagne and Dressler's strange
accent, Lily didn't understand a word they were saying, but she
knew that those hard black marbles were fastened on her face and
that Mr. Wirtz had stopped touching her and become all business
again. You didn't have to be terribly smart to sense that something
was up.

Dressler went on staring at her for a few minutes, then he stood
abruptly. "I can't hear myself talk. And I can't see Miss Storey.
Come back to my house for a nightcap. Both of you." Dressler left
the rest of his party staring after them.

Even after three months in Hollywood and the handful of private
parties the studio had sent her to, Lily had never seen anything like
Gustave Dressler's house. Outside it looked like all the others, a
big sprawling animal lurking behind a tall privet hedge and carpet
of manicured lawn. As they drove up the wide circular drive, Lily
noticed the requisite pool in the back. But the inside was something
else. There was no mirrored bar, no billiard room, no gaudily dis-
played Oscars, though she knew Dressler had won at least one and
probably more. Instead there were walls and walls of books and
pictures. At first the pictures confused Lily, because some of them
were familiar. She'd seen them before, but then they'd been in
books or taped to other people's walls, not framed in gilt like this.
She stood staring at one that had been in her high school history
book. Gustave Dressler watched her. When he finally spoke, he
didn't ask whether she liked the painting or what she thought of it.
"My first Corot," he said, and went around the room turning on
more lights. When the room was bright as daylight, he led Lily to a
sofa and sat beside her. The hard black eyes were focused on her,
but he was speaking to Wirtz.

"You've certainly been keeping her under wraps, Freddy, in
view of those big plans." Wirtz started to answer, but Dressler cut

him off. "What has she done? Besides the pinups and the publicity.
I'm not interested in making a career on barracks' walls."

Wirtz mentioned the two pictures in which Lily had had bit parts.
Dressler shook his head. "I saw them. I see everything. Even the
garbage. In the first you made her a sexpot, in the second you tried
to make her a comedienne. In other words, Harlow and Lombard,
only Harlow and Lombard did it better."

He took a linen handkerchief from his pocket and began to rub
at her face. Gradually the eyebrows returned to their natural line,
and the contours of her mouth emerged from beneath the greasy
red lipstick. Dressler began pulling the pins from her hair. It tumbled around her shoulders. He ran his long skeletal fingers through
it, then took her chin in his hand and lifted her face until the light
cast no shadows. She dropped her eyes. Her mouth trembled. "The
eyes can break hearts, the mouth make grown men cry. You take a
face like an angel—a vulnerable, wistful angel—and a body that's
the stuff of a million male fantasies in this repressed country of
yours, and you turn her into a second-rate imitation. Tell Alec Zeal
to go back to his pushcart. And you can go back to selling shoes.
That's all you're good for."

Wirtz sipped his brandy and smiled. "I take it that tirade means
you want to borrow Miss Storey for a movie. I don't know if A.Z.
will loan her out."

"Miss Storey," Dressler repeated. "Jeanne Storey." He spat out
the words as if they had a bad taste. "What's your real name?"

"Lily," she said. "Lily Hartarski."

Dressler's laughter started quietly and gained momentum like
water running downhill. "You fools! The imagination of a pushcart
vender. The vision of a shoe salesman. You take Lily Hart—Lily
Hart!" he shouted to the high-timbered ceiling—"and turn her into
Jeanne Storey. Oh, you'll loan her out, all right, because you know
by the time I give her back you'll have a star. The only question is
how much you'll loan her out for. The pushcart vender likes to
haggle."

Lily started to speak, and Dressler turned back to her and took
her face in his hands again. "Don't worry, Lily Hart. World will
loan you out to me. Alec Zeal would loan out his own wife for the
right price. I'm going to make a picture with you. Not with Harlow
or Lombard, but with you, Lily Hart."

Wirtz stood. "This is a matter for lawyers. I'll get them to work on it first thing in the morning. Come on, Lily."

"But, Mr. Wirtz—"

"It's after two, Lily. And you're going to need a lot of strength if you're going to make a picture with the great Gustave Dressler. He's a genius, but he's also a tyrant."

"But—"

"Freddy's right," Dressler said, and began walking Lily toward the door. "Go home, Lily Hart. Go home and have sweet dreams."

"But, Mr. Dressler—"

"I'll take care of everything."

Lily stopped at the door and faced the two men. "But, Mr. Dressler," she said again, and this time she kept going. "I'm not under contract to World. I haven't been since midnight. They didn't pick up my option."

"Oh, baby," Fred Wirtz wailed.

"I'm sorry, Mr. Wirtz," Lily said.

But Gustave Dressler began to laugh, and again it gained momentum until it overtook the whole room and drowned out everything else.

20

ANDY BARNES had warned he wouldn't write. He was as good as his word. All news of him came through Spence, who wrote of Andy's way with the plane, the crew, the English women. It never occurred to Spence that his sister might not want to hear about the last. He shared a room, a cockpit, exhaustion, danger, and fear with Andy Barnes. Isabel suspected he was beginning to share his philosophy of life, if that was what you could call it, as well. For a flyer in the Eighth Air Force stationed in England in the winter of 1943, there were weather conditions and bombing raids; the terrain of France and Germany and the welcoming green fields of Suffolk and Cambridgeshire; briefings and debriefings; eternal cold and dampness; sleep, food, and an occasional trip to London. Life was a matter of immediate exigencies and temporary pleasures. Spence wrote about them. Every now and then he did ask about Sally, so maybe he wasn't turning into Andy Barnes after all.

On the home front life was more complicated. The OPA banned all pleasure driving. The meat shortage grew worse. Point rationing went into effect, and every housewife became a mathematical wizard over night, calculating the point value of food against the cost and adding in her family's tastes, if, that is, there was any choice in the market. The army began drafting fathers.

"And to think I almost got married and had a baby just to be safe," Sam joked.

"At least you would have had someone to take care of you," Isabel said, and put the flowers she'd brought in a vase on his night table. He'd been felled by a vicious winter cold. So, it seemed to Isabel, had half the city and most of the network news staff.

"I don't need a wife to take care of me, Isabel. I've got you."

Actually Isabel had come as much for herself as for Sam. Her hours at the station were long and frantic, but there was always that moment, whether at six or nine or midnight, when she went home alone to the big empty townhouse. The rooms that remained open had a desolate air, and in the corridors she walked past too many closed doors. Occasionally Cora, who still believed in the dignity of private service and disapproved of the quick money to be made in war work, waited up for her, but though Cora was a good woman, she was not good company.

Grace begged Isabel to come down to Palm Beach for a vacation. Isabel countered with several slogans, half of them written by Sam Wicker, discouraging nonessential travel. "I can't imagine what you're doing rattling around in that empty house," Grace said.

"I'm working, Mother. Harder than ever. Everyone's come down with a cold, and we're shorthanded, but the war's still going on."

From the telephone table in the sun room of the house in Palm Beach, Grace looked out over the carpet of green rolling down to the bay. No troops marched along her private beach as they did farther south in Miami. It was hard to believe from where Grace sat that there was a war on, though she never for a moment forgot that there was, or that her son was fighting it. "If you keep this up," she said to Isabel, "you're bound to get sick yourself."

"Not possible. I'm disgracefully healthy. It comes from having a mother who had the sense to find Cora who made sure I ate my spinach and drank my milk. She's still making sure of it."

Isabel continued to hammer away at her own job and pick up the slack for any number of invalids. Some were grateful, others wary.

"Why's she working anyway," one of the newscasters asked over

a drink with Lew Packer, the man who was considered the authority on Isabel Childs because he'd found her in a Long Island gas
station. "She doesn't need the money."

"No, but we need the extra hands," Packer answered. "She's
okay."

"Oh, she's okay," the newscaster said. "Great legs. Good ass.
Nice body, if you like them without much meat. But I don't trust
her. She's after my job. She's after all our jobs."

Packer knocked back the last of his drink. He'd watched Isabel
around the newsroom. The man was right. She had great legs. And
she was after a job, but these days there were more than enough
jobs to go around. "Take it easy," he said. "All you have to do is
stay relatively sober and keep your voice, and she can't touch you."

Packer was right. If the newscaster had been home in bed nursing his cold rather than out in a bar with Lew Packer trying to
drown it, he never would have had to worry. But the man believed
rye was a miracle drug. He and Packer drank till one. The next day
his throat ached, his nose ran, and his head throbbed in protest. He
made it to the newsroom seven minutes before two. Isabel told him
he looked awful. He ignored her, picked up a script, and staggered
into the broadcast booth. The second hand inched toward twelve.
The newscaster studied the script. Isabel studied him through the
window of the booth. His face was covered with a film of perspiration. He gestured for water. Someone poured a glass and handed it
to him. The minute hand hit twelve. The commercial announcer
swung into action. Silk and Satin Soap, the soap that knew that
keeping your skin soft kept your fighting man's spirits up, brought
you the news at two. The newscaster leaned toward the microphone. He opened his mouth. He moved his lips. There was silence
in the studio. He tried to clear his throat. No sound came out. He
moved his mouth again. "Like an actor in an old silent film," someone said later when the story was raging through the industry.

"What the hell's going on?" the head of the newsroom shouted.

"Get him off!" someone yelled.

"Get somebody on!" the head screamed.

As she told the story later, Isabel said she just happened to be
standing outside the door to the broadcast booth. Sam laughed and
said it was a good place to be standing, though they both knew she
could have got across that room if she'd had to. She was inside the

booth in a second. On the clock above the window the hand had already swept through eight of dead time. She grabbed the script from the newscaster's hands. *Good afternoon. This is the two o'clock news. In the wake of the Russian victory at Stalingrad . . .* Thank God it was Stalingrad. At least she could pronounce Stalingrad. *In North Africa General Eisenhower in command of all allied forces . . .* Not too fast, she warned herself. Only amateurs read the news as if they're racing against a stopwatch. *On the homefront, the OPA has announced . . .* She tried to keep her voice low, authoritative but not pompous, warm but not too cozy. *And on a lighter note, plans to mobilize man's best friend in a Canine Corps . . .*

She finished and looked up from the script. Across the way in the control booth, someone signaled wildly. She'd finished exactly on time. The newsroom went crazy. Some of the people were applauding her and some were berating her and men were screaming and one secretary was crying and the phones were ringing.

Twenty blocks north in the quiet of his sickroom Sam Wicker turned off the radio, lay back against his pillows, and smiled. He'd know Isabel's voice anywhere.

"You weren't bad," Matthew Gardner said. Isabel glanced beyond his shoulder at the skyline. Afternoon sunlight glanced off the steel towers. The city was shimmering just for her. "Your pacing was good. Of course, your diction's perfect." He leaned back in his swivel chair and made a church steeple of his fingers. He had a habit of squinting at people. He knew it gave him an air of serious concentration. "Have you spent much time in England?"

Isabel brought her eyes back from the skyline. "I had an English governess."

He sat up again. "Well, you sounded pretty good. For a woman. But that's the point. News is serious. Especially war news. People don't want to hear it from a woman. I'm not even sure they'll believe it from a woman."

"And yet women are good enough to cover it."

"Don't get carried away. You've picked up some stories off the wires. You've gone to a couple of OPA briefings. That isn't covering the news."

Isabel thought of the broadcaster she'd stepped in for this afternoon. "It's more than some of the men do. You're lucky if they turn up in time to look over the script before they go on."

Gardner leaned back in his big leather chair again. "I know. The good ones, the really good ones, are the boys who cover the news and write it and broadcast it themselves. And they're the ones who're going off to cover the war firsthand. We're left with the lightweights."

"I'm not a lightweight. I can do all three."

"The public would never stand for it."

"You mean you won't stand for it. You've never given the public a chance." Isabel leaned forward in her chair. "Who listens to the two o'clock news, Mr. Gardner? Men in their offices or on their jobs? Not by a long shot. Women. Women cooking and cleaning and taking care of the kids. Or women who leave all that to someone else while they play cards."

"That's true," he said, "but not entirely in your favor. For every woman who wants to hear another woman reading the news, there are two or three who won't believe it unless it comes from a man. It's an unfortunate fact, but it is a fact, and that's what I deal in, Miss Childs. Facts. If those women don't like our newscasts, they'll turn to another station."

"Why don't you give it a month, a week, and see what happens? I did a good job today. I can keep it up."

"I'd like to. God knows we're shorthanded." Gardner swiveled his chair until his back was to Isabel. The silence dragged on. He turned to face her again and went on staring. Finally he spoke. "I really would like to." He paused. "But I can't take the chance. You can lose a lot of listeners in a month. And it takes another six to get them back." He stood and walked around the desk. "But you did an excellent job today. Excellent. Please accept my congratulations."

Isabel considered telling him what he could do with his congratulations, but the buzzer on his desk was ringing. He pressed a button and his secretary's voice announced that Mrs. Gardner was on the phone. As Isabel left the room, she thought of the woman in the silver frame on Gardner's desk. She was probably one of those women who didn't believe the news unless it came in masculine tones, one of those women who thought her husband's word was law.

Isabel was about to leave her desk a few hours later when the call came from upstairs. Mr. Gardner wanted to see her again. This time there was no skyline behind his head. Blackout curtains shut out the city. Gardner followed her eyes. "I know. I miss the view too. It's wonderful during the day, but it used to be even better at night. Before the war I used to love that view. It was like a diamond necklace."

Isabel sat in the chair opposite his desk without answering. She didn't know why he'd dragged her back up here, but he could save the diamond necklaces for his wife. The little woman. Or his mistress.

"I had an interesting talk after you left my office, Miss Childs. With my wife." When Isabel still didn't answer, he went on. "She called to ask me who broadcast the two o'clock news."

"Presumably she didn't believe a word of it. I hope you reassured her that the Russians have broken the siege of Stalingrad even if the news did come from a woman."

"You're sulking because you did one broadcast and we didn't turn the news department upside down to suit you."

"I'm angry because I did one broadcast—well—and you need me to do more, but you won't let me because of some stupid sexual prejudice."

He squinted across the big desk at her. His face gave away nothing, but she thought from the way he toyed with a silver cigarette lighter that he was angry. Nonetheless, when he spoke, his voice reminded her of maple syrup. "On the contrary. She was impressed by the broadcast and the broadcaster. She said you were the closest thing she'd heard to a female Murrow. She also said there was something about a woman's view of the news that made it more comprehensible. I pointed out to her that it was the same news, it was only being read by a woman. She said she knew that, but she still found it more—I believe the word she used was sympathetic—coming from a woman."

"So you're going to try me out after all."

Gardner leaned back in his chair again. "You have a peculiar view of the world, Miss Childs. This afternoon you were incensed because I told you that most women deferred to men. Now you expect me to reverse a professional decision because my wife calls and gives an opinion."

"Then why did you call me up here again?"

He came forward in his chair and leaned across the desk toward her. "Because my wife wasn't the only woman who called. You weren't entirely wrong about those women who were home cooking and cleaning and taking care of the children. Or the ones playing cards. Apparently some of them do like hearing the news from a woman. At least from this particular woman. The switchboard was busy all afternoon." He picked up a sheaf of papers and rifled through them. "You sounded 'intelligent,' 'nice,' 'like the Queen of England,' 'understanding,' 'like my daughter who's a nurse somewhere in the Pacific,' and 'like a female Murrow.' That last opinion is from another caller, not my wife. Several women said you made the news so much clearer. Don't let that one go to your head and start ad-libbing."

"That means you're going to give me a chance."

"We'll start you with the two o'clock news. If that works out, we'll branch out to the one, three, and four broadcasts."

"What about noon?"

"My God, I give you a hand and you ask for an arm. The noon broadcast is too important. You'll start tomorrow."

Isabel stood and held out her hand. "You won't be sorry."

He took her hand. "Don't you even want to know how much money you'll be getting?"

Isabel laughed. She'd completely forgotten about the money. "How much?"

"We're doubling your salary. You'll be making eighty dollars a week."

"The newscaster who lost his voice this afternoon is making two hundred."

"We're taking a chance on you. Don't forget that. If it works out, you'll get a raise in six months."

"I'll work out." She turned and started for the door.

"One more thing," he said when she reached it. She turned back and looked at him. "You'll get a lot further in this world if you don't go around accusing the people who can hire and fire you of stupid prejudices."

She smiled. "It seems to me I'm doing pretty well as I am. For the moment."

21

MICHAEL'S LAST LEAVE was a replay of his first, except that this time they went to a hotel because they no longer had a home of their own. Thanks to his lingering connections in the city, he managed to get a room at the Plaza. It had a view of the park, a double bed, and a good-sized bathtub. The air of strangeness worked in their favor. They didn't even try to pretend that things were as they'd been. This was an interlude. They wrung every moment of pleasure from it. And every opportunity. By the time they said goodbye in Penn Station, Eliza was sure she'd conceived.

The next time he called her it was from New Jersey. "Practically across the river," he said when she asked where in New Jersey because a sign above his head warned him that Hitler was listening.

"Then I can come see you!" Eliza said. "Or can you get into town?"

"Neither, sweetheart. This is a staging area."

"What's a staging area?"

"The last place we go before we go."

"Oh!" she said, and her voice sounded like a tiny balloon bursting. "When?"

"Soon."

"But you'll call me again?"

"Everyday until . . ." His voice trailed off. "I've got plenty of time to stand in line for the phones. All we're doing is getting innoculated, again, being issued new equipment, and standing inspection to make sure we haven't lost what we've just been issued."

The next day he called with his APO number. For the first time Michael believed he was going to war. He didn't tell Eliza that, or any of the rumors that circulated over endless crap and poker games in the grim, anonymous barracks. They were being sent to England, the Canal Zone, Africa.

They were put on alert and told to hold themselves ready for moving out.

"Christ!" the man lying on the bed beside Michael's said. "Why wasn't I 4-F?"

"Don't sweat it, kid," a second soldier answered. "We're sure to get another six months training wherever they send us."

"Naw," a third man said. "My brother went straight from basic to the Solomons."

The alert was taken off. Michael called Eliza.

For the next week they were put on alert and taken off almost daily. The men grew less frightened and more angry. Wives and girlfriends began to lull themselves into security. He's not really going at all, Eliza thought. Against all reason, Michael was beginning to agree with her. And so when they really said goodbye, they didn't say goodbye at all.

"I love you," Michael said.

"I love you," Eliza answered.

"Kiss Teddy for me."

"Will you call tomorrow?" she asked.

"Sure thing."

But he never did.

The next day Eliza got her period.

By the spring of 1943 shortages were growing worse. There were no lipsticks because the cases had gone to make cartridge shells. If you wanted to buy toothpaste or, Eliza thought longingly, shaving cream, you had to turn in the old tube. In the unlikely event you found a laundry that was still open for business, they were probably too busy to take your work. And that April the newspapers reported a new crime. They called it "mugging." Thanks to dimouts and blackouts, people were being hurled into dark doorways, beaten, and robbed. Eliza figured the safest place to be was at home, and her parents agreed.

But even in that apartment insulated by so much family love there were dangers. Two weeks after Michael shipped out, Eliza came down with a terrible cold. Her mother took over the care and feeding of Teddy. Teddy didn't mind. Grandma gave him almost anything he wanted. Grandpa gave him anything. Only Aunt Pam was mean. One day when Teddy had turned over a bottle of nail polish that she'd already warned him not to touch three times, she actually spanked him. Teddy went running to his grandmother, who enfolded him against her enviable chest. "Aunt Pam didn't mean it," she said.

"I did mean it," Pam insisted. "Someone has to discipline him."

"But not you," Eliza said, clutching her robe around her. The sound of Teddy's crying had brought her from her sickbed.

Teddy turned to his mother and held out his arms, but his grandmother held him firm. "Germs," she said. "Mommy has germs." Teddy accelerated his sobs.

"My God, I didn't hurt him," Pam said.

"That's not the point," Eliza said, but she knew better than Pam what the point was. Her son was being—and she hated the term—spoiled rotten. She swore that as soon as she felt better, as soon as she was up and around, she'd do something about it.

Eliza was over her cold by the end of the week. Then the headaches started. At first two aspirins took care of them, but gradually the pills became less effective. After several weeks either the headaches or the aspirins began to affect her stomach. Half the time she was too nauseated to eat. She lost twelve pounds. Her clothes hung on her as on a hanger. Her mother took her to the doctor. They had to wait two hours in the cramped, overcrowded reception room. Children screamed. Mothers scolded. People sneezed and coughed and occasionally groaned in agony. The doctor examined Eliza quickly and pronounced her fit but thin. "Eat a little more," he said. "We don't want that husband of yours coming home to a scarecrow, do we?"

But she couldn't eat. She didn't have to take care of Teddy. She even stopped reading. There was no way to pass the interminable days, because days without Michael at the end of them had no definition. She began to knit again. Michael could use another sweater. She knitted and knitted and knitted. Sometimes she thought about knitting baby clothes. Then she found herself crying. The day she packed the sweater to mail it to Michael she was crying so hard her tears made the APO number printed carefully on the brown wrapping run until it was illegible, and she had to wrap it all over again.

Several weeks later Michael wrote from what Eliza's father was certain was North Africa that he loved the sweater. It was perfect for the cool nights. "You see," Mr. Stern interrupted as Eliza read the letter aloud, "it must be North Africa." He could also, Michael assured her, use it as a blanket. It reached, he wrote, to the top of his boots.

The headaches lingered and the stomach aches grew worse. Mr. Stern got the name of a specialist in Manhattan. The internist examined Eliza and gave her the name of another specialist. This one was a psychiatrist. Sarah Stern was horrified. "My daughter's not crazy," she said.

The specialist glanced at the clock on his huge mahogany desk and sighed. "I never suggested you were crazy," he said to Eliza. "You're suffering from a syndrome we're seeing a good deal of these days. Among the wives of absent servicemen. Inability to eat and sleep. Psychosomatic complaints."

"She has something wrong with her stomach," her mother said.

"An inability to recall what their husbands look like," the doctor went on as if Mrs. Stern hadn't spoken. "I asked you to describe your husband, and you said he was big. Then you said you guessed he wasn't so big after all and told me about the sweater."

"But what can a psychiatrist do?" Eliza asked.

The internist stood. "For your problems, I don't know. All I do know is that I can't help you. Unless of course you'd like a job. My receptionist is leaving to follow her husband to San Francisco." He was easing them toward the door. "I'm not joking, Mrs. Kramer.

I'm desperately shorthanded, and I think a job might help you get your mind off your problems."

"My daughter doesn't have to work," her mother said. "She's not crazy, and she doesn't have to work.

"At least he says you're not sick," Sarah said when they were outside the office. "But as for the rest, he's the one who's crazy. We'll go have a nice lunch. You'll forget all about it."

Eliza's stomach lurched at the mention of lunch, but she didn't want to upset her mother any more than she already had. They took a bus down Fifth Avenue and got off in front of Schrafft's.

The worst of the lunch hour crowd was gone, and they had to wait only twenty minutes for a table. "Would you look at that," Sarah said when they were sitting across from each other. Eliza turned to look at the sign above her head. *Please be nice to our help. We can always get more customers.* "I don't know what this world's coming to."

They took a long time over the menu. Mrs. Stern considered Eliza's choices carefully. Chicken was soothing, but red meat would build her up. Of course, if she just wanted something light, a salad would be good, or eggs. They were still debating when Sam Wicker approached the table.

Sam Wicker was not the sort of man anyone expected to find in Schrafft's but a meeting with a client had run late, and he had another meeting back at his office. Schrafft's was convenient and fast. He'd grabbed a sandwich at the counter and was on his way out when he spotted Eliza and her mother. He just had time for a cup of coffee, he announced, and pulled up a chair.

He asked Eliza how she was. He swore he'd been meaning to get out to see her, but the agency was a madhouse these days. "We're so shorthanded." Then he looked at her again, really looked at her. "Are you sure you're all right?"

That was her mother's cue. Mrs. Stern proceeded to tell him the whole sad story. The only thing she omitted was the part about the psychiatrist.

Sam's response was not what she'd expected. "You don't have to work for a doctor, Eliza. It'll just depress you more. I've got a job for you in my office. Can you type? It doesn't matter," he went on before she could answer. "If you can't, you'll pick it up."

"Eliza doesn't have to work," her mother said for the second time that afternoon.

Sam turned from daughter to mother. His eyes, under the thick, spikey lashes, were full of understanding. "I know that, Mrs. Stern. I know Mike can take care of his wife. And you and Mr. Stern can take care of your daughter. Eliza doesn't need the money but these days the country needs her."

"When did you become so patriotic?" Eliza asked.

Sam turned back to her with the smile she'd seen him use on dozens of women. "Okay, the agency needs you. *I* need you."

"Besides," Mrs. Stern went on, "Eliza's a mother."

"Lots of mothers are working these days. Mothers who don't have their own mothers there taking care of their children. If I know you, Mrs. Stern, you don't even let Eliza near Teddy."

"The whole idea is ridiculous," Sarah insisted.

Sam glanced at his watch. "I've got to run. Think about it, Eliza. At least it would get your mind off yourself."

His parting words were no aimless shot, and Eliza knew it. She'd always railed against women who spent their lives worrying about clothes and hair and makeup and nails, as if they measured the world by the limits of their own physical bodies. It was that attitude, Sam used to say each time he broke up with another blond beauty, that made Eliza such a good wife and mother.

He called Eliza a few days later. "I got a letter from Mike today. He sounds okay, considering. He told me about the sweater. What do you say, Eliza? Give up the knitting and come work for me."

"I can't. I don't know anything about working in an office."

"A piece of cake. You'll catch on in no time."

"Michael wouldn't want me to."

"Then we won't tell him."

Eliza was shocked. "I couldn't do that!"

"I was joking, Eliza. Mike wouldn't want you to sit home making yourself sick worrying about him either."

"I just can't do it, Sam."

By the time Eliza got off the phone, her mother was already halfway through Teddy's bath. "I'll take over now."

Teddy threw a wooden duck—all the rubber ones had gone to war long ago—into the air and watched it fall back to the tub with a splash. "No! I want grandma to."

Mrs. Stern beamed. "I'll finish. You go lie down. Your stomach's bothering you again, isn't it?" Eliza nodded. "I can always tell. Go lie down. I'll bring you some tea after I finish giving Teddy his bath."

Eliza went to her room, turned down the spread, and lay down on her bed. She didn't bother to turn on the light, because a headache was gathering force to join the stomachache. She thought of getting up for aspirins, but that would only make her stomach worse.

Pam came in and sat on the other bed. "Are you all right?"

"There's nothing wrong with me, if that's what you mean. Ask all the doctors. But I feel awful."

The darkened room was silent for what seemed like a long time. "Take Sam's job," Pam said finally. "Or the doctor's. It doesn't matter which. Just take one of them."

Eliza turned her head on the pillow, but she couldn't see her sister's expression. "Are you serious?"

"Dead serious. I've been thinking about it for weeks. It's hard not to these days. It used to be if a strange man started talking to you, he had something shady in mind. Now wherever I go I get propositioned for a job. I took one this afternoon. In the library. I was returning some books, and Mr. Goetz said I spend so much time there I might as well get paid for it."

"But I don't know anything about working."

Pam turned on the small lamp on the night table. Eliza blinked against it. "You ran a house. You took care of Teddy. Once upon a time, back at Hunter, you belonged to a million clubs and were always organizing something. You even had that story published in *Mademoiselle.*"

"That was before I married Michael."

"That's right. Now all you do is lie around the house all day listening to the news. And I'm no better. If we don't get out and start doing something, we'll both go crazy. Or I'll go crazy, and you'll become an invalid."

"What about Teddy?"

"It'll be the best thing in the world for Teddy, and you know it. He'll have only one woman fussing over him. Maybe he'll have to stop playing you and Mommy off against each other. Come on,

Liza, you're not going to let your baby sister outdo you. Give it a try."

"What if it doesn't work out?"

"We'll have lost nothing but time, and God knows we've got plenty of that on our hands."

They went into the kitchen, where Mrs. Stern was feeding Teddy an early dinner, and broke the news. She began to cry. They told her there was no reason for tears, but Mrs. Stern knew better. "I have this awful feeling. I'm sure of it."

"Of what?" Eliza asked.

"Don't ask me how I know. I just do."

"Know what?"

"If you take those jobs, if you take any jobs, you'll never be satisfied to be housewives again. I just know it."

Both girls told her she was just being silly.

Sam was right. The job was a piece of cake, which was not to say it wasn't exhausting. It simply wasn't difficult. Eliza might not be handy, as Michael had frequently reminded her, but she was efficient and organized and intelligent, as he'd often failed to mention. Within a week she'd learned which people to put through immediately and which warranted polite excuses, the routing of ads and the niceties of mediation between the copywriters and the illustrators, who thought they were artists, and the clients, who knew their place in the business world. The more she did, the more Sam gave her to do. He always had been good at delegating duties. Soon she was filling in for him in his absences and following him around to meetings. If Eliza had been ambitious for professional success, she would have seen the opportunity and seized it. But Eliza had no ambitions in that area. As she'd explained to the personnel director when she'd taken the job, she was simply trying to pass the time till her husband came home. The personnel director, a desperately myopic 4-F, had beamed approval. He didn't have to go through his usual warnings against getting funny ideas about feet in the door. "Once the men come home," it ended, "you gals go back to the kitchen. Back where you belong."

Despite the long hours and constant pressure, Eliza's headaches dwindled and stomachaches disappeared. And after a full day at the office, a long subway ride, and a couple of hours romping with

Teddy, she was too tired not to sleep, though she still awoke in the middle of the night in trembling terror. Only when she got her bearings and realized where she was and that Michael was not there with her, did she remember what she was in terror of.

Work wasn't a panacea, but it was a respite between the loneliness of the nights, and between the morning and evening editions of the newspapers. Eliza told herself you could never really know what was going on from the news, but still the thud of the paper against the door each morning and the sight of those big black headlines spread out on the stands each evening terrified her. It was hard to remember there'd been a time when newspapers had been little more than harmless vehicles for ads from Lord & Taylor and Peck and Peck. Still, the job allowed her to forget Michael and the war for whole minutes at a time, and to feel useful.

Sarah Stern, however, took a different view of things. "You're going to make yourself sick."

"I was sick," Eliza pointed out as she picked Teddy up for bed, though he was capable of getting there under his own steam. "I'm better now."

"No," Teddy shrieked. "No sleep!"

"Yes, sleep," Eliza said. "I'll read you a story, and then it's time for bed."

"No!" The cry rang through the house as if Teddy were being murdered.

"Let him stay up a little longer," her mother urged.

"It's already an hour past his bedtime."

"What's a few more minutes?" Mrs. Stern asked.

"Grandma," Teddy screamed, and held his arms out toward her.

"Mother!" Eliza pleaded.

"Don't argue with your mother," her father said without looking up from his *World Telegram.*

"I'm not arguing with her," Eliza insisted. "I'm trying to put my son to bed."

"What's this *my* son?" Sarah asked. "He's not our grandchild? Our only grandchild?"

Pam tossed aside the issue of *Life* she'd been leafing through, stood, and started for her room. "Leave me out of this."

"I'm just trying to help," Mrs. Stern said when Eliza came back from putting Teddy to bed. Despite his protests, he'd fallen asleep halfway through the story.

"I know. And I'm grateful. But giving in to Teddy's every whim isn't helping."

"That's right. Tell me how to raise children. I did such a terrible job with my two daughters."

Eliza apologized. Sarah went into the kitchen to make tea for everyone.

By the time Eliza reached the office the following morning, the crisis was already under way. Buddy Morton, the funniest man on radio next to Benny and Allen, the man paid twenty-two thousand a week to plug Mintfresh gum, had threatened to take his program away from the sponsor. Like Lucky Strike Green which had gone to war, Mintfresh had taken advantage of the war to change its packaging. *Because of special materials in the familiar green Mintfresh package,* the announcer repeated again and again, *materials crucial to the war effort, Mintfresh has gone mint white. So to win the war tomorrow, chew Mintfresh today.*

Buddy Morton had complained about the slogan when they'd first introduced it, but he'd finally backed down. Then, yesterday, he'd received a telegram. "The Secretary of War desires me to express his deep regret . . ." Morton's son had been killed in the Aleutians. The telegram did not add that the boy had been killed not by the Japanese, who'd already withdrawn, but by accidental "friendly fire." Morton had wanted to strike out at the war. Instead he'd had to settle for a single exploitation of it.

"Poor Morton," Eliza said.

"I'm sorry for Morton," Sam answered. "But at the moment I'm more worried about us. Unless we have a new campaign by tonight, Morton walks."

She glanced at the morning newspaper tossed aside on Sam's desk. ALLIES BROADCAST FROM ALGIERS ALERTING ITALIANS TO IMMINENT INVASION "Goddamn you, Sam! Morton's son is dead, all over Europe Jews are being murdered, Michael's probably on his way to Italy right now, and you sit here safe as houses worrying about your accounts and your own precious skin."

He sat behind his desk smiling up at her. "As they say in the movies, Eliza, you're cute when you're mad."

"Go to hell," she said, and walked out of his office.

"Easy for you to say," he called after her, "but with all the magazines cutting back on advertising because of the paper shortage, Mintfresh needs a radio show."

"I'm sorry," she said when she handed him the typed script for the new commercial fourteen hours later.

He took it from her and put it in his briefcase for the next morning's meeting. "No need to be. You're turning into an interesting woman, Eliza."

"Because I lose my temper and curse?"

"Because you aren't afraid of everybody and everything anymore." He smiled. The cleft in his chin deepened. "You aren't even scared of me."

"I was never afraid of you."

"The hell you weren't." He stood and walked around his desk. "How about a drink? I think we deserve one."

She could think of about a dozen reasons to say no. She didn't drink, except for an occasional apricot sour when Michael took her out to dinner. She didn't think she ought to go out for drinks with other men, even other men who were her husband's best friends. She didn't trust Sam Wicker. But the arguments all came from Eliza's past, and she knew how provincial they'd sound to Sam. "Thanks, but it's much too late. I really have to get home."

Sam glanced at his watch. "My God, it's almost midnight."

"That's what I mean." She started out of his office. He followed her to her desk. "You can't go home now. You'll have to stay in town."

She smiled. "Brooklyn is town, Sam. There are five boroughs, or haven't you heard."

"I picked up a rumor to that effect, but I didn't believe it. Anyway, you can't take a subway at this hour, and you'll never get a taxi."

He had a point.

"I've got a place for you to stay."

Eliza's background, provincial or not, reared its head. "No, thank you."

He started to laugh. "I'm sorry, Eliza. It's not that funny, but you should see your face. I didn't mean you could stay at my place.

Though you could, and I promise you nothing would happen. You could, but you wouldn't. This is a friend's place."

"Another of your tall, blond *shiksas?*"

"Well, she's tall and she's not Jewish, but her hair is kind of coppery, and she's definitely not just 'another.' In fact, I'd like you to meet her."

"At this hour?"

"If I know Isabel, she isn't even home yet."

"Still at El Morocco or the Stork Club, no doubt."

"Still in the newsroom."

"That Isabel? The one you always listen to on the two o'clock news?"

"The two, three, and four o'clock news. This one has a mind behind the body and face."

"I couldn't just barge in on someone like her in the middle of the night. Anyway, she probably doesn't have room."

"She has an entire townhouse."

"Now I really couldn't think of it."

"That's the old, timid Eliza talking. Not the exciting woman I saw stomping around here this morning."

"Stop calling me an exciting woman. I'm supposed to be your best friend's wife."

"You're supposed to be Mike's wife or I'm supposed to be his best friend?" He saw the color creeping up her throat. "I'm only teasing you, Eliza. Come on, you need a place to stay."

Isabel Childs was even more intimidating than Sam's description of her. She opened the door wearing a woolen robe and an air of total self-possession. It was as if all of Sam's tall, aristocratic-looking girls had been only imitations. This was the real thing. She held out a long slender hand to Eliza and said she was more than welcome. "If Sam's kept you working till this hour, you must be starved."

Eliza said she wasn't hungry, though in fact she was ravenous, but Isabel insisted, and they all trooped down to the kitchen. Eliza was fascinated. Even without the long pantry with dozens of cabinets and glass-fronted closets, the kitchen was huge, and hopelessly old-fashioned. The stove and sink were practically antiques. Only the refrigerator looked up-to-date. Then it dawned on her. If you had plenty of servants, you didn't need any other conveniences. Only there were no servants around now, and Isabel seemed perfectly competent moving between the big old appliances.

"Will bacon and eggs be all right? It's one of the few things I know how to make."

Eliza said that really she didn't have to bother, but her mouth watered at the words. She was glad Isabel had suggested bacon. Ham was more problematic, and no one she knew ate pork chops.

"What I could really use is a drink," Sam said. "Where are you hiding that bottle of scotch I brought?" Isabel said it was in the pantry. Sam went down the long hall and came back carrying a bottle of Haig and Haig pinch. "Isabel has a peculiar set of scruples," he said as he took three glasses from a cabinet. Eliza noticed that he knew where things were kept. "She complained when I brought the bottle."

"It's black market," Isabel interrupted as she began beating the eggs.

"Strictly speaking, it can't be black market, because booze isn't rationed. On the other hand, I admit that it comes from a special cache that my liquor store saves for special customers who are willing to pay special prices. Anyway, the point is," he said, taking a seltzer siphon from the refrigerator, "Isabel won't drink it alone, but she will with me."

Isabel took the glass he handed her. "That's only because I don't want to let you drink by yourself. It's a dangerous habit. Cheers," she said to Eliza.

Eliza took a sip of the drink. It burned her throat.

They sat at one end of the long wood table and ate the bacon and eggs and toast and drank the scotch. Eliza found the taste was growing on her. She found Isabel Childs growing on her, or maybe that was only the scotch after all. It wasn't until the next morning that she realized that for the first time since Michael had left, she'd let a day pass without writing to him.

Isabel was at the table in the dining room when Eliza came down that morning. She looked crisp and efficient in a navy linen suit, and Eliza felt crumpled and shabby in yesterday's dress.

"I thought of offering you something to wear," Isabel said, "then I realized you'd swim in anything of mine."

"I'm too short," Eliza said.

"You're not too short. You're just shorter than I am. And height is a mixed blessing. These days I like it, but it's no fun when you're twelve and a head taller than all the boys in dancing class." Isabel stopped. She sounded like a new girl, babbling nervously, trying desperately to make friends.

Eliza spent the morning trying to think of a thank you gift for Isabel Childs. What did you send a woman who had everything? Finally, she gave up trying to be original and settled for flowers. The next day Isabel called to thank her. "You're welcome any time," she said. "And I'm not being polite. I mean it."

The Mintfresh gum crisis continued. Sam went through several more campaigns before everyone was happy. Eliza stayed at the townhouse on East Sixty-seventh Street three times in the next two weeks. Her parents were scandalized. "I knew you never should have taken that job," Mrs. Stern said.

Eliza was beginning to think her mother was right. Days in an office and nights in town were all very well for a career girl, but Eliza was no career girl. She was a mother who'd made the mistake of taking a job.

"He wouldn't go to bed," Sarah said. "I read to him and then Daddy told him a story and finally he had some milk and cookies. I think it was after ten by the time we got him to sleep."

Eliza knew it wasn't fair to her parents, or to Teddy. What child wouldn't put off bedtime—if he could get away with it? She told Sam she was quitting.

"You can't do this to me, Eliza."

"I can't do this to Teddy."

"What can I do to convince you to change your mind?"

"Nothing."

"More money?"

"You know that's not the problem." It wasn't the problem, but it had become a secret pleasure. Eliza liked making money. The fact surprised her because both her father and Michael had always given her everything she'd wanted. But there was a difference, she discovered when she got her first paycheck, between asking or hoping for something and simply deciding to buy it for yourself. There was no doubt about it. Eliza was going to miss the job.

The next morning Isabel Childs called and asked if Eliza would like to have lunch. They didn't go to Schrafft's. Isabel knew of a little French place on Forty-eighth Street. "It must be authentic because the crew from the *Normandie*—at least the ones who are still here—eat there."

The restaurant was small and dark and redolent of roasting meat and garlic. Eliza thought she'd never seen or smelled anything quite so exotic in her life. Isabel was sitting on a banquette talking French to a group of men at the next table. "That's the *Normandie* contingent," she said when Eliza joined her. "Funny, I crossed on it twice with mother in the summer of '36, but I never got to know the crew then." She laughed as if it were funny in more ways than one.

They ordered omelettes *fines herbes,* or rather Isabel ordered one, and Eliza said she'd have the same, because despite her Hunter French she was too shy to pronounce *fines herbes.*

"Sam told me you're quitting," Isabel said as soon as the waitress had taken their order. "And he told me why. I have a solution. Why don't you and your little boy move into our house? You'll be doing me a favor. For one thing I'd like the company. For another, I'd stop feeling that I was sabotaging the war effort single-handed. Every time I see another article on the housing shortage, I cringe."

"It's generous of you," Eliza said, "more than generous. But I don't see how I could. I mean, I wouldn't have the long subway rides anymore, but what would I do with Teddy."

"Cora could take care of him. In fact, I can't think of anything she'd like better. She's a first-rate children's nurse. Came to work for us when my brother was born, and stayed on after I went off to school. She was sure that by this time I'd have given her another generation to care for, but I've let her down. I have the feeling I'm never going to come through for Cora, but that's another story."

The waitress brought a basket of bread and two pats of real butter, not the awful sickly white margarine some copywriter had christened Uncle Sam's Spread.

"Don't you want children?" Eliza asked. She'd never met a woman who didn't.

Isabel shrugged. "That's a postwar problem. But in the meantime come stay with me. There's plenty of room, including a fully equipped playroom for your son."

The idea was tempting. But impossible. "What would my parents say?"

Isabel stopped buttering her bread and looked across the table at Eliza.

Eliza noticed the tilt of Isabel's head. Isabel wasn't looking at her, she was looking down at her. Eliza was sure of it.

"How old are you, Eliza? Twenty-five?"

"Twenty-six."

"You're twenty-six. You're a married woman. You have a child. Do you need your parents' permission?"

The waitress arrived with their lunch. Eliza was hoping it would distract Isabel. Isabel was not so easily distracted.

"Well, do you?"

"I don't think my husband would approve either."

Now Eliza was sure Isabel was looking down at her. "Does your husband have to approve of everything you do? You don't have to answer that. But there's really nothing to disapprove of. All over the country servicemen's wives are moving in together. Well, I'm not anyone's wife, but I've got an empty house in town, and you need a place to stay in town. I can't believe your husband wouldn't approve of that. Assuming he's a reasonable man."

Michael was a reasonable man. And Isabel had a reasonable point. Eliza was a grown woman. Why couldn't she live where she pleased? And the idea of living in the townhouse pleased her. She liked the beauty of the place, and the freedom, and the excitement. She'd been missing all three since she'd become a child in her parents' house again. But there was one more problem, and she didn't know how to broach it. "It's kind of you. Really. But I don't see how I could afford—I mean, I don't make very much at the agency." That sounded as if Michael didn't take care of her. "Of course, my husband left—"

It had never occurred to Isabel that Eliza would regard money as the stumbling block. Isabel rarely thought about money. These days she had to remind herself that others did. "I couldn't take money from you. The house is there whether you live in it or not. Cora's wages are taken care of."

"But not by me. I'd have to pay my share."

Isabel started to argue, then thought better of it. "All right." She turned to the table next to them and said something in French. One of the men handed her his newspaper. Isabel began to leaf through it for apartment rentals. Then she started to laugh. "There are no apartments for rent. I should have thought of that." Again she turned to the Frenchmen. Her accent was impeccable. "He says five dollars a week is a fair price. I'll take five dollars from you every week and contribute it to the Free French. As for Cora, that's between the two of you. Fair?"

Eliza said it was fair.

"Now everyone's happy. Including the Free French and FDR because we're alleviating the housing shortage."

"Everyone but my mother." Eliza was wondering how she was going to tell Sarah.

Isabel laughed. "Mine still hasn't forgiven me for taking a job. She says nice girls really don't."

Eliza started to laugh too. "That's even worse than my mother. All she's worried about is that I'll never want to stay home again."

"You probably won't," Isabel said, and was sorry when Eliza stopped laughing abruptly.

Eliza moved into East Sixty-seventh Street the following weekend. Mrs. Stern sobbed. Mr. Stern stood in front of the Brooklyn apartment building with his hands folded across his chest shaking his head back and forth as his daughter and grandson drove off in Sam Wicker's car.

Cora opened up the old playroom. There were electric trains and a small jungle gym and a model of Noah's ark with a parade of animals that was so long it went twice around the entire room. There were bikes and wagons and scooters and a garden out back and a park half a block away.

That Friday, payday for Eliza, she came home from the office and handed Isabel a five-dollar bill. Isabel looked up from the tomatoes she was picking in the small victory garden she and Cora had planted. Behind her the evening sun slanted over a high stone wall. A late summer breeze ruffled the leaves of the sycamore shading the yard. "Why don't you just make out a check to the Free French?" Isabel asked.

"Michael's father has the checkbook."

Isabel stood and wiped the dirt from her hands. "Your husband went off to the army and left the checkbook with his father?"

Eliza wished Isabel wouldn't sound quite that way. "I'm not awfully good at figures."

"Sam says you're terrific at figures, but that's not the point." Isabel started to say something, then stopped. Eliza was glad. She could tell from the tone of Isabel's voice that she wouldn't have liked whatever it was. Isabel bent to the tomato plants again. "As soon as I finish this, we're going inside, and I'm going to teach you to balance a checkbook. It's child's play. Teddy could do it. Then Monday, you're going to the bank first thing in the morning and open an account."

"In my own name?"

"Not in Winston Churchill's."

"What will Michael say?"

Isabel had some idea. She decided not to answer.

Eliza went inside to write to Michael. She didn't mention the checkbook. He was having enough trouble getting used to the idea of a job, even if it was a job working for Sam, whom he'd trust, he wrote, with his life.

22

THE MORNING AFTER World Pictures failed to pick up Jeanne Storey's option, Gustave Dressler signed Lily Hart for two hundred dollars a week. Lily was under personal contract to him. When six months later he left Elysian Films for World, he took Lily along. This time she signed with World. Half a year earlier they could have renewed her contract for a hundred and fifty dollars a week. Now her agent got her two thousand. In the interim Lily had made three pictures with Gustave Dressler, but one was all it had taken to change her life.

The first movie was called *Desire.* It was about a poor but beautiful girl named, absurdly, Miranda, about the men who desired her and the men and things she desired. Lily didn't have to act. All she had to do was remember. And all Dressler had to do was decide which angle to shoot from to best capture the tragic longing of those wide beautiful eyes and the tremulous desire of that full sensuous mouth. The critics raved. They acclaimed Gustave Dressler a genius. They christened Lily Hart a presence, a force, the most exciting discovery of the decade. No one used the word "actress."

Moviegoers flocked to the theaters. When Lily moved to World, Fred Wirtz assigned six secretaries to answer Lily's fan mail and fulfill the requests for her photograph. Gustave Dressler had said he didn't want to build Lily's career on barracks' walls, but there was a war on and millions of men who'd fallen in love with Miranda in *Desire* were living in barracks. Fred Wirtz scheduled a shooting for a new Lily Hart pinup.

"No pinup," Gustave said. He and Lily and Fred were in the dressing room trailer Dressler had insisted on for Lily. World had footed the bill, but Gustave had chosen everything in it, including a painting Lily hadn't understood or even liked until he'd explained it to her. After that she'd liked it a lot, and Gustave was pleased because he'd said he hated to think that someone as beautiful as Lily couldn't appreciate the beauty of Cezanne.

"What do you mean no pinup?" Wirtz asked. "There are a couple of million GIs out there who are clamoring for a pinup of Lily Hart."

"Like Betty Grable in the bathing suit or Rita Hayworth in the nightgown?"

Lily thought of Tom. She'd sent him some of the stills from *Desire*. He said none of the guys could believe she was his girl. She'd heard from Rose and Iris too. They'd written that the night *Desire* opened in Duquel, the line in front of the movie had gone all the way around the block. They'd also said their father had forgiven her. Lily had written to her mother and sisters and enclosed a check. She hadn't mentioned her father in the letter. "Not a nightgown," she said. Neither man paid attention to her.

"I want her in a dress," Gustave insisted. "Not low-cut."

"For Christ sake, Gus. What do you think we're selling? Tickets to a church supper?"

"I know what we're selling, and there's nothing more erotic than the imagination. I want her in a black dress. With long sleeves and a high collar. A beautifully cut black dress that reveals nothing and makes you think of everything."

"I think you're crazy," Wirtz said.

"I'm not the one who let her option lapse," Gustave answered. "Leave the photography to me."

"You're the boss," Wirtz conceded.

"As long as it's not a nightgown," Lily said, but neither of them heard her.

The shooting took an entire day, but Lily didn't mind. Working with Gustave wasn't really work. She'd discovered that the first day on the set of *Desire*. Other people—cameramen and assistant directors and grips—said Dressler was a terror to work for, although there were actresses throughout the industry who would trade their souls and had traded their bodies for the chance. He shouted and threatened and bullied everyone on the set—everyone except Lily. To her he made love. When he turned her face a fraction of an inch, his hands were a caress on her skin. When he moved a strand of hair, his fingers were a kiss. In his mouth even the most mundane orders—"A little to the left, Lily." "Not so big a smile, Lily."— became compliments. Sometimes when Gustave touched her or talked to her that way, she found herself thinking of Tom and wondering what he was doing at that minute. She basked and glowed in the attention that was warmer and more flattering than any lighting, and the pictures showed it. They showed a woman adored.

At the end of the shooting that day Dressler saw her to the limousine he'd made World buy for her. He did that every night, but he never got in with her. Each night he sent her home alone to the house in Beverly Hills he'd picked out for her with a script he wanted her to study or books he wanted her to read. The nights out arranged by World's publicity department were a thing of the past. Occasionally Gustave took her to dinner or a party given by what he called Hollywood royalty. Lily could tell from the way he pronounced the word that he didn't mean it. But that night there would be no dinner or party. Gustave wanted her to study the script of *Too Little Time.* It was about a girl and a soldier who meet and have a single weekend before he goes off to war.

The driver brought the car to a stop on the big circular drive in front of her house. The maid Gustave had hired for her opened the door. He'd wanted to hire a butler as well, but these days they were all on assembly lines or front lines.

The mail lay on a table in the hall. Among the piles of invitations and solicitations were a letter from Rose and two from Tom. She took the three letters and climbed the wide carpeted staircase to her room. It had a canopied bed and curtains and wallcoverings of a blue and beige print that told stories of shepherds and milking girls and love. Gustave said it was called *toile de Jouy*. He'd modeled the room on one in a French chateau where he'd spent the summers of his youth, though he wasn't French. Lily never could find out where he'd been born, but she knew he'd lived all over the world.

The maid brought a crystal goblet with mineral water on a silver tray. Lily would have preferred a Coke, but Gustave had forbidden her to drink Coke. "It's the bane of your country," he said. "Like the Russians and vodka. It rots the mind as well as the teeth."

The maid asked if Lily would like her to run a bath. Lily said she would. Whenever Mary offered to do anything, Lily accepted, but she still couldn't bring herself to ask to be waited on.

The bathroom was bigger than the room she'd shared with Rose and Iris. The tub was huge. Lily waited till Mary had left, then took off the satin underwear Gustave had chosen for her. She was still too shy to undress in front of Mary and refused to let her hold a towel for her when she stepped out of the tub or a phone to her ear while she was in it, though Mary insisted she'd done all those things for the women she'd worked for previously. Lily eased herself into the steaming scented water, lay back against the rubber pillow, and looked at the two tissue-thin envelopes with Tom's big unruly handwriting. The letters were her only company for the night. She wanted to make them last as long as possible. Finally she put one down on the towel which Mary had folded on the chair beside the tub and tore the other open along the perforated edge. The thin V-Mail paper crackled in her hands.

I guess you're wondering why you haven't heard from me in a while, it began. *Well, this time it wasn't just the fleet postmaster's fault. About a week ago I ran into a little trouble.* Lily sat up in the tub. *I can tell you this now because everything's all right. There's a little piece of real estate here that goes back and forth between the Japs and us.* The next two lines had been blacked out by the censor. *So we had to take it back. Well, one minute my buddy Dan and I are making a big push and the next thing I know I'm waking up in a hospital.* The sweat from her fingers made the ink on the paper run. *The shell landed, the medic told me later, about two feet away. It blew my pants off and knocked me out, but except for a few scratches, that's all it did. You'll know I'm telling you the truth when I tell you they're going to send me back to my company in a week or two. So keep writing to me there. I expect to find a whole mess of letters and packages waiting for me when I get back. And send more pictures. I've got one tacked on the bamboo strut next to my bed. One of the guys asked who it was. I said my girl. He said the same thing all the guys do. "Come on, no one's got a girl who looks like Lily Hart."*

Lily tore open the second letter. This one didn't mention his wounds at all. Tom wrote about how soft life in the hospital was. *I've actually got a bed and mosquito netting. Pretty cushy. But I bet old Dan is lonely in the old fox hole.* They'd brought in some frozen beef and he'd had steak the night before. *The first real meat I've had in months.* The weather was cooler. *Only about a hundred today.* There were a few blacked out lines, then a paragraph about a buddy who'd died of Dengue fever. *It's worse than the Japs, and they're bad enough. Don't ever let anyone tell you they can't see—or fight. They're damn good soldiers. But the marines are better.*

Lily sank back into the cooling water and read the first paragraph through several times. A few scratches! What did that mean? She tried to picture Tom with a maimed arm or a limp. The image was too awful to be real. She thought of his face. Please God, she crossed herself, don't let anything happen to his face. Or his eyes. Or . . . She sat up again. Once you started imagining things, there was no stopping. She leaned forward in the tub, turned on the hot water, and let it run until the tub was warm again. Then she settled back and read through the letters a second time. They were sending him back to his company. That was the important part. They wouldn't be sending him back if there were anything really wrong with him.

On the other hand, why shouldn't there be something wrong with him? A tiny wound that wouldn't hurt him. A little scratch that couldn't be seen. A wound just serious enough to keep him from being sent back. That would be even better. She closed her eyes and thought about his homecoming.

Lily reread the letters several times. When the tissue paper had gone limp from being turned again and again in her damp hands, she put Tom's letters aside and opened the one from Rose. The words shot off the page like bullets. *Eloise and Marion weren't in school. A telegram to the Lunds. "The Secretary of War desires me to express his deep regret. Missing in action. Presumed dead."*

At the sound of her scream, Mary came running into the bathroom. Miss Hart was sitting bolt upright in the tub, still as a mannequin. A letter floated in the water.

Mary managed to get her out of the tub and into a robe. Lily followed all her directions—first one arm, then the other, a towel for her hair—like a docile child. Mary got her into bed, then went downstairs and called Mr. Dressler.

Gustave was there in minutes. "It's Tom," she said, but he'd known that the minute the maid had called him.

"Did you get a telegram?"

"I'm not his wife," she said, and Gustave wished he could capture the expression in her eyes on film. He was already memorizing her voice which he knew he'd want her to use in a movie someday.

"Didn't his family call to tell you?"

"They didn't approve of me. They were very rich. And very important. In Duquel."

Gustave picked up the phone on the night table. He wasted no time trying to get through to the rich and important of Duquel. Instead he went straight to his contact in the War Department. The colonel promised to get back to him within half an hour. He called in twenty minutes. Lund had rejoined his company only a few days earlier. They were on their way from Guadalcanal to—"well, I can't tell you where, but another of those damn godforsaken islands"—when his ship was torpedoed and sunk. They picked up a couple of survivors and some bodies. "Lund wasn't among either. And the Japs didn't take any prisoners. There isn't a snowball's chance in hell the boy's still alive. Not with the Japs and the sharks."

Gustave stared at the picture of the young man in uniform on the table beside the phone. He looked like a child, younger even than Lily. But the picture had been taken a long time ago. He'd been in battle for the last year. He would have been an old man by the time he died. War did that, especially to children. War did that, Gustave knew, though he'd never been in war himself. He felt a flash of the terrible secret triumph the living feel over the dead. Then he turned to Lily to tell her what the colonel had said, and all the time he was telling her he kept thinking perhaps he should change the ending of *Too Little Time*. Perhaps the young hero shouldn't come home from the war after all.

By early the next morning, the wheels of World Pictures had begun to turn. Alec Zeal's secretary sent a floral arrangement so huge it redefined the word "tasteless." Fred Wirtz came to Lily's house to deliver his condolences in person, and pick up a photograph of Tom Lund, the YOUNG MARINE LILY HART LOVED AND LOST. The headlines had been racing through Wirtz's head ever since Dressler had called.

Lily and Gustave were in the solarium when Wirtz arrived. In the harsh morning light her skin looked translucent. The real tears in her eyes were better than glycerin. When he told her how sorry he was, her full lower lip trembled. He wished he'd brought a photographer, but of course there were limits. Even in this business there were limits.

"Now don't worry about hurrying back to the studio," Wirtz said. "A.Z. told me to tell you to take as long as you want, as long as you need."

"Lily has a costume fitting in two hours," Gustave said. "We start shooting tomorrow morning."

Lily said nothing.

"Isn't that a little premature?" Wirtz asked, though he was secretly relieved. A.Z. had said to tell the kid to take as much time off as she wanted, providing she didn't want more than a few days. "I'm not paying her two thousand a week to sit on her ass. It's worth too much on the screen."

Like millions of American women whose world had been turned upside down, Lily needed something to hang on to. She turned to the church, and for the second time in her life the church failed her. All she wanted to know was that she and Tom would be reunited in eternity. The priest inquired after the state of Tom's soul. Had he been in the habit of confessing to the chaplain before battle? Lily shook her head. "He wasn't a Catholic," she said.

"You mean he wasn't baptized in the church?"

"He must have been in his own church."

The priest moved his head from left to right. "I'm sorry, my child." Then Lily found another life raft, the wording of the telegram. *Missing in action. Presumed dead.* Who was the government to presume Tom dead? There was no body, no proof. He could have been picked up by another ship, taken prisoner by the Japs, swum to safety. Lily's heart pounded out the possibilities. But Gustave deflated each hope. Tom's name was not among the survivors. The Japanese had taken no prisoners. The ship had gone down among flames and enemy fire miles from land in shark-infested water. Gustave had it all on the authority of his colonel, who had it on the authority of the War Department. Lily had to come to terms with Tom's death, Gustave said gently. And she had to go on with her life. Work was the answer.

Gustave Dressler brought *Too Little Time* in nine days early and exactly on budget. Work had been the answer, work and Gustave. He and Lily were together constantly. He had a room fitted out for her at his house with a second wardrobe and extra copies of the books he wanted her to read and paintings that he changed every few weeks.

Each night after dressing for dinner they met in Gustave's library at seven-forty. There he permitted her sherry rather than mineral water while he had two fingers of scotch. Promptly at eight they went into the dining room. He sat at the head of the long table and she sat on his right while the butler poured and served and Gustave talked. He talked about books and paintings and music and movies, about food and wine, about men and women and life. As she sat and learned how to eat an artichoke and how not to hold a wine glass and watched Gustave's long skeletal fingers moving over the heavy silver and thin crystal, she learned how small her world, even when it had expanded to include Tom and Carrie Snyder and her contract at World, had been. Gustave told her about other countries and other customs and other times. And she took every word as gospel, except those that desecrated the gospel. Gustave hated the church. He hated all churches. He said organized religion was responsible for most of the hatred and violence through the ages. "First the Romans fed the Christians to the lions. Then the Catholics broke unbelievers on the rack. Now the Pope stands by while Hitler kills Jews all over Europe."

"Are you Jewish, Gustave?"

He ignored her question. He ignored all personal questions.

"Scratch a true believer, and you'll find a bigot."

"I'm not a bigot," Lily said.

"You're not a true believer either. You're just a victim of circumstance."

"I go to church."

"Not as often as you used to before Tom died. You don't need the church anymore, Lily. I've given you something else to believe in."

"I suppose you mean you." Sometimes she thought Gustave went too far.

He put his hand over hers on the table. His face, long and pale and serious as an icon's, creased in an unusual smile. "Not me, Lily, but truth and beauty and art. You must admit mine is a more pleasant religion."

One night she asked him if he'd ever been married. He said until he'd reached Hollywood he'd never been in one place long enough. "Were you ever in love?"

"Constantly," he said.

She began to think he might be like some of the young men the studio had set her up with when she was first under contract. They liked other boys. She asked him to tell her about some of the women he'd loved. He did. Lily knew from the way he talked that he wasn't making them up. They were flesh and blood women. And she hated them.

"I hear you're living at Dressler's these days," Fred Wirtz said to her one afternoon in the commissary.

"I stay there sometime. I don't like being alone since . . ." She let her voice trail off.

Wirtz looked across the table at Lily. Tragedy had defined her features. The beauty was more heartbreaking than ever. It was a pity she hadn't ended up with her marine. It was a shame she hadn't ended up with him. He and the marine would have treated her right, but he didn't trust Dressler. He liked and admired him, but he didn't trust him, especially where women were concerned.

"Just be careful, Lily."

"There's nothing going on. Really."

Wirtz laughed. "Look, honey, you're a big girl now. And a star. You can do what you like—as long as it doesn't get in the papers or the mags. I don't care who you shack up with, but I care about you, so just be careful."

That evening when Lily left the studio she went to her own house. That's why she was there when Jerry Crowley called. "I didn't think you'd take the call," he said. "Now that you're a star. I didn't think you'd even remember who I was."

"How could I forget? If it weren't for you, I wouldn't be a 'star.' "

"The hell you wouldn't. You've got what it takes, Lily. You didn't need any help from me."

Lily loved to hear it, but she never knew what to say when she did. "How's Carrie?"

"Never better. Her husband's back. The poor guy lost a couple of fingers, but at least he's alive."

"I'm glad," Lily said, and Crowley noticed that her voice sounded funny.

"How's that marine of yours? Tom, right?"

She told him.

"I'm sorry, Lily, really sorry."

There wasn't much to say after that, and they got off the phone. It wasn't exactly a brush-off, Crowley thought. She'd sounded pretty broken up. Anyway, what had he expected? She wasn't a pretty kid on the assembly line anymore. She was a movie star, and she had a lot bigger fish to fry than forty-dollar-a-week union organizers with broken noses and just enough internal injuries to qualify as 4-F.

Lily spent the rest of the night studying the new script Gustave had given her. The following evening she returned to his house.

23

BY THE END of America's second year of war, Hollywood had undergone changes. The shortage of hairpins made it necessary to check them in and out of the dressing rooms. They were used, sterilized, then reused. All over town directors, actors, and lesser lights were wearing elbow patches on their sleeves. "Use it up, wear it out, make it do, or do without," went the slogan, but most of the patches were new and came from Abercrombie and Fitch. Henry Fonda, Jimmy Stewart, Robert Cummings, and Gable himself had signed up. Alec Zeal managed, thanks to a series of training and sex hygiene films, to have himself made an Air Force colonel. He bought five custom-made uniforms and wore a different one to the studio each day. But the business of entertainment went on. The USO Clubs alone required a thousand prints of films a week. The Hollywood Victory Committee managed to convince the same number of contract and free-lance players to contribute their services in camp shows. Lily volunteered for the Foxhole Circuit, the one that toured overseas. She was hoping to be sent to the South Pacific. The Army said they needed her in North Africa. But that was several weeks and countless inoculations off. In the meantime there was the premiere of *Too Little Time.* The war had put a temporary end to search lights, but there was still plenty of glitter—in the sequins of the silver dress Gustave had chosen for her; in the popping flashbulbs as he helped her out of the limousine; in the eyes of the thousands of fans hungry for a glimpse of her. "Lily!" they cried. "Lily Hart." "You're beautiful." "You're wonderful." "We love you, Lily."

Later there was the heat of the applause that went on and on as the closing credits crept past the last frame of Lily's face, and the sparkle of the icy champagne at the party, and more words of adoration, not from anonymous fans, but from powerful men.

"I love you, Lily," Fred Wirtz said. "I always knew you had it in you."

"I love this girl," A.Z. said to his entourage as he hugged Lily for the photographers.

"How does it feel to be loved by the whole world?" Gustave asked as he held the front door open for her. All the way home in the limousine he'd been silent.

"Cold," she said. "The house is cold."

"You're developing a flair for irony, Lily. I like that."

He followed her into the living room. "Perhaps this will warm the evening." She turned back to him. He was holding a long velvet box out to her. She took it from him and opened it. A chain of emeralds lay like a bright snake on the white satin. He lifted it from the box and fastened it around her neck. The stones were cold against her skin, but his hands were warm. His hands traced the line of her shoulders, then he turned away and moved to the brandy tray.

He poured two snifters and held one out to her. He usually didn't allow her brandy, especially at this hour, but he said tonight was a special occasion.

"Is that why you gave me the necklace?"

"I gave you the necklace because you've been a good girl, and I'm proud of you."

"Is that all?"

He sipped his brandy and looked at her. She remembered the first time they'd met. She'd been terrified by those eyes that seemed to see right into her. She was no longer terrified, but she still believed in their power. "What more do you want, Lily?" he asked as if it were a serious question, as if he really didn't know. "If there's something you want, something you need, you have to tell me. You know I'll do anything to make you happy."

They stood at opposite sides of the room staring at each other. What could she say? That she loved him? She wasn't even sure she did. That she wanted him to touch her, to make love to her? Right now, right here. On the living room sofa or floor or wherever he said. That she'd do whatever he wanted? She drained her glass and put it down on the table. She felt as if she were playing a scene, one of Gustave's scenes. "Nothing. I don't need or want anything. You've already given me everything."

By the time she reached the top of the stairs she could feel the heat in her face. She didn't know if it was from anger or embarrassment or simply the brandy.

She went to her room and took off the sequin dress. She wore nothing beneath it but step-ins, and now she sat on the side of the bed staring at the dress that hung from the back of the chair like an icicle. It reminded her of the straps of the dress she'd made for Tom's going-away party. She'd been so proud of that dress. Poor Lily Hartarski had had so little. Lucky Lily Hart had everything. Only that night Tom had driven to the bluff overlooking the river and made love to her until the sun began melting over the horizon and the two of them were pale and silent with exhaustion. And tonight Lily Hart would sleep alone.

She took the sequin dress from the chair and slipped it over her head. Then she walked down the hall to Gustave's room.

He was sitting in a chair beside the bed, wearing silk pajamas and a silk foulard dressing gown over them. He looked up from the book in his lap.

"Did you want something, Lily?"

"I never said thank you. For the necklace."

"I hope you like it."

Another minute passed. The clock on the night table seemed to grow louder. He went on staring at her with those hard black eyes. "Why don't you say what you mean, Lily?"

She didn't answer.

"Do I have to direct this scene for you too? All right, you walk into the room. You close the door behind you. You stand just as you are now with your face half in shadow. You're developing a sense for that, Lily. And then you say, 'Gustave, I want you to make love to me.' "

"I didn't—"

"You did, Lily. That's why you're here. That's what you want. And it's what I've been waiting for. For you to realize that you want me as much as I want you. I won't be just another one of those men, drooling over you, scheming for a casual touch, maneuvering you into bed."

"Then why did you buy me the necklace?"

"I told you. Because you've been a good girl and I'm proud of you." He was still sitting in the chair beside the bed staring up at her. "Now why are you here, Lily?"

"You want to humiliate me."

"I want to make love to you. When you admit you want me to."

"I—" She stopped. "Please, Gustave." A strange sound broke from her throat. "Please make love to me."

He stood and crossed the room. She lifted her face to his. He kissed her lightly without touching any other part of her, then stepped away.

Slowly, still without touching her, he slid the thin straps from her shoulders and peeled the dress down her body. Her hands moved instinctively to her breasts. He took her hands in his and drew them to her sides. He slipped her step-ins down her legs, held her hand while she stepped out of them. Then he moved away from her. When she started to follow him, he stopped her. "Don't be so impatient, Lily. You're young. You have all the time in the world."

He stood staring at her for an agony of time. Yet gradually the embarrassment drained away. It was as if they were on the set again, and his admiration clothed and protected her. Finally, he led her to the bed, and she lay down on it. She held her arms up to him, but he sat on the side, still clothed. His hand traced the contours of her face. Though she was naked except for the emerald necklace, he still hadn't touched her body. Finally his hand moved to her breast, slow, gentle, adoring. "You like that, don't you, Lily?" She closed her eyes, embarrassed to see the effects of his hands on her body, then opened them wide. His hand continued its pilgrimage. Finally it found its way between her legs. She moaned softly. "You've been waiting for me a long time, Lily. Longer than you know."

He stood and took off his robe and pajamas. His body was long and pale. In the light from the night table the prominent blue veins made him look like a marble statue.

"Aren't you going to turn it off?" Lily asked as he lay down beside her.

"Why, Lily, do you want to hide from me?"

She turned toward him and hid her face against his chest, but he lifted her head and looked into her eyes. "You can't hide, Lily. I already know all there is to know about you." He kissed her then, her eyes, and her lips, and his mouth worked down her body as his hands had. It went on that way, through slow, endless waves of pleasure, one after another until when he finally entered her, she sobbed in exhausted fulfillment.

She awakened in Gustave's arms. He was staring at her. "There's a new softness to your face."

She supposed there was. She was happy again. Not the way she'd been with Tom. Tom had given her passion. Gustave had given her pleasure. She tried not to think about the skill behind the pleasure, because it made her feel disloyal to Tom, and because it made her afraid of Gustave. He'd said he wanted her to let go, and last night he'd pushed her farther and farther, to the edge of abandon and beyond, but he'd never let go himself. She didn't want to think of that, of her abandonment and his reserve. She was happy again. She felt as if she belonged. She wondered if they'd talk about marriage.

"Where were you born?" she asked him on the way to the studio that morning.

"In Europe."

"I know that. Where in Europe?"

"Now you're going to become curious about my past."

"I've always been curious about your past, but you'd never talk about it."

"And now you expect me to?"

"When were you born, Gustave?"

"I'm old enough to be your father and young enough to be your lover."

"In other words, you don't want me to know anything about you."

"Lily, we've been working together for a year, living together for half that time. Now we make love and sleep together. Do you really think the facts of my birth are going to tell you anything new about me?"

She couldn't complain. She wouldn't complain. He continued to worship her with a camera every day on the set. He found new ways to please her every night. She told him that once, and he laughed. "They're not new, Lily, but you're young. And you've been shaped by a young and puritanical culture."

Louella predicted marriage. Hedda reported rumors of it. Lily read both columns and waited nervously for Gustave's reaction. "I see Freddy's been at it again," he said, but for once in his life Gustave was wrong. Wirtz hadn't planted the rumors.

Fred still didn't like the idea of Lily and Dressler offscreen. "I see you and the genius really are an item these days," he said to Lily one Sunday afternoon around A.Z.'s pool, where the great and the near-great had been summoned to play croquet, tennis, and studio politics.

She laughed. Hollywood was coloring her outlook. "Don't sound so judgmental, Fred. I seem to remember a night at the Troc, the night my contract had expired, when you were working pretty hard to get me where Gustave has me."

"I wasn't being judgmental. And you didn't know the word till you met Gustave."

"I didn't know anything till I met Gustave."

"Maybe that's what bothers me."

"What do you mean?"

He glanced across the pool to the clay courts where Dressler was playing doubles. "I wish to hell Tom had lived."

She sat staring at her perfectly painted toenails in silence.

"I'm sorry, Lily."

"Don't be. I still think about Tom."

Wirtz sipped his gin and tonic. "Why don't you fall in love with some nice leading man. Look at Hepburn and Tracy. Wyman and Reagan."

"I don't like actors. I can't stand competing with their egos. What do you have against Gustave anyway?"

Wirtz thought about the question. It wasn't that Dressler was bound to cheat on Lily. Fred took that as a given of Hollywood in particular and men in general. It wasn't even the streak of decadence that ran through Dressler like the undercurrent of his accent. What people did in the sack was their own business. It was something more subtle. Fred was the worst kind of cynic, a romantic one. He still believed people oughtn't to own other people. But he didn't know how to explain that to Lily. "Just be careful, honey."

"That's the second time you've said that to me."

"Then I must mean it."

The next morning Wirtz threw himself into the plans for Lily's USO tour. At least Dressler wouldn't be going along.

He did, however, take her to Union Station to see her off on the Superchief. All around them military boots sounded like shots on the marble floor of the waiting room. Khaki and blue uniforms fought for the oversize leather chairs. Accents from every part of the country babbled through the huge space. Lily thought of the last time she'd been in a railroad waiting room. This time Gustave's hand at her elbow steered her through the madness toward the correct track. World had managed to get her a drawing room. It was filled with roses and calla lilies and baskets of fruit. Gustave told the porter to leave her overnight case on the rack—the rest of her luggage was in the baggage car—and handed him a folded bill. The porter thanked him half a dozen times and said he'd take care of Miss Hart. There'd be no stale ham sandwiches on this trip. Lily went into the bathroom, her own private bathroom, to check her makeup. The metal sink gleamed. There were piles of snowy towels. The sign caught her eye. *Passengers will please refrain . . .*

When she came back into the compartment, Gustave was arranging the books and magazines he'd bought for her to read on the train. He took good care of her.

"Gustave," she asked, "have you ever thought of having a child?"

He turned and smiled. "An heir to carry on my name?"

"Or a daughter." Lily thought she'd prefer a daughter, a beautiful little girl to dress up and take places and teach things. Gustave could teach her the serious things, but Lily thought she had a few lessons of her own, at least for a little girl.

"You have a point, Lily. Any male raised in this country would probably turn into a barbarian."

So there it was. He wanted a daughter too. "I wish you were going with me on this trip," she said. It would be exciting to conceive a child on a train. And then they'd have to get married.

24

SAM WICKER was a man of many talents, and talent, in the civilian sector, was in short supply these days. The more time he contributed to the government writing slogans encouraging meatless Tuesdays, discouraging absenteeism, and warning against loose talk, the more time the government wanted him to contribute. He'd inched from advertising to public relations. Somehow that had taken him into bond drives. He organized a massive one and enlisted Lily Hart, who was passing through New York on her way to North Africa, to appear at a lunch hour rally in Wall Street. In two hours she sold three hundred thousand dollars worth of bonds, and that didn't include the hundred thousand from the sale of the portrait of her as Miranda in *Desire.* He also arranged for Lily to be interviewed by Isabel Childs on the afternoon news. The last was no easy task.

"I do a news broadcast, Sam, not a gossip program," Isabel said when he raised the subject over dinner.

"Why are women so suspicious of each other? Just because she's beautiful, it doesn't necessarily follow that she's stupid." He leaned

across the table toward her, though 21 was not a place for intimacy
or even privacy. "You're beautiful, and you're not stupid."

"I'm not beautiful, and I'm smart enough to keep Hollywood's
latest sex symbol off my news program."

"*My* news program. Aren't we getting proprietary."

"In a word yes. I cover the news, and these days that means the
war. Or are you too busy eating black market steaks to remember
there's one going on?" She put down her fork. "Last month we
bombed the German ball bearing factories at Schweinfurt—" Her
voice caught on something.

"And you think your brother was in one of those B-17s. Your
brother and that flyboy?"

"I think the news is no place for Lily-the-Body-Hart."

Sam put down his own fork. "Today while you were reporting
your five minutes of war news, she was raising close to half a million to fight that war. And if you give her two minutes, one even,
on your program, she'll probably bring in another half mil."

"I do the afternoon news, Sam. My listeners are mostly women.
Women don't like Lily Hart. Maybe because men like her too
much."

Sam motioned to the waiter for the check. "I think I've heard this
argument before. When you were bucking to do the afternoon
news. Then it was suggested that women didn't want to hear the
news from another woman."

"Sixty seconds," Isabel said. "Sixty seconds at two o'clock, and
not a second more."

"I thank you. World Pictures thanks you. The war effort thanks
you. And we'll all be twice as grateful if you invite me up for a
nightcap now," he added as he signed the check.

"I have to get up early tomorrow. Besides, I don't want to disturb Eliza."

"What I had in mind, Isabel, wouldn't disturb Eliza. It's all done
very quietly."

"I still have to be up early."

Outside the restaurant a galaxy of stars hung over the blacked-
out city. The small jockey statues gazed out over a street empty of
cars. Gasoline and tire shortages had finally solved New York's
traffic problem. Two full taxis passed, then an empty one. Sam
hailed it. "If we start now, we can be in bed early."

"You're incorrigible."

"That's right. Incorrigible and entirely unsuccessful. At least with you."

"You're just angry that I've ruined your batting average."

"The way that flyboy has ruined yours?"

She pulled away from him. "Sometimes I forget you're not as nice as you pretend."

"And you'd be even less interested in me if I were."

Lily Hart didn't so much arrive in the newsroom as occupy it. At least her entourage did. There were two PR men from World, a woman of indeterminate purpose, and Sam Wicker. In the middle of that crowd of protectors Lily Hart looked very beautiful and extremely ill at ease. Isabel had been prepared to dislike her. Instead she felt sorry for her.

Sam introduced them. Isabel held out her hand. Lily's grip was insubstantial, like her voice. The second was more detrimental to the work at hand. Isabel decided her only hope was to get Lily away from her retinue. The more they fussed over her, the more nervous she became. She even began to stutter. Isabel suggested they move to a private office for a few words alone. The flunkies protested. Sam said he thought it was an excellent idea.

"Would you like some coffee?" Isabel asked when they were off by themselves.

"I guess you can tell how nervous I am."

Isabel looked across the desk at Lily. She was wearing a meticulously tailored and beautifully simple gray suit with a gray hat that shadowed her huge eyes. She would have looked gorgeous in a housedress. A few days from now she'd look sensational in an army uniform. "What I can't understand is why. You've starred in movies. You've stood up in front of huge rallies. Pictures of you have gone on bombing raids and submarine missions and just about everywhere in the world the American military has gone. And all you have to do here is say a few words on the afternoon news."

"Where they can't see me. My voice isn't anything special. Even with all the lessons and Gustave's coaching. Gustave Dressler, my director. Not like yours. Gustave would go wild if he heard your voice. And I don't have anything to say. I'm not clever. People on the news are smart."

Isabel looked across the desk at Lily, more carefully this time. She'd underestimated her. Lily Hart's instincts had reached the same point as her own reasoning. "Are you telling me you're afraid to go on radio because it's the one place you can't sell your biggest asset, your appearance?"

"My only asset. I told you I'm not smart, at least not smart enough to have anything worth saying on the radio."

"Don't you believe it, Miss Hart. You're one smart cookie. And you're going to do splendidly." Isabel laughed. "Especially since Mr. Wicker has written out exactly what you're supposed to say. I'm afraid no one around here trusts women to think on their feet."

"Even you?"

"I get to write my own stuff now, but I had to fight tooth and nail to do it. First they let me write the news. Then they let me read it. But for some reason they wouldn't let me do both at the same time." Isabel stood. "We'd better get moving or the next thing we know they'll be saying women can't broadcast cause they're never on time."

Lily stood too. "You're not anything like what I expected. I was sure you were going to high-hat me."

"But you're the star. I'm just a newscaster."

"Sure, I'm a star, but I don't know anything. Gustave says I'm totally uneducated. But he's working on that."

"If you don't mind my saying so, Miss Hart, your friend Gustave sounds like the worst thing to be visited on womankind since menstrual cramps."

Lily's translucent skin went dead white. Then she started to laugh. She was still laughing when they went into the broadcast booth.

"What's she like?" Eliza asked Isabel that night. "I never met a movie star."

"Gorgeous. She absolutely drips glamour. And simple as a kid. Not stupid, which incidentally she believes she is, but naive."

"Naive. That's a funny word to use. I bet she's had lots of affairs. All those movie people do."

"Judging from the way she talks about him, she's having an affair with Gustave Dressler—you know, the director—and it sounds like hell."

"What do you mean?"

"Gustave says this. Gustave says that. Gustave is either Svengali or God."

They were silent for a moment. When Eliza spoke, her voice sounded almost as uncertain as Lily Hart's had that afternoon. "I guess I do that a lot too. Quote Michael, I mean."

"Only right after you get a letter. Sometimes, especially when you're busy at the office, you go for days without mentioning him."

"You never mention that air force lieutenant of yours."

Isabel stood, crossed the room, and threw herself into another chair. "I don't get letters. Besides, he's not mine. Not by a long shot."

"And what about Sam?"

"I like Sam. I really do. Maybe I even love him. But I'm not in love with him."

Eliza smiled. For the first time Isabel seemed young to her. "I never understand those distinctions."

Isabel laughed. "I'm not sure I do either, but it seemed like a good thing to say."

"Of course, if you had any sense, you would be in love with Sam. He's handsome and successful and crazy about you. And he's safe."

"Safe?"

Eliza smoothed the tissue paper letter on her lap. "He's not flying missions over Germany. Or fighting in Italy. He doesn't want to play hero. I'm not blaming him for that. There was a time when I did, but not anymore. Besides, I like Sam. I never used to, but since he met you, he's changed."

"Are you sure you aren't the one who's changed?"

Eliza laughed. "Maybe a little of both." She picked up Michael's letter. Isabel was right. She was changing. And the letter said—all of Michael's letters said—that he remembered everything about her and couldn't wait to come home to his Eliza.

Just as Sam had got in the habit of taking Eliza along to meetings, the head of the agency, Carter Oliver, had got in the habit of having her there. "What do you think of it, Mrs. Kramer?" he asked after a copywriter had presented his new brainchild for Colombian Gold coffee.

"Well," Eliza equivocated, "it's interesting. And I don't suppose it matters what kind of an ad they run, since people are desperate for coffee anyway."

"But we have to keep the product name in the public eye," Oliver reminded her. "So after the war when people can buy coffee, they buy Colombian Gold." Oliver leaned back in his big swivel chair, put a cigarette in a holder, and the holder in his mouth. He had a habit of going that far, then forgetting to light it. The arrested gesture made Eliza nervous. She always wanted to strike the match for him. "And you don't think this ad will make them do that, do you, Mrs. Kramer?"

"I don't think any wife likes to be called a nitwit, even a 'sweet little nitwit.'"

"But the husband in the ad is saying that with affection," the copywriter protested.

"If he's so fond of her, why does he call her a nitwit?"

"But by the end," Sam pointed out, "the husband's the one who looks foolish because the wife's the one who had the sense to buy Colombian Gold to put in his thermos on the graveyard shift."

"I don't read ads to the end," Eliza said. "Does anyone?"

Oliver took the unlit cigarette from his mouth. "I think Mrs. Kramer has a point." He replaced the cigarette holder in his mouth. "I had a talk with Sam this morning, Mrs. Kramer. Between his volunteer work for the OWI and the OPA and God knows what other alphabet soups and his accounts here, he can't keep up. Sam's my best man, and I don't want to lose him to battle fatigue. So how would you like to take over some of his smaller accounts?"

"What do you mean?" She couldn't believe Oliver was saying what he seemed to be saying.

"How would you like to be the AE on Colombian Gold and a few other accounts, Mrs. Kramer?"

"But I don't know anything about being an account executive."

"You know about production and traffic and all that. Sam says he's never going to find another secretary who can keep things moving the way you do. You have good instincts about how to sell things, especially how to sell things to women. As for business lunches, most of our clients are men. They'll be standing in line. And incidentally, we'll double your pay. You'll be making almost as much as you would in a war factory."

Sam called Isabel to tell her the news, and Isabel called Cora and

asked if she could lay her hands on enough sugar to make a cake to
celebrate. Cora made a layer cake and coq au vin—chicken was not
rationed—that was as festive as any steak.

"Mommymommymommy!" Teddy flung himself at Eliza when
she came in the door just as he used to at Michael. "Cora and I
made you a cake!"

Eliza thought guiltily of her mother. Sarah would do anything for
Teddy except let him help in the kitchen. He made too much of a
mess, she said. "And besides," her father always added, "he doesn't
belong in the kitchen. He's a boy."

"What kind of a cake?"

"White with lots and lots of chocolate icing. I got to lick the
bowl."

There was a letter from Michael on the hall table. She tore it
open and glanced at it just long enough to make sure he was all
right. Then she took Teddy upstairs to bathe him and put him to
bed. Eliza was scrupulous about that. Cora might take care of him
during the day, but she had her time with him every night. He fell
asleep halfway through chapter two of *Emil and the Detective*.

She turned out the light, took Michael's letter, and went to her
room. Strange, she thought as she kicked off her shoes and
stretched out on the Adam bed, how quickly she'd grown accustomed to townhouses, priceless antiques, and trusty family retain-
ers.

She unfolded Michael's letter again. His humor was growing
blacker, but it was still humor. *Remember all those travel ads for*—The
censor had blacked out several words. She inserted sunny Italy. *The
tourist bureau lied. I've been wet for so long my feet are webbed. But I'm not
as cold as some of the men. I've got my love's sweater to keep me warm.
What really worries me is that K and C rations are actually beginning to
taste like food to me. I hear there are still people who wash and shave in a
sink rather than a helmet, but I find that hard to believe.* He said the
only good thing about the weather was that it had put an end to the
war, at least temporarily. *Everything is stuck in the mud.*

Eliza tried to imagine life in a foxhole. Sleeping in mud, eating
unheated food out of a can, being eternally wet and cold. She
looked around the room in shame.

*I still can't get over the fact that my little Eliza's working. I don't mind
telling you that at first I was a little worried. I didn't like the idea of my*

wife working, and I especially didn't like the idea of my wife turning into a hard-nosed career woman. But then I remembered how you can worry, and I realized Sam was doing us both a favor by giving you something to take your mind off me and this damn war. Only don't take your mind too far off me, sweetheart.

As for this new living arrangement, I figure Sam wouldn't get you mixed up in anything funny. Isabel sounds like a nice girl. According to Sam, she's the greatest thing since sliced bread. And the house doesn't sound bad either. But don't get accustomed to it. I plan to get home someday, and when I do, we're going back to the old apartment, or maybe a new one with more rooms for more kids. The first thing we're going to do is get to work filling those rooms.

Eliza lay staring at the ceiling. She tried to remember what it had been like to make love with Michael. She thought of the night before he'd gone off to basic training when neither of them had been willing to waste a moment in sleep, the weekend they'd checked into the Plaza and hadn't even left the room for the first twenty-four hours. The memories were faded and dusty, like a photograph from another era. She thought of Michael's plan to fill all those rooms in a new apartment. She remembered all the weeks she'd spent waiting in hope that she'd conceived, and all the disappointments when she'd discovered she hadn't. She felt as if time were slipping away.

She heard Isabel and Sam calling her from downstairs. They were home to celebrate her new job. She had the new job, but they had each other. She added Michael's letters to the cache in the overflowing drawer. She felt as if her life were slipping away.

In her room at the hotel Lily had to wait for close to an hour to get a long-distance line to California. Then Gustave wasn't home. She called three times in the next two hours. Each time the butler said he'd give Mr. Dressler Miss Hart's message as soon as he came in. Lily paced the room and reminded herself of the time difference. Gustave was probably still at the studio.

She tried to concentrate on the book he'd given her for her trip to North Africa, but T. E. Lawrence was no match for her own imagination. She pictured Gustave dead in a car wreck. She pictured him in bed with another woman. She closed the book and turned on the radio.

Good evening. It's eleven o'clock eastern war time, the voice on the news said. Lily waited another fifteen minutes for the long-distance operator. The butler said Mr. Dressler had still not returned home. Lily reminded herself it was only a little after eight in California.

She took one of the pills Gustave sometimes gave her after a long day on the set when she was too overwrought to sleep, then got into bed. She left the radio and one lamp on. The room seemed less lonely that way.

When she awakened there was a dull buzz on the radio. The station had signed off. In the dim light from the single lamp the clock said three-thirty. Twelve-thirty in Los Angeles. She picked up the phone. This time she didn't have to wait for a long-distance line.

Gustave answered on the first ring. "Are you all right?" he asked when he heard her voice.

"I was worried about you. I kept imagining the most awful things."

"One moment," he said, and she heard garbled words. He'd put his hand over the mouthpiece to speak. She must have awakened the butler.

She told him about the bond drive. "Plus a hundred thousand for that picture of me as Miranda. The radio program went well too. I liked the newscaster. She was a woman." Lily thought of Isabel's judgment of Gustave. Now with Gustave on the other end of the line it seemed blasphemous. Isabel Childs was nice, but she obviously didn't know anything about men.

Lily babbled on about her day. Gustave made noncommittal sounds. Then Lily heard the voice. She would have recognized it anywhere. For years she'd sat in darkened movie theaters listening to it. Only on the screen it was softer, like a muted saxophone. Now it was all brass.

Are you ever getting off that phone, Gustave?

"You're not alone!"

"As a matter of fact, I'm not. Why don't I give you a call in the morning, Lily?"

"You're with—"

"Lily!" he silenced her. "It doesn't matter whom I'm with."

"But you had an affair with her, and now you're with her again. The minute I leave."

"Would you rather we met while you were here?"

She began to cry. "It's not funny."

"All right, Lily, I'll be serious. Did I ever promise I'd give up other women for you?"

Again Lily heard the voice in the background. *You haven't trained this one so well, Gustave.*

"She's listening to all this and laughing!"

"You're right, Lily. The scene is vulgar. We're not going to play it. I want you to go to bed now and get a good night's sleep. We'll speak in the morning."

"You can't just hang up on me that way!"

"Lily," he said, and his voice was gentle again. "Don't be so selfish. Do I give you less pleasure because I give another woman pleasure as well?"

My God, the voice came from the background again. *I thought that one went out with the silents.*

Lily hung up then. She sat on the side of the bed waiting for the phone to ring. Gustave would call her back. He always took such good care of her, always knew what she felt. He wouldn't let her suffer now.

She stared at the phone. It had to ring. Her body strained toward it. Gustave would make it ring. She put her hand on the phone. It was cold to the touch. She lifted the receiver, then put it down. He'd be angry if she called him again. But he'd call her. He had to.

She sat that way for a long time. The phone was silent. The room was quiet. She thought of Gustave. He was doing the things he'd done to her to that woman. She could picture the room, his coal black eyes in the shadows, his long hands moving ceaselessly, expertly. She began to cry again.

She went into the bathroom and ran cold water over a washcloth. On the shelf above the sink the small bottle with the pills Gustave had given her caught her eye. She wouldn't take too many. She didn't want to die. She especially didn't want to die that way and be condemned to eternal damnation. She just wanted to make Gustave sorry, so sorry that he got on the next train and came east to apologize.

She shook the pills out into her hand. They looked like small shiny jewels. She put a few back into the bottle, then went into the bedroom and poured a glass of water from the pitcher on the night table. She tossed the pills into her mouth and took a swallow of water. They caught in her throat. She gagged and swallowed more water. It spilled on her nightgown, but the pills went down. She crept under the covers. Maybe he'd fly east. That would be even better. And after he apologized, they'd be married.

"Get me the Waldorf," Sam told his new secretary the following morning. "Miss Hart's room. On second thought, get the desk. I'll ask for the room." You didn't keep a star like Lily Hart hanging on the phone, not if you were in public relations.

The phone rang several times. Sam was about to hang up when a voice answered. It sounded like Lily Hart speaking from the bottom of an ocean. She was either very sick or very drunk.

He thought of calling World—she was their baby—then decided to do the job himself. He didn't take the time to question whether he was acting out of altruism or curiosity.

Twenty minutes later he knocked at the door of her room, politely at first, then more violently. If she was still in there—and Sam would bet from the sound of her voice on the phone that she hadn't gone anywhere—she was either unwilling or unconscious. A little charm and a few dollars convinced a maid to open the door for him.

Lily Hart was asleep in one of the twin beds. She slept on her side with her knees curled up and her fist in front of her mouth. She looked peaceful and innocent as a kid.

"Miss Hart," Sam said. Her lashes didn't even flutter. He touched her shoulder. No response. He shook her more roughly. Her hand fell away from her mouth and she rolled over on her back, but she didn't wake up.

Sam looked around the room. There were no whiskey bottles. He tasted the liquid in the glass on the night table. Plain water.

He went into the bathroom. There was a bottle of pills on the shelf. It was half empty, but then it could have been that way to begin with. He knew one thing for sure. If she'd taken only a few, she wouldn't thank him for rushing her to the hospital. He picked up the bottle and looked at the prescription. It was made out to Gustave Dressler.

Sam told the long-distance operator it was an emergency. He got a line in fewer than five minutes. He told Mr. Dressler's butler the same thing. Dressler got to the phone in less than one.

"Do you know how many pills were in the bottle?" Sam asked.

"About twenty."

Sam hung up the phone before Dressler could say anything else and called Dr. Katz. In an emergency, Sam, like most people, reverted to the familiar. As he waited for Katz to come to the phone, he emptied the bottle on the table and counted the remaining pills. "I don't think she could have taken more than six or seven," he said after he'd explained the situation to the doctor.

"In that case, you take care of it, Sammy. I've got one son in Italy and another in the South Pacific, and I'm covering three practices here. Give her lots of coffee and keep her walking. She'll be all right. But now you see what all this running around with *shiksas* gets you. Movie stars," he said with a mixture of wonder and disgust and hung up.

Sam called room service and ordered several pots of coffee. Before the girl could warn him about the wait, Sam said yes, he knew there was a war on, but there was a two-dollar-bill in it for her and another for the girl who delivered it, if they got it there fast.

By noon Lily had drunk nine cups of coffee and was sitting up. She looked like death but was alive. Dressler had called four times before she was in any condition to speak to him. When she finally was, Sam went into the bathroom and closed the door to give them privacy, but he could still hear Lily's voice. Between the tears she kept apologizing.

Finally she called Sam out of the bathroom and handed him the phone. Dressler was polite and extremely grateful. It was obvious, to Sam at least, that he'd already run a check on who Sam was, what he was doing there, and whether he could be trusted. "I wish I could get east, but that's impossible right now. You've been a big help, Mr. Wicker. I take it I can trust you to get her on that transport plane."

"Do you think she's well enough to go?"

"There's nothing wrong with her, Wicker. Miss Hart took a few too many pills by mistake. She explained the whole thing to me. When she thought the first one wasn't working, she got up in the middle of the night to take more. But she was groggy and accidentally took too many. Besides, she has several days before she leaves. She'll be fine by then."

The guy, Sam thought, was all heart. He called Isabel. "She shouldn't be alone now. And it's only for a few nights," he explained.

Isabel said she'd be glad to have her. "At this point one more guest isn't going to matter. Last week we had two WACs who'd met Spence in Texas before he shipped out and an ensign whom Jack Livingston knew from Newport. At least FDR can't call me a real estate parasite anymore. We've got more military transients than Penn Station. Teddy's becoming a pro at identifying ranks."

Lily moved into the guest room next to Eliza's. *Poor darling,* Eliza wrote Michael that night, *while you're shaving in a helmet, I'm sharing a bath with America's sex symbol. The funny thing is that she's more like a timid kid than a glamour girl. Don't misunderstand me. You wouldn't be disappointed in the packaging, but underneath I get the feeling she's just a kid waiting for someone to tell her what to do.* And who am I to talk, Eliza thought as she sealed the letter.

Gustave Dressler called several times during Lily's stay. Cora called him "that man with the foreign accent." Isabel insisted his voice had an ersatz silkiness to it, like rayon or another of the wartime substitutes. Each time Lily got off the phone with him she cried. "You don't have to speak to him," Isabel said finally.

"What do you mean?"

"We'll say you're not here."

"I couldn't lie to Gustave." Lily sounded as if she were speaking of confession.

"All right, we won't lie. We'll say you can't come to the phone at the moment."

"I couldn't do that to Gustave," Lily said again.

They were in the second-floor sitting room. Isabel glanced up at the portrait of her mother hanging over the mantle. It's none of your business, Grace would say. "Gustave doesn't seem to be quite so considerate of you."

"He is," Lily said. "Without him I'd be nothing."

"He really has you believing that!"

"But it's true. I owe him everything. And he's very good to me, really. That woman the other night didn't mean anything. He explained it all."

Isabel and Eliza exchanged glances, then looked away.

"If it meant so little," Eliza asked, "why did he do it? You don't have to answer that," she went on quickly. "I'm just an old-fash-ioned housewife with a lingering affection for fidelity."

Isabel glanced at the photograph of her father that stood on the piano. "I don't know anything about fidelity or infidelity." She stopped suddenly and looked at the other two women. "Unfortu-nately, I don't even know very much about sex. But I do know what I've been seeing ever since I met you, Lily. You get along perfectly well without Gustave Dressler. In fact, the only time you can't manage is when he comes into the picture."

25

CHRISTMAS OF 1943 was the leanest of the war. The shelves were empty of gloves, leather goods, and toys. Isabel saved the day for Teddy by unearthing some of Spencer's old playthings in the attic. Even Sam was having trouble getting whiskey and gin. Isabel gave Sam a ballpoint pen. Eliza gave Isabel the same thing. Ballpoint pens were new and, temporarily, in supply. Eliza and Isabel had sent off boxes of sweaters and food and still more ballpoint pens to Michael and Spence months earlier. Isabel had debated whether to send anything to Andy. It seemed unpatriotic not to. She finally decided on a parcel of food. He couldn't misconstrue a fruitcake, which was one of the gifts recommended for servicemen because it lasted and wasn't made of the cheap chocolate sold in the PX.

Then Andy surprised her. She stared at the return APO number on the small package in disbelief, then tore off the paper. Inside an old box from Turkish cigarettes was a wad of newspaper. At first she thought it was a joke. She began opening the newspapers. A black onyx art deco pin fell out. A few words were scrawled on a scrap of paper that looked as if it had been torn from the back flap of an envelope. *Won this in a poker game. Didn't know what to do with it. Thought it looked like you. Happy Boxing Day, as they say over here. Andy.*

Isabel laughed. He was trying too hard. No one was that tough. She looked at the scrap of paper. It had a pink lining. Perhaps Andy Barnes's mother, the Southern belle, wrote on pink stationery. Or perhaps a dozen other girls did. Isabel didn't care. He'd sent her the pin.

In Teheran, Stalin met Roosevelt and Churchill for the first time. The Japanese boasted that "a million men could not take Tarawa in a hundred years." A few thousand Americans took it in seventy-six hours—and added another place name to the glossary of bloodshed.

Nineteen forty-three turned to nineteen forty-four. Isabel slipped away from a noisy party on Sutton Place to stand alone on the terrace for a moment, staring eastward into the icy night. From the other side of the French doors Sam watched her and knew what she was thinking and what she was planning to do.

On Sixty-seventh Street Eliza sat alone in the library among the expensive leather-bound books and first editions trying to write a letter to Michael and thinking about the uselessness of words.

And somewhere over the Atlantic Lily was on her way to North Africa and, though she didn't know it, General Chester (Buzz) Skeffington.

January set in. On the afternoon news Isabel introduced the name of another obscure foreign town into American history. Anzio. It was an innocuous, faintly musical name. No one guessed how heartbreaking it would come to sound. That morning more than thirty-seven thousand American and British troops had been put ashore under massive air and naval cover. By nightfall the beachheads were consolidated, the port facilities captured intact, and U.S. troops had moved seven miles inland. It was a moment for rejoicing, if you were looking at the war on a large map. But if you were a woman whose husband was a man in a platoon in a company in a battalion in a division that had participated in the invasion, you might be a little more reluctant to start celebrating.

On the way home from work Eliza bought all the evening papers and forced herself to read every account. She was sure Michael was in it, had been in it. The delay in time was terrifying. While she sat here thinking about Michael in the present tense, his body might be lying on a beach somewhere south of Rome. She went to the drawer where she kept his letters and took out a handful. They were all that kept him alive for her.

Soon there was nothing to celebrate. A Panzer division counter-attacked and other German units moved down from northern Italy. The newsprint of the accounts stuck to Eliza's sweating fingers after she finished reading the papers. In an attempt to get her mind off the war Isabel and Sam dragged her along to a movie. Over the past few months Eliza had practically given them up. War stories frightened her. Love scenes had an even more unsettling effect. But Isabel and Sam insisted she go with them that night to see *Casablanca*. The attempt at escape was unsuccessful. Even the line about the problems of three people not amounting to a hill of beans didn't take her mind off Michael. She started paying attention when the newsreels came on. *The first footage of American troops on Anzio,* the announcer began. Eliza found herself gripping the armrests. *As American men wade ashore . . .* "It's Michael!" She grabbed Sam's hand. "Look, right there. It's Michael. I'm sure of it." But the camera had already moved on. "Didn't you see him?" Eliza insisted, and no one around them told her to be quiet.

"I don't think you can really tell—" Sam began.

"It was Michael! I saw him. I'm sure of it."

All the way home from the movie Eliza kept insisting she'd seen Michael wading ashore at Anzio. There was no point in arguing with her. For all Sam knew it was Michael. He'd seen no one in the newsreel who resembled his old friend, but then he hadn't been looking as hard. He wasn't a wife. And the belief seemed to cheer Eliza up. Michael was real again, at least for a day or two.

The news from Italy grew worse. Casualties mounted in the Marshall Islands. On every broadcast Isabel reported heavy fighting somewhere in the world. Sam said there was an urgency in her voice when she did. "You sound just like all the seventeen-year-old kids I know. You can't wait to get in it."

He was partly right. For months now she'd been scheming and

fighting to get overseas. But he was wrong about one thing. Unlike those kids Sam compared her to, she wasn't after the glory of war. She knew without having been there that there was none. What she wanted was to understand why men thought there was. And she couldn't learn that on the homefront.

Again Isabel was lucky as well as ambitious. The correspondent in England was less fortunate. The jeep he was driving through a fog thick and soft as cotton candy had careened off the road and down a rocky slope on the north coast of Devon. About that time the government released a new statistic. Noncombat deaths had finally exceeded combat deaths in the war. Isabel picked the news up off the wire and included it in her broadcast. It would be her last from 485 Madison Avenue for several weeks. She was leaving for England that night.

"Now remember," Gardner said from behind the big desk with the silver-framed picture of a smiling Mrs. Gardner, "forget the battle reports. I have enough war correspondents. I want the human side. Hundreds of thousands of American boys are over there staging for the big push. I want you to tell their wives and mothers how they're getting along, what they're eating and wearing and sleeping on. What they dream about. What they do when they're not training." He swiveled to face his own private corner of the New York skyline. "You're going to have to be careful about that. The *Atlantic* ran a short story about a married GI who had a one-night stand with an English girl—all very polite and cerebral—and more women than I thought read the *Atlantic* wrote in to protest. I don't think our listeners are ready to hear about the army looking the other way from local whorehouses either. Am I shocking you, Isabel?"

"No, but you're trying to."

He turned his chair back to her. "Tell us about all those nice clean American boys who spend their time handing out chewing gum to English kids."

"The two pursuits aren't mutually exclusive."

"Anyway, you get the idea. I want firsthand stuff, and I want it fresh."

Isabel was determined to give him all that and more. He said he wanted her to tell the women of America what it was really like for their men over there. That meant what it was like on a bombing mission to Germany as well as a weekend pass in London.

She said goodbye to Eliza at the house. Eliza cried. "It's not fair. Lily left for North Africa, you're going to England, and I'm the one with the husband overseas."

"I'll give him a kiss if I run into him," Isabel said.

Eliza blew her nose. "Don't you dare. Not the way you look in that uniform. He'd forget he even had a wife."

Sam drove her out to Mitchell Field. She remembered the evening she'd taken Andy and Spence there. The night had the same feeling of unreality.

Her pass got them onto the field. An Army C-54 was waiting for her, several other journalists, and a handful of VIPs.

"What's wrong with this picture?" Sam asked as he pulled the car up to the edge of the landing field. "I'll tell you what. The wrong one of us is going off to war."

"I'm not going off to war."

"Tell it to Gardner. I know you better."

They got out of the car, and he lifted her duffel from the back. Then he took off the soft civilian hat and looked down at her. "Damn it, Isabel, I feel as if I ought to salute you or something."

She touched his thick black hair and pulled his face down to hers. "The something will do."

The kiss tasted a lot like Andy's, only this time she was the one leaving.

"Take care of yourself," he said, and his words made a small balloon of mist between them.

"I will."

He kissed her again.

"Watch out for the Blitz. Even if they're calling it the Little Blitz these days."

"I will." She turned and started to walk away.

"And that glory boy."

She looked back over her shoulder and waved, but this time she didn't answer.

The plane was freezing. Isabel spread her coat over her like a blanket. The engines started up. The noise was deafening. Beside her one of the VIPs said something, but she couldn't hear a word.

She clutched the arms of her seat as several thousand pounds of steel shuddered and hurled itself down the runway and lifted into the night.

The VIP took a silver flask from his briefcase and offered her a swig of whiskey. She took it gratefully. The whir of the motors began to sound reassuring. She pulled her coat up beneath her chin. Just as she was dozing off, she thought she heard a catch in one of the engines. Two thoughts sprang out of the mists of half-sleep. If she died now, it would be over quickly. And if she died now, she'd die a virgin. Somewhere over the drone of the motor she heard the deep rumble that was Andy Barnes's laugh. Then she slept.

The VIP woke her when they started the descent to Gander. They filed off the plane. The terrain was barren and icy. She felt as if she'd landed on the moon. A brutal wind cut through her great-coat and uniform. In the officers' mess she drank several cups of black coffee. It had never tasted so good.

She learned something on the second takeoff. It didn't get any better with practice. They were nearing Europe. She wasn't exactly in danger, but she wasn't home safe in the house on Sixty-seventh Street either. She thought of Andy again. She'd written Spence that she was coming.

They landed at a base in Cambridgeshire. As she waited for the plane to taxi to a stop, she told herself to be sensible. The Eighth Air Force was spread out all over this part of England. The Army wasn't likely to deliver her directly to him.

The engineer pushed the door open and she smelled England before she saw it. Isabel hadn't thought you could smell a color, but she smelled the green she remembered from earlier trips, and the heavy metallic aroma of airplane fuel. The night was black and thick with fog. She started down the steps. It was like walking through a cloud. Gradually she made out a line of jeeps and several men huddling around them. The passengers were moving in a crowd toward the jeeps now, the VIPs first, then the correspondents. Isabel shivered. The dampness crept into the bones that fast.

But it was more than the dampness because one of the officers had broken away from the group around the jeeps. He was wearing a leather flight jacket, the fur collar turned up against the cold, the zipper left open in defiance of it. She'd know that walk anywhere.

She wanted to break away from the group and run into his arms. Instead she forced herself to keep walking. Then she was standing face to face with Andy Barnes.

"The funny thing about war," he said, "is that you keep running into the damnedest people in the damnedest places. Welcome to England, Isabel." Then he bent down and kissed her as if he'd been waiting for a long time.

Spence hung back until he couldn't stand it anymore. Then he told Andy to knock it off, and he and Isabel hugged for a long time. Finally they got into the jeep and drove toward the sprawl of Nissan huts in the distance.

They took her to the officers' club. After the unrelieved darkness of the blackout, the light hurt her eyes. She blinked several times. Their faces swam into focus. She was shocked. The bones showed beneath Spence's skin. The blue vein at his temple was like a scar. Andy's face had been honed to an ax blade.

She glanced around the club. It was not a room that deserved to be brilliantly lit. Brown leather chairs and sofas spilled their guts like wounded men. A scarred plywood bar stood at one end and an iron stove managed to dominate the center of the room without giving off much heat. Officers sat playing cards or reading torn, dog-eared magazines or doing nothing at all. Every one of them looked up when Isabel walked in. A few called to Andy or Spence, but most of them just went on staring as if they didn't know they were staring.

Spence went off to get drinks, and Andy found them a corner. He kept touching her, as if he wanted to make sure she was real. His hands were warm, but his eyes were colder than she'd remembered, as if all those hours spent in high thin altitudes delivering death, fleeing death, witnessing death, had frozen any feeling that might have lurked there. The eyes were beautiful blue cadavers in his long handsome face.

Spence came back and they talked about the English weather and her flight over and a million foolish things because it was too soon to talk about anything that mattered. Or maybe, Isabel thought looking from one razor-edged face to the other, it would never be time.

Spencer wanted to know about Sally. "The flame still flickers,"

Andy explained. "Though God knows I've recruited enough WRENs and Red Crosses for him to put it out."

"I don't see much of her lately," Isabel said. It wasn't exactly a lie. She'd run into Sally only once in the last few months. She'd been wearing a navy lieutenant on each arm.

"News travels fast around here," Spence said looking past Isabel toward the door. "Here comes the Old Man. The CO to you, Isabel. He must have heard there was a new woman within spitting distance."

Isabel turned. A few officers stood in the door. None of them looked like an "Old Man." "Where?" she asked.

"Right there in the door," Spence said. "The guy with the colonel's eagle."

Isabel looked toward the door again. "That's the Old Man?" She was incredulous.

"The Old Man is twenty-nine," Andy said, but as the CO approached, Isabel saw what they meant. The features were still boyish, but the lines around his eyes and mouth were carved as if into a fossil.

The colonel joined them. Spencer introduced him to Isabel. A curious thing happened as she reached out to shake the colonel's hand. Andy's arm, which had been stretched across the torn leather back of the sofa, came to rest on her shoulders, as if he were laying claim.

The colonel started to speak, but his words were drowned out by another voice. It crackled through the wet night like lightning, rattling the windows and shattering the tenuous exhaustion that passed for peace in the room. Later she'd learn it was a loud speaker system called the Tannoy. All she could think at the moment was that it was a voice of doom. The base was on alert. There would be a mission in the morning.

Andy's arm fell from her shoulder. The colonel excused himself. Men stood and stretched and cursed. The bar closed. Isabel watched the flyers as they shuffled out of the room. Their faces were secrets that couldn't be told.

Andy walked her back to her room in one of the Nissan huts that had been fixed up—that is, mildly heated—for VIPs. The fog was so dense they kept wandering off the paths into the mud.

"How can you fly in this?" she asked.

"We can't. The word must have come down from Stormy—that's the group meteorologist—that it's going to lift."

"It seems impossible."

"It's possible, but not likely. The ground-grippers just like to get us up at two in the morning, brief us, get us out on the field, postpone for a couple of hours, then scrub. Except when they keep us going all the time. Last week we had a run of weather and flew four missions in five days. Fifteen hours sleep in five days."

They stopped in front of the door to her hutment. In the darkness his face was the deepest secret of all. "Take me with you," she said.

"No way."

"Correspondents do it all the time. Even women correspondents. Margaret Bourke-White took pictures on a bombing mission over Tunis."

"Not from my plane, she didn't. This isn't joyriding, Isabel."

She wanted to slap him for that. "I know it isn't joyriding. I'm terrified, but I want to go."

"To prove something?"

"To learn something."

He brought his face close to hers. "No way," he said again. He kissed her then, and she could taste the anger in it, anger at her for asking to go, and anger at that awful ghostlike voice for making him go.

"See you tomorrow." He turned and disappeared into the fog, leaving the words hanging in the cold, wet air like a terrible temptation to fate.

The next day went as Andy had predicted. At two in the morning while Isabel slept, the company waker-upper shined a cruel flashlight into the eyes of Andy and Spence and several hundred other men and was rewarded with a stream of sour-smelling obscenities. The men staggered into longjohns and silk socks and coveralls and woolen sweaters, staggered into the foul-smelling latrine, staggered through the chill darkness to a breakfast of powdered eggs and bacon limp with grease. On mornings when there were missions they were supposed to get real eggs, but army life was full of unfulfilled promises. Then they shuffled into the briefing room, some in leather caps with the ear flaps hanging down and some in knitted caps, some bitching, some joking blackly, some silent, and waited for the news of whether it would be a milk run to the coast of France or a suicide mission into the heart of Germany. Then the Old Man got up to tell them it would be something in between, and S-2 said there wouldn't be much to worry about from fighters. He got some flak from the men on that. Finally they synchronized watches.

The morning crept on, as the pilots and navigators and gunners went to their separate briefings and the trucks took them out through the fog that was still thick and white to their planes. The Forts were lined up, some with paintings of women and some symbols of prowess and some only a name, and the ground crews worked over the planes, tinkering and tuning and readying them for flight. A sergeant came through in a jeep and called through the fog that Wing had postponed for another two hours and Andy and Spence and several hundred other men yelled back what Wing could do with itself. The men stood around in their bright blue electrified flying suits waiting for the waiting to be over. Someone told a story about a girl he'd picked up in Westminster Abbey, and someone else topped it with a graphic account of what a girl he'd found in a local pub had done for a tube of lipstick, and Andy took a tarp and spread it on the wet ground and lay down and thought about Isabel. It was okay, he reasoned, to think about her when she was there. You only got in trouble when you started carrying a torch. He thought about the polished copper glow of her hair in the harsh sick light of the officers' club, and the sound of her voice, smooth as a perfectly tuned engine in the foggy night, and the soft secret feel of her body beneath the rough khaki uniform. Then the sergeant came through in a truck again and said Wing had scrubbed the mission.

By that time Isabel was miles away. She was not, as Gardner had reminded her, an accredited war correspondent, but a guest of military PR. Planning was well under way for the greatest amphibious operation in military history. There was a lot the military didn't want her to see, but a lot they did. She had a jeep and a driver whose job it was to distinguish between the two. For the next week she talked to airborne troops and infantry, LST commanders and medics, sergeants so hardened in the regular Army they could barely get through a sentence without expletives and kids so scared they could barely speak at all. She ate with enlisted men and officers, listened to gripes, boasts, and propositions, and wandered through villages where young Yanks drank warm beer in old pubs and shook a quiet and stable civilization until its foundations rattled and, in some cases, began to crumble. She talked to English girls who adored them and English parents who didn't trust them; she had tea with a dowager duchess who'd lost a son at the Marne and a grandson at Dunkirk and every Sunday welcomed the GIs into her ancestral house, and she listened to a shopkeeper repeat the now familiar chestnut that the trouble with Yanks was that they were overpaid, oversexed, and over here. And each day she went to London to broadcast to the women of America what she'd seen and heard and learned. Gardner was satisfied. Isabel was not. She knew she still didn't understand.

At the end of the first week her schedule took her back to Andy's base. It was close to nine o'clock. He and Spence, she discovered, had gone into the village. In the officers' club dozens of men remained. Most of them were eager to talk to her. She was fairly sure that one would agree to take her up as well. It took her less than a quarter of an hour to spot the one. His face was wide with thick smug features not yet eroded by death and exhaustion. Maybe that was because he'd flown only four missions. Or maybe four had been enough to take whatever was human out of him. Different men, she was beginning to see, reacted differently to the same experiences. He told her he could fly rings around the rest of these throttle jockeys. He smelled of Vitalis and held his glass and cigarette in the manner of a small-town boy who'd just learned the word "sophisticated." He was called Chip.

Isabel flirted with him as she never had with any man who interested her. When he walked to the bar to get her a drink, she saw him give the man beside him an elbow and a wink. He had it made. Then as if she'd arranged it herself, the ghostlike voice crackled and boomed over the base again. There would be a mission in the morning.

Chip loomed over her. Isabel looked up at him as she'd seen Sally Sayre look up at dozens of men including Spence. She asked if he'd take her along. He opened his mouth as if he were flexing a muscle. "If it's a milk run, honey."

Andy came awake to the same sharp light in his face, the same sick dread, the same smell of too many men living and sweating and being frightened together. He heard Spence taking clothes from his metal locker. He'd be looking for his silk ski socks. Andy grabbed a stained T-shirt. Every flyer had his talisman. He took his shaving kit and shuffled to the latrine like a dead man, or at least a sleepwalker.

At two-thirty in a latrine the conversation is not elevating. The usual hostilities were exchanged. The usual crudities expressed. Except for Shoyer. You'd think Shoyer was going to a goddamn prom. He was singing, for Christ sake. He was singing "You can't say no to a soldier."

"What's wrong with Shoyer?" someone asked.

"He's got a date."

"Sure. With a couple of 109s."

" 'If he's gonna fight he's got a right to romance,' " Shoyer sang.

"He's taking that reporter babe up," someone growled.

Shoyer smiled at his own fleshy image in the filthy mirror. "I never got it in a plane before."

"The only thing you're getting in a plane today, Shoyer, is flak from Gerry."

"First one, then the other," Shoyer said. "It's a long way home."

The razor tore a piece of flesh from Andy's chin. He wished to hell he had a styptic pencil. The blood ran onto his lucky T-shirt.

During that mission Isabel came to understand everything—except how they did it again and again and again.

Chip came to get her before dawn. It would be a milk run, he told her. A piece of cake. At the analogies to food her stomach heaved. That was all right. She'd read enough to know she was supposed to be afraid. A little diversionary mission, he added, to drop a package on the French sub pens while another wing hit Gerry where he lived. She climbed into the electrically heated suit he'd brought her.

She rode out to the dispersal point in a weapons carrier with Chip and his crew. The air was thin and dry as kindling. In the east a line of pink hugged the horizon. The day reminded her of football games and ski parties. There'd be no scrubbing this morning.

The ground crew was fussing over the plane as if it were a baby. Isabel saw the name on the side. She knew that the pilot had the right to name the ship. Andy's was Unicorn. Chip's was Hubba-Hubba Girl. A half undressed woman sprawled across the top of the letters.

A truck came around and dispersed K rations and fruit juice and candy bars. The men groused about the candy bars. "Where the hell are the Milky Ways?" demanded the ball turret gunner, whose skin showed the ravages of too many Milky Ways. He was that young.

"The Milky Ways been diverted to the doggies," the sergeant said. "You glory boys will have to settle for Hersheys."

The ball turret gunner suggested that the sergeant do something obscene with his Hershey bars. Isabel watched the exchange as if it were part of a dream.

Once aboard the plane Chip found her a place to crouch between the bombing seat and the navigator's desk in the greenhouse and forgot about her for a while. He and the copilot checked and rechecked and checked again. Then he crawled back and went over the flight plan with the men. As Isabel watched, the first rays of light filtered through the green-gray plexiglass, casting a lifeless pall over their faces. She stared at her own hands. They looked like the hands of a dead woman. It occurred to her, stupidly, that if she was going to die, she didn't want to die with Chip Shoyer and a bunch of strangers. She wondered where Andy and Spence were in the formation.

The engines started with a deafening noise. More waiting. Finally they began to taxi. As they passed the two English ambulances at the side of the runway, the navigator turned his face away.

The planes were stacked up on the runway now, miles of planes, and still the waiting went on. "I hate this part," the navigator said. "All dressed up and no place to go." Finally they started to roll.

Below them England had never looked more beautiful, a patchwork of greens rolling for miles and miles in sunlight that sparkled like crystal. Isabel thought she'd never seen so many shades of green. She wondered why she was leaving it.

They were turning, circling, trying desperately to form up. Planes careened toward them and sheered away. The ship bounced wildly in prop wash. Her breath caught in her chest as the wing of the next plane appeared to come right toward her, then veered off. It was called flying formation, and it was sheer hell.

They were over water now. In the air around them puffs of smoke appeared suddenly as if some magician were doing his stuff. Isabel heard the crack of guns and felt the ship shudder like a ride in an amusement park, but as Andy had said, this was no joyride. Inside her helmet her hair was wet with sweat. "Just testing," the navigator said.

They climbed higher and went on oxygen. The tight mask chafed at her face. She'd lost all feeling in her fingers and toes. Electric suits didn't quite do it for the extremities. She remembered a story Spence had told about a gunner who'd lost a hand because of frostbite. The copilot came around checking everyone's oxygen. There were a dozen ways to die that had nothing to do with the enemy.

It all began to happen quickly then, too quickly for Isabel to make sense of it. The men were screaming on the interphone, and in the air around them the harmless-looking puffs of smoke were coming more quickly as if the magician had gone mad. Planes came at them and veered away, or maybe they were the ones who veered away. Isabel couldn't tell. She felt dizzy and sick to her stomach. She hoped she wouldn't throw up. She'd been told of men who'd thrown up into their oxygen masks and suffocated.

The bomb doors opened and a rush of icy air cut her like a knife. The doors closed. Far below them Isabel glimpsed more puffs of black smoke, larger now, a more powerful magician at work. She tried not to think about the fact that there were people in that smoke. Then she heard a sharp crack and stopped thinking entirely. The gunfire was constant now. The ship bucked and rocked. There were puffs of black smoke everywhere. Just below them flames appeared as if someone had turned on a gas range. "I got the son of a bitch!" a gunner screamed over the interphone.

Finally the coast of France was behind them, but still the gunfire went on and the clouds of smoke kept popping up around them. Planes appeared and disappeared in her view. It was nothing but acrid-smelling, trembling confusion. Then she saw a larger cloud of smoke, and a plane, a Fort just like theirs, spiraled endlessly toward the ocean and slipped beneath the smooth gray-black surface. "Any chutes?" someone asked over the interphone, and someone else said there hadn't been any.

Later, Isabel didn't know how much later, they came off the oxygen. When she took off her mask it was full of saliva.

Chip turned the controls over to the copilot and came swaggering back through the plane. She told him she was going to be sick. Then she was.

She wasn't sure how she'd got back to her hutment. Her legs were like rubber. When she lay down on the cot the springs vibrated from her trembling. Though she was still wearing several layers of clothing, she kept shivering, but sweat covered her face and ran down her sides.

There was a knock at the door. A voice said that it wasn't locked. The voice must have been her own, but Isabel didn't recognize it. The door opened. Even in the gathering dusk she could see the anger in Andy's face. He stepped into the room and closed the door behind him. His eyes were as pale and terrifying as the sky over the French coast. He stood there staring down at her, and she felt the same rush of cold she'd felt when the bomb doors had opened that afternoon. She reached up and touched his arm. She felt no life beneath the leather jacket.

He sat beside her on the bed, but his face didn't soften and his eyes didn't thaw. She reached up and touched his chin where a thin red line attested to the fact that he did bleed. A muscle in his jaw twitched. Then he put his arms around her and held her, and she began to cry.

They lay that way for a long time. First the tears stopped, then the trembling. The room grew darker. Her skin tingled as the heat crept back into her body. He lifted his head and looked at her. She wondered if there was a new coldness in her own eyes. "Are you all right?" he asked. She nodded. "Really?"

"Really," she whispered, but her voice still didn't sound right.

He brushed his mouth across hers. Somewhere deep within her a small wounded bird fluttered its wings. He kissed her again. She tasted life and strained against him.

They were a tangle of jackets and sweaters and heavy boots. He sat up and unlaced hers, then his own. She stroked his back as he did. He pulled his sweater over his head, then hers. They kissed again and fumbled at the buttons of each other's shirts.

Beneath all the layers of clothing his skin was warm, the warmest thing in this whole chilling world. Still, she shivered again. They slid beneath the rough sheets and heavy blankets and he wound long arms and legs around her. She stroked his back and shoulders. There was a line of scar tissue where his wing would be if he weren't real. She thought that someday she'd ask him how he'd got it. Her hands wandered over his body, tracing the cords of tense muscle. He was so beautiful to the touch that she wanted to cry. And perhaps she did begin to cry again because he kissed her face and then her mouth and she tasted the salt on his tongue.

His mouth continued down her body and the small bird of life within her flapped its wings wildly. His fingers were long and beautiful and thrilling, and her own moved with a will she hadn't known. His body, like his face, was lean and hard and honed to an exquisite edge. She sharpened her pleasure against it, moving with him, slowly at first, luxuriously, stretched and turning and touching. Then she felt his urgency and her own and time fell away as it had in the plane that afternoon, not in panic now but in pleasure, and she felt as if she were sailing through a midnight black sky, spinning away from earth faster and faster until she heard her own voice, stranger than ever, and saw a galaxy explode in a million tiny lights.

They didn't talk much that night, and they must have slept a little, because when she opened her eyes again the hands of his watch glowed in the darkness carving a thin wedge from the pie of time. It was a little before nine. She stirred against him, and he turned toward her in sleep, and his mouth found hers. They began again, slowly, sweetly, but soon they were spinning out into the night away from the narrow iron cot and the icy room and the death-infested base. Then all around them the darkness crackled, and the terrible voice booming out alerts and missions wrenched them back to earth.

The next morning the sky was pale and cold as a sheet of ice. Wing wouldn't scrub. Isabel wandered the base, trying to interview some of the ground crew, trying to keep her mind on her work, but it was no good. By late afternoon she knew it was no milk run. They'd been gone too long.

The afternoon wore on, a thin, frayed fragment of time. She could feel the apprehension stealing over the base. A wan sun came out in time to set. Men began to drift down to the control tower to sweat them in. There were a few Red Cross girls there too. They stood about and sat on the grass, but even from a distance you could tell this was no picnic. Isabel joined them.

"God, why don't they come?" one of the Red Cross girls said. No one answered.

Another Red Cross girl hugged herself against the cold. An enlisted man slapped his hands together for warmth. The sun fell behind some trees. Night waited in the wings like the heavy in a melodrama. Isabel felt as cold as she had in the plane.

"Where the hell are they?" a sergeant said. No one answered him either.

In the distance the Nissan huts were beginning to fade into the darkness. Soon the whole camp would disappear into the blackout.

Memories of the previous night floated through Isabel's mind. A voice screamed in her head like the roar of engines. One night wasn't enough! She felt sick to her stomach again. Was that what war was? Constant nausea?

Then she realized the roar was real. The first group came over the field, and the low squadron peeled off. The high group followed. The sergeant was counting out loud.

"Look at that formation," the Red Cross girl said.

The sergeant kept counting.

"They must think the generals are down here watching," another man said.

Isabel found herself counting along with the sergeant. She felt like a child playing hide-and-seek, and she was it. Would the count never stop? Would the game ever be over?

"They're in," the Red Cross girl cried. "They all came back."

Isabel stopped counting and sat down on the grass hard, but she knew the game wasn't over. Not by a long shot.

Andy managed a weekend pass. They went down to London. He wrangled a room at the Savoy. It had a big bed with a silk spread, water that occasionally ran hot, and an old Victorian tub. More important, Andy said as he locked the door behind him, it had no officers or enlisted men, no one but the two of them. They were in bed within minutes.

But escape was not that easy. The first night Isabel thought she was dreaming. Then she realized Andy was dreaming, and his shouts had come crashing into her sleep. "Bail out, Pollock! Bail out, damn you!" The bed shook with his thrashing as the plane had when it fired. She put her hands on his shoulders and called his name. "Bail out, goddamn you!" he shouted.

"Andy!" she screamed.

His eyes opened. They weren't cold anymore. They were blue-white fires. His body was drenched with sweat.

He turned on his side with his back to her. She put a hand on his shoulder tentatively. "Who's Pollock?"

"Another pilot. He went down over Shweinfurt. No chute."

"I'm sorry."

He turned on his back, shaking off her hand. "Oh, yes, Isabel, we're all *sorry.*"

She lay back on the bed staring at the ceiling. It was pale in the darkness, reminding her of the sky Andy had taken off into the previous morning.

Finally he turned to her and drew her to him. His skin was dry now, but she could taste the salt of his panic. "It's just a dream," he said. "Everyone has them. Sometimes in the middle of the night the place sounds like a goddamn soundtrack for some crazy movie with too much action going on at once."

Isabel put her arms around Andy and held him. She could hold him, but she couldn't protect him.

The next morning they made love and had eggs that weren't powdered and kippers on a tray in bed and made love again. When they finally opened the curtains, they discovered the day was clear but half gone. They went out then and wandered the city. There were too many uniforms and too many Americans and too many holes where buildings used to be, but there was still London with barges and boats on the river and Big Ben and a hundred images from books read long ago. They talked to an RAF bomber over tea at the Ritz and a Free Frenchman over scotch at the Dorchester, but Andy shook both of them quickly, and they took a bus to nowhere in particular and the underground back. As they waited for the train they watched a few early arrivals settling into their bunks for the night.

They went back to the hotel and drank a little more scotch because of the cold and then it was warm enough to take their clothes off. She asked him about the scar on his back where his wing ought to be, and he told her a story about a boyhood that was so far distant it made her want to cry again. She kissed the scar and the mouth and eyes and body she was coming to know so quickly. They were becoming schooled in each other, in secret places and predilections and pleasures. And they fell deeper into those secrets, beating back the war and time and death with a few moments of ecstasy that left them both gasping and sweating in the shock of it.

They went to dinner and the theater and laughed at Noël Coward lines as air raid sirens wailed in the distance. But the sirens reminded them of the real world so they went back to the room and made love again.

"This is all there is," Andy said later in the darkness.

"What do you mean?" she asked without lifting her head from his chest.

"Food and sleep and sex, that's all there is." When he spoke, the words rumbled in her ear like thunder.

"And that's what you're flying for?"

"Are you selling something else?"

They lay there in the darkness for a while, her head rising and falling with his breath.

"There's a four-letter word," he said. "It's slang for what we've spent a good part of this weekend doing, and the military couldn't get along without it. It's used as a verb and a noun, an adverb and an adjective. Just about everything but a conjunction. The officers use it about the enlisted men and the enlisted men use it about the officers. Men use it to express anger and excitement and misery and homesickness and longing. It's the military man's all-purpose word. And if you didn't know the language, and just listened to us talking, you'd go back and tell the American public that was what we were fighting for. And maybe you wouldn't be far off-base." He stroked her hair. "Because there's nothing but now, Isabel."

They said goodbye at Charing Cross Station. All around them were uniformed men and tense women, some with proverbial stiff upper lips, others with cheeks wet as the English countryside. Boots crashed on the pavement and whistles screamed and smoke hung dense and gray in the evening air. It occurred to Isabel that at least part of this war was being fought in railroad stations. She looked up at Andy. In the soft privacy of the hotel room, his face had begun to lose its cutting edge, but now it was hardening into the sharp lines again.

"Listen," he said, and she knew what was coming. "About the last few days . . ."

"I know they didn't mean anything."

"I wasn't going to say that. They meant something. But you've been up there, Isabel."

She saw the plane glinting in the sunlight as it spiraled down to the sea, smelled the acrid gun smoke, heard Andy's voice screaming at Pollock to bail out. She touched his cheek. There was a faint red line where he'd cut himself shaving again. "Take care of yourself, flyboy," she said, and turned and walked away.

She wandered through the misty dusk for a long time and finally got on a bus and didn't begin to cry until she'd closed and locked the door to the suddenly empty hotel room behind her.

26

THE FIRST THING that struck Lily when she emerged from the transport plane on a base "somewhere in North Africa," as the dispatches always said, were the palm trees. She remembered the first ones she'd ever seen outside the train station in San Diego. Maybe they were the emblems of change in her life. Then Lily Hartarski had taken the first step on the road to becoming Lily Hart. Now Lily Hart was on her way to becoming her own woman, not Tom Lund's girl or Gustave Dressler's creation or World Pictures' property. She'd sworn that to herself, and to Isabel and Eliza.

The motley band of entertainers—Lily, a comedian, a minor league male vocalist, and several chorus girls—straggled across the heat-baked airfield. Spears of sunlight pierced her dark glasses. Her cotton uniform already stuck to her body like hot glue. She wondered how men carried equipment, built airfields, and fought in this heat. She could barely move.

A group of officers was waiting to welcome them. Lily brightened. She had to admit she liked men in uniform, even limp, sweat-wrinkled uniform. They piled into several jeeps and started for town. This first stop was the luxurious part of the tour. They'd be staying in a hotel. There'd be mosquito nets over real beds and running water, or if the water didn't happen to be running that day, servants to carry it. Later on there'd be tents and bedrolls, and nothing, Lily was to learn, was colder than a bedroll in the desert two hours before dawn. Maybe that was why she broke her resolution.

The road to town was clogged with traffic. Jeeps and trucks nosed their way among camels and horse-drawn carts loaded with grapes and guns and God knew what other exotica. The captain beside Lily kept up a running commentary.

The hotel was more luxurious than comfortable. There were lots of marble and minarets and servants who smiled enigmatically and clearly didn't understand a word she said. In any event, she had only a few minutes there before she was back in the jeep on the way to the amphitheater. They did two shows that night. At first Lily had been sure she was too terrified even to go on. For one thing, she wasn't a song and dance woman, though everyone assured her the men would give their right arms to see her sing or dance or simply stand centerstage and smile. For another, she'd never worked before a live audience. Lily didn't know it at the time, but she'd never again find live audiences quite like these. They were mosaics of sweat-shined faces, each one raised to her in love and longing and aching homesickness. Their applause was like the roar of a huge adoring animal. Lily could have gone on performing for them all night, but the brass had other plans.

After the second show there was a reception back at the hotel. By the end of the tour Lily would have entertained, by *Variety*'s estimate, half a million GIs. She entertained the enlisted men, but she was permitted to fraternize only with officers. Dozens were crowded into the suite at the hotel. Lily was surrounded by them when General Buzz Skeffington entered. The group didn't exactly part like the Red Sea, but it did get ready to disintegrate. Buzz Skeffington wore only one star, and as generals go, he wasn't terribly important, but in that breeze-swept Moorish room filled with American boys, he had rank. A captain got him a drink. A colonel brought him over to Lily. Sure enough, the circle around her began to spread like ripples in a still pond after a pebble has been tossed.

It has been said that every West Point plebe looks in the mirror

and sees a President of the United States. Buzz Skeffington had
been no exception, and in his case the image fit. He had a strong
face with a jaw stiffened by righteousness and eyes that couldn't
have been kinder. A reputation for physical bravery gave him the
slightest hint of a swagger. Like all professional soldiers, he thought
of himself as a man's man with a powerful if fleeting taste for
women. He looked down at Lily Hart and thought again how much
he liked this war.

General Skeffington sent a major off to get some more ice for
Lily's drink. "It's all right the way it is, really," Lily insisted, but the
general said what in the Sam Hill was the good of the new ice
machine if it couldn't turn out a few cubes for Miss Hart's drink.

He said she was a feisty lady—that was the phrase he used—to
come over here to cheer up all these boys. "You can't imagine what
it means to them to see a nice American girl again. What it means
to all of us."

"It seems to me, General, that I entertained quite a few nice
American nurses and Red Cross girls tonight."

He laughed and said it wasn't quite the same. "They're as war
weary as we are. You're like a breath of spring."

Gustave, Lily thought, would have laughed at the line—it was
too trite even for a movie—but the general made it sound fresh and
sincere.

"Now if you need anything, anything at all, you just give a hol-
ler." He put a strong hand with fine dark hairs and a West Point
ring on Lily's shoulder and said his men were like sons to him and
as long as Lily was in his theater he hoped she wouldn't mind if he
thought of her as a daughter. Anyway, he was going to look after
her. The face that was meant to stare out from the pages of a history
book stared down at her somberly.

Gustave would have said he was absurd, and she had to admit he
was corny, but he was nice too, and nice was one thing Gustave
definitely wasn't. Besides, she was through seeing the world
through Gustave's eyes. She looked up at the general from under
thick dark lashes. She knew the effect that look had. "Thank you,
General."

"Call me Buzz. Everyone does."

Lily almost laughed. So far this evening no one had called him anything but general or sir. But she didn't laugh. She just went on looking up at him. "Thank you, Buzz," she said.

Buzz Skeffington had promised to look out for Lily, and for the four days she spent entertaining his troops, he did just that. When she got back to her hotel, there was always a bowl of ice from the general's ice machine waiting. When she misplaced her toothpaste and had to brush with grapefruit juice, the general located some for her and sent it over with his aide. When he discovered Lily was a Catholic, he arranged for a chaplain to celebrate mass in one of the rooms of the hotel and even attended it with her, though he explained he'd been brought up a Presbyterian. When Lily left on the next leg of her tour, she was genuinely sorry to say goodbye to Buzz Skeffington. He said she'd never know how much her tour had meant to his men. "And to me," he added, and the kind eyes turned morose. "Command is lonely, Lily. For a little while you made it a little less lonely."

Lily didn't expect to see Buzz Skeffington again. That was a shame, but it was also war. She continued the tour, playing in Nissan huts and tents, Moorish theaters and makeshift hospital wards. There was no more ice, and now she was grateful if she could find grapefruit juice to use when the toothpaste ran out. The days were an agony of heat. When she performed, the sweat ran down her body, drenching her costumes. Between shows she lay on a cot, a bedroll, the floor, thinking she would suffocate. By evening a chill set in. One night her teeth chattered so badly she was sure she'd caught some strange fever. She wouldn't be surprised. She didn't think she'd had more than four hours sleep at a stretch since she'd started the tour.

By the time Lily reached Algiers she'd lost fifteen pounds. Her costumes hung on her. Her violet eyes seemed even bigger in her newly honed face, and more tragic. She'd seen things. She'd seen boys with the faces of old men in death. She'd seen kids laughing in maniacal fear because tomorrow they were flying another mission. She'd seen hospital beds filled with maimed bodies and burnt flesh and nothing more than mounds of bandages encasing voices that sounded, on the rare occasions they spoke, like whistling in the dark. She'd seen as much of war as she could see without actually pulling a trigger or dropping a bomb or taking a hit herself, and at odd times, during a performance or in the middle of the night, she'd go into a cold sweat and begin to tremble. That was the condition she was in when Buzz Skeffington found her at the St. Georges Hotel in Algiers, where he'd been summoned to headquarters.

"Lily, you've got battle fatigue." He led her to a chair.

"I've got two more shows to do tonight."

"Cancel them," he said as if he were giving an order.

She thought of the sea of faces she'd been looking out on four or six or eight times a day for the last three weeks. "I can do it. It's just two more shows."

The eyes measured her as if she were one of his troops. "All right, Lily, but I'm going to be in the wings through both of them, and if I think it's too much for you, I'm going right out there and carry you offstage. Someone's got to look after you."

Lily managed to make it through both shows. When she came off for the last time, the general was waiting for her. He told her she was a hell of a soldier, then apologized for his language, but Lily felt his strong hand at her elbow, saw the way he separated the crowd for her on the way to his waiting jeep and driver, and didn't think he was in the least corny.

He told her what she needed was a good thick American steak and maybe a little whiskey with real ice to calm her nerves, and he was going to see that she got them. There was no point in wearing this star, he said, if you couldn't get your hands on a few necessities every now and then.

General Skeffington rated a suite at the hotel. Carved ivory screens shut out the city, and gauzy curtains danced in the night breeze. Lily had the eerie sensation of being on a movie set. The general showed her the bathroom and told her she could freshen up while he got the wheels moving. By the time she came back into the sitting room a tray with glasses and the miraculous ice had appeared. Steaks, Buzz reported, were on the way.

"It's a little like being a king," Lily said when they'd finished dinner and the table had been cleared. Buzz was right. The food and drink had helped. The war seemed far away.

The general swirled his brandy around in his glass thoughtfully. "I suppose all this looks pretty soft." When she started to say something, he went on quickly. "But this is the exception. I'm not bragging, Lily, but I'm a good officer. I go where my men go, and I don't ask them to do anything I don't do myself."

She believed him. What was more, later, when she no longer wanted to believe him, she found out it was true. Buzz Skeffington was a good officer who was known for going among and in front of his men.

He asked if she wanted another brandy. She shook her head. "Feeling better?"

She was stretched out in an easy chair. He was sitting on its ottoman. "Almost as good as new," she said.

"Now when you get home, I want you to pamper yourself." He put his hand on her ankles. "You deserve it after this stint." He was massaging her bare feet now. There was nothing erotic about the gesture. It was paternal, affectionate, as if he was showing her how to take care of herself. "I'm going to miss you, Lily."

"I'm going to miss you too," she said, and was surprised at how intensely she meant it. With Buzz she felt protected and cherished and safe.

"Damn this war!"

She said nothing.

"I keep thinking what it would be like if we'd met somewhere else, some other time."

She wanted to tell him the war couldn't go on forever. They could meet somewhere else, some other time.

Suddenly he laughed and began stroking her calf. "What am I saying? If there weren't a war on, if you weren't out here, we wouldn't have met at all. You'd be back in Hollywood with all those handsome boys and rich men. You wouldn't be sitting here with a guy old enough to be your father"—he flashed a smile that made boys believe they were men—"almost, a guy who hasn't got much more than the uniform on his back."

"Maybe I'd rather be here talking to you."

"You're a nice girl, Lily, even if you don't mean it." He patted her knee beneath her skirt.

"But I do mean it."

He sat staring at her in silence for a moment, and she thought she knew why men followed him. She reached out and touched his jaw. Then suddenly he was kissing her. His mouth was bruising, his hand beneath her skirt insistent. She pulled away, looked up at him, stroked his cheek. He read the gentleness of her touch. "I've been at the front for too long." He kissed her again, gently this time. Then he stood, just as the hero in *Desire* had, picked her up, and carried her to the bed, and Lily had the peculiar feeling that Gustave was standing somewhere in the shadows directing the scene.

But soon she stopped thinking of Gustave because Buzz was all around her, ardent, urgent, overpowering. And later she told herself that she was silly to worry about her own pleasure. For the moment it was enough that he'd needed her so desperately. The rest would come with time. When he woke her in the middle of the night with slow hands that lingered over her body, she knew she was right. And if he was more abrupt if no less ardent in the morning, well, that was all right too. Buzz was a general, and there was a war on.

They said goodbye in his suite. He told her again that she couldn't know what meeting up with a nice American girl like her had meant to him. He said he wished they could see each other sometime stateside. "You'd like Martha-Ann and the kids."

"Martha-Ann and the kids?" she repeated.

"Sure. There's Buzzy—he'll be at the Point in a few years—and Linda and Suzy. Real army brats. They're all back in North Carolina with Martha-Ann's folks. I bet you and Mudgie would get along great. Oh, she's not glamorous like you, Lily. But she's got a good heart like you."

Lily turned away and began buttoning her jacket. A good heart. A heart of gold. The hooker with a heart of gold. She wanted to hurl the words back in his face, the words and Mrs. Buzz Skeffington with those army brats who hadn't existed last night. Then she remembered another scene from *Desire*. She turned back to the general and held out her hand. "I hope we can all meet someday, Buzz. In fact, I'm looking forward to it."

The strong face arranged itself in a smile of approval. She'd earned her good conduct medal.

27

"THERE MUST BE something wrong with me," Lily said. She and Eliza were curled in chairs on either side of the fireplace in Isabel's bedroom watching Isabel unpack. Lily had returned from North Africa two days earlier, Isabel from England that afternoon. On the wall above the mantle a Childs's ancestor looked down her aquiline nose at the daughter of a Polish Catholic factory worker and the wife of a Jewish politician with populist leanings.

"There's nothing wrong with you," Isabel said. She took a sweater from the duffle. It smelled damp and musty, like the rooms she'd slept in for the past several weeks. "There's something wrong with the men you choose. General Skeffington sounds like a real prince."

"Poor Mrs. Skeffington," Eliza said. "Poor good-hearted Mrs. Skeffington."

"I suppose he takes care of her," Lily said. "In his way."

"The way he took care of you?" Isabel asked.

Lily leaned a face covered with cream she didn't need on her fist.

"The funny thing is he did. What happened at the end doesn't change that."

Isabel flung a pair of boots on the floor and sat on the end of the bed facing Lily. "For God's sake, Lily, he got you some ice and toothpaste and a good steak. He didn't take care of you. You don't need taking care of. Look at the way you held up on that tour. Most women, men too, would have cracked under the conditions and the strain."

"There was even a quote from Bob Hope in one of the columns," Eliza added. "He said Lily Hart had gone places even he hadn't hit."

"Exactly," Isabel said. "So don't fool yourself that you need General Buzz Skeffington or Gustave Dressler or anyone else to take care of you. Go to bed with them if you want, but don't expect too much of them. And don't think so little of yourself."

"I take it from that outburst that you saw that flyer while you were over there," Eliza said.

"I saw him and I went to bed with him—so you're not the only fallen woman, Lily—and it doesn't mean anything."

Eliza pressed her lips together. The gesture made quite a statement.

"You don't approve?" Isabel asked.

Eliza shrugged. "It isn't up to me to approve or disapprove. I just wonder if you believe it yourself."

Isabel thought of Andy's lecture on military language. "I believe it."

"Don't you love him?" Lily asked.

It was a question Isabel couldn't afford to consider. "Did you love Buzz Skeffington?"

"I thought I could."

Isabel stood and went back to unpacking. "No, you didn't, Lily. You didn't even know him. But you liked the idea that he might love you. You liked the idea of having a man around again. I don't blame you. I like having a man around too. But that doesn't mean I need to have a man around. And neither do you. That's what I've been trying to make you see."

"Unless, of course, all that casual sex has repercussions." There was no mistaking the disapproval in Eliza's voice now.

"For God's sake, Eliza!" Isabel tossed another sweater to the pile on the floor. "You're the married woman, the one who's supposed to know about these things. There are what we politely call precautions. I knew a girl at school who went into Boston and actually bought her own diaphragm. But the military makes things easier. They hand things out. And sell them at the PX."

"Only they don't always work," Eliza said.

"Thanks for the warning! In case I wasn't already worried."

Lily thought of the baby she'd been sure of that hadn't existed after all. "Sometimes," she said, "I wonder about all the women through all the centuries who have worried about the exact same thing. I suppose everyone of them thought how unfair it was, but not one of them could do a thing about it."

Isabel could hear Andy's voice as if he were in the room with them. *You knew what you were getting yourself into.* But she didn't need Andy to tell her that. She had her own warning signal. It had gone off the night she'd driven him to the airfield to leave for England and any number of times since. The warning signal kept going off, and she kept ignoring it. You had to be out of your mind to get mixed up with a flyer.

She sat on the end of the bed again facing the two women. "I went on a bombing mission while I was over there."

"You're kidding."

"You must have been out of your mind."

"I was trying to learn something. To understand what they're going through." She looked from Lily to Eliza. "What I want to know is why none of them ever tries to understand what we go through?"

Later that night Isabel knocked on Eliza's door. She was sitting up in bed writing a letter to Michael. The letter was not coming easily. Her mind was on the conversation they'd had earlier. Sex without marriage. Life without love. She was confused and a little frightened and would have liked Michael's reassurances, but she didn't dare write him about any of it. She knew what the return letter would say. Get out of that house immediately and go back to your parents, back where you belong till I return. But Eliza didn't want to go back. She wasn't that frightened.

"I'm sorry if I shocked you before," Isabel said.

"You didn't shock me," Eliza lied.

"Then offended you."

Eliza put the pen and paper aside and hugged her knees to her chest. "If you want to know the truth, I think you scared me more than anything else. I'm glad I'm older. I'm glad I met Michael and fell in love and got married before this whole thing started."

"You think that's protection?" It was a genuine question.

"Of course!" Eliza said, and picked up the half-finished letter.

There turned out to be nothing for Isabel to worry about. Girls got pregnant immediately upon losing their virginity, she told Eliza, only in cautionary tales and movies with moral messages. Still, the fact that she was no longer worried didn't fill the silence that said Andy didn't give a damn. She threw herself into her work. She'd collected enough material for a month of special reports. And there was Sam. As Isabel had said to Lily, she didn't need a man around, but she enjoyed a man around.

He showed up at Isabel's office the day after she returned. When she looked through the broadcast booth window and saw him standing there in a perfectly tailored army uniform with captain's bars, she lost her place in the script, and for the first time the women of America heard Isabel Childs stumble over a phrase.

"Don't let it fool you," Sam said when she'd finished the broadcast. "The only things I fire off are PR memos. It's up to me to convince press like you that the army is just a bunch of good-hearted guys who have your boys' best interests at heart."

They went to 21 for lunch. When the headwaiter called him Captain Wicker, Sam smiled like a kid at his own birthday party.

"Don't let it go to your head," Isabel said.

Sam laughed. "Why not? I can't stand those guys who strut around in uniform, taking all the salutes and deference and pretending they hate it. At least I'm honest enough to admit I get a kick out of it."

They talked about England all through lunch. He asked the right questions. More important, he really listened to her answers. Then, as he was helping her on with her coat, he asked one more.

"How's the glory boy?"

"Don't call him that!" She was shocked at the sound of her voice, sharp as a piece of broken glass. "I'm sorry, but there's no glory over there."

Sam didn't answer. Out on the street he put on his officer's cap. The brim cast a shadow of seriousness over his too perfect features. "I hope you didn't do that for me." Isabel indicated the uniform.

"Can you think of a better reason?" He took her arm and started walking east on Fifty-second Street. "After all, Isabel, a man needs something to fight for."

On March fourth, Eighth Air Force planes bombed Berlin for the first time. Isabel read the news into the microphone and thought of that haunting voice floating over the base announcing alerts night after night after night. The allies advanced in Italy against fierce German resistance. Eliza listened to the news and grew more furious. She spent her days at the agency turning out ads telling how America was winning the war through chewing gum and coffee and fountain pens. She filled hour after hour creating needs that couldn't be met only to find her days emptier than ever. One night after an afternoon spent on a deodorant ad that invited every woman to "Be the thrill in his furlough!" she stopped in at a hospital she'd visited with Lily on one of her USO tours. The nurses and the aides were glad to have her. The men were even happier. A few remembered her from Lily's visit. "Where's Lily?" some of them called.

"Sorry to disappoint you," Eliza said, "but I'm all you've got tonight."

A naval officer who was older than the rest looked up from his book. "You're more than enough, Mrs. Kramer."

She began going to the hospital a few evenings a week after she'd read to Teddy and tucked him in. She wasn't sure why. On the way downtown she always had a moment of panic when she thought she couldn't face it again. She hated the nauseating smell of human suffering cut by antiseptic cleaning agents. She cringed at the sounds of anguish that escaped from behind closed doors. She dreaded meeting the old eyes in the young faces. But still she went. She was bargaining with fate, bargaining for Michael.

Everyone warned her not to grow attached to any of the patients, but after a few weeks she had her favorites. There was Stephen, the boy with his entire upper body in a cast, who liked to dictate letters to his girl back in Kansas about the birds he saw outside his window, and Nick, who kept touching the bandages on his eyes while she read to him from Dickens and the sports pages, and John, the older one who'd remembered her that first night and kept a picture of a little girl on the table beside his bed. The child, who couldn't have been more than two, had large sad eyes like the officer in the seersucker hospital robe in the bed beside her. The other men called him professor because he was older and before the war had taught literature at Swarthmore. When the war started, he could have stayed on at the college, but he'd decided to take a lesson from his students and had enlisted in the navy. "I chose the navy," he told Eliza, "because like a true Midwesterner—I grew up in Minnesota—I was crazy about the sea." Eliza went on listening with half her mind while the other part slogged through the drenched Italian earth beside Michael. Right after John had enlisted he'd married the prettiest girl who'd ever sat in the first row of his transcendental lit course. That was where Lucy, the little girl in the photograph, came in. He'd been lucky enough to be stateside long enough to see her born and twice more before he'd been assigned to the *U.S.S. Beatty*. He'd been in the fighting in North Africa and in Sicily too, and it was on the way back from Sicily, he told Eliza at the end of her second week at the hospital, that he'd picked up this damn collapsed lung and all the shrapnel in his leg from some German planes. He didn't mention that he'd picked it up because he'd volunteered to take over for the signalmen after they were wounded. The heroism was just one of several details he didn't mention, but Eliza didn't find that out till later.

"Hey, Mrs. Kramer," he said when she came into the ward one night after she'd stayed away for several evenings nursing Teddy's cold, "where have you been? The boys all blamed me. They said I'd bored you to death." He had a square face with a granite jaw, but when he talked about Lucy or teased Eliza, the dimples came out. He straightened the wire-rimmed glasses he wore as if they were a protective shield for the soft sad eyes that changed from blue to gray like the sky on an unsettled day. Her mother, Eliza thought, would say he looked like the perfect *goy*. "I was about to come out on my trusty crutches and track you down," he said. "Face it, you can't get away from me."

That was the way they all talked, as if they were trying to remember what it was like to be whole enough to flirt with a girl. Like Nick, who was always asking her about Lily Hart. Each time he did,

Eliza promised to get him a date with Lily as soon as he got the bandages off his eyes. Then Stephen would pipe up and say Nick could have the movie stars. All he wanted was his girl back home. "I'm not even waiting till I get out of the hospital to get married," he told them at his going-away party the night before he was to be transferred to a hospital in Wichita, and his girl.

"Some wedding night with both arms in casts," one of the men joked.

"It isn't his arms he's going to need," another shouted. "Sorry, Mrs. Kramer," he added.

"And so they married and lived happily ever after," John said, and Eliza turned to look at him because he'd never sounded that way before.

"You were married awhile before the war, weren't you?" he asked a few nights later.

"Five years. Pearl Harbor was my anniversary."

He straightened the wire-rimmed glasses and looked at her carefully. "You must have been just a kid." She didn't answer, because she was there to listen rather than talk. "My wife was just a kid too."

Occasionally Eliza gave blood at the hospital. She and Michael had the same type. She lay there among the signs warning that loose lips sank ships and reminding her to buy war bonds and asking if she'd relieved a sailor for duty today and thought of her blood flowing into Michael's veins. Please, God, she prayed, though she wasn't sure she believed in God, please don't make him need it.

"You've been giving blood again, Mrs. Kramer," John said when she went upstairs.

"Am I late?"

"No, you're pale. White as a sheet."

If it had been one of the other men, one of the younger men, the joke would have followed. Why don't you lie down here with me, Mrs. Kramer? There's plenty of room in my bed, Mrs. Kramer. But John wasn't like the rest of the boys. He left it at that.

The following week the doctors told John he was ready for his first outing. "Come with me," he asked Eliza. "We'll go to the Metropolitan Museum. Or a concert. Or lunch. Or all of them. Whatever you want."

Eliza told him she worked on weekday afternoons and spent weekends with her son. After all, her responsibility stopped at the hospital walls.

"How was your outing?" she asked him a few nights later.

"Terrific. I went to the Metropolitan and the Modern, rode a double-decker bus, and ate whipped cream in the Palm Court of the Plaza." He might have done all that alone, but it was unlikely. His eyes were too soft, his dimples too deep, his lean, war-hardened body in its lieutenant's uniform too attractive, even on crutches, maybe especially on crutches. Women would be eager to take care of him. Eliza was glad.

"I brought you a present," he said, and opened the drawer of the small bedside table. He took out a brown paper bag, the kind they use for inexpensive reproductions of museum paintings, but before he closed the drawer, she caught a glimpse of a poster lettered like the one in the blood bank, but with a truncated slogan. *Have you relieved a sailor today?* So Lieutenant Whelan was no different from the other boys after all, just a little more sophisticated and subtle. Only later alone in her room back on Sixty-seventh Street did she look at the reproduction. It was of a Monet landscape, all soft rioting color and secret shadows. "It reminds me of you," he'd written on the back. Eliza tucked it into the corner of her mirror.

"How on earth did Michael get hold of this in Italy?" Isabel asked a few nights later.

"It's not from Michael. One of the men at the hospital gave it to me. The one they call the professor."

"Uh oh."

Eliza whirled to face her. "What does that mean."

"For God's sake, Eliza, I was only kidding."

The mail brought a windfall from Michael. What had the Army Postmaster been doing with them all this time? His company had been moved back, giving some of the newcomers a chance to win the war, he wrote. He was well behind the lines. The only danger was from a surfeit of spaghetti and chianti. His buddy Conte spoke the language, and the night before, a local dignitary had bestowed on them several dozen bottles that he'd managed to hide from the Germans. *There's an artillery barrage going off in my head this morning, but I'm in better shape than Conte. It seems he's engaged to the local dignitary's daughter, or so the L.D. decided when he stumbled upon them in the early hours of the morning.*

"I'm thinking of growing a mustache," John said when she got to the hospital that evening. "It'll give me something to do while I'm stuck here. What do you think?"

"My husband has a mustache. At least he had one before he went into the army."

John looked up from the hand mirror he was pretending to study. "You miss him a lot, don't you."

"Like my right hand," Eliza said, but in fact at that moment her right hand was busy addressing a letter for a boy who had no hands at all.

28

"I'VE WASHED MY HANDS of the problem," Eliza's mother said, and Eliza knew, even though they were talking over the phone, that her mother would be pantomiming the gesture. "You're a grown woman. If you want to make yourself sick, go ahead, make yourself sick."

"I'm not making myself sick."

"And what about Teddy?"

"He couldn't be happier. Or less spoiled."

"You're saying I spoiled him."

"I'm not saying anything of the sort. Listen, I'm late for a shoot— a photography session. I have to run."

"Sure, run. That's all you do. Don't expect me to come take care of you when you get sick."

Eliza laughed. "Of course I expect you to come take care of me if I get sick. Isn't that what mothers are for?"

She'd laughed but the arguments were wearing her down. Everything was a struggle. She thought of Michael battling through the mud of Italy and felt guilty at her self-pity. Juggling the ration books, laying hands on a pair of rayon stockings, and fighting the advertising war weren't exactly hardships. Any more than getting drunk with the local populace, Eliza thought, and felt even more ashamed. She ran her last pair of stockings rushing for the photographer's studio.

It was bedlam. Seven different scenes were being shot in the single huge skylighted room converted from an old indoor tennis court. A woman at a vanity table was modeling a girdle, though Eliza hadn't seen a new girdle in a store for months. She was still wearing her old ones, though Isabel and Lily had given them up entirely. Several girls wearing skirts and sweaters and carrying books were standing ankle deep in paper leaves for the cover of the September issue of a magazine. A handful of male models were defeating the axis from behind sandbag props to promote the virtues of Commando Fruit, aka Florida grapefruit. That was Eliza's account. She tried to forget the opportunism of the ad and concentrate on the fact that at least Michael had fresh fruit in Italy. John had said that when he was at sea he'd dreamed of apples and peaches and grapes.

One of the commandos was getting friendly with the girl in the girdle. The photographer told him to get back to his sandbag. He told the photographer to hold his water. Eliza heard her own voice telling the commando there were plenty of other unemployed actors and models in town. He shot Eliza a filthy look and went back to his post.

The shoot went on forever. The simulated gunsmoke kept obscuring the picture. The photographer wanted more dedication and less blood thirst from the commandos, who owed their prowess to the sunshine state's citrus. What am I doing here, Eliza asked herself. "What am I doing here?" she said aloud.

"You're trying to get this damn ad shot," the photographer answered, but by that time Eliza had closed the studio door on the commandos and the woman in the girdle and the girls going back to school and was halfway down the stairs to the street.

She walked home through the damp late afternoon. The chill made her think spring would never come. She wondered how the season arrived in Italy.

Teddy came running to the door with his usual war cry. "Mommymommymommy!" There were two letters from Michael.

Isabel and Sam were in the library. They were sitting at opposite ends of the long leather sofa, foot to foot, as Eliza and Michael used to in the old days. She felt the cold wind of her own loneliness whistling around her. "Sam's on his way to Washington for a few days," Isabel said.

"The Pentagon can't get along without me."

"I'm quitting," Eliza said.

Sam groaned. "This is where I came in," Isabel said.

"I'm tired of exploiting the war to make money for some fat, cigar-smoking businessman. You know what I mean, Sam. You left the agency to enlist."

"Are you planning on enlisting?" he asked. "Or just going back to knitting oversized sweaters and nursing psychosomatic complaints."

"I'll find something to do. I'll work full time at the hospital."

"Speaking of the hospital," Isabel said, "a Lieutenant Whelan called. He said to tell you Nick's bandages come off next week so you'd better get to work on that date with Lily Hart."

Eliza remembered an incident in the hospital a few nights earlier. When she'd come onto the floor, a doctor had been listening to John's lungs. She could still see the black disk of the stethoscope against his bare chest. She stood. "All right, I'm over my outburst. I'm not going to work at the hospital. And you can relax, Sam. I'll keep the agency fat and functioning for your safe return. I just wish this damn war was over."

"Now there's an original thought," Sam said.

Eliza didn't go to the hospital that night. Her boys, as John called them, noticed. "So did I," he said the following night.

"Do Nick's bandages really come off next week?" she asked. John said the doctors had sworn to it. "Then, they think he'll be able to see?"

He turned his face away from her. "All they're talking about is the bandages."

"He's nineteen," she said.

"Twenty. Not that it makes a difference."

She was busy all that night, reading to the men, writing for them, taking a hand of cards and trading jokes and being there. She stayed later than usual and she was more exhausted than she'd ever been. Maybe that was why it happened. She was walking quickly down the aisle between the beds, calling good night to the men, and her foot caught the IV of one of them who was sitting on the end of his cot and toppled it. The bottle didn't break and the man was fine and nothing had happened, except that Eliza slumped to the floor and began to cry. The men stood staring in a silence that only accentuated her sobs. This was not a side of her they knew. This was not a side of her they wanted to know. John hobbled toward her on one crutch and lifted her to her feet with his free hand. He couldn't believe how light she was.

He led her out into the hall and told her to wait there. When he returned he was wearing his coat over his uniform and limping along on both crutches. He handed her a handkerchief. "Come on," he said, and started moving down the corridor.

He was all right in the elevator, but the door to the street was too heavy for him. She held it open. He started walking east toward the river, and she fell in step. Finally she stopped crying and stuffed the crumpled handkerchief into her pocket. "I'll launder it and bring it back."

"Good," he said. "I was worried about that." They walked half a block in silence. "You didn't get bad news today, did you?"

She stopped and faced him. Even in the dimmed out street the horror was visible in her face. "Oh, my God, no! You don't think . . . I mean, could I have sensed . . ."

He leaned on his crutches and put one hand on her shoulder. "Take it easy, Eliza. You didn't *sense* anything. I don't believe in that junk, and neither do you."

She wondered how he knew her name. He'd never called her anything but Mrs. Kramer.

They started walking again. "There's nothing wrong with your husband, but you've got a bad case of shell shock. You've been running yourself ragged."

Eliza took his handkerchief from her pocket and blew her nose again. "First everyone said I was sick because I wasn't doing anything. Now everyone's telling me I'm sick because I'm doing too much."

"Sounds to me like you go to extremes."

They'd reached a small cul de sac overlooking the river, and he took his weight off his crutches and leaned against the wall. "I didn't even know this existed," she said.

"It's a good place to go when you're supposed to walk and don't have anyplace to walk to."

"When are your wife and Lucy coming up to see you?"

He looked out across the river. No lights decorated the opposite shore. "It's almost like being aboard ship," he said. "Only not so cold. And no torpedoes."

"Were you frightened?"

"Sometimes. I'm no hero."

"You got those medals."

"They give them out in crackerjack boxes."

"Your wife must be proud."

He turned his back to the river and stared at her. "Are you proud of your husband's medals?"

"I don't care about the medals. I just want him to come home."

"Then why should my wife be proud of mine?"

He turned back to the river. "You feeling better?" he asked after a while.

"I'm okay. It was nothing. I got so fed up at work yesterday, at the hypocrisy of it all. And then I got home and Isabel—that's the girl I share a house with—was there with Sam."

"That her boyfriend?"

"I guess so. These days. And my husband's best friend."

"You know what you need, Eliza? Time off. Have dinner with me. They let me go out and masquerade as a normal human being these days. I can't take you dancing, but I can buy you dinner. Tell me the difference between talking to me in the ward or over a good steak?"

"My husband. Your wife."

He turned to face her again. His jaw was very square. "I'm asking you to have dinner, Eliza. If I wanted anything else, I wouldn't be wasting my time with you. You know what the boys call you? The mine. They say you look as if you'd explode if anyone so much as touched you." She turned her face away, inexplicably stung. "I like talking to you. I like being with you. Maybe that's because I'm lonely, but you're lonely too. So why won't you have dinner with me?"

"Because you're right." Her face was still turned away from him. "I am lonely. And I'm afraid."

He turned her face to his. "There's a war on. Everyone's afraid."

His face was coming closer now. There were no dimples, but his eyes behind the wire-rimmed glasses were soft. His mouth was soft too, and so hungry it made her dizzy. She pulled away and started to run. He called after her, but she kept running. At the corner she looked back once before hurling herself into a cab. He was standing there, leaning on his crutches, watching her disappear.

He called her the next day. "You didn't have to run. I can barely keep up when you walk."

"Are you playing on my sympathy?"

"I would, if I thought it would work. Eliza," he began.

"Don't talk to me in that tone."

"All I want to do is have dinner with you."

"That's not all you want," she said, and this time he didn't argue.

On the day the allies conceded that the campaign to take Monte Cassino was a "temporary failure," two doctors and Miss Nelson, the nurse everyone called Nellie, came into the ward and pushed several screens into place around the bed belonging to Nick, the twenty-year-old with the bandages over his eyes. John tried to go on reading. Several other men pretended to play cards. Someone turned on a radio. Hospital life seemed to go on as usual, but the air in the room felt suddenly thin.

The words on the page swam before John's eyes as if his own vision were impaired. "You playing cards or you sleeping?" someone taunted someone else. Still, there was no sound from behind the screen.

John tossed his book aside and walked up and down the aisle between the beds. All he could see through the slit between screens were three white backs leaning over Nick's bed. Around the card table somebody won and somebody else cursed.

That was when they heard it. "Nellie!" Nick yelled, "Nellie, you're beautiful!"

John went down the hall to the pay phone and dialed Eliza's office number. "Nick got his bandages off."

There was a silence. She was afraid to ask the rest.

"You better go to work on that date with Lily Hart because now he'll be able to see her."

Eliza began to cry. Her reaction caught her off guard, but it didn't surprise John in the least.

The following week Lily came to town, partly on a public relations tour, partly in flight from her current leading man, who, she'd discovered too late, was a better lover on screen than off. Eliza told her about Nick and the promised date. Isabel said they'd turn it into a dinner for Nick and John and a few other ambulatory patients. It would have been inhuman of Eliza to refuse.

Teddy came in while they were having drinks before dinner. He surveyed the uniforms and insignia with a practiced eye, then zeroed in on John's ribbons. "What do they mean?" he asked.

John looked at Teddy man to man. He didn't try to take him on his lap or ingratiate himself in any way. "Mostly that you happen to be in the wrong place at the wrong time. You get them just for being in action."

"That means when my daddy comes home he'll have a whole bunch of them."

"So I understand," John said.

"What about this one?" Teddy tapped John's chest. Eliza thought of the poor damaged lung within.

"I got that for trying to signal to another ship."

"My daddy's in the army," Teddy said. "In Italy. He was at Anzio. He drove back a whole Panzer division. He—"

Eliza stood and said it was time for bed. Teddy went reluctantly but without a battle. John was standing in the hall when she came down again. "He's a nice boy."

"I think so."

He touched her bare shoulder, improbably white against the red chiffon. "He looks like you."

She turned away. "He looks exactly like his father."

They went in to dinner. Cora had got out the old Lowenstoft and some of the bigger silver pieces that hadn't been used since before the war. She'd even managed to find two maids to come in to do the serving.

Lily told stories about North Africa and Hollywood, which she maintained was even stranger, and Isabel talked about England; Nick told them about Australia and New Caledonia and Sam made jokes about the Pentagon. None of the other men seemed to mind that Sam's uniform had never seen action. They'd all seen enough of it to know it had nothing to do with glory. Eliza said wasn't it strange that among them they'd been all over the world. Except for her, she thought, who'd never left New York but had come quite a distance nonetheless.

Isabel was just about to cut into the devil's food cake and wondering how Cora had found the sugar for it when the phone rang. Cora padded into the room and whispered into Isabel's ear. "It's for you," Isabel said to Lily. "Long distance."

But Lily no longer jumped for every long-distance call. She asked Cora to take a message.

Cora returned a moment later. "It's Mr. Wirtz," she whispered to Lily. "He says it's urgent."

Lily excused herself. Nick went on with a story about some New Zealanders who'd planned to send the women and children to the hills in the event of a Jap invasion.

"No!" Lily's voice rang down the hall. "Oh, no," she repeated, though her voice was saying oh yes, oh yes, oh yes.

The conversation stopped. The entire party sat eavesdropping. "Yes," she said, and "yes" again. "Tonight. I'll get a plane tonight."

By now every face in the room was turned to the doorway. Lily appeared. She had a dazed look, as if the wine had got to her. She put a hand out to steady herself against one wall. Gustave would have said it was a nice piece of business, but Lily wasn't acting. She stood staring at them. Again Gustave would have approved. She was building suspense.

"Are you all right?" someone asked.

"What happened?" someone else added.

She went on staring at them, her eyes wide with disbelief. They stared back.

"Lily," Isabel said finally. "What is it?"

"Tom," she said. "Tom's alive."

It took some time to sort out the story, partly because it was so unbelievable, partly because Sam kept going to the phone to arrange for a priority flight, and each time he returned, Lily had to repeat what she'd just said.

When Tom's ship had been torpedoed, he'd been lucky enough to be wearing his life jacket, and so, despite the fact that he was unconscious and thanks, miraculously, to the absence in the imme-

diate area of sharks, he'd washed up on one of those atolls too tiny
to rate a name or, fortunately for Tom, much Japanese attention.
That was all Lily knew so far. How he'd lived on the island and
how he'd managed to get off it were still mysteries. All Lily knew
was that Tom was alive and well, or as well as could be expected
after almost a year on a Pacific atoll, and that the first thing he'd
done when he'd reached the navy hospital back on Guadalcanal was
try to get word to her.

And the first thing Fred Wirtz had done when word had come to
his office was set the publicity wheels in motion. The marines
weren't adverse to getting a little mileage out of their latest hero.
They were willing to send Tom home to make some personal appearances. And Wirtz was going to see that Lily was there to meet
him—and that all of America was witness to the reunion of those
two clean-cut kids.

The dinner party broke up early. Sam had managed to get Lily
space on a flight. He didn't mention to anyone that it had meant
bouncing a PFC to do it. He and Isabel drove Lily to the airport.
After they left, the men shrugged into their coats and stood in the
foyer trying to prolong their stay in the world of the healthy. John
lingered behind the others. "You could ask me to stay," he said.
"For a nightcap."

"No, I couldn't."

"Eliza," he began in the voice she'd told him not to use.

"Please!"

"Okay." He touched her cheek with his thumb, then traced a
line to her mouth. "But I still say Teddy looks like you."

After they left, Eliza wandered through the downstairs rooms but
there was nothing to do. It wasn't like the aftermath of the dinners
she'd given when she was with Michael. Cora had supervised the
maids. The maids had taken care of everything.

She drifted into the library, her favorite room in the house.
When she'd taken John into it, he'd looked around at the books for
a long time, then the dimples had deepened. "Sometimes on the
ship when I was reading the same torn paperback of Max Brand or
Forever Amber for the fifth or sixth time, I used to dream about a
room like this filled with books like these." He'd taken a step toward her. "But I never knew the dream would be this good." She'd

moved away then, and she left the library quickly now. There was no place to hide.

She went to her room and took a handful of Michael's latest letters from the drawer. There was a long story about a restaurant overlooking the sea where there was no meat and patrons brought their own bread, but the shellfish and chianti remained plentiful and the waiters sang Santa Lucia endlessly. Conte had managed to get out of his engagement. The next letter was grimmer. His unit was on the move again. There was something about a monastery but the censor had blacked out the name. Eliza hated that anonymous officer who read Michael's letters before she did, deciding what Michael could tell her and what must remain secret. She wondered if censors enjoyed their jobs. Did they laugh at the funny lines, get a vicarious kick from the intimate ones? Did they ever censor nonmilitary information on a whim? She pictured an officer who'd just got his own Dear John letter stamping out *I love you,* or a paternal type deleting a confession of infidelity for the soldier's— and his wife's—best interests. Maybe the Army ought to censor mail going the other way as well. She sat up in bed. She was being absurd. Her mother always said she had too much imagination for her own good, though Eliza was sure imagination was one trait she was sorely missing. Oh, no, a small voice that sounded very much like a conscience said. That's not true. What about all the things you've been imagining with John Whelan?

She threw herself back on the bed and lay staring at the ceiling. She tried to picture Michael eating spaghetti and drinking chianti. She tried to picture him curled in a foxhole under the sweater she'd knitted. She tried to picture him. John's face swam into view.

She got up and went into Teddy's room. She tripped over the rocking chair and stumbled against a shelf of toys. Teddy whimpered and opened his eyes. "Don't worry," Eliza said. "Everything's all right. Mommy's here. Mommy will stay until you fall back to sleep." In fact, she sat in the rocking chair singing the songs Teddy liked until long after he was asleep and wishing she'd had another child before Michael had left. A baby would have kept her too busy to think.

On the way uptown to the Triborough Bridge Lily made Sam stop the car in front of a Catholic church. "You don't have much time," Isabel said.

"I have enough time for this."

She came out of the church a few minutes later. The longing in her mouth that tugged at millions of American heartstrings had been smoothed into a peaceful curve.

The airline terminal was crowded with tired-looking men and women in uniform and disgruntled civilians. Sam carved a path between them for Lily. Heads turned from private concerns and exhaustion to stare. Isabel heard the name "Lily Hart" flit from mouth to mouth.

Sam went to the desk to take care of Lily's ticket, while the two women stood waiting. "I still can't believe it," Lily said.

Isabel fought the urge to tell Lily not to get her hopes up. If a mistake had been made once, it could be made again. The warning seemed too cruel.

"I can't imagine what it's been like for him," Lily said. "Except it must have been awful. And he must have changed a lot."

"You've changed a lot too, Lily. Just since I've known you. Imagine how much you've changed since you've seen Tom."

Lily's eyes wandered off to the middle distance for a moment, then returned. She smiled. "I haven't changed that much. Not where Tom is concerned."

Sam returned with Lily's ticket, and the three of them walked out of the terminal into the cool spring night. A bitter wind defied the season. Lily kissed them both and started across the field to the plane. As she walked, she turned her collar up and pulled the fur coat close around her body. Even from behind she looked glamorous. The lush body and silky blond hair belonged to the beautiful kid who'd worked behind the counter in the five-and-ten, but the mink coat was the property of a different woman.

Lily strapped herself into the seat, arranged her coat over her as a blanket, and leaned her head against the window. She closed her eyes. That would discourage overly friendly traveling companions.

"Lily. Lily Hartarski."

She opened her eyes wide at the sound of her old name. She no longer thought of it as her real name.

Jerry Crowley smiled down at her. "Or should I say Lily Hart?"

He took the seat beside her. As he did, the overhead light caught the scar that cut through his eyebrow and kept him on the unfortunate side of handsome. Still, he was looking good. The old confidence was there, and a double-breasted pin-striped suit lent an air of success. "What luck. On these flights I usually end up next to some poor homesick GI who wants to tell me about his girl or some management Joe who wants to tell me how the unions are keeping the country from winning the war."

He talked until the plane took off. He was working for the government now on postwar labor plans. He hadn't seen Carrie but heard she was well. "She had another baby. She and her chief petty officer." He asked about Lily, and that was when she told him about Tom. He laughed and said that was wonderful and laughed again and leaned over to kiss her on the cheek. Then the cabin fell into half darkness and the plane roared into the air and he told her above the drone of the engines that he'd let her get some sleep. The flight attendant brought her a pillow, and she tried wedging it against the window, but that didn't work well. Finally Jerry took it from her and rested it against his shoulder and told her to go to sleep. She hesitated a moment, then put her head on the pillow. Her mind was full of Tom and, as she grew drowsier, all sorts of confused thoughts. She thought of Jerry and Carrie and a night they'd all gone dancing. Afterward she'd gone home alone and cried herself to sleep. She remembered a time when she was first working for World and was still Jeanne Storey. Jerry had come to visit and asked her to dinner. When he'd taken her home, she'd wondered if he was going to try to kiss her, but he hadn't.

The plane hit an air pocket and jolted her half awake. Tom was home. She didn't have to think about the might-have-beens anymore. And she didn't have to think about what had been. She didn't have to think about Gustave or Buzz Skeffington or any of the others. Tom was home now, and he'd wipe out all the memories and all the mistakes.

The house was dark by the time Isabel and Sam got back to it. He followed her across the foyer and up the stairs to the library as if he belonged there. He even poured a brandy for each of them without asking.

"Something's bothering you." He sat beside her on the leather sofa that still carried the aroma of Eliot's cigarettes.

"Lily. I'm afraid she's going to find out you can't go home."

"Lily's a big girl."

Isabel stood, walked to the hearth, and rested her arms on the mantle, keeping her back to Sam. "And Eliza."

Sam remained on the sofa watching her. "Eliza's a big girl too. Are you worried about them, Isabel, or envious of them?"

"Why would I be envious?" she asked, her back still to him.

"Love. Passion. Sex. All those words that have never been mentioned in this room till now. They're living the war, not just reporting it." He stood, walked to the mantle, and touched her back where the dress dipped low. His fingers traced a lazy pattern. He bent and kissed the back of her neck. She shivered, then moved across the room to put Eliot's desk between them.

He shrugged, put his hands in the pockets of his uniform, and leaned against the mantle. He knew how he appeared, and it was a lot more casual than he felt. "Look, Isabel, this war isn't going to go on forever. Pretty soon you won't be able to go running off on bombing missions. And your family's grown accustomed to your job. So you're going to need a new form of rebellion. I'm volunteering. Think of it. 'Daddy, Mummy—'"

"I don't call them daddy and mummy. Especially not mummy."

He smiled the smile that had won million-dollar accounts. "Don't interrupt me. I'm getting to the good part. 'Daddy, Mummy, I'm in love with a dyed-in-the-wool, one-hundred-percent Jew.'"

She laughed in spite of herself. "You're not so dyed-in-the-wool."

He crossed the room and moved around the desk to her. "For you, Isabel, I'll give up bacon, shrimp, anything." He put his arms around her waist. "I'll change my name back to my name." He kissed her, slowly, carefully, as if it were all part of the joke. And like a good comedian, his timing was perfect. Soon she was kissing him back. Why not, she thought. The pressure of Sam's body answered the question in hers. You didn't have to be cheating death every day to want to snatch as much life as you could while you could. But she pulled away from him finally, put her hands on his shoulders, which weren't as broad as Andy's but were nice and broad nonetheless, and turned him toward the door. They walked downstairs together. He kissed her again, and she kissed him back again, and it started all over, but she broke away again, and finally closed the door behind him. "Why not?" she said aloud to the empty foyer, but she was sure she didn't mean it.

29

ELIZA DIDN'T GO to the hospital the evening after the dinner party. The following day John showed up at her office. The pool of secretaries and typists turned to stare as the receptionist led him, limping with the aid of a single cane, to her office.

"I see you've graduated." Eliza's tone was so gruff the receptionist glanced at her curiously as she left the office.

John leaned on the back of a chair and saluted with the cane. "From crutches to cane with the help of a good woman. I've come to take you to lunch to celebrate." He pushed the door closed with the cane.

She started to open it, then decided she didn't want the whole office listening. "I'm busy."

John sat in the chair on the other side of her desk. "Fine. Then we'll have dinner."

She sat on the edge of her desk. Her skirt, cut according to skimpy war regulations, hiked up above her knees. She slid off the desk. "John," she began.

"Do you realize that's the first time you've called me by my name."

"Lieutenant—"

"Yes, Mrs. Kramer?"

"If you're so much better, why don't you go home to see your wife? And Lucy."

Something pulled at the side of his mouth. Then he smiled again. "She took Lucy back to her folks in New Orleans. The doctors won't let me travel that far. Not for another couple of weeks."

"Then why doesn't she come see you?"

He traced an aimless pattern in the carpet with his cane. "Too busy with her war work. Thinks it's unpatriotic to ride the trains for nonessential business."

"I think you're essential."

"Good." He stood. "I'll limp by for you around seven. Think of some place expensive. I've got a couple of months' back pay burning a hole in my pocket."

That evening Eliza and Isabel passed in the front hall of the house on Sixty-seventh Street. "I'm off to Washington," Isabel said. "Sam set up an interview with a four-star general who never, ever talks to the press. Wish me luck."

"I'm off to dinner with John. Maybe you ought to wish me luck."

Isabel stopped and stared at Eliza. "I have faith in you."

"What does that mean?"

Isabel picked up her overnight bag. "That you're stronger than you think. Whatever you do, you'll be all right."

By the time John arrived, Eliza had already put on and taken off Michael's favorite dress, one she'd worn when he'd come home on his first leave, and three others. Finally she grabbed a black dinner dress with a high neck and long sleeves, very proper, very demure. Only halfway down the stairs did she remember that everytime she'd worn the dress, Michael had commented on the way the skirt hugged her bottom.

They went to a French restaurant where the food was good and the noise level low enough for conversation. The first was wasted on them. Neither of them ate much, though in her nervousness Eliza drank three glasses of wine. They talked about Edith Wharton and Scott Fitzgerald and John Marquand, about Teddy and Lucy, about his childhood in Minnesota and hers in Brooklyn. He told her his father was a minister and had wanted him to be one too, but somewhere in his adolescence, he'd started thinking about religion and come up without a god. And she said that was funny because she'd done the same thing.

"I've never had dinner with a minister's son before."

He looked across the table at her, and the dimples punctuated his smile. "I'm willing to bet you've never gone out with a gentile man before."

She could feel the heat, full and red as the wine, rising in her cheeks. "I must seem awfully, well, provincial to you."

He reached across the table and put his hand over hers. "Do you want to know how you seem to me, Eliza?"

She pulled her hand away. "No, please, don't."

He paid the check then and they took a cab to Café Society Uptown to hear Mildred Bailey. After that he suggested El Morocco, but she said El Morocco was for dancing. By that time they were already in the cab, so John gave the driver the address of the house on Sixty-seventh Street.

His arm moved around her shoulders, and he began to toy with a whisp of hair that had escaped from the upsweep. She'd been afraid he was going to try to kiss her in the cab. He didn't. He just went on toying with the wisp of hair. The fear turned to disappointment, then mounted in her like a panic. What if he really had wanted only dinner?

Four stairs led from the street to the house. Without a word he put his arm around her shoulders and she put her arm around his waist, and they climbed them. His weight was not unpleasant. He followed her through the grille and glass outer door. The vestibule between it and the heavy wooden inner one was dark. She turned to him and held out her hand. He took it and drew her to him, as she'd been waiting for him to. He kissed her. "Don't," she whispered, but her mouth found his again and turned the word into a lie.

He took the key from her hand and opened the inner door. They stopped in the hall and kissed again, more hungrily this time. His hands found their way beneath her coat. Her own stroked his smooth fine hair, the back of his neck, the familiar roughness of beard. This time she said nothing.

They took the stairs slowly, their arms wound around each other, stopping to kiss and touch and, in the dim light of the landing, look at each other. "Eliza," he began.

She kissed away the word. If she could keep him from speaking, this wouldn't be real, he wouldn't be real.

She opened the door to her room and stood aside to let him go in. "I'll be right back." Her voice was hoarse.

"Where are you going?"

"To check on Teddy."

"Let me go with you."

"No!"

He winced as if she'd slapped him.

She went into Teddy's room. His small arm was thrown across Teddytoo. The bear had grown ragged and worn over the past few years, but Teddy still clung to it. She kissed her son's cheek. He didn't move. She went back into the hall and closed the door behind her.

She'd told John she was going to check on Teddy, but there was one more thing she had to do. She wasn't a girl, and this was no seduction. She went into the bathroom and took the diaphragm she hadn't used since Teddy had turned two from the medicine cabinet. She opened the compact. It looked dusty and unused. She'd felt the same way until John. She could still taste him on her mouth. Then it came to her. She didn't know why it hadn't occurred to her before. He wouldn't be circumcized. The idea terrified her. He wouldn't be like Michael. He'd be different, foreign, alien.

She couldn't go through with it. Then she looked in the mirror and knew she couldn't not go through with it. At this moment he was all she wanted. She took the diaphragm from its case.

He was standing with his back to the door staring at the Monet print she'd stuck in the dresser mirror. He'd taken off his jacket and shirt and was wearing only his trousers. His back was a smooth strong V. She closed the door behind her and locked it. He turned. She crossed the room to him, saw the angry scars left by the shrapnel, reached out and touched one beneath his heart. The tissue was rough and jagged.

He took off his glasses. Without them his eyes were even softer, and sadder. She put her arms around his neck and swam up into those eyes.

Suddenly she realized something was different. The picture of Michael on the night table. He'd turned it face down. She knew exactly how he'd done it. Gently, apologetically, without triumph.

A long line of buttons ran down the back of her dress. He worked at them carefully, as if he were unwrapping a costly present, and all the time he kept kissing her, touching her, tracing the lines of her body with his free hand. Her own moved to his belt buckle.

Finally they stood naked, looking at each other. Then she moved into the circle of his arms. She wondered how she could ever have been afraid of him.

In bed he whispered her name again. She put her fingers over his mouth to silence him, but he kissed her fingers and went on repeating her name, Elizaelizaeliza. His mouth moved over her body, searing the word into her flesh, and she knew she'd be marked by it forever.

It took a long time for his breathing to return to normal. "Are you all right?" she asked. "I mean, were you allowed to . . ." Her voice trailed off.

"Just let them try to stop me."

"I'm serious."

He smoothed the hair back from her face. "Yes, I'm allowed to, Eliza. Anyway, I'm not breathing that way because of my lung, I'm breathing that way because of you."

They lay in silence for a while. Their bodies were still entwined, but Eliza's mind had begun to wander off. She turned on her back and lay staring at the ceiling. She could remember Michael's face now. It stared down at her in disgust. She felt as she used to as a child when, overcome by guilt at some transgression, she'd pray to God to turn the clock back a few minutes so she could not do what she'd just done.

She felt John looking at her. She refused to meet his eyes. "Eliza," he whispered. She didn't answer.

How could she have done it? How could she have gone to bed with this stranger? She hated him. She hated herself.

He tried to turn her face to his. She got out of bed, crossed the room to the chair where he'd tossed his uniform, took a cigarette from his jacket, and lit it.

He was sitting up in bed now watching her. "I've never seen you smoke."

As if on cue, she coughed. "I don't smoke."

"In that case, why don't you give that to me."

"You're not supposed to smoke either," she said, but she handed him the cigarette.

He caught her hand and pulled her down beside him on the bed. "You're having second thoughts."

"It was a mistake, a terrible mistake," she said, but she didn't pull away from him because she didn't hate him. She wished she could.

"Terrible?"

"Oh, God, I didn't mean *it* was terrible. I meant it was a terrible thing to do."

"Why?"

"Because I have a husband and you have a wife."

His hand was stroking her back, molding the length of her body to his. "They're not here now."

This time she did pull away from him. "I can't understand you. Don't you even feel guilty?"

He pulled her to him again. "I feel happy. For the first time since I went overseas, I feel happy."

"What about your wife?"

Now he was the one who broke away. He rolled over on his back and lay staring at the ceiling. "I don't have a wife," he said finally.

She sat looking down at him in silence. Even in the dim light he could see how pale she'd gone. He reached up and touched her cheek.

"I don't understand. What about the picture of Lucy?"

"I didn't lie to you. I just didn't tell you the whole truth. A little less than a year ago, about the time we hit Sicily, I got a Dear John letter." His laugh sounded like a fingernail being drawn over a blackboard. "In this case it really did start 'Dear John.' Not a particularly original story. She got tired of waiting, found someone else, wanted to marry him. She's going to as soon as the divorce comes through."

Eliza was sitting up now, her back straight against the headrest. She pulled the sheets up to cover her. "Why didn't you tell me?"

"Because if you thought I was single you would have been even more wary."

She didn't say anything.

"And because I didn't want your sympathy. Poor Lieutenant Whelan. A gimp. Can't walk. Can barely breathe. Can't even hold on to his wife."

She got out of bed again. This time she put on a robe. Then she went to his uniform and took another cigarette.

"I thought we agreed you didn't smoke."

"I do tonight." She puffed furiously. "This is my night for taking up new vices. Tobacco. Adultery. You name it, and before the evening is over I'll probably commit it."

"I don't see what you're so upset about."

She ground out the cigarette. "Don't you? Come on, professor. You're a smart man. You have a Ph.D. Knowledgeable about art and music and literature. It's the first time I've been seduced on Edith Wharton."

"It's the first time you've been seduced, and just for the record, I like to think there was some mutual seduction going on. I pursued you, Eliza, but I didn't force you into anything."

"I'll remember to tell that to my husband."

He sat up. "I would hope you wouldn't tell any of this to your husband."

"Are you giving marital advice now? Because I don't think you're exactly in a position to."

"Don't get bitchy, Eliza."

"Don't tell me what to do. And don't tell me any more lies. The happily married man."

"I never said I was happily married."

"You said you were married. I thought we both had too much to lose."

"So that's it. Now you're the only one with something to lose. And you think I'm going to make trouble."

"You already have."

"Is that what you call this?"

"What do you call it?"

"Love, but you don't want to hear that. You don't want to hear anything."

"Not from you. Not ever again."

He was out of bed, hopping awkwardly on one foot, pulling on clothes. "Fine, that's fine with me."

She sat on the end of the bed pulling her robe tight around her. Behind her she could hear him muttering and cursing as he dressed. At one point he must have lost his balance because she felt the bed shake as he caught the post to steady himself.

She stood. "Do you need help?"

"Not from you, Mrs. Kramer."

30

FRED WIRTZ had been on the phone with various Marine Corps officers for the past thirty-six hours, but he still managed to get to the airport to meet Lily. So did several hundred reporters who had been alerted by Wirtz's department. People were tired of death and destruction. Here was a romantic war story, one with a happy ending. The press crowded around the arrival gate, jockeying for a good position from which to fire cameras and questions.

As the plane taxied to a stop, Jerry Crowley peered over Lily's shoulder out the window. "And to think I knew you when."

The cameras started clicking as soon as she appeared in the door of the plane. Crowley followed her down the stairs. He noticed that she stopped every few steps to give the photographers a crack at a flattering and seemingly natural pose. It was hard to believe this was the frightened kid he'd met two years earlier. Only the sway of those beautiful hips was the same.

Fred Wirtz was waiting at the bottom of the stairs. He put his arms around her and kissed her on the cheek. "I'm happy for you, Lily. I mean, I'm crazy about all this." He nodded toward the press.

"You've given me a story any self-respecting publicity hack would kill for. But I'm happy for you too."

He guided her to the waiting limousine. The cameras kept clicking until the driver had closed the door and they'd driven off. Only days later did Lily realize she'd never bothered to say goodbye to Jerry Crowley.

"Is Tom here yet?" she asked.

"Another day. Two at the most. I'm having a little trouble with one general who thinks Tom ought to go right back to fighting the war. He's in that good condition. I've just about convinced the general that Tom'll do more for morale—and recruits—on the home front. We're setting up appearances for him. And the press is going crazy over the homecoming. It's going to take half the MPs in San Diego to control them."

"Couldn't you tone it down a little, Fred? I haven't seen Tom in two years. We need some time alone."

"Of course, you'll have time alone. Hell, Lily, we're not going to follow you into the bedroom. Just the usual stuff. Tom coming out of the plane. You running to greet him. The first kiss. My God, Gustave could make a movie out of it."

"I don't want Gustave there."

He turned to look at her. "It's your show, Lily."

"Sure." She turned to look out the window at the palm trees she'd come to take for granted. "As long as everything goes according to your plan."

Fred didn't bother to answer her. He spent his life humoring men and women who'd clawed their way into the spotlight only to complain about how bright the glare was. Lily was nicer than most of them. She hadn't clawed much—she hadn't had to—and she didn't complain often.

"Then there's the wedding," he said. *"Life* wants to cover it. The only trouble is they want an exclusive, and the fan magazines are screaming bloody murder. But don't you worry. I'll take care of everything."

"Aren't you moving a little fast, Fred? No one's said anything about a wedding."

"You were going to get married before he shipped out. You two kids are made for each other, Lily. America's dying for you to get married. A.Z. thinks it's a great idea too."

"As long as we keep A.Z. happy."

He turned to look at her again. "I can always tell when you've been with your friends in New York. Well, just remember one thing, Lily. To the rest of the world you're a star, but in this town the studios still call the shots, and A.Z. still runs one of the biggest studios. I'm not saying he can break you, but he can hurt you."

"I'll keep it in mind."

"Incidentally, I wasn't joking about Gustave's making a picture of your story. A.Z. loves the idea. Small-town kids in love. The war turns everything upside down. He goes off to the Pacific and disappears. Presumed dead. By now she's a big movie star, but still true to his memory. Remember, this has to pass the Hays Office. Then he turns up, they marry and live happily ever after. Love triumphs over all."

"Isn't anything sacred to you, Fred?"

"To me, not much. To A.Z. nothing. But you just concentrate on making that poor kid happy. Jesus, I envy him."

"Eleven months on a Pacific atoll?"

"Coming home to you. And every other fighting man's going to agree. We'll need a new pinup."

That night Fred managed to set up a telephone call between Lily and Tom, who'd reached Hawaii. The following day one of the tabloids carried a banner headline. LILY'S FIRST WORDS WITH LOST LOVE. Beneath it was a fairly accurate record of their conversation. Lily didn't even bother asking Fred how the paper had got hold of it.

Tom was due home the following afternoon. Gustave stopped by Lily's house that morning. The maid said Miss Hart was around the pool. Gustave said he knew the way.

"He's going to like the tan lines."

Lily opened her eyes, though she'd recognize that soft guttural accent anywhere.

"It's very exciting," he said. "He'll look at your face and arms and legs, all bronze from the California sun, and think how beautiful you are. Then he'll look at the tan lines, the lines of demarcation between the public Lily Hart and the private, and touch that white flesh untouched by the sun and think how lucky he is to be the one. Or perhaps among the ones."

"You're a bastard, Gustave."

"And you're not the sweet girl I discovered. Thank God. Or maybe thanks to me. Your marine ought to be grateful."

"What do you want?"

"I brought you a gift." He dropped some papers on the table beside her lounge. "Story outline. A.Z. has four writers on it even as we speak. A tale of war conquered and love triumphant. Trash, but I can make it into art. A.Z. wants to borrow Garfield to play Tom."

She sat up and looked at Gustave. She'd had time to get over the shock. Now the fear had started to set in. "How can you write the story? You don't know how it turns out."

"This is Hollywood, Lily." He lifted her face to the sun as if he were posing her for the camera. She still found his touch unsettling. "You two kids live happily ever after."

Fred Wirtz picked her up that afternoon. A cavalcade of cars had already assembled for the drive to San Diego. Lily Hart's reunion with her true love would be almost as well documented as the coming invasion of Europe. Fred said he'd drive down in the limo with her and return in one of the other cars. "Don't worry, Lily, you'll have your time alone."

Tom's plane was late. Lily sat in the hot car pulled up beside the sunbaked runway while Wirtz went to work the other cars, spreading Hollywood salve over the cynical reporters and suspicious marine brass. At one point he returned with a woman who considered herself the heir to the Louella-Hedda mantle. "I don't want to talk to anyone now," Lily said.

"Just a few words," Fred urged. "She's got a lot of readers."

"I don't care if the whole goddamn country hangs on her every word. I'm not giving interviews now. I'm too nervous."

Fred slid across the backseat and put his arm around Lily's shoulders. "I know how you feel, honey. But think of all the girls across the country who are still waiting for their guys to come home. You owe them this."

"What about privacy?"

"You want privacy, go back to working on that assembly line. Just a few words, Lily."

She did her duty.

The afternoon dragged on. The car grew hotter. The leather

upholstery stuck to the back of her legs. Fred brought a marine colonel over to be introduced. He had a hard handsome face, long on strength and lacking much feeling. He reminded her of Buzz Skeffington.

Fred heard the engines before she did. He looked out the limo window. "This is it, Lily." The plane came taxiing down the runway. Her stomach was churning like the propellers.

Fred helped her out of the car. The press was already crowding around the gate. A few of Fred's henchmen and some MPs carved a path for her. The runway shimmered in the heat. The wind churned up by the propellers was hot. The engines roared in her ears. The heavy door of the plane swung open. A man in uniform appeared in it. Lily stopped several yards from the plane and stood staring up at him. The sun was in her eyes, but the sun wasn't the problem.

She knew it was Tom, but it wasn't her Tom. His face was black from the sun, his hair yellow, his body so thin he looked as if he might break in two. He started down the stairs. His step was military, but there was something stealthy and hunted about his bearing. When he got to the bottom of the steps, he stood looking around as if he didn't know where he was.

Lily kept walking toward the stranger. His mouth smiled but the wary look in his eyes remained. He put his arms around her. They were nothing more than sticks. She hugged him. He was a bundle of kindling. She remembered Tom's body and started to cry. That was what they'd been waiting for. The cameras began clicking.

He kissed her. He didn't even taste like Tom. Or had she forgot Tom's taste? He let her go. The colonel and his entourage were approaching. Tom saluted. He seemed a little more familiar now.

Finally they were alone in the backseat of the limousine. He kissed her again. It was easier than trying to talk, as easy as saluting.

They drove for several minutes in silence, one of those thick voids that amplifies other sounds. The horn of another car screamed past them. Tom snapped his fingers several times, realized what he was doing, stopped. Lily coughed. "You look wonderful," he said finally. "Like a million bucks." His smile was thin, as if he realized the aptness of the expression. He hadn't thought about money for eleven months but he was thinking about it now. The scale between them had tipped the other way.

"I'm still the same, Tom." She took his hand to cover the lie.

"Sure, we both are."

The first few days were halcyon, or so they assured each other repeatedly. Tom was silent, sometimes maddeningly so, Lily thought, but she reminded herself of his recent ordeals and conveniently forgot how little they'd talked before he'd gone away. The attraction between them had been powerful but not articulate.

And Tom sat in the Hollywood sun, a pale replica of the tropical glare he'd just escaped, and felt his natural reticence hardening into silence. At home in the familiar house on the bluff overlooking the Mississippi he might have tried to talk. He might have tried to explain about his buddy Sharp and that business with the gold Jap teeth and then the look on Sharp's face which wasn't a face anymore at the end. He might have tried to describe the island with the violent growth that seemed to overrun things in hours and the natives who were only a generation or so away from cannibalism and the girl with the jet black hair and face like the book of paintings on Lily's coffee table. But here he couldn't even try to talk about them. Maybe that was why, because here they'd be nothing more than a source of entertainment, like that book of Gauguin's pictures. Like him. A source of entertainment, an oddity, a trophy to be exhibited by the marines and the Hollywood moguls and even Lily.

It wasn't that he didn't trust Lily, only that he didn't know her anymore. She looked the same, only better, but she didn't talk the same, thanks to all those lessons the studio had given her, and she didn't say the same things. One morning he heard her on the phone telling that director Gustave Dressler that she didn't care if it was unprecedented, she wanted script approval. "Without me you haven't got a movie, Gus, and without script approval you haven't got me. And tell that lecherous old bastard A.Z. it won't do any good to threaten suspension. I could use a vacation." She hung up the phone then and turned to Tom with that sweet smile he'd carried with him across the Pacific, and he hadn't known where he was.

Where he was, he frequently reminded himself, was a fifteen-room mansion in Beverly Hills. He'd been surprised when Lily had told him he could stay with her. "What will people think?"

"They won't think, Tom, they'll know. This is Hollywood, not

Duquel. Nobody cares what you do as long as it doesn't affect your box office."

So Tom moved into Lily's house and Lily's bed, and there for a while the strangeness disappeared. Everything was all right in bed. Lily refused to admit to herself that it wasn't any more than all right. No one could have lived up to her memories of Tom, but Tom managed to live up to the expectations Gustave had heightened and honed. Tom was no Buzz Skeffington.

When they weren't in bed, they were rarely alone. Fred Wirtz saw to that. There were interviews at which Lily and Fred did the talking and Tom managed to smile for the camera. There were personal appearances at rallies and bond drives. There were meetings at the studio about the movie based on their story. When someone suggested testing Tom to play himself, he looked around the room as if he were searching for an exit and said to count him out. And there were parties. Everyone wanted to meet the shipwrecked hero who'd played Robinson Crusoe on a desert island for eleven months. "It wasn't deserted," Tom insisted. "There were natives. And a Dutch planter who sobered up long enough to find the stuff for me to put together that radio that finally got me off. And every now and then a Jap patrol." But no one listened. Tom's story didn't play nearly as well as the one the studio and the press had cooked up.

"What do you say?" Tom asked the morning after a party World had thrown for Lily and him at the Coconut Grove. "Isn't it time we went home for a while?"

Lily sat up in bed. "Home?"

"Duquel. I've been back for more than a week, and I haven't even seen mom and dad."

Lily sat staring at the thin sunburned man who all the papers said was the love of her life. Maybe if you grew up in a big house overlooking the river, Duquel was home, but if you'd been thrown out of a foul-smelling shack down near the docks, it was just a gritty town filled with mean-spirited strangers. "I am home, Tom."

He crossed the room and sat in one of the chairs. He was wearing only undershorts and his skin was black against the pale upholstery. "But I'm not, Lily." He went on staring at her. "I've been away for a long time, and I want to go home."

"Oh, darling!" she said. The word still sounded phony to Tom, but the frown that pulled at her mouth was real. "I'm so damn selfish. Of course, we'll go home. I'll have the studio make all the arrangements." It was, she told Isabel when she telephoned her later that day, the least she could do for Tom.

"In other words, you're going to make it all up to him," Isabel said. "Guadalcanal. The torpedoing. Everything he's seen and suffered."

"What's wrong with that?" Lily asked.

"Not wrong," Isabel answered. "Just impossible."

31

THE MORNING after Eliza and John quarreled, he forced himself to wait until eight-thirty to telephone. He wasn't playing games, merely trying not to disturb the rest of the house. Cora said Mrs. Kramer had already left for her office. He'd wanted to begin calling there immediately but had been forced to limp off to his physical therapy session.

When Eliza got to her office, there were no messages waiting. She closed the door and sat staring at the telephone. She wasn't angry at John anymore, but she was furious at herself. If only he'd call, she'd tell him so. She went on staring at the phone. Why didn't he call? Michael always called after a quarrel. She winced at the memory. Her husband was overseas risking his life, and she was home screwing around. That was the term. She knew it even if she'd never used it. She was screwing around.

Eliza put her head in her hands. She'd cheated on Michael and turned on John and made a mess of everything. Well, she couldn't undo what she'd done, but she wouldn't make things worse. She was glad she'd fought with John. It would make never seeing him again easier. That was when the phone rang. She picked it up. "I'm sorry," he said.

"Oh, God, so am I. I'm so sorry."

"Can I see you tonight?"

She opened her mouth to say no. It came out yes.

They went to dinner at the French restaurant frequented by the crew of the *Normandie*. John knew as soon as they arrived that Eliza had taken him there for more than the food. It was dark. It was not the sort of place people she knew, or more important, people she had known, were likely to turn up. But Eliza wasn't the only one changed by the war. They were halfway through their escargots, which she'd never had and John had convinced her to try, when she looked up and noticed the woman standing in the door. The man wore the uniform of a captain in the army. The woman had lived down the hall from Eliza and Michael in the building on Central Park West.

Eliza put down her fork and shifted position so her back was to the door. She kept her eyes down, as if her refusal to look at the woman would keep the woman from seeing her.

"Are you all right?" John asked.

"That woman," she whispered. "Don't look," she hissed as his eyes moved to the door.

He turned back to Eliza. "We're only having dinner. I wasn't even holding your hand."

"You don't understand," she said.

But he understood perfectly. He signaled for the check, paid, and waited until the woman and the officer she was with had taken a table before steering Eliza out of the restaurant.

A soft spring rain was falling and misty coronas hung about the street lights. "I'm sorry," she said.

"It's all right." He started walking. His cane made a lonely sound on the pavement.

She fell in step beside him. "You had to pay for the whole dinner. All that food we ordered and didn't eat."

"It's only money."

She started to say something, then changed her mind.

"That guy she was with wasn't her husband," John said.

Eliza stopped walking. "I know, but how did you?"

He turned to her and shrugged. "Just a guess. They didn't act as if they were married."

She started walking again. He caught up with her. "Then why were you so worried?"

She whirled on him. "Because maybe I don't want to be like her. Or like you. Or like anyone else who uses this damn war as an excuse. It's only money. It's only sex. Spend. Eat, drink, and be merry. Screw around. Do whatever you damn please and justify—"

"Eliza!" His free hand grabbed her arm and shook her into silence. "I don't have to justify anything. I love you."

"Of course. You love me. That captain back there loves my former neighbor. And if he doesn't, he's probably shipping out tomorrow. Great lines of World War II."

His hand tightened on her arm. She looked up at him in the misty darkness. The line of his jaw was hard, his mouth thin as a razor. "You don't think much of me." He ran a finger over her cheek. "But you don't think much of yourself either."

She began to cry then. He put his arms around her and she buried her face in his chest and they stood holding each other as if their embrace were a shelter from the rain.

A few days later John was discharged from the hospital. He had a month's leave before he had to report to Newport and, he assured Eliza, a cushy desk job. She convinced him to visit his daughter and parents. He was back in New York in a week. His parents had been overjoyed to see him, but they didn't seem to know what to do with him. Lucy knew the word "daddy" but used it to refer to her mother's new boyfriend. John managed to get a seat on a plane back to New York. He went straight from the airport to the house on Sixty-seventh Street. There he got the kind of welcome Eliza had sent him home for.

"We ought to go away," he said to her the next day. "We ought to get away from the war and everyone and everything and spend some time together."

"I can't go away with you."

"No one would know."

"I'd know. Besides, it's too dangerous."

"It's the only chance we have," he pleaded. "It's the only time we'll ever have." But she was adamant.

He managed to find a small apartment on West End Avenue kept by a fellow officer who rarely got to use it. They spent long hours there, weaving intricate patterns of aimless conversation that stitched them closer and closer together, waiting out the silences that Eliza plunged into when some casual word or action reminded her of what she was doing, and making love again and again in a desperate battle against time.

A week before his leave was over he convinced her to stay the night. Eliza lay awake in the narrow bed in the strange apartment and watched the sky turn from black to gray. Gradually a pink blush spread, and the gold disk of the sun climbed above the city.

"Are you up?" John whispered.

"I didn't think you were."

His arms tightened around her. "I can sleep later. I can sleep for the rest of my life." He pulled her on top of him. "I don't want to waste now."

A week later he left for Newport. They said goodbye in the borrowed apartment. John had never heard the word sound so final.

32

ALL OF DUQUEL turned out to welcome its marine hero son and movie star daughter. "That's not saying much," Lily observed as the train pulled into the station. "All of Duquel, I mean."

Tom didn't answer her. He was too busy looking out the window. He wasn't the patriotic kid he'd been when he'd left this station. He didn't think war was the greatest game since football. He knew that the Japanese could see—and fight. He was more cynical or at least realistic about the brass and the government and his own importance in the world. And he could do without the band blaring and the flags flapping and the mayor standing there with that dumb-looking oversized key in his chubby little hands. But he was damned if he wasn't glad to be back. He wondered now why he'd been so hot to leave.

Hypocrisy, Lily thought. Gustave had taught her the word. It was one of his favorites. She looked at the pattern of faces lifted to the train windows. Mrs. Lund was in a smart blue suit and hat that must have exhausted her clothing rations for the year, or did the irreproachable Mrs. Lund patronize Mr. Black? Her own mother stood beside Mrs. Lund, looking like a sad worn imitation now that her father had a job in a war factory and Lily sent money regularly. Her father, slick and dapper, had edged ahead of the others, his thin face split by a smile revealing long neglected teeth and hubris. Even Fathers Feary and Wade were there. Where had everyone been when she'd left?

Only Iris with her smooth blond pageboy and mouth that was a mirror image of Lily's seemed untainted. Rose had found her own way out by joining the WAC. Iris would get out too. Lily wondered why she'd come back.

The train chugged to a stop. The band went on playing. Two porters were gathering their luggage. A third placed the small wooden platform at the bottom of the stairs. Tom stood and tugged his uniform into place. He held out his hand to Lily. She had no choice but to take it.

Fred Wirtz had taken care of everything. He and the press occupied the two good hotels in town. Lily and Tom were to stay in the Lund house on the bluff. It was, Wirtz's advance scout had reported, a perfect Hollywood version of the quintessential American home, which meant that few Americans could afford to live in it.

The house was a surprise to Lily. The rooms had shrunk. And she'd forgot all those prints of dogs and horses on the walls and that fake spinning wheel in the sun porch. Mrs. Lund said she was so pleased Lily had agreed to stay with them, and this time she wasn't pretending. She showed Lily to a guest room that smelled of soap and furniture polish.

Mrs. Lund said she'd leave Lily alone so she could freshen up before dinner. She started for the door, then turned back. "I'm glad you're home, Lily. I've learned a lot in the last year. I've learned what matters and what doesn't."

Lily looked from Mrs. Lund to the freshly laundered eyelet bedspreads, the magazines on the night table, the vase of golden tulips on the dresser. The room had certainly been prepared for her. She wondered if Mrs. Lund would have learned quite so much if she'd still been Lily Hartarski rather than Lily Hart.

"It's nice of you to have me, Mrs. Lund."

"Call me mother," Mrs. Lund said. "Please."

Overnight the house became a cross between a movie set and a public building. Camera crews, reporters, city officials, old friends, and would-be hangers on came and went. And Mrs. Lund presided over it all. The first morning Lily came down to find her giving an interview to a woman's magazine. "Lily and I were always close," she was saying. Fred Wirtz had nothing on Mrs. Lund.

Joseph Hartarski was in the dining room. From the look of him sitting alone at that gleaming table set with Irish linen placemats he might have been breakfasting off fine china and silver all his life.

"Aren't you going to give your father a kiss?" he asked when he looked up and saw Lily standing in the doorway.

As if on cue a reporter with a camera appeared. Lily kissed her father on the cheek, then went to the sideboard and poured herself a cup of coffee. Her father joined her there and helped himself from a chafing dish of bacon and eggs. Mrs. Lund must have cornered the black market.

"Aren't you having any, Lily?"

"Just coffee."

"Have to keep that million-dollar figure, eh?" He patted her bottom. She twisted away and went to the table. He followed her.

"Shouldn't you be at work?" she asked.

"I quit. The father of Lily Hart shouldn't pack meat, even meat for the armed forces. They'll have to win the war without me."

Lily sipped her coffee. "I send a check to ma every month. It's up to you two how you live."

"That's one of the things I got to talk to you about. I don't want the money going to her. Or these special bank accounts for your sisters' college. I'm the head of the family. I take care of the money."

She looked at him over the rim of her coffee cup and smiled sweetly. "As I remember it, you take care of spending the money."

"You're not too old for the back of my hand."

"Only the back of your hand? I got a lot more than that last time I saw you."

He put down his fork and pushed his plate away as if he had no stomach for it. "Lily," he said, and his eyes misted over. "My little Lily. I was just trying to take care of you. To keep you a good girl."

"By beating me up?"

"A girl gets out of line, she has to be taught a lesson."

"By throwing her out?"

"Throwing you out?" The thin face creased in pain. "I sent you to be with Tom. I even gave you money for the ticket. Seventeen dollars."

"Ma gave me that."

He smiled now, on safer ground. "You think she could have given you that if I didn't want her to? I knew she had the money, and I knew she gave it to you." He tapped his thin chest with his thumb. "I'm the man of the family. I know what we got and where it goes. Look, Lily," he said, and his voice and face changed, quick and elusive as a chameleon. "Maybe I was a little hard on you, but you gotta realize what I was going through. My little girl. My Lily. Remember when you were little and we used to go to the drug store for ice cream? Didn't I always let you have extra?"

"I'm not a little girl looking for ice cream now," she said, but the words were no armor against the memory.

"And the time we went up to Kelly's bluff. Remember that?"

She nodded almost against her will.

"You were always my favorite, Lily. That's why I was so hard on you." He took her hand in his. His fingers reminded her of Gustave's. "It isn't easy when a father finds out his little girl is a woman —and another man wants her. It wasn't easy to let you go. But now you're back."

She wasn't going to cry, damn it. She rubbed her eyes with her free hand. He recognized the gesture, took the hand, and kissed it. "You see, Lily. You're still my little girl, and I'm still your papa. That's the way it always was and always gonna be."

Joseph Hartarski was uneducated but far from stupid. He didn't mention money again that day, and by the time the subject came up a few days later he'd managed to learn the name of Lily's lawyer from Wirtz. "Don't you worry about a thing," he told her. "I'll talk to the man and take care of everything."

Fred Wirtz had got permission for the press to photograph Lily at mass Sunday morning. On Saturday afternoon she was permitted to go to confession alone.

Unlike the rest of the city, the church had not shrunk with time. The gothic arches still rose imposingly above her head. The aroma of candles and incense and age assaulted her. After the warmth of a May afternoon, the musty air felt cold against her skin.

She remembered the last time she'd come here to confess. It had all seemed so simple then. She'd admitted her sin with Tom. Father Wade had given her penance. She'd said her Hail Marys and been cleansed. Only life didn't work that way. But old habits died hard. She didn't want to go to mass without taking communion and she couldn't take communion without going to confession. So here she was, confessing the same sins. It was like stepping back in time.

She thought of all the confessions she'd made over the years. The first awkward fumblings with Tom, the night they'd finally gone all the way, the time after that week in Laguna Beach. At first she'd even confessed the things she'd done with Gustave, but gradually she'd stopped going to church, at least while she was in the throes of an affair.

She gazed up at the statue of the Blessed Virgin that had listened to so many of her youthful prayers. Why did all her confessions revolve around sex? Why had she never confessed her hatred for Alex Zeal or her envy of other actresses or the terrible complicated feelings she had about her parents? Why did she confess only her pleasure? Lily rang the bell for the confessional. Today would be different.

The dusty plush curtain felt familiar in her hand. The screen made the same grating sound as Father Wade lifted it. But she was not the same person.

"Bless me, Father, for I have sinned," she began, and cataloged her lack of generosity toward the people she lived and worked with. But Father Wade knew his business. The sins of the spirit were all very well, but it didn't do to neglect the sins of the flesh in their favor. Years of experience had taught him the questions to ask. Years of habit had trained Lily to answer. In the murky, sick-smelling half darkness of the confessional the trembling joy she found with Tom, the only thing she still shared with Tom, became sin.

In fact, Lily had not sinned with Tom since they'd arrived in Duquel. Though Tom could easily have slipped across the hall from his room to Lily's, he didn't.

Each night Lily lay in the one of the narrow twin beds and listened for Tom's step. She heard Mr. Lund's as he came upstairs from turning out the lights and Mrs. Lund's as she padded down the hall to the girls' rooms, and sometimes Marion's or Eloise's coming in late from a date, but never Tom's. Then on Tuesday night, when the imprint of confession and communion had begun to fade and Lily's loneliness had grown, she crossed the hall to his room.

She opened the door and closed it quietly behind her. In the moonlight filtering through two windows she could see the outline of Tom's body in the single bed. "Lily?"

She crossed the room and got into bed beside him. He sat up and turned on the lamp. She'd crept into bed beside a man. The light revealed the room of a boy. Banners decorated the walls, sports trophies lined the shelves, and pictures of an innocent prewar life stood everywhere.

Tom got out of bed and put on a cotton robe. Like everything else from that earlier life, it didn't quite fit. "We can't, Lily."

"What do you mean we can't?"

"Not here. Not in this house. Not with them down the hall."

"They're asleep. They won't come in here."

"That's not the point."

She was beginning to get the point. "It was okay in your Buick. It was okay in my house. But not here, not on mom's holy ground."

"Your Hollywood standards don't apply here, Lily."

She got out of the bed where he'd spent so many nights dreaming of having her. "And I don't belong here."

"You used to think you belonged with me."

"I used to think a lot of things."

"Can't we give it time, Lily? We spent two years apart. We ought to give being together more than two weeks."

"Sure," she said. "Of course." She owed him that much. After all, he'd risked his life to keep her safe.

She crossed the room and kissed him lightly on the mouth.

"Watch that," he said. "I'm not made of stone." But he was only joking. At that moment he might as well have been.

The next morning Mrs. Lund was waiting for Lily in the sun porch. "Have your coffee in here with me," she said in a voice so sweet it made Lily's teeth ache. "Would you like toast? Or I can have the girl bring you some eggs." Lily said coffee was all she wanted. She knew from the way Mrs. Lund was fussing with the papers on the coffee table in front of her that she had more than breakfast on her mind.

"I have a small problem, Lily. And I need your help. It's about the wedding reception. I know that's up to the bride's family, and your mother's been such a help, but Mr. Wirtz and I decided it ought to be at the country club—he was very pleased with the club when we drove out yesterday afternoon—so, of course, that leaves most of the arrangements to me." She looked down the chintz-covered sofa at Lily. Her smile flooded the room like the spring sunshine. Lily smiled back no less brightly. After all, she was a professional. "Not that I mind. I'm enjoying every minute of it. Or I was until Father Feary called this morning. It seems he insists on saying some sort of blessing at the reception."

"Father Feary likes to bless. Years ago when I was small I remember he blessed the old secondhand Ford my father bought."

This time Mrs. Lund's smile was a little pained. "I'm sure that's very amusing, Lily, but you understand the problem."

Lily understood, but she saw no reason to make things easier for Mrs. Lund. "The problem?"

"Well, dear, it's only been the last few years that Catholics have been allowed in the club at all. Of course, you're a special case entirely."

"Because I'm a movie star?"

"You have to admit you've come a long way."

"Oh, I admit that. If I hadn't, I wouldn't be sitting here with you now."

Frown lines gathered on either side of Mrs. Lund's mouth. "People are prepared to like you, Lily, if you'll just make some effort yourself."

"Like speaking to Father Feary?"

"I'd appreciate that."

"But it seems to me Tom and I are going to need all the blessings we can get."

That was when Tom turned up. Mrs. Lund appealed to him to make Lily see reason. Lily said she was being reasonable. Tom laughed. "Leave me out of it," he said, and held up his hands as if he were surrendering to the enemy. "Weddings are women's business."

Lily went into the hall and called Fred at the hotel. She'd told

Tom she'd give it time, but she didn't have to give it time in Duquel. "I hate to take you away from all your wedding arrangements, Fred, but I want you to get me space on a train to New
York. You've got more material than you need, and I've got to get
out of here."

"Nerves. Everything will be okay when you two kids are married."

"You'd better watch it. You're beginning to believe your own
publicity."

Wirtz knew trouble when he heard it. "Listen, Lily, the studio
has a lot riding on this. *Life*'s going to cover the wedding. Gustave
plans to start shooting the movie in a month, six weeks at the outside. This isn't just some kid romance. This is big business."

"I'll keep that in mind. Now will you get me reservations to
New York? I'll even make a couple of USO appearances while I'm
there, if that'll make you happy."

"That's my Lily. You're worth a hundred of those prima donnas.
Have a good time in New York. The studio says you have to get
married, honey. They don't say you have to act married—as long as
nothing gets in the papers."

Lily got off the phone and thought about the men in her life, the
men who were trying to run her life. Her father wanted her to be a
good girl, and if it took a little roughing up to keep her that way, it
was okay with him. Father Wade didn't want her to make love. Fred
encouraged her to play around. A.Z. and Gustave said she had to
get married and live happily ever after, off screen and on. Tom only
wanted to love her—on his terms and his timetable. And the worst
part of it was that she was beginning to listen to them, again. She
had to get away.

It was still dark when Tom awakened, and it took him a minute to
wrench himself out of the dream and into the world. The smells
brought him home. Instead of the stomach-heaving stench of death
or the overripe aroma of rotting tropical vegetation, his senses recognized the immaculate smell of clean sheets and furniture polish
and cinnamon, the smell of the house he'd grown up in. A breeze
wandered through the open window carrying the scent of open
fields.

It had been one of those confused dreams filled with the wrong people doing the wrong things in the wrong places. He'd been on the atoll, but the atoll had been overrun with Japs and instead of Sharp beside him, poor Sharp whose bits and pieces were still rotting somewhere on Guadal, there was his father screaming the way Sharp had screamed when his face had been sliced off by enemy fire. His mother was on the atoll too, and Lily, only sometimes Lily became the girl with the blue black hair and sometimes the girl with the blue black hair became Lily. But they were all there, and the Japs kept coming back, at night especially, they'd come swarming over the island, and in the dream it was up to Tom to take care of everyone. The dream still lingered in the fresh-smelling darkness. He turned over and switched on the light. The room fell into place. He was home. They said he'd have to go back. He might even have to go back into action. But he'd made it through once, and he'd do it again. Then he'd come home for good.

33

THE ALARM WENT OFF with a horrible jangle. Isabel's hand slammed it into silence. She squinted at the clock. It was only a little after five. She'd got home from the office just before one. She deserved more sleep. She needed more sleep. Then she remembered. She couldn't afford more sleep. Not today. She kicked off the covers and staggered into the early morning gloom. Not today, not yesterday, not last week. She'd been on alert for too long. She'd been waiting for D-Day for so long she was sure it was never coming.

Forty minutes later she growled good morning at Lew Packer. He looked up at her with a face so bleached and wrinkled it looked as if it had been laundered too many times. "You're early," he said.

"Haven't you heard? We're expecting an invasion."

"I'll believe it when I see it," he snarled and went back to his coffee.

Sam Wicker hadn't bothered to go home to sleep. You didn't have to have intelligence clearance to sense that something was up.

He'd hung around the Pentagon all night. Not that he'd had anything to do. That was one of the signs. All the generals who were always on the phone asking his particular general to borrow him for this speech or that article were silent. For the moment the army had forgotten about PR. Sam was sure this was it. He sat at his desk and thought about the thousands and thousands of men hitting the beaches of France. He remembered an army study that had come across his desk a few weeks earlier on a very unmilitary subject. Fear. The army had found that 65 percent of the men wounded admitted to being so filled with fear during combat that they could barely function. Sam had run down the list of symptoms with a sickening fear of his own. Violent pounding of heart. Trembling. Sick stomach. Cold sweat. Feeling faint. Vomiting. Losing control of bowels. Urinating in pants. He tried to imagine how he'd feel if he were on an LST heading for a French beach right now. Would he be praying to a God he hadn't believed in since childhood, crying, checking his equipment, puking his guts out from fear and seasickness? It was a question he asked himself more and more these days and one he was never going to answer.

The squadron waker-upper shined the light first in Spence's face, then Andy's.

"Christ, I never even got to sleep," Spence cursed.

Andy looked at his watch. Twenty-nine minutes past midnight. "Maybe it's D-Day," he joked, because that was what it had become, a joke. Every time they were awakened in the middle of the night for a mission, someone said it was D-Day.

"Breakfast at one, briefing at two," the waker-upper said.

They made their way to chow through faint moonlight muted by a low overcast. RAF planes flew overhead. In the mess there were tables full of majors and colonels and captains. "Looks like the brass had a hard night," Andy said, but there was a tense edge to his voice. There were too many of them to be merely the dregs of poker and bridge parties.

It started to come together in the briefing room. "You are in support of ground troops. . . . Tanks on the beach at 0725 . . . troops at 0730. . . . There will be eleven thousand aircraft in this area. . . . You must stay on briefed course . . . no deviations . . . no abortions."

They synchronized their watches. It was D-Day, all right. Couldn't be anything else.

"Those poor bastards on the beach," Spence said.

Andy zipped his leather jacket. The metal coming together made a tearing sound. "Yeah. From now on it's their show, and we can take it easy."

Michael stood leaning against a wall of the stone courtyard, looking up at the sky that covered Italy like a soft blue blanket. He had to lie down or stand up. It was too painful to sit. He'd been warned about that and had sworn he wasn't going to take the injections in his buttocks, but after the first thirty-six hours his arms had throbbed with pain. It didn't matter where you took the injection. The pain was general. The shame couldn't be localized.

Some guy came running across the courtyard shouting. It was the first time Michael had heard anyone raise his voice since he'd been in the camp. The men generally spoke in terms of quiet dejection, as if they were exchanging some terrible secret. The man who was shouting was rumored to have been a captain. The rumors were meaningless. There were no ranks within this camp. When a man was sent here, he was stripped of standing as well as hope.

As the man who may or may not have been an officer came through the courtyard shouting, others began getting up off their cots, coming out of the tents, and gathering in excited clumps. The words spread from one group to another like a contagious disease. "Invasion!" "D-Day!" "The real thing."

For the rest of his life Michael would remember that camp where he'd spent one week of the war, though he never mentioned it to anyone. And he always remembered one thing about D-Day. Not a single man had joked about how lucky they were to be interned in a camp run, no matter how vindictively, by Uncle Sam instead of with those poor bastards on the beaches of France. But then he'd always remember something else. There hadn't been many jokes at that camp. Even at the front there'd been black jokes, but not at that camp where they were finally, thanks to the miracle of penicillin, safe.

John Whelan heard the noise outside his door in the BOQ. That was odd. Arguments rarely occurred in the morning. He shut out the noise in the hall and went back to composing the letter in his head. He didn't know why he bothered. The letters he'd already sent had disappeared into a dark silence. Eliza had told him it was over. Still, he continued to write. He lay in bed staring at the ugly green ceiling of his room. It was, Eliza had told him during the hours they'd talked endlessly about books and everything else, his chief failing. "The trouble with you, Professor," she'd said, and he could hear her voice as clearly in this ugly military barracks as he had in that borrowed apartment, "is that you put too much faith in the written word."

"You think so?" he'd challenged her.

"Yes, I think so."

He'd pulled her down on the bed then and said that, being the professor, he'd have to teach her a lesson, and they'd laughed until gradually the laughter had turned to sighs.

He went back to composing the letter in his head. The noise in the hall was mounting. This was no isolated argument. The words broke into his consciousness. John was out of bed in seconds. Other doors were being thrown open, radios turned on. Men hung around them, weighing and debunking, cheering and cursing. For the moment all cynicism was suspended. Gradually they began to drift off to their individual jobs, but this morning there were no complaints about the tedium of the work or the stupidity of the men who assigned it. Everyone of them had it easy, and knew it.

Only in the shower did John remember the letter he'd been composing to Eliza. To paraphrase Churchill, who'd paraphrased Talleyrand, this really was the beginning of the end. Her husband would be home soon. And then even the letters would have to stop. He toweled himself vigorously, dressed in the neat uniform quickly, and hurried to the mess. All that time around the radio had made him late. He had so little time.

Lily went straight from the station to the house on Sixty-seventh Street. Eliza was in the dining room with Teddy. The radio, a permanent fixture of the George III tea tray on the sideboard, was on. Isabel's voice, charged with a current of excitement, filled the room. *I repeat communique number one from Supreme Headquarters Allied Expeditionary Forces. "Under the command of General Eisenhower*

allied naval forces supplemented by strong air forces began landing allied
armies this morning on the northern coast of France."

"It's begun," Eliza said.

"It's begun," Lily repeated, and crossed herself inadvertently.

Teddy, who'd been listening in confused and unwilling silence to
Aunt Isabel's voice on the radio, picked up the current between the
two women. "What, Mommy? What?"

"The invasion of Europe," Eliza said, and pulled him onto her
lap.

"Is Daddy there?"

"No, Daddy's not there." She hugged him to her. "Thank
God." She turned to Lily. "I think I have a cousin who is. What
about you?"

Lily thought of the hundreds of thousands of troops she'd entertained. "No one."

Like the rest of America, Eliza and Lily stayed glued to the radio
all that day. There were no commercials or regular programs. Everything gave way to the news from Northern France. Broadcasters
continued to spell each other. Again and again Isabel came back
with news of landings and bridgeheads, official communiques and
discounted reports picked up from Nazi broadcasts. Eisenhower
spoke on a recording. George VI was picked up on the BBC. FDR
asked them to join him in prayer. Occasionally a bulletin came in
from Rome, which American troops had entered the day before.
"That's where Daddy is," Eliza said to Teddy. "I think." But the
real news came from the invasion. Allied paratroopers had landed
on the islands of Jersey and Guernsey. Allied war ships were bom-
barding the coast of Normandy. Allied planes had cleared the skies
over France of German fighters. Allied troops were piling onto the
beaches. The allies were deepening their bridgehead. By evening
Isabel's voice was hoarse, the nation was jubilant, and millions of
women were sick with worry. The news had been coming in all
day. When would the telegrams begin to arrive?

Isabel got home close to midnight. She announced she had time
for a drink, a bath, and an hour's sleep. They agreed not to break
out champagne. It would be tempting fate.

Isabel poured a drink for each of them. "To absent friends," she said.

"To the end of this damn war," Lily added.

And Eliza burst into tears.

34

IN THE DAYS AFTER D-DAY Eliza found herself thinking more and more of the night she'd gone to see *Casablanca* with Isabel and Sam and recognized Michael in the newsreel. It was all very well to remind herself that she and Michael and John were nothing compared to the largest amphibious invasion in history, but the invasion wasn't happening to her. It wasn't even happening to Michael. The rest of this mess was.

"Are you absolutely sure?" Isabel asked. The three women were in the yard of the house on Sixty-seventh Street. There was no Victory Garden this year—the war had gone on for too long, people were too tired for special efforts—but the roses had bloomed and their fragrance hung heavy in the June air. Lily was stretched out on a chaise longue. The sun filtering through the sycamore tree dappled her dress into a camouflage pattern. Eliza and Isabel sat in chairs opposite. Isabel looked tired, Eliza haggard. Blue-black shadows, soft as crayon smudges, lay beneath her eyes. As she talked, she kept a wary lookout on Teddy, who was waging an armored battle on the flagstone patio.

"I've been sure for a month," she said. "As of this afternoon the doctor's sure too. So much for my diaphragm. When I think how much I wanted another baby before Michael left . . ." She let her voice drift off.

"Have you told John?" Lily asked.

"This has nothing to do with John."

"It's his child too," Isabel said.

Eliza thought of the picture of Lucy that John had kept on the table beside his hospital bed. He'd look on another child as a gift, but it was one she couldn't afford to give him. "I haven't told him, and I'm not going to. No one's going to know except the three of us."

"What are you going to do?" Lily asked.

"I wish I knew."

"Do you want me to find you a doctor?" Isabel asked. "I know a reporter who's had three abortions."

"I know an actress who says she's had six."

"I'm not a reporter or an actress. I'm a wife and mother. And I want another baby. Michael and I were trying to have one when he enlisted."

"This isn't Michael's child," Isabel said quietly.

"It doesn't matter. I still couldn't get rid of it." She glanced at Teddy. "Any more than I could give up Teddy."

"Then you're going to have to divorce Michael and marry John," Lily said.

"I don't want to divorce Michael. I love Michael." She looked from one woman to the other. "Don't say it. I've been saying it to myself for months. If I love Michael so much, what was I doing with John?"

"I wasn't thinking that," Lily said.

"Neither of us was," Isabel added. "I know you love Michael. And that doesn't stop you from needing John, maybe even loving John too. Anyway, stop wasting time on self-flagellation. You did what you did, and neither of us blames you. The question is what are you going to do now."

"Tell Michael, I guess."

"In other words, you won't divorce him, you want him to divorce you."

"Maybe he'll understand."

Isabel stood and paced the length of the garden and back. "Look, Eliza, I never met Michael. All I know is what I've heard from you. He doesn't sound like the kind of man who would forgive something like this. If you're lucky he'll leave you. Otherwise he'll make your life a living hell. And the baby's. Michael may have wanted another child of his own before he went overseas, but what kind of father do you think he's going to be to a bastard?" She saw Eliza flinch at the word. "And that's the way he's bound to think of this baby."

"That's a chance I'll have to take."

"It's not a chance. It's a certainty."

"Tell John," Lily said. "He's your only hope."

"But I don't love John. At least not the way I love Michael. I love Michael more than anyone or anything." She glanced across the garden again. "Except Teddy."

"Then you can't have this baby."

"Isabel's right," Lily said. "You have to choose between Michael and the baby."

They went on that way, around and around in a desperate cyclical argument. At one point Eliza left to bathe Teddy. When she returned, the blue haze of dusk hung over the garden. They resumed the conversation. As the night air grew cool, they moved inside. The discussion continued. By 1 A.M. they were all exhausted. The smudges beneath Eliza's eyes had darkened. Her cheeks were raw from being rubbed dry with a handkerchief. She was going to have an abortion.

They agreed it was the only thing to do. Eliza said it was immoral. Lily secretly agreed. Isabel believed in it in principle but kept thinking about Teddy. She said she'd take care of all the arrangements. It was clear that Eliza couldn't.

None of them slept much that night. At one point Lily heard Eliza go into Teddy's room. She followed her. "Do you want company?" she whispered. Eliza just shook her head.

Four days later the three women took a taxi to 106th Street. Eliza's skin looked like a corpse's.

The doctor's office was on the ground floor of a small apartment house. The building had an air of having seen better days. The doctor's office reminded Eliza of the waiting room of her old family doctor in Brooklyn. She remembered the day her mother had taken her there for all those psychosomatic complaints. She wished she'd listened to that doctor. She wished she'd never gone to the specialist in New York. If she'd stayed home with her parents, if she'd never got a job or moved in with Isabel, she wouldn't be here now.

A nurse in a white uniform came into the waiting room. She looked soft as a pillow. Her voice was reassuring. Isabel had said the doctor was in this on principle rather than for the money. The nurse told Isabel and Lily they could wait there, then led Eliza into a small examining room. It looked no different from her gynecologist's. The nurse gave her a gown, told her to undress, went through the familiar instructions. It reminded Eliza of dozens of doctor's visits. Only it wasn't like any of them.

The nurse left her alone. She took off her clothes and put on the white gown. The rough material scratched her skin. The irritation was minor. She almost longed for the physical pain that would drown the guilt.

She climbed on the table and sat with her legs hanging over the side. The office was silent. She wondered where the doctor was. Did he perform many of these a day? If he was with another patient, where were the screams of pain, the sobs of guilt?

The minutes dragged by. Still, no one came. The room was cool, but she was perspiring heavily. She remembered all the times she'd sat this way waiting for the doctor when she was pregnant with Teddy. She hadn't minded the time then. She'd played games with herself. Guessing games. Was it a boy or a girl? Planning games. Theodore for a boy after Michael's paternal grandfather Tevya. Nina for a girl just because she liked the name. Hope games. The child would be beautiful and brilliant with a sunny disposition. And she hadn't been disappointed. She had a handsome little boy who was quick and bright and happy. She'd been lucky. So lucky that the first year of Teddy's life she'd been terrified that something would happen to him. Fate couldn't be this good to her. She didn't deserve it. So, she'd kept a constant and careful vigil. She'd sterilized bottles and made her own baby food and called the doctor for every cough and sniffle. And still she'd lain awake at night imagining all the terrible things that might happen to this wonderful gift that had been given her.

The office was no longer silent. Someone was crying. Loud painful sobs wracked the air. It took her a minute to realize they were coming from her. She slid off the table and began pulling on her clothes. She caught a foot in her girdle and almost fell. Her hands were trembling so badly she couldn't button her dress.

She pushed her way into the waiting room. "I can't do it." She squeezed out the words between sobs. "I just can't."

Neither Isabel nor Lily argued with her.

35

EVERYONE KNEW the war was as good as over. Everyone except the men slogging it out up Italy and across France and throughout the Pacific. Paris was liberated, DeGaulle marched down the Champs Elysées, and in Rockefeller Center in New York, Lily Pons stood in a USO uniform and sang "La Marseillaise." Rationing was removed. Beaches and summer resorts were mobbed. Women bared their backs and shoulders and arms as never before. Someone was always liberating a bottle to celebrate the liberation of Europe. The nation was awash in optimism.

Lily's future looked less bright. She'd stayed in New York a week after that night in the garden. Tom hadn't come after her. On her way back to California she stopped in Duquel. She had only a few hours. She and Tom went for a ride in his old Buick convertible and parked on the bluff overlooking the river. He turned to her. She still wasn't sure what she was going to do.

"You want to stay here, don't you, Tom? You feel as if you belong here."

"You used to."

"No. I never did. Even if the war hadn't come and neither of us had gone away, it wouldn't have worked." She saw the relief flicker across his face. "Your mother would have seen to that. Boys like you date girls like me, Tom, they sleep with girls like me, but they don't marry girls like me. At least not in towns like this."

"Do you really hate it?"

"As much as you love it. Except for you, it wasn't very good to me."

"I can't believe we're splitting up over a town."

"It's a lot more than that, and you know it."

They were silent for a moment. She knew now that he'd expected it, perhaps even wanted it, but he still had to get used to it.

"What will you do now?" he asked.

"What I've been doing all along. Go back to work. What about you? Your leave's almost up."

"Funny how hot I was to get away last time."

"Will they send you back to the Pacific?"

He shrugged.

"That means yes. Take care of yourself, Tom. Take care of yourself and come home and marry some nice girl and live happily ever after in a house on the bluff."

"I'll never love her the way I loved you."

She noticed that he used the past tense. She touched his cheek. He was beginning to fill out into the contours of the old Tom. "No, I don't think you will. And I'll never love anyone the way I loved you. And neither of us will ever be so young and so beautifully innocent again."

"The war saw to that."

"If the war hadn't, life would have. War's just faster and more cruel."

Lily had told Tom that she'd go back to work, but Alec Zeal had other plans for her. Fred Wirtz had pleaded with her. Gustave Dressler had cajoled her. Now Zeal was going to threaten her.

She'd been summoned to his office for a ten o'clock meeting. She arrived at ten-thirty. He kept her waiting till eleven. Fred and Gustave were already in the office when she was shown in. They were sitting at opposite ends of a sofa under a Renoir painting that Gustave had been trying to buy from Zeal for years. A.Z. stood, a small plump man behind a vast sleek desk, and held out his arms to Lily as if she were a long lost child.

"Lily. My own little Lily." She was, in fact, several inches taller than he. "You look beautiful this morning, Lily. Like a bride."

"But I'm not a bride, and I'm not going to be one in the near future."

Zeal jerked his head toward Dressler and Wirtz. "So the boys told me." Only in Hollywood, Lily thought, would two men whose combined ages came close to a century and whose annual incomes added up to almost half a million, be called boys. "A lovers' quarrel?"

"This isn't one of your movies, A.Z."

"My movies have been pretty good to you, Lily."

"And I've been pretty good to them. I've made you a lot of money."

"I haven't exactly sent you to the poorhouse."

"Fine, I'm glad we appreciate each other."

"Appreciate, yes, but we don't understand each other so good. I want you to get married, Lily. America wants you to get married."

"Can we leave America out of this?"

He shook a fat finger at her. "A star who forgets her fans isn't a star for long."

"I haven't forgotten my fans. I'm back and ready to work. I've been sitting around my pool all week waiting for a script."

He looked at the two men. "She's waiting for a script." He turned back to Lily. "Freddy got you a couple of million dollars' worth of free publicity. Gus has a movie up his sleeve's gonna win us a bunch of Academy Awards. And you turn it all into *dreck*. You know what *dreck* is? Translate for her, Freddy. Freddy's a *goy* like you, but he learned Yiddish to survive out here. Tell her what it means, Freddy."

"Shit," Wirtz said quietly.

"That's right. You turn it all into shit because you won't marry that guy. A hero. A genuine A-number-one hero, and you won't marry him."

"Can we leave Tom's heroism out of this, too, A.Z.? There are some things even you ought to respect."

Zeal splayed both hands on his desk and leaned toward her like a battering ram. "I seen broads like you before, Lily. You get ideas."

He pronounced the word as if it were smut. "Start to think you're Lynn Fontanne or Helen Hayes. Well, let me tell you what you are. Tits, ass, a pair of legs, a face. You're a piece every man wants to get his hands on, a picture little boys jack off over. That's what you are."

"I never knew you had such a way with words, A.Z."

He slammed his fist down on the table. "Don't get fancy with me. I've been buying and selling tramps like you all my life."

There it was again, that word. The minute she did something some man didn't like, she was a tramp.

"You'll marry that kid or you'll be on the street peddling your ass before you know it."

"I have a contract."

"You never heard of suspension?"

"For refusing to marry someone?"

"I got a bunch of smart-assed lawyers. Harvard and Yale men. They'll find me a reason. By the time you can work again, nobody'll remember who Lily Hart was."

She turned to the two men on the sofa. One had been her lover, the other the closest thing she had to a friend in this business. "You agree with him?"

Gustave smiled. "I can make them fall in love with you, Lily, but I can't make them like you."

"The public isn't going to plunk down its quarters to see a girl who jilted a war hero," Fred said. "Marry him, honey. Just for a year or two."

"Thanks for the vote of confidence." She turned back to A.Z. "And thank you for the vacation. I need a rest."

"You'll never work in this town again!" he shouted after her. She would have laughed at the old chestnut, if she hadn't been so frightened.

36

LILY RETURNED TO NEW YORK. There was nothing for her to do in California. There wasn't much she could do in New York either, except sit in the house on Sixty-seventh Street trying to find a way out for Eliza.

"Face it," Eliza said one night at dinner, "there's no hope. I'll write Michael, tell him the truth, and let him take it from there."

"That's right," Isabel said. "Let Michael take over. Put it all in his lap. It'll be just like old times."

"There's no need to get bitchy," Lily said.

Isabel put down her fork and rubbed her forehead with her thumb and forefinger. "You're right. I'm sorry. But the whole thing is so damn frustrating." She turned to Eliza. "You won't do anything. You just sit here waiting for some act of God to make everything all right."

"I'm not waiting for an act of God to make everything all right," Eliza said. "I'm waiting for a baby. I know you're impatient, Isabel, but this is one thing you can't rush."

"Are you sure you won't consider adoption?" Lily said.

"We've been through this. Can't either of you understand? I want this baby. I've wanted it for a long time."

"You've wanted a baby for a long time," Isabel pointed out. "Not necessarily this baby."

"You don't pick and choose. It's my child, and I'm going to have it."

"I'm not saying you shouldn't have it," Lily said. "I just think you ought to consider adoption. You could go off and have it quietly, then give it up for adoption. I almost wish I'd married Tom. Then I could adopt it."

"I keep telling you. I want to have the baby and keep it."

Isabel put down her fork and stared at the other two women. "That's it!"

"What's it?" Lily asked.

"Why didn't we think of it before?"

"Think of what?" Eliza insisted.

"You'll adopt the baby. You and Michael."

"What are you talking about?"

"I'm talking about taking Lily's plan one step further. You go off somewhere and have the baby quietly. Then you write Michael and tell him about this marvelous child you want to adopt."

"You're out of your mind. Why would I want to adopt a child? Especially since everyone says the war's going to be over soon and he'll be coming home. He'd never believe it."

Isabel sipped her wine and sat thinking for a minute. "You want to adopt this baby precisely because of the war. Because this baby is a war orphan, and you want to save it. At least that's what you'll tell Michael."

"Make sense, Isabel. Where would I find a war orphan?"

"She has a point," Lily said. "I don't think Michael will buy it for a minute."

"Do you two have a better suggestion?" Isabel looked from one to the other. "All right, I'll tell you where you'll find a war orphan. Through me. The baby's due in December right? Gardner promised me I could go overseas after the invasion. I'll go in December when I will just happen to fall head over heels in love with a helpless baby orphaned by the war. Now everyone knows I can't adopt the baby. I'm not married, and I wouldn't make much of a mother if I were."

"Too busy tracking down the news," Lily agreed.

"And Lily can't adopt it because she's not married either. And she's always on the road too. So naturally I turn to you. You and Michael. I dare him to turn down a plea like that. Especially when we send pictures of the baby. And don't worry about the adoption papers. I know a lawyer who'll take care of everything, including an Italian birth certificate. For a fee, of course."

"I still think it sounds fishy. Michael will suspect something. No, he won't suspect, he'll know. Besides, people are bound to find out."

"Not if you go away. We've got a house in Maine no one's used since before the war."

"What about Teddy?"

"You'll take him with you. If you watch your girlish figure and wear loose clothes, he'll never notice. A little while before the baby's due one of us will bring him back here."

"And why am I going to Maine?"

"Do you have to have a reason?"

"Don't you think it looks a little funny if I don't?"

They were silent for a while.

"You see," Eliza said, "I told you it was impossible."

"It's not impossible," Lily insisted. "We've just got one more wrinkle to iron out."

"You're going to write a book," Isabel said.

"What!"

"A book, Eliza. You know, a cover, pages inside, the written word. Sam's always said you should. Books by servicemen's wives are big these days. There's that one on how to get along after your husband ships out and another by that woman who followed her husband from base to base and even that collection of letters between a marine and his wife. Sam said you ought to write about your experiences after Michael left. From housefrau to high-powered account executive. He said he could make a bestseller of it."

"He was kidding."

"Sam doesn't kid about things like that. Anyway, there's your excuse."

"I still don't think it will work."

"Maybe not," Isabel said. "But you've got nothing to lose by trying, and everything to lose if you don't."

Of course, it wasn't quite as easy as it sounded. There were a dozen hitches. Every night Eliza thought of another. "Are you up?" she asked from the doorway of Isabel's room one midnight.

"I am now."

"I'm sorry, but I just thought of it. What if the war's over before I have the baby? What if Michael comes home when I'm nine months pregnant?"

Isabel sat up in bed and turned on the light. "Listen, Eliza. I spend half my life listening to politicians and generals and anyone who has inside information on the war. Not one of them thinks it's going to be over that soon. And even if it is, it will take months and months to bring the men home."

"But what if they're wrong? And what if Michael is the first to be shipped home? God, I never thought I'd be hoping Michael wouldn't get back soon."

"You can stop worrying, because he's not going to."

"But what if he does?" Eliza insisted.

"We'll worry about that when and if it happens."

The next night Eliza woke Lily. "He'll never believe it. You'd have to be an idiot to believe a story like this, and Michael's no idiot."

"But Michael trusts you."

"Michael used to trust me. He used to have reason to trust me."

"He'll believe you."

"Lily, if you were a man away for a couple of years and your wife suddenly wrote that she wanted to adopt a baby, would you believe her?"

Lily was silent for a moment. "You're going to have to make him believe you."

Eliza met Isabel in the front hall that evening. "Teddy's bound to notice," she said before Isabel had even put down her briefcase. "He's too old not to notice."

Isabel took off her hat, ran her fingers through her hair, and sighed. It was almost ten o'clock. She wanted dinner and a drink and felt guilty that she could have both because the news from

St.-Lo was grim and she couldn't help thinking of all those boys who couldn't have either.

"We've been through this, Eliza. You're going to have to be careful not to gain too much weight, but that shouldn't be hard considering how you're always fighting not to lose it. When you begin to show, you can complain about getting fat and pretend to go on a diet. Like your mother. Even Teddy knows your mother's always worrying about her weight."

"What if the baby looks like me?" Eliza asked the next morning at breakfast.

Isabel put down the *Times.* "Eliza, who does Teddy look like?"

"Michael." She remembered that night John had come for dinner. He'd insisted Teddy looked like her, but everyone in the family knew he took after Michael.

Isabel turned to Lily. "Who do you think Teddy looks like?"

"Well, he's got Eliza's nose."

"And what about you, Lily? Do you look like your mother or your father?"

"Neither."

"Exactly. Depending on which side of the family you're talking to—the Childs or the Spencers—I'm the spitting image of my paternal grandmother or my great Aunt Abigail. And this baby isn't going to be any different. It's going to look like itself."

"I still say the whole idea is crazy," Eliza said.

"That's right," Isabel said. "It's crazy, but it's your only chance."

"Michael will never go for it," Eliza repeated for perhaps the hundredth time, and in fact she was right. Under normal circumstances Michael would have seen through the story in a minute.

Lily went to Maine with Eliza and Teddy. Isabel had called ahead to have a woman from town come out to get the cottage ready for them. It was simple, almost ostentatiously rustic, but comfortable enough. They settled into a routine. The war had taught the two women how to wait.

Their connections with the rest of the world were tenuous. Teddy went to the local school. Once a week they went into town to buy groceries. Each day they listened to Isabel's voice broadcasting the news. Fred Wirtz telephoned occasionally. Eliza wrote to

Michael nightly. Mail from him was still erratic, and not only because of the Army Post Office. According to the dates on his letters, ten days had passed without his writing at all. When the letters resumed, Michael said that the fighting had bogged down again in heavy rain and flooding. He sounded as if his spirits had bogged down too. He wrote that it had been twenty-three months since he'd seen her face, twenty-two since he'd heard her voice. *And the worst part is that it doesn't get any easier. I'll never again believe that line about time healing all wounds. It hasn't healed the wound they left when they tore you out of my life.* The night she got that letter she lay in bed with the sheets of tissue-thin victory mail propped up on the sleeping mound of her stomach and read it over and over until the tears blurred her vision.

The next afternoon she was at her desk working when she heard the sound of the engine. She reached the window just in time to see John climbing out of the car. His dark blue uniform was a blot of ink against the snow. As he glanced up at the house, she stepped back from the window, but before she did she caught a glimpse of his eyes. Behind the wire-rimmed glasses they were the same bleak gray-blue as the winter sky.

Hanging back from the window, Eliza stood watching as Teddy came bounding across the yard and tackled John. They went down together in the snow and wrestled wildly. When they stood, John pounded Teddy on the back and called him "old man." Then they disappeared under the porch roof into the house.

Eliza was still standing at the window when she heard Lily's footsteps behind her. "Tell him I'm not here."

"He'll know I'm lying. He saw Teddy."

"I can't see him. Not like this." Her hand moved to her stomach.

Lily stood in the doorway for a moment. "You should see his eyes."

"I saw his eyes!" Eliza's voice snapped like a dry, thin branch under the weight of snow.

"But—"

Eliza whirled to face her. "Don't you think I want to see him! I'm dying to. But I can't afford to. So go tell him I'm not here, or I don't want to see him, or I never gave a damn about him in the first place. I don't care how you lie to him, as long as you get him out of here."

Lily went back down the stairs. A few minutes later Eliza heard the front door of the cottage open and close. She stood to one side of the window again peering out at the yard. Teddy walked beside John, his short legs crossing like a fast little scissors to keep up with the longer dark blue ones. John's hand rested on Teddy's shoulder, the slender fingers pale against the red snowsuit. God, how well she remembered those hands! He turned and looked back at the house, lifting his hand to shade his eyes. It could have been a salute or a farewell gesture or just the motion of a man who'd been temporarily blinded by the sun.

He turned back to Teddy and held out his hand. Teddy shook it solemnly. Then John bent and scooped the boy up in his arms, and for a moment Teddy forgot his age and clung to John as he used to cling to his father before Michael had gone away.

John pried Teddy's arms from his neck and got into the car. He turned it carefully and started back down the driveway. Teddy stood looking after him, a crimson stain against the snow.

The last few weeks of waiting were the worst. The closer they got to the baby's arrival, the more impossible the plan seemed. Eliza had been so happy when she'd been pregnant with Teddy. Now everything was hopeless.

The nation had sunk into the same mood. Though no one knew that the gassings at Auschwitz had stopped, everyone was beginning to realize that the war was still going on. The Germans launched a massive attack along a forty-mile front in the Ardennes forest. Eventually someone would call it the Battle of the Bulge. V-bombs continued to fall on London. Japan took advantage of constant westerly winds and began launching incendiary balloons. A few reached the continental United States and killed six Americans. War factories and military units were short of manpower. Cigarettes disappeared from the shelves again. Rationing was reinstated. On the third anniversary of Pearl Harbor, Nina entered a bleak, war-exhausted world.

Isabel left for Italy a week later. She'd had no trouble convincing Gardner to let her go. "The entire press corps is in France, except those who're in Germany," she'd argued. "Those poor men in Italy are actually getting letters from home telling them how lucky they are to be in a safe place. But they've been through two bitter winters, and they're still dying. It's the Forgotten Front, and I want to go to it." Gardner agreed immediately. "After that I'll swing up to France," Isabel added on her way out of his office.

Spence was in France. Andy was too, though of course the news had come from Spence. Both had completed their tours of duty and were eligible to be rotated home. Both had signed up for a second tour of duty, which was unusual but not unheard of, and switched from flying bombers to fighters, which only a handful of men had managed to do. *It's a hundred times better,* Spence wrote. *I told you once I wanted to prove something. I guess I have.* They were stationed somewhere in France, living in pitched tents in the snow and ice of one of the worst winters in recent history. Life on the permanent base in England looked luxurious in retrospect.

"So you're going to France to see the glory boy," Sam said the night before she was due to leave. He was living in Washington these days but had come up to say goodbye.

"How did you know he was in France?"

Sam laughed. "Because you're not going to England. And when your brother switched, I figured he was following in our hero's footsteps."

"You don't have to be sarcastic."

"Hell, I'm not sarcastic, I'm jealous. He's got a chestful of medals. And he's got my girl."

"I'm not your girl. I'm not his girl. I'm not anyone's girl."

"You give a good imitation. I'm just wondering what's going to happen after the war. He's going to have to stop being a hero someday."

"For a man who doesn't believe in heroism you spend an awful lot of time talking about it."

"That's because I had the misfortune to fall in love with a woman who spends so much time thinking about it."

"You're not in love with me."

"What do you call it?"

"Wanting something you can't have. I'm just the first girl who didn't fall over backwards when you snapped your fingers."

"Like you and the flyboy?"

"Why do you keep bringing him up?"

"Isabel," he said, and stroked her hair, "I don't have to bring him up. The bastard's between us all the time."

Isabel spent her first forty-eight hours in Italy at a field hospital. It was no more than a series of tents, marked by huge red crosses on the top and filled with suffering young old men and exhausted doctors and nurses. Gardner was delighted with her interviews, especially the one with the kid from Brooklyn. Everybody at the hospital had loved the kid from Brooklyn, but his popularity hadn't helped him. He'd died thirty-six hours after Isabel had talked to him. Gangrene, the scourge, one of the scourges of the Italian campaign, had set into his wounded leg. "The sulfa does wonders in that department," a doctor told her, "if they take it right away, but they don't always have it in their packs. Sometimes the boys have already used it up."

"For what?"

"Gonorrhea. They're more afraid of that than gangrene."

Isabel left the field hospital and headed toward Bologne. Thanks to her own military connections and the help of General Buzz Skeffington, she had no trouble tracking down Michael. He was in a town, or rather the ruins of a town called Livergnano, or, as the boys who were there called it, Liver-and-Onions.

She arrived early one morning. The snow was deep and the wind bitter. A frozen waterfall cascaded into a faint trickle of ice water. A group of men were collecting it in their helmets for a frigid bath. Her guide pointed out Private Kramer. Isabel wouldn't have recognized him from the picture on Eliza's night table. In place of the smooth symmetrical face punctuated by a carefully trimmed mustache were features honed to a razor's edge and camouflaged by a scruffy growth of beard. Despite the cold, he'd stripped to the waist to bathe. Every rib showed. Isabel felt a wave of pity, followed by disgust for herself and Eliza and the job at hand.

Even before she told him who she was, he didn't look at her the way she'd become accustomed to being looked at over here. There was no sexual interest in his eyes. She felt worse than ever. She introduced herself. His grin was like an opening door.

They went into a tent and she gave him the pictures of Eliza and Teddy, the packages of food and clothing and soap, and the letter that, he said, still smelled of Eliza's perfume. He put the envelope in his pocket. Isabel could tell from the way he buttoned the flap that he was going to put off reading it. The anticipation had to be savored.

They talked for hours. He had a hundred questions. She was in no hurry to get to the one she'd come about. She was beginning to think Eliza was right. He'd never buy it.

"I spoke to Eliza two days ago. From Rome." Isabel saw the look of hunger that tore at his face. She felt as if she were describing a banquet to a starving man.

"I haven't heard her voice in two years. Instead of dreaming up new weapons, someone ought to come up with a Victrola and record you can carry in your wallet, like a picture. It's hell—" He stopped abruptly. He didn't want to admit that he could no longer remember what Eliza's voice sounded like.

"I called her because I had a favor to ask." Isabel hesitated. They'd been crazy to think this would work. "She said to ask you." Isabel dropped her eyes. She couldn't bear to look into his. They were so hungry. "You were in Rome a few months ago on R & R, weren't you?" Suddenly his eyes turned wary, the way they'd been when she'd first approached him that morning.

Michael sat staring at the woman who had become his wife's best friend and tried to keep his face impassive. He'd been in Rome, all right, for R & R and its aftermath. But she couldn't possibly know about that. The army said it kept those records confidential. But she was a reporter, and reporters had a habit of snooping around in confidential matters. He wondered if she'd told Eliza. He couldn't remember her voice, but he could imagine the look of revulsion on her face. He thought of that goddamn chaplain who'd told him it was God's punishment for his sins. "You can never go near a nice girl again, my son." Michael fought to bring his mind back from the camp and concentrate on what this woman was saying. Something about a kid found in the ruins of a bombed building.

"It was a miracle she survived. She was only a couple of weeks old. Some soldiers found her and took her back to Rome. I ran across her in the hospital there. It was love at first sight." Isabel took out the photograph. Why hadn't she seen the resemblance to Eliza before. She handed it to Michael. "You know what it's like for kids over here these days. Begging food and gum and cigarettes from GIs. Sleeping in streets like bedraggled kittens. Selling their bodies once they're old enough." Michael winced. "The idea of leaving her to that breaks my heart. I wanted to adopt her, but the nuns won't give her to a single woman. That's when I thought of Eliza and you. She's crazy about the idea, but she said she wasn't sure how you'd feel."

How he'd feel! He hadn't felt this good since he'd reported to the dispensary that morning in Rome and been handed the pink slip. Wasserman—Pos. Kahn—Pos. Not me, he'd wanted to say. Not Private Michael Kramer. Not the man the boys had kidded and called Pops all through training because he was so much older and because on Saturday nights when they went into town to pick up amateurs or wait in line for the pros at the whorehouses, he'd stayed on the base and gone to the movies or read or sat around drinking 3.2 beer and writing to Eliza. They'd kidded him because they were kids. What did they know of marriage and loyalty and trust? At night they'd lie on their cots bragging about "pieces of ass" and "tail" and "getting laid," and Michael had felt sorry for them, and more than a little superior. But battle is a great equalizer, and he'd lost his sense of superiority somewhere in the mud of Italy. By the time they'd clawed their way up the Italian boot, he was just another GI drowning in misery and fear, desperate for a little comfort or a moment's pleasure. But still he'd kept some remnants of his former self, some shred of fastidiousness. Not for him the rough impersonal comaraderie of the whorehouses, the tawdry twenty minutes of paid-for pleasure. He'd found a girl with a shy half smile who wore a cross between her breasts and liked to cook him the eggs and meat he managed to procure from government supplies. She was a nice girl who'd found herself in decidedly unnice times. And a few weeks later Michael had found himself standing in the dispensary staring with disbelieving eyes at that pink slip. He'd taken the first step on the assembly line of shame. Next came the doctor. In civilian life they would have been equals, the physician and the attorney addressing each other with respect. Now Michael was nothing more than a number and a disgraceful disease. "You're one of the smart guys, eh?" the doctor snarled. "Think it can't happen to you. Take down your pants."

And it had gone on from there. The corporal who'd typed his orders had lectured him from the vantage point of superior wisdom and sheer luck. "I find a babe and stick to her," he said. "A nice girl. Not one of them tramps that'll do it for anyone. That way I figure I'm safe." Michael hadn't answered.

And the doctor at the camp. "We're going to make your life a living hell. Because you men have got to learn to be careful."

That was when Michael had finally brought himself to speak. "Can I be cured, sir?"

The doctor had shrugged. "It's a new treatment. We don't know an awful lot about it. Penicillin. You'll get an injection every three hours. By the time we're finished a POW camp is going to look good to you."

And then there was the final indignity, worse than being herded into the long hall every three hours, worse than the sadistic orderlies wielding their cruel needles, worse than his stinging sore flesh. They'd taken away his uniform and personal possessions and issued fatigues. On the back, two huge black letters spelled out his dishonor. V.D.

At the end of a week he turned in the fatigues and slipped into the camouflage of his uniform. Another doctor, one with more faith, said he was cured. "For the time being. We don't know about the long-range effects yet."

"What about my wife?" Michael had asked. "What about children?"

The doctor shrugged, the uncaring gesture of a safe, superior man. Michael remembered it from civilian life, his own days of untouchable power. "We'll know more in a few years."

He didn't have a few years. Or at least he hadn't thought so until this woman had dropped into camp like a barrage of propaganda pamphlets bringing good news from the right side. They could have another child. And a new baby would mean precautions against other new babies. This time he'd take the responsibility. A new baby would give him an excuse to protect Eliza. Michael felt like a man reprieved.

He took the picture Isabel was holding out to him. The baby looked like all babies, a wizened old man, but she was suddenly beautiful to him. "I think it's a terrific idea," he said, and Isabel noticed that his eyes were dangerously damp. "Eliza always wanted a daughter." He looked at the picture again. "She's even got Eliza's hair. I've got a running start on all those guys who're always talking about the population explosion they're going to set off after this war is over. And some poor Italian kid gets a break." He rubbed his eyes with his thumb and forefinger as if he was tired. "It's about time someone got a break in this goddamn war."

Isabel heard gunfire in the near distance, but for the moment she wasn't afraid. Everything had turned out all right. Michael wasn't even suspicious.

37

ISABEL HAD WRITTEN Spence that she'd be in Paris by New Year's. That didn't mean, she warned herself, that Andy would find a way to get there. For one thing, the military reasoned, accurately for once, that liberated Paris was the single city every fighting man was fighting to get to. Therefore, it was declared off-limits to most of them. For another, her luck couldn't hold. He'd been waiting for her in England. He wouldn't turn up again in Paris. A year was a long time, even for steadier men than Andy Barnes.

Isabel's predictions turned out to be correct. Andy wasn't in Paris. And Paris wasn't Paris. Thanks to fuel shortages, the city of light was dark and bitterly cold. There was no electricity until 5 P.M. each evening. During the occupation the Parisians, Isabel reported in her first broadcast to the States, had lost an average of forty pounds. The tuberculosis rate had risen 20 percent. Everything was in short supply, or lacking entirely, including soap, which resulted in a rash of skin problems. The most beautiful city in the world and its most fashionable inhabitants hadn't fallen on lean times; they'd grown accustomed to them. Fresh fruit and vegetables were nonexistent. Eggs sold for twenty-four dollars a dozen, butter eight dollars a pound. Milk was scarce and fine French wines had disappeared with the retreating Germans. The other side of the smiling GI handing out gum and candy to hungry French kids was the smiling GI selling American cigarettes for five dollars a pack on the black market. That particular broadcast got her in trouble with Gardner. He said the mothers of America didn't want to hear that their sons who were dying on French soil were also getting rich on French suffering.

Isabel managed to get a room at the Hotel Scribe. Under the occupation the venerable nineteenth century hotel had served as the German press center. After the liberation it was assigned to American journalists. The lobby was cluttered with the helmets and bedrolls and ubiquitous typewriters of news men and women in transit. The basement bar overflowed with the men and women themselves and newly liberated champagne. The first few nights Isabel had to share a room with a woman from a Newhouse paper, the next several with one from a wire service. Perhaps it was just as well Andy hadn't turned up.

She made no effort to track him down. If she'd crossed the Atlantic, he could find his way down from northern France. Besides, she was in Paris to work. She couldn't get accredited to the front, but she did manage admission to a confidential Army briefing. It was strictly a public relations affair intended to woo the press rather than inform it, the kind of operation Sam would have dreamed up.

The briefing was held in a large bare room in one of the headquarters buildings. A guard at the door checked Isabel's credentials. Confidentiality lent a whiff of melodrama. The collapsible chairs were already half filled with her colleagues who'd also picked up the scent. On a platform at one end of the room several maps were covered with cloths. She remembered a story Andy had told her about preflight briefings. When the flyers filed into the room, the maps were always covered, but the men learned to tell how long the mission was by the spool of yarn hanging from the side of the map that was used to trace the course. If the spool was almost full, it would be a milk run; if it was pulled all the way out, that meant Berlin or Posen or Munich. Then she reminded herself she'd decided to stop thinking of Andy.

A PR officer with a smooth, creamy manner indigenous to the

breed, including Sam, stood and reminded them that this was a "guarded room" and everything that would be said in it was Confidential, which was one step below Secret. He added there would be no note-taking. Then he introduced a two-star general, who told a tired joke about strategy—clearly this general didn't have Sam writing his speeches—and launched into an explanation of what was going on in the Ardennes. Next came the color. The PR officer produced a wounded second lieutenant and two wounded privates who would tell the press what it had really been like at the front, as if anyone could tell such a thing. The PR officer returned and said the air force wanted to bring them up to date on their part in the show. The door through which the two-star general and the first lieutenant and two privates had entered opened again, and Captain Andy Barnes came strolling in as if he wished he were somewhere else. His uniform was a little too rumpled for regulation and threadbare at the elbows. His face still had that lean sharpness honed by too many hours in the air and too much waiting on the ground. He paced to the podium like a wild cat trapped and caged for public display. When he tried to smile at the group, it came out as a grimace. Isabel knew he was hating this. He spoke briefly and grinned, really grinned, only once, when a woman reporter asked a question about air aid to Bastogne. The PR officer seemed glad when Andy's turn was over. He was too surly to make good press.

After the briefing there were drinks in the offices downstairs. With peace on the horizon, the army had become solicitous of the press. A crowd gathered around the general. Isabel fought her way to the bar. "Better ask for a double." Andy's voice behind her was infuriatingly casual, as if they'd met only yesterday, or as if they'd never met at all. "The scotch is running out in Paris. Even among the brass."

He got drinks for both of them, and they moved to a corner of the room. "I'd congratulate you on your talk," she said, "except I have the feeling you're not particularly proud of it."

"I never was much on public speaking."

"More intimate situations are your style, if I remember correctly."

"You're angry."

"About what?"

He decided not to answer that.

"Tell me about Spence." She moved to safer ground. "Is he all right?"

"About as you'd expect, under the circumstances."

She felt suddenly dizzy, and it wasn't from the scotch. She'd heard from Spence ten days ago. In war ten days was a lifetime, or enough time for countless deaths. "What do you mean 'under the circumstances'?" Her voice pierced the easy social hum like an air raid siren. "Was he wounded?"

"Only by friendly fire. Your old friend Sally Sayre."

"I thought that was over."

"Not quite. Sally has good timing. Whenever he did start to get over her, a letter arrived. Somewhere around D-Day she decided she was in love with him after all. Maybe the rest of her pen pals were in the Pacific, and she figured Spence would be home sooner. But then some navy guy beat him out. This time she didn't even bother to write a letter. Just sent a wedding announcement." He finished his drink in a single swallow. "I understand you folks at home are having a hell of a time during this war."

"You can't judge everyone by Sally."

He gave her a long, hard stare. "I go on the evidence I have. Spence didn't sober up for a week after he got that damn announcement. And he wouldn't even take himself off duty. I had to go to the doctor and do it for him." He was still staring at her. "Have you ever been in a fighter plane, Isabel? I mean, we all know you're an old hand at bombers, but have you ever been in a fighter?"

"No."

"Well, things happen pretty fast. So you've got to react pretty fast. A week-long binge slows down your reflexes. A broken heart does the same thing to your mind. I've got Spence back in shape. It took half a dozen girls to do it. Now when he goes up, Sally's face is mixed up with all the others."

"In other words, now you have him flying for nothing rather than something."

"In other words, now I've got his vision clear. And I'm not taking any chances with Mrs. Barnes's little boy either."

She put down her drink. "Then you better lay off this stuff. It's hell on the reflexes, as you pointed out. But as for a broken heart, I wouldn't let it worry me if I were you. I don't think the government issued you that particular organ."

She turned and walked away, and he didn't follow her. By the time she found her coat, he was talking to the woman reporter who'd asked about Bastogne.

Isabel went back to the Hotel Scribe. Anger had its advantages. For the first time since Andy Barnes had shipped out, she wasn't worrying about him.

38

BY MID-FEBRUARY the Battle of the Bulge was history and the war had entered its violent death throes. The allies were bombing Berlin round the clock. In two days they devastated Dresden. U.S. marines invaded Iwo Jima. Everyone was making plans for peace—including, at Yalta, Churchill, Stalin, and a desperately ill Roosevelt—but there was little of it in the world.

The house on Sixty-seventh Street was far from calm. Officers and enlisted men and women continued to come and go. Lily, who no longer had World Pictures organizing her professional and personal life, was trying to lose herself in a frantic social one. The men who pursued her filled the house with flowers and tied up the phone endlessly. The new baby made her demands known. There were many jokes by visitors about the tiny war orphan who had Eliza's hair, Lily's eyes, and Isabel's experience at the front. Only Sam noticed that all three women laughed a little too hard at the comments, but these days Sam had other things on his mind. He kept thinking about a line that was making the rounds. "What did you do in the war, Daddy?" Damn little was the answer. And so early in April he jumped at the chance to conduct a group of magazine writers on a tour of air force installations in the Pacific. The week before he was due to leave, a week spent drawing all sorts of jungle equipment from the quartermaster, including a forty-five which gave him no sense of safety at all, Eliot Childs slumped forward over the desk he'd been toiling at as a dollar-a-year man for the past three years and was rushed to the hospital. The doctors diagnosed a heart attack.

Grace Childs took the train up from Palm Beach. Isabel took one down from New York. Sam met her at Union Station. Overhead huge banners reminded them to stay on the job till the war was won and keep buying war bonds. "I just came from the hospital," Sam said. "The doctors used that wonderful euphemism. He's resting comfortably. I'll take you there now."

"Will you do me a favor instead? Go to his apartment at the Mayflower. If there's a woman there—don't look surprised; I'm not a child, though I was when I found out about him—get rid of her. And any traces. Someone has to do it before mother gets here, but I don't have the stomach for the job."

He went on staring down at her as the crowd swirled around them. "You think I'm hard?" she asked.

"I think you're strong, but not as tough as you like to pretend."

Eliot Childs didn't look as if he'd suffered a heart attack. His face was pale and drawn with exhaustion, but it had often been that way after a polo match in Palm Beach or the Newport-Bermuda yacht race. Isabel asked him how he was.

"Fine, but I'd be a good deal better if they'd let me have a martini. I don't suppose I could convince you to smuggle one in."

She sat in the chair beside the bed. "No martinis. I'm on your side in this war. Mother should be here tomorrow." There was a moment's silence. "I asked a friend to . . . to get your apartment ready for her."

His thin mouth curved into an unrepentant crescent. "You're a good girl, Isabel. If only you were a little more forgiving. Like your mother."

"I don't think this is the time to go into it."

"That's exactly what I mean. Is the friend Sam Wicker? That fellow I met when you were down last time?" She said it was. "He's a Jew, isn't he?"

"Does that bother you?"

He laughed. "You don't know me nearly as well as you think. No, Isabel, it doesn't bother me, but I think you were hoping it would." He lay back on the pillow. "I haven't seen much of you during this war, but it's nice to know I'm still an influence."

Grace arrived from Palm Beach the following day. She looked tired from the trip but, like her husband, better than Isabel had expected. As she came down the red carpet from the Pullman car, Isabel noticed a dusting of peace, fine as powder, on her impeccable features. The realization came to Isabel then. This was what her mother had been waiting for, the old age that would bring back the young man who'd once loved her. Isabel shivered. She'd grown accustomed to grieving for lives snuffed out in youth. She'd never considered the tragedy of lives spent waiting for age.

The next afternoon Eliot threw his daughter out of his hospital room. "You act as if you're at a wake, Isabel. Look at your mother. She knows how to cheer a man up. Go out and have your hair done. Or have lunch with Captain Wicker. I'm sure he'd love to show you the Pentagon. He's very successful there, you know. Started out writing speeches for one general, then others got wind of how handy he was and were fighting to borrow him."

"My father says you're a hot ticket at the Pentagon," Isabel said to Sam over lunch. He'd taken her to the field grade officers' cafeteria, where both fresh fruit and brass were plentiful.

"I wish you were as impressed as your father."

"I'm impressed."

"No, since I signed up, you're just a little less disdainful."

After lunch they both went back to work. Gardner had decided not to waste Isabel's trip to Washington. The network had set up an interview with Mrs. Roosevelt. The first lady spent twenty minutes telling Isabel what she wanted to tell the women of America. Isabel thought she seemed preoccupied. It was a journalist's job to go for the jugular, but for once Isabel held back. She didn't ask about the President's health.

Isabel made two broadcasts from Washington that afternoon, then finally managed to flag down a lady cab driver—all the cab drivers were women these days—and went back to the Mayflower. Washington, she complained to Sam when he came to pick her up for dinner, was like the rest of America these days, only more so.

There were too many uniforms and not enough laundries or telephones or cigarettes or whiskey. No matter what you wanted you had to stand in line for it. And still there was a frantic ambiance that had all the hedonism of life at the front and none of its danger.

"You're just tired," Sam said. "You'll feel better after a dry martini and a rare steak."

"Black market, no doubt."

He poured two drinks and handed her one. Beyond the hotel windows the lights of Washington proclaimed that the blackout was a thing of the past and peace close at hand. "What are you going to do when this war is over, Isabel? When the world's a finer and easier place, or so they tell me? It's going to be harder to keep proving yourself."

Her head tilted to that angle of impossible arrogance that always reminded him of a Gainsborough portrait. Then, as if she realized her own absurdity, she relaxed and laughed. "You know me too well, Sam."

He came and sat beside her on the sofa. "There are still some surprises."

"Like what?"

"Like the fact that you asked me to take care of that business with this place. You don't like to ask things of people, Isabel. Especially men."

"I don't like to be obligated."

"And you think you are to me now?"

She pushed the silky page boy back from her face. Sam recognized the gesture. It meant she was worrying a problem. He liked this look better than the Gainsborough one. "I think you've done a lot for me, from the very beginning."

"I'm not an altruist. I expect to get my just deserts in the end."

"The end?"

He finished his drink and stood. They'd been having these conversations long enough for him to know the cutoff point. He was pressing for love, not pity. "Ah've waited for you longer than ah've waited for any woman, Scarlett."

"You do a lousy Rhett Butler." She finished her drink. "But you make a mean martini. Almost as good as my father's." She stopped abruptly as if she'd said something wrong.

"Not every man is like your father, Isabel. Though you seem determined to have one who is."

"That's over." She spoke quietly, but all through dinner the words kept going off in his head like an artillery barrage.

The hedonism of the city was like a contagious disease. The harder you tried to resist it, the more likely you were to succumb. In the dim, discretely expensive restaurant candles flickered, wine glowed in deep crystal goblets, and all around them men in exquisitely cut khaki and blue leaned across snowy tablecloths toward beautiful women. Isabel decided the whole world must be in love, at least for the night. The waiter kept her glass full and Sam kept her laughing about generals and protocol and snafus that seemed funny only this far from the war. And gradually she stopped thinking about her father and Andy, or maybe she only started to think like them.

On the street the air held a promise of spring and peace. "Thanks to a favor I did for a chicken colonel I have a bottle of Napoleon brandy that's older than we are. Can I lure you to my apartment?"

Sam's apartment—two and a half rooms of it—was splendid by current Washington standards, the brandy rich and resonant, and Sam perfect as an ad for custom-tailored uniforms.

"It's going to be dull seeing men in mufti again."

"Thanks a lot." He switched on the radio. Glenn Miller crept into the room, the sweet, smooth sound of escape from the war that would always be associated with the war.

They danced for a while, because it seemed the logical thing to do, and because they were both good dancers, and because their bodies matched so perfectly. He wasn't as tall as Andy, and there was something to be said for that. Her head fit in the hollow of his neck neatly as relevant information in a parenthesis. And pretty soon it seemed only logical that he turn his face a little and she lift hers. The brandy was even richer on his tongue, and Glenn Miller's music flowed around them binding their bodies together with a sweet sinuousness. Finally, they stopped dancing but went on kissing. He unzipped her dress. She shrugged out of it and the slip. He drew her to him again. The rough wool of his uniform chafed at her skin. Her fingers worked at his buttons.

"We can continue this inside." His voice was hoarse, as if from a long thirst.

In the bedroom he turned on a small lamp. That was when she saw the pile of materiel stacked against one wall. He'd collected a helmet and combat boots, canteen and quinine, all the accoutrements of jungle warfare, including the mean-looking little forty-five. She stopped half undressed in the middle of the room. "What's that?"

He told her about the tour of the Air Force installations in the Pacific.

"But you never said anything."

"I was going to. It's no big thing, Isabel. You've done it twice."

She sat on the side of the bed in her step-ins and bra. Her face was flushed and crumpled as if she were going to cry. "Damn it, don't sound so cavalier. I thought you were the one man who didn't want to be a hero."

"Who said anything about being a hero. It's only a PR tour with a bunch of magazine writers. You know how the military's treating the press these days. We'll probably have more scotch than we can drink—with ice."

"There's still a very nasty war going on in the Pacific, you know."

"That one you visited in Europe wasn't too nice either."

She'd composed her face by now. She stood and put her arms around his neck. "Don't do anything stupid, Sam."

"I won't do anything stupid," he murmured against her mouth. He unhooked her bra.

She slid the webbing of his belt through the metal buckle. It made a whispering sound. She pressed herself against him. "Not when I'm just finding you."

He kissed her mouth again. He kissed her neck. His tongue licked like small warming flames at her breasts. He straightened and looked at her from under that fringe of lashes. "Then I especially won't do anything stupid."

They were quick with the rest of their clothing then, as if the mention of the war had set a clock ticking in the room. They got into bed and kissed and touched and, once, drew back and looked at each other and smiled at this miraculous discovery they were making. She clung to him then and his body was lithe and tough and his mouth was soft and capable of giving exquisite pleasure. She'd been right when she'd said he knew her too well. His hands sensed every desire. His mouth fulfilled needs she hadn't known. And suddenly she found that making love to Sam was loving Sam, and she wanted to give him the same pleasure he gave her. And gradually there was no giving or receiving but only a joy that doubled and quadrupled like some astonishing mathematical progression that finally consumed them both in its explosive exhilaration.

The following morning, April twelfth, he took her to Union Station. Their eyes were glazed, their mouths soft and bruised from making love. There was a red patch on her cheek from his beard. His earlobe carried a faint stigma, identical to her teeth. They lingered in the station restaurant, tangling fingers over untouched coffee cups. That was the kind of war he was fighting, he told her, a desk war that allowed mornings off for love affairs.

"Stop trying to reassure me," she said. "It makes me think I have something to worry about."

They stopped in front of the steps to the Pullman car and turned to each other. "It's about time you started worrying about me."

They kissed and held each other and kissed again, a long kiss that was too intimate for public display. Before the war, people would have turned to stare and disapprove, but during the last three and a half years the public had grown accustomed to excesses as well as shortages.

On the train ride up, Isabel tried to work, but images of Sam kept intruding. When the man in the swivel chair across the aisle tried to start a conversation, she realized he'd thought she was smiling at him. She blushed then because she was afraid her face had shown what she was really thinking.

As she got off the train, her mind was still tangled up in Sam and Sam's bed and she was still smiling, so it took her a while to notice that around her a great many people were crying. The late editions of the afternoon paper were already on the stands, but she didn't need them to know what had happened. Around her, servicemen and civilians wore the same mask of mourning. An eerie hush hung like dusk from the great overreaching ceiling. She forced herself to look at the black headlines on the newsstand. FDR DEAD.

A porter walked past, his cheeks bisected by two rivers of tears.

A woman in a straw hat and yellow coat made for happier spring days sat on a bench in the waiting room and rocked back and forth in silent grief. Isabel went straight to her office. Though there was no real news, only a continuing chronicle of official plans and personal sorrow, she stayed at her desk until well into the night, almost as if she were keeping a vigil.

It was close to midnight by the time she returned home and found the letter that had been lying on the table in the front hall of the house on Sixty-seventh Street for two days. Andy Barnes had finally decided to break silence.

He wrote, he said, because he thought she'd like to know about Spence. He was fine. Sober as a judge, flying like an ace, and shacked up with a French girl. *So, as you put it, he's flying for something again rather than nothing.*

I've been thinking about Paris. I guess I was pretty much of a bastard. I don't know. Maybe Sally's announcement got to me too. Anyway, I figure I was dumb to throw away Paris. On the other hand, you threw it away too. You were the one who walked out.

Something no one's ever done to Captain Andy Barnes, she thought and crumpled the letter in a ball. The thin paper made a crackling sound, almost like gunfire. She was tired of explosives and danger and death. She was tired of men who were too busy proving their manhood to care about women. She decided to call Sam to say good night. His voice was warm and safe, the safest thing in this whole violent world, and she wrapped herself up in it and went to sleep.

39

LIKE MANY WOMEN who have worked all their lives, Lily was no good at idleness. For a while she followed the new baby around hungrily, but with a full-time mother and a professional nanny in the house, Nina didn't need another caretaker.

Lily invited Rose to New York on her next furlough. She barely recognized her younger sister. Army life had claimed thirty pounds, age had healed her skin, and independence from Lily had done wonders for her confidence. So had the new fiancé on her arm. Lily was delighted for her sister. She said she wanted to do something for them. She meant she wanted to do everything for them.

She offered a big wedding, but Rose and Charlie wanted to be married in the army chapel among their friends. She offered a house, but Charlie said he'd inherited his parents house in Indiana, and they wouldn't be able to live in that because after the war he planned to go to college.

"Then let me pay for that," Lily said. "I put money away for

Rose's education, but now she says she doesn't want to go to college."

Charlie said that was mighty nice of Lily—he said it three or four times—but added that the GI Bill took care of all that.

"But I want to help you," Lily insisted.

They told her, again, that was mighty nice of her, then added they didn't need any help.

She invited Iris east for a few weeks and took her on a tour of New England to visit colleges. Lily wanted her sister to go to Smith as Isabel had. Iris fell in love with Smith. She also fell in love with Wellesley and Radcliffe and Mt. Holyoke and Vassar. At least there was something Lily could do for her. Unfortunately, paying for Iris's education would not consume any of Lily's time.

Her social life grew more frantic. A.Z. didn't want her, but a good many other people did. Among them were another general, two bankers, the owner of a newspaper chain, an alcoholic writer, a man who'd got filthy rich on the Norden bomb sight, and an exiled Polish count. She went to bed with the newspaper owner and the Polish count, but the experiences were unrewarding. She was looking for love. They were pursuing the celluloid myth.

At the end of April Jerry Crowley called to say he was passing through New York and knew from one of the columns that she was in town too. He didn't add that he gathered from the piece in the column linking her with a Polish count that she hadn't married her marine after all. He asked Lily if she'd like to have dinner. She thought of the Polish count. A little Slavic moodiness went a long way. She told Jerry she'd love to have dinner.

He looked even better than he had on the plane. He had that facile self-confidence that is perhaps the only thing that comes easily to a self-made man. Lily stood in the townhouse foyer staring at the slightly battered face and perfectly tailored evening clothes. Then she laughed. "You've come a long way from organizing the assembly line."

He kissed her on the cheek. "We've both come a long way. Maybe that's why we get along so well."

"Do we get along well?"

"I always like seeing you. And you felt comfortable enough with me to sleep on my shoulder halfway across the country. In some states that's grounds for marriage."

He took her to El Morocco. Heads turned to stare at Lily, but the waiters paid deference to Jerry. Chauncey Gray's orchestra alternated with Chiquito's rumba band. Jerry was a smooth dancer and an even better talker. He told wonderful stories about organizing and striking and fighting the big boys in Washington. He had her laughing over Jerry Crowley, the poor Irish kid from Philadelphia, who'd finally made his way to a White House dinner only to be fed the same terrible hash he'd grown up on.

"But hash on White House china is a different story."

He looked at her for a long minute. "You must think I'm a real sellout. I admit I like eating hash with the President and being able to take you to El Morocco. I like power and I like money, and I haven't met many men, or women, who don't. But I haven't forgotten where I came from, Lily, or what my job is. After the war all hell is going to break loose with labor. The no-strike pledges didn't work during the war. Imagine what's going to happen when management can't bring patriotism into the argument. Unlike most of my colleagues, I don't think anybody really wins anything from a strike, especially a bloody strike. So I'd like to head off some of the trouble. If I have to work for the government to do that, I will, but I haven't forgotten where my allegiance lies." He leaned back and looked at her with a wicked smile, the altar boy gone wrong again. "Jesus, I didn't mean to get up on a soapbox. Don't ever repeat any of this. Even to me." He motioned to the waiter to refill her glass. "Now tell me what you've been doing."

"Not nearly as much as you. I haven't made a movie in a year." She told him about her suspension from World.

"You need to get back to work."

"Like the time you marched me back into the factory? Maybe I should have let you draw up my contract."

"How long till it expires?"

"Another eighteen months. Alec Zeal's right. By then there'll be a whole new crop of girls on the scene, and no one will remember who Lily Hart was."

He took a long swallow of wine, and she had a picture of him sitting around Carrie's kitchen table drinking beer. "It's a damn shame."

"I can't complain. I brought it on myself. And I had an awfully good time while it lasted."

"You're not having an awfully good time these days."

"Does it show?"

"Only to someone who's interested."

She shrugged.

"Don't do that."

"Don't do what?"

"Move like that. All night long I've been looking at you in that dress. You remind me of that painting by Sargent. The woman in the long black dress. You know the one I mean?"

She said she did. Gustave had treated her to a lecture on the uses of light and dark, color and composition in *Madame X*.

"In that dress you look just like that picture. With twice the impact. So don't shrug like that. The way you move around inside that dress gives me too many ideas."

She turned the wine glass around in her fingers.

"I'm sorry," he said finally.

"No, it's not what you said. Every man I go out with makes a pass."

"That wasn't just a pass. I have more than a one-night stand in mind, Lily."

She looked at him for a long time. "You said we're old friends, and maybe we are, Jerry, so I'll tell you something. They all have more than a one-night stand in mind. After all, I'm something of a trophy. But with the exception of Tom, poor sweet Tom, and . . . and one other man, it's never any good. And I'll tell you why. Because everyone of them goes to bed with Miranda and wakes up with me."

He reached across the table and took her hand in both of his. His hands were wide and strong with powerful knuckles. "Lily, I'm probably the only man in America who never saw *Desire*. And somewhere in the back of my mind I still think of you as Lily Hartarski, the kid who stood up to that son-of-a-bitch foreman and half an aircraft factory."

"Is that a proposition?"

"It's an invitation. You've been on my mind for a long time. When I first met you, you were still a kid. The next thing I knew you were a big star, and I was just some guy trying to organize factories and keep one step away from management's rough stuff.

But things have changed a little, so why don't you come back to my hotel, Lily Hartarski, and let me make love to you?"

She couldn't think of a single reason not to.

At first they laughed at the idea of the two of them—the poor Polish girl from Duquel and the tough Irish labor organizer—coming together in his suite at the Waldorf among all the gilt and satin and ersatz Louis Quinze and Seize. But soon they stopped laughing.

Tom had brought her youthful passion, Gustave worldly lust, but Jerry offered knowing desire and an affection so tender it surprised her. They brought to each other experience and disappointment, failed affairs and new hope, an urgent longing and a sweet, unexpected closeness.

The next morning she awakened to the warmth of his body. He rolled over on his side and looked down at her. "I like waking up with Lily Hartarski." He slid the sheet down her body. "I like waking up with all of Lily Hartarski."

40

ON MAY 7, 1945, a colleague of Isabel's, Edward Kennedy, an AP correspondent who'd pledged on his "honor as a correspondent and as an assimilated officer of the United States Army not to communicate the news until it is released on the order of the Public Relations Director of SHAEF," scooped the world by flashing the story that Germany had surrendered unconditionally. For the rest of their lives a generation of Americans would remember what they'd been doing on a handful of days. Pearl Harbor came first in that category, then V-J Day, the real end of the war, but May seventh would be etched in memory as well. Millions of American men could suddenly count on the fact that, barring assignment to the Pacific, they'd have a chance to grow old. Millions of American women stopped fearing a future alone. And millions of American parents rejoiced at an end to the upside-down state of nature that had the older generation burying the younger.

There was no doubt about it. May 7, 1945 was a momentous day. Isabel would remember it for the rest of her life, but she wouldn't rejoice at the memory. It seemed to her later that the minute she'd seen the flash over the wire, she'd had feelings of foreboding. If the German high command had surrendered unconditionally on May seventh, why would the fighting not end until 11:01 P.M. on May ninth? She thought of Spence. She tried not to think of Andy. Damn these men who played war as if it were a game. Would a boy killed in the interval be any less dead? Would his widow be less alone? The closer they got to the end of the war, the more terrifying it became. Who wanted to be the last man to die in the ETO? She must have had some premonition, or was that only hindsight?

For the other two women in the house on Sixty-seventh Street the day had happier associations. Years later Lily would come to see it as a turning point in her career. And Eliza, who'd celebrated her own personal peace in Europe and Michael's safety several days earlier when the fighting in Italy had finally been declared over, would remember with a sweet nostalgia the day that her first book had been published.

There'd been so much fuss about the baby that none of them had paid much attention to the book Eliza had written during those long months in Maine. The work had been therapeutic, but the expectations for it hadn't been great. Who wanted to read about one more woman's experiences as a lonely serviceman's wife? A great many people, promised a publisher friend of Isabel's. He'd given Eliza a contract and an advance and rushed the book through production for returning servicemen and their wives. Publication day was, by fortunate accident, May seventh. By that time a Broadway producer had already got hold of a set of galleys. He too had his mind on all those returning servicemen and their wives. They'd have money in their pockets and be out for a good time. They wouldn't want to see plays about the front, but they'd get a good laugh out of a warm, sentimental play about what had gone on at home.

"You're looking," Lily said when Eliza returned home from her meeting with the producer, "awfully pleased with yourself." Liquid late afternoon sunshine poured through the sycamore into the small yard behind the townhouse. This year there hadn't even been talk of a victory garden. Victory itself seemed that close.

"Like the proverbial cat that swallowed the proverbial canary," Isabel said.

Eliza took time to admire a gold star Ted had won at school that day, then bent over the carriage and inhaled the sweet baby smell of her sleeping daughter. "Why shouldn't I look pleased? I just spent the afternoon with a man who actually wants to pay good money to put my book on the stage."

"It's more than that," Isabel said. "I can tell by your smile."

Lily sat up on the chaise longue. "It's Michael. He's on his way home."

Eliza's smile melted in the dwindling sunshine. "If only that were true. I haven't heard a word yet."

"Then tell us about your meeting," Lily said.

Eliza sat in one of the wrought iron chairs. "That's all you ever say anymore, Lily. Especially since Jerry Crowley went back to Washington. Isabel and I come home every evening, and there you are asking us about our day. The way I used to when Michael came home at night. I really think you ought to get back to work."

Lily was stung, Isabel shocked. Eliza had been known to lash out from her own misery, but never with gratuitous cruelty. Perhaps she was turning into one of success's casualties.

"What do you suggest I do?" Lily asked. "Go back to an assembly line?"

Eliza stood and crossed to the baby carriage again. She might as easily have rubbed Lily's face in her own life. She had a husband, children, a suddenly successful career. Lily had nothing but a new and tenuous affair and a quickly fading celebrity.

Eliza sat again, crossed her legs, smoothed the skirt of her smart new suit. "I think you ought to go back to what you do best, acting."

"There's a minor hitch called a suspension."

"I didn't say movies, Lily, I said acting. On Broadway. I have just the vehicle for you"—she laughed—"as we say in show biz."

"It's a brainstorm," Isabel said. "I can't believe we didn't think of it before."

"We didn't have a play for her before," Eliza pointed out.

Lily turned from one to the other. Her eyes were like saucers. "But that's just the point. I'm not a legitimate actress. I'm a movie star. I can't act."

"Who says so?" the two other women demanded.

"Gustave Dressler, for one."

"That's right, I forgot," Isabel said. "It was Gustave up there on the screen in *Desire* and all the other movies. It was Gustave half of America and every GI fell in love with.''

"I was nothing before him. World was about to let my contract lapse.''

"I thought you were free of him,'' Isabel said.

"I'm just facing facts.''

"No, you're not,'' Eliza insisted. "You're just giving in to your old fears. Look, Lily, I'm not saying Dressler didn't help you a lot, and teach you a lot. I'm not even saying you don't owe him a lot. Though just for the record I think you've made payment in full. The point is you aren't just a creation of Dressler or World Pictures. You're a woman with beauty and presence who—and this is the important part—was smart enough to learn from Dressler and all the rest of them. You were great in those movies. And I think you're going to be great on the stage. So does the producer. He said he'd never have thought of you, but once I had, he didn't want anyone else for the part. And he wasn't being kind. Producers like to make money on their plays, in case you haven't heard.''

"What if I flop?''

"I admit it's a possibility, but would you rather spend your life lying here in the garden remembering the old days?''

"But it's your play. What if I let you down?''

A whimper rose from the carriage. Eliza walked to it and rocked it gently. "What if the play lets you down? You aren't exactly taking on Eugene O'Neill, you know.''

"Neither of you is going to let the other down,'' Isabel said. "I can see the reviews now. A dazzling performance in a brilliant play. Or maybe the other way around. Anyway, I'm so sure of them that I'm going to start celebrating right this minute. Let's open a bottle of champagne. We'll drink to the two of you and the end of this damn war, at least the European part of it.''

Impossible as it seemed later, she'd had no premonitions. She'd stood there laughing in the late afternoon sunshine, laughing in sheer joy at Eliza's good fortune and Lily's and the imminent end of the war. Spence and Andy couldn't still be flying missions, not at the eleventh hour. She'd been about to go in to get the champagne when Cora had come out into the garden and said there was a call from the newsroom. And even then, Isabel had suspected nothing. A routine call. Just business. She'd crossed the patio, trailing a hand over Ted's small dark head, and gone into the house. She'd hesitated a moment, giving her eyes a chance to adjust to the indoor gloom, then climbed the back stairs leading from the kitchen to the second floor. The aroma of Cora's victory meatloaf followed her, and she was thinking that despite everything they'd had an awfully good time of it. She went into the library to take the call and thought as she sat behind the big desk that soon her father would be reclaiming the room and they'd all be adjusting to a new postwar world. That made her think of Sam, who said she'd have to stop proving herself after the war, and of Andy, who was going to have a hard time coming down from the clouds himself. She picked up the phone then and was surprised to hear Lew Packer's voice. The story had just come over the wires. A minor story about a minor person. Nothing like the death of Ernie Pyle or the disappearance of Glenn Miller. No one in the newsroom had even noticed it. No one except Packer, who knew a little about Isabel's life. An army communique had reported that a plane carrying Sam Wicker, a public relations officer and former advertising executive, had collided with another plane while forming up for a mission. There were no survivors.

Lew said he thought Isabel would want to know. Isabel thanked him. By the time she hung up the phone her hands were trembling uncontrollably. The receiver made a terrible clattering sound as she tried to replace it.

There'd been no reason for Sam to be on that bombing raid to Japan. It hadn't been part of the tour. None of the magazine writers had gone. There'd been no reason, Isabel knew, except her.

She felt something black and brackish rising within her. All along she'd been saying that she hated war. She was mixed up in it only because she wanted to understand why men loved it. But Sam had seen things differently. He'd seen beneath her talk of hating war to the fact that she'd fallen in love with a man who loved it. So Sam had set out to love it too, or at least conquer it. He'd set out on a cruel stupid quest that had ended in waste.

The nausea was rising within her again. She went upstairs to her bathroom and was painfully and violently sick as she had been after the bombing mission. But this time there was no relief. Afterward, all she felt was an aching black emptiness.

41

THAT SUMMER Okinawa fell, Japan burned under a barrage of
fire bombing, and President Truman weighed the number of American boys who would be lost in an invasion of the Japanese home-
lands against the terrifying cost and terrible implications of a fearful
new weapon. Meanwhile, magazines and newspapers turned their
attention to the returning veteran.

Psychologists, sociologists, clergymen, educators, politicians, and
editors of ladies' magazines all had an opinion. Coddle him. Don't
make too much of a fuss. Encourage him to talk about his experiences. Don't force him to dwell on the war. Be prepared for
strangeness; your man has seen and suffered a great deal. Most men
come out of battle pretty much the way they went into it. Give him
time to readjust. The sooner family life gets back to normal the
better.

Eliza read all the articles. After her book came out, she was even
asked to write several. She agreed to do a piece for *Vogue.* The
article was easy. It was Michael's return that worried her.

His letters promised it was imminent. The military had announced that men would be discharged according to a system of credits earned for time in service, time in overseas service, combat record including medals, and number of dependent children. Michael wrote that he ranked high in every category, including the last, thanks to Teddy and Nina. *Just got the picture of the three of you taken in the garden. I think I'm going to like our daughter.* There was only one catch in this credit system. No matter how high a man's rating, he would not be discharged if he was considered essential to the war in the Pacific.

A great many hopes that had skyrocketed in May were sinking by midsummer. Then, on July sixteenth, President Truman received word at Potsdam, where he was meeting with Churchill and Stalin, that a bomb called Fat Man had been successfully exploded at Alamogordo, New Mexico, and two more bombs would be ready within ten days. Summer melted on. Truman issued an ultimatum. Japan replied. The two new bombs were dropped. Historians would argue the implications and immorality of the act for generations, but at that moment America was ecstatic. People cried and shouted, danced and drank, but the true celebratory gesture was the kiss. All over the world American servicemen who suddenly had a future were kissing women. In Times Square a sailor grabbed a nurse in white, bent her backward, and kissed her. A photographer named Alfred Eisenstaedt caught that single moment of euphoria on film, and just as a photograph of several marines raising the flag on Iwo Jima had come to symbolize the war, so this one became the emblem of its end. Peace had broken out.

But among the celebrants there were those who didn't shout or dance or drink or kiss. There were those who simply stood in silent homage. And when Isabel Childs broadcast the news of peace, the catch in her voice spoke to those people.

And still the waiting went on. When would the boys come home? What would they be like? Michael was no boy, but Eliza shared the anxiety.

At least his voice hadn't changed. Her fingers tightened on the telephone receiver. She began to tremble. "Michael," she breathed. "Michael," she repeated again and again, as if the very fact of his voice were a miracle.

He told her he was at Fort Dix, the closest deprocessing center.

He said with any luck and without any snafus he'd be out in a day or two. He added that he couldn't wait to see her, her and the children. And all she could do was keep repeating his name. "Say it again," he said just before they hung up.

"Michael."

"Nobody else in the world says it the way you do."

He didn't call the next morning, though he'd promised to. That afternoon she was sitting at her desk in the Central Park West apartment she'd reclaimed a few weeks earlier trying to work on another magazine article and not to worry about Michael's return when she heard the doorbell, not the buzzer from downstairs, but the bell outside the apartment. That was odd. Louis the doorman never let anyone up without calling from the lobby first. As she walked to the door, she was so busy worrying about Michael's homecoming that it never occurred to her that it was Michael's homecoming.

She didn't even have a chance to look at him. He stepped into the apartment and took her in his arms that quickly. She clung to him and began to cry. He laughed, but it was a choked sound. They stood that way for a long time, as if they were afraid to let go of each other. Only later did Eliza realize it was as much fear of seeing each other as of losing each other.

Finally they broke apart. She put her hand on his upper lip. The mustache was back, but it didn't camouflage the strangeness. His cheeks were hollow, his thick hair receding by a fraction of an inch, his dark eyes wary. She said something stupid about not letting her know, about how awful she must look, but he told her she looked wonderful, and she could tell from the way he said it that he meant it. He pulled her to him again.

Finally they let each other go. He looked around the apartment. "Where is everyone?"

"Ted's at school. Cora took the baby to the park."

"Cora?"

"The nurse. She used to work for Isabel's family, but now she belongs strictly to Ted and Nina."

They went into the living room. He sat in one of the chairs. She sat on the sofa. "Do you want something?" she asked. "Coffee? A drink?"

"Not yet. I just want to sit here." He took a pack of cigarettes from his uniform pocket, started to take one, then caught himself and held it out to her.

She laughed. "I don't smoke, Michael. Remember. You never wanted me to."

He took a cigarette from the pack and went through the ritual of tapping it on his watch and lighting it. At least it gave him something to do.

"Maybe I'd like that drink after all."

She was up like a shot. "I'll get it. Oh, and I'd better make a call."

"To tell my folks I'm home?"

"No, I hadn't thought of that. To cancel something. I was supposed to meet some people for drinks tonight," she called over her shoulder on her way out of the room.

He sat in the living room smoking his cigarette and listening to her on the hall phone explaining that she couldn't make it that night. "Michael's home." There was a silence. "Michael. My husband."

He stubbed out the cigarette.

She came back into the room and handed him a drink. He caught her hand in his free one and pulled her down on the arm of the chair. "Who was that?"

"Just some people from the play."

"The play?"

"I wrote you about the play, Michael. Based on the book. It's opening in a few weeks."

She'd written him about the play and the book and the children's nurse, all right, but none of it had been real until now. He looked up at her. "My wife, the celebrity."

"It's all about you," she said. "About missing you and learning to live without you—" She stopped abruptly. She bent over and kissed him. "Oh, God, I missed you so much."

He stood and paced the room a few times. "It looks as if you got along pretty well." He didn't sound angry, only a little hurt.

The doorbell rang. He watched her leave the room again. She hadn't worn trousers before the war, because he hadn't liked women in trousers, but he had to admit she looked wonderful in them. His hands curled as they always had when he'd looked at that beautifully rounded bottom. An image of a long line of GIs waiting for their injections flashed through his mind. He tried to think of the doctor who'd said he was cured rather than the chaplain who'd warned him he was forever tainted.

"Daddy," he heard Eliza's voice singing in the hallway. "Daddy's home."

Michael squatted like a baseball catcher at the ready and waited for his little boy to come hurling into the room. A strange kid came and stood shyly in the archway. He had Michael's eyes and Michael's neat well-proportioned features and Michael's way of standing with his hands in his pockets and his weight on one foot, but he was still a stranger.

Eliza gave him a gentle push into the room. "Go on, Ted, kiss your father hello."

The boy stood there for another moment. Michael straightened. Eliza gave another gentle shove. Ted crossed the room and held out his hand. Michael took it, pulled the boy toward him, and hugged him. The tears in his eyes made Eliza's water.

They arranged themselves around the living room again in a pantomime of family closeness. Ted was curious about his father's ribbons.

"The first thing I'm going to do," Michael said, "is get out of this uniform, and I'm not getting back into it. Not ever."

Ted surveyed the private's uniform with a practiced eye. "Uncle Sam was a captain. Uncle John was a lieutenant in the Navy."

"Who's Uncle John?"

Eliza started to speak, but Ted didn't give her a chance. "He used to come around the big house all the time. He had a medal for Sicily too. Only he was wounded there. He walked with a cane."

Michael laughed. "Sorry if I let you down, Teddy, but I was damn glad I wasn't wounded in Sicily. Or anywhere else."

"I didn't mean that."

Michael took another cigarette from the pack. "I know you didn't."

Ted turned to his mother. "Can I go out and play now? There's a game in the park."

"You most certainly cannot. Daddy just got home."

Michael stubbed out the cigarette. "What do you say, Teddy, you and I go out and toss a ball around?"

The boy looked at his father for a minute. "Sure." He hesitated. "But the guys call me Ted."

Eliza stood in the window and looked down at the street. Michael and Ted came out of the building into the golden Indian summer afternoon. The doorman shook Michael's hand again and even threw an arm around his shoulders. Louis, at least, was having no trouble readjusting. She watched her husband and son at the curb. The light changed. Michael reached for the boy's hand. Ted put it in his pocket. Michael followed his example.

By the time they returned, Cora had brought the baby back. Michael picked her up and smiled at her and tickled her and made foolish faces for her benefit. Eliza remembered how frightened he'd been the first time he'd held Teddy, as if the baby were a fragile objet. He didn't look nervous now. He looked more at ease than he had all afternoon.

"She's beautiful," he said. "Absolutely beautiful. Look at those eyes. Where did you get those big, blue eyes?" he crooned to the baby. "Poor little Nina with the big blue eyes, you haven't had an easy time of it, have you? Not between Hitler and Mussolini on one side and our bombs on the other. But everything's going to be all right now. Daddy'll see to that." He looked at Eliza, and for the first time since he'd stepped into the apartment, she saw the old Michael behind the wary, ill-at-ease stranger. "I'm going to like having a daughter."

After dinner, Eliza and Michael went into the living room again. He had two highballs and was surprised when she did too. Their words glanced off each other like the ice in their glasses when they rattled them. A little before midnight he stood and said he guessed he'd call it a night. Eliza stood too. "I forgot to check the frig. I bet we're out of eggs."

"It's all right, I don't need eggs for breakfast."

"But it's your first breakfast home. I'll go out before you get up. I'll get eggs and bagels and lox."

"It's all right," he said again. "Just relax." But he was standing in the center of the room as if he were at attention.

They went into the bedroom. Michael continued on to the bathroom. The shelf where he'd kept his toiletries was cluttered with makeup. He balanced his dop kit on the side of the sink. He looked at himself in the mirror and rubbed his hand against his cheek. He'd bathed before dinner but hadn't shaved. He took the shaving cream and razor from the kit. His eyes met their image in the mirror. All this fastidiousness. Like locking the barn after the horse is stolen. But the doctor had said cured. That was the word he'd used. Cured.

Eliza sat up in bed turning the pages of a magazine that was nothing but a blur. He was a stranger, as much a stranger as John had been that first night. What if she made a slip? What if she called Michael by John's name? She remembered a tasteless joke she'd heard at the theater about a man who talked in his sleep. Or wouldn't she have to say anything to give herself away? Lily said she'd learned something from every man she'd gone to bed with. Had Eliza learned too much from John?

Michael came into the room and got into bed beside her. She tossed the magazine aside and turned to him. "You smell good," she said.

"So do you."

She stroked his cheek. "You shaved." Silly words, she thought, masking what's really going on inside.

He kissed her. "You taste the same," she said.

His hand found its way beneath her nightgown. "You feel the same," he said.

"Michael!" Her voice snapped.

"What?" he asked. "What is it?"

The answers tumbled about in her mind. John. Infidelity. Betrayal. Nina. She opened her mouth. "I'm afraid."

His arms tightened around her. "That makes two of us," he whispered, and they got down to the long sweet process of reacquaintance.

Eliza didn't go out to get breakfast the next morning. Michael had said he wanted to find her there beside him in bed when he opened his eyes.

He opened his eyes earlier than she'd expected. He turned to her. Neither of them was frightened anymore. She traced the lean hardness of his chest. He stroked her skin and thought of velvet and satin and all the words that had had no meaning for years. He rolled over on top of her. The door opened and they sprang apart.

Eliza sat up in bed, holding the sheets to her. Michael reached for his pajamas that lay in a tangle on the floor from the night before. Ted stood in the door, looking at them suspiciously.

"I came in to say goodbye."

"Don't you knock first, Teddy? Ted," Michael corrected himself.

The boy didn't answer. Neither did he cross the room to kiss his mother as he usually did before leaving for school.

"He always comes in to say goodbye in the morning," Eliza explained after he'd left.

"Does he always come in without knocking?"

"There was never any reason to." She could taste the lie behind the technical truth. She swallowed painfully and wondered if the years would work as an anesthetic.

Michael started to say something, then thought better of it. He laughed. "No, I guess there wasn't. Well, I'm sure as hell not going to complain about that. But I think we're going to have to start making some new rules around here."

The phone began ringing at ten. Eliza told Cora she wasn't home, but of course, there were exceptions. The coffee and eggs Cora had gone out for grew cold as Michael and Eliza dealt with the outside world.

"We're going away for the weekend," Michael said when Eliza came back into the dining room after her third call of the morning. "Just the two of us. To New England. I'm going to find an inn that has no phone. We're going to see how the leaves have changed." He looked at her with a thin smile. "And how we have."

It was a halcyon weekend that, for the rest of Eliza's life, was imprinted in her mind as vividly as the violently colored leaves dying all around them. They walked and rode horseback and ate hugely and well. They began to talk. They never stopped making love. And the excitement of being together again drove away, at least for the moment, the fears that had come from being apart so long.

They stayed at the inn for two extra days. Then the air that had been clear as glass since they'd arrived grew heavy and the sky that Michael had said was as blue as Nina's eyes turned a metallic gray. They packed their things and returned to town.

The mail and phone messages had piled up in their absence.

"I've got a very important wife," Michael said as he rifled through them.

The next morning he announced he'd better start making some calls himself. "I can't let my wife support me forever."

"I'm not supporting you," she said. "Besides, you'll be running for office, and winning, in no time."

"First I need an organization, and before that I need backing."

"That's what I'll do with my ill-gotten gains," she said. "Make the first contribution to the Michael Kramer campaign chest."

"Like hell you will!" She flinched at the sharpness of his voice. "I'm sorry, Eliza, but that's your money. From your book and your play—"

"We hope."

"—and I'm not taking money from my wife."

"I took money from you all those years. I still do. We're living on your investments."

"That's different."

"Why?"

"Because it is."

"That's a good explanation."

"I don't want to discuss it."

"That's even better." She started for the hall, stopped, and came back into the dining room. She sat beside him and put her hand over his. "Please don't do this, Michael. I'm not an idiot. I know how to balance a checkbook. I've been managing the money you've been sending home and I've been bringing in. I'm not the 'little wife' you left behind three years ago."

He pulled his hand out from under hers. "I can see that."

"All I meant was that I wish we could share things more."

"Like all this fuss about your book and your play?"

She reminded herself of mud and fear and death and all the warnings about readjustment. "Like decisions."

"I thought you didn't need my help there. You know how to manage money. And bring it in. You can run the house. Raise Teddy. It was damn white of you to ask me about Nina and not just spring her on me when I got home."

She closed her eyes. She'd been waiting for this.

"And don't look so damn pained about it. As if I'm one more

cross to bear, one more responsibility to manage." He stood abruptly, spilling the coffee in his cup, and stomped into the hall.

"Where are you going?"

"For a walk. You won't miss me."

Michael returned home a little after five. He wasn't carrying flowers, but he was wearing the sad smile he'd worn when he used to come home carrying flowers. And he didn't say he was sorry, which was funny because in the old days he'd been awfully glib with apologies. She asked him where he'd been. "Trying to see some people who used to have trouble getting in to see me. Do you still want to go to that cocktail party you mentioned?" he went on before she could begin reassuring him about his bright future again.

The party wasn't a disaster. A few of the men remembered who Michael had been. Several women were curious about who he was, since most of the servicemen hadn't come home yet.

"You have a lot of friends," he said in the cab afterward. Something in his voice was cold and dry as the martinis he'd been drinking, and it frightened her.

"They're not friends, only acquaintances. From my old job at the agency. From the book. From the house on Sixty-seventh Street. People were always coming and going."

"Must have been a lot of fun."

"It was mostly lonely."

"I could see that tonight."

She didn't answer him, and he paid the cab driver and followed her into the building in silence.

"Who was that guy with the cigarette holder?" he asked after Ted had gone off to do his homework and they were alone at the table. "What was his name? Oliver? Carter Oliver."

"The head of the agency. Sam used to say he was the smartest man in advertising. Next to Sam."

"You two were pretty friendly."

"He was telling me how sorry he was he couldn't take me back as an AE now that all the men were coming home, but he said there was always a place for me at the agency as a secretary."

Michael started to say something, then seemed to think better of it. He leaned back in his chair at the head of the table and lit another cigarette. "What did you tell him?"

"I said I wasn't interested."

"Good girl."

"I told him I was through with advertising."

Michael's smile was growing broader.

"I told him I need some time off to get to know my husband again."

"I like the sound of this."

"Then I have some ideas for another book. I figure that's something I can do at home."

The smile didn't slide from his face. It just tilted slightly. "That's a nice idea, Eliza, but do you think you'll be able to carry it off? I mean this book about your life after I went away was cute, but it was kind of a fluke, what with the war and so many people in the same boat and everything. Do you really think you have something else to say, sweetheart?"

"You don't think I'll be able to write another book. Or sell it?" She was questioning rather than arguing.

"I just don't want to see you hurt."

His voice was soft, as soft as his eyes. He just didn't want to see her hurt. It had been a long time since anyone had taken care of her. And maybe he was right. He always had been in the past. Maybe the book had been a wartime fluke, and it was time to stop kidding herself and go back to real life.

She looked across the table at Michael. She thought of the children down the hall, Ted doing his homework in his room, Nina sleeping in her crib. There was nothing wrong with real life. And she was being given a second chance at it, a chance to stay home and be a good wife and mother and make amends to Michael for the terrible thing she'd done to him.

42

ELIZA KNEW all about Broadway openings. In the old days when she'd had time for two morning papers and an evening one every day, she'd read about the celebrities arriving in limousines before and the parties at Sardi's where the champagne flowed and wit flew afterward. She'd been prepared for all that, but she hadn't been expecting Ted to catch his first cold of the season and run a fever of 102 degrees or Nina to spit up on her five minutes before she was due to leave. Fortunately, Eliza hadn't put on her dress yet, so all she had to do was take off her robe and change her underwear. When she was finally dressed, Cora refused even to allow her in the baby's room. But Michael insisted on going in to say good night. Eliza had the feeling he'd like an excuse to stay home. His mouth was a tight line. His prewar dinner jacket hung on him as if on a scarecrow. Eliza apologized for not having thought to get it out sooner and have him try it on. He didn't say anything.

"What if they hate it?" Eliza said in the taxi going downtown.

Michael still didn't answer.

"What if all eight critics tear it to shreds?"

"All eight critics have never agreed unanimously on anything, Eliza. I doubt they're going to start now. Besides, they'll blame it on the guy who did the script, not on you."

"What if people say awful things during the intermission? What if they get up and start walking out before the intermission?"

Michael put an arm around her shoulders. "This is what I mean, sweetheart, when I say I don't want you to be hurt."

The opening was, in fact, like those Eliza used to read about. Flashbulbs exploded. Limousines drove up, spilling out women in sable and chinchilla and men in somber black and white. There were only a few uniforms in sight.

Isabel arrived looking beautiful and thin and a little stark in black satin. They went backstage to Lily's dressing room. Lily's face was deathly white. Eliza's turned crimson at the sight.

"How did I ever think I could do this?" Lily asked.

"I know how you feel," Eliza answered.

She and Isabel went back out to the lobby, where Michael was waiting. He'd said he'd just be in the way backstage. He and Isabel went down to their seats. Eliza said she'd stand in the back for the first act. "That way I can make a quick getaway."

For a while she thought she might have to. It started that badly. When the hero entered, a doorknob came off in his hand. Lily was so rattled she blew her line. Having no cue the actor blew his. The audience stirred and whispered and giggled. Eliza put her head in her hands.

Lily recovered. The male lead went off to war. Eliza heard a woman in the last row sniffle. Lily returned alone to her empty apartment. The woman sniffled again, and Eliza saw the man beside her take her hand.

"A little saccharine, don't you think, darling?" Eliza heard a woman in a dress without any back say during intermission.

"I know exactly what you mean," her companion answered. "The women I met during the war weren't quite so, shall we say, devoted."

But not everyone was so cynical.

"Clever," Eliza overheard.

"Light, but I'll be damned if it doesn't give me goose bumps."

"I never knew Lily Hart could act."

Jerry Crowley, who'd joined them in the lobby, whirled around and stared long and hard at the man who'd spoken.

"Now you understand," the woman who'd sniffled said to the man who was still holding her hand.

Lily took four curtain calls. The applause made her as beautiful as Gustave Dressler's camera ever had.

As they pushed up the aisle Eliza basked in the overheard comments.

They went backstage. The director kissed Eliza and told her she was a genius. He told Michael he was a lucky man. The producer hugged her and said they were going to make a nice piece of change together. He told Michael he'd better hold on to her. The line of Michael's mouth was getting tighter.

They went back to the producer's penthouse. There was champagne and more whiskey than Jerry Crowley said he'd seen since before the war. There was smoked salmon and caviar. And after a while there were the reviews. Michael had been right. The critics didn't agree. One recommended that theatergoers stay away in droves. Another found the play cloying but Lily Hart a bright new light on Broadway. A third thought the play was the most heart-warming story to come out of the war he'd yet seen but added it needed a stronger leading lady than the wooden Miss Hart. Four liked the play and Lily Hart. One urged the mayor to close all bridges and tunnels from the city in order to keep Lily Hart from returning to Hollywood and predicted a great literary future for Mrs. Kramer.

Michael didn't say much on the way home, and what he did say had a terrible hollow ring to it.

"Michael," she began when they were back in the apartment. She'd turned her back to him so he could unzip her dress. "Before the war, when the mayor first appointed you to office, every time you moved ahead, every time your picture was in the paper, I was happy for you. Genuinely happy."

He turned away from her and went and sat in the chair in front of the window. "I know." He put his head in his hands. "I really do know that. And I feel like a heel."

She stood alone in the middle of the room, holding her dress to her.

"But that was different," he said without looking at her.

"Why?"

"Because I still needed you. To come home to. To talk to. To know you were here."

She sat on the end of the bed. "And you think I don't need you?"

"For what? You're making plenty of money."

"Is that what our marriage is based on? Your money?"

"What else do you need me for? You proved you can get along without me. Run the house. Take care of the kids. You've got plenty of men after you."

She swallowed the awful metallic taste of lies again. "I don't have any men after me. I don't want any men after me."

"That's not the way it looks from where I sit. And I'm beginning to wonder what was going on while I wasn't sitting here."

She looked across the room at the stranger with the thin face and hard eyes. "Why don't you ask? You've been hinting about it ever since you got home." Her voice was climbing. She wished he would ask, and then she could blurt out everything and be finished with it. "Why don't you ask?" she screamed. "Then I'll ask you about Italy. All that wine you kept liberating. And the buddy who kept ending up engaged to the local girls. What were you doing during all that? Playing chaperon?"

"Nothing happened on those parties!" His voice drowned out hers. Nothing had happened then, but a great deal had happened later.

Her head drooped on her neck, wilted as the flower still pinned to her half-open dress. "And nothing happened here, so I wish you'd stop implying it did."

"Am I supposed to be grateful that my wife didn't screw around while I was away."

"Damn it, Michael," she shouted. "You're supposed to—" She stopped abruptly. They could go on this way all night, screaming at each other, hurling accusations, goading each other's anger until there was nothing but anger left. She took a deep breath. "We're both supposed to be happy," she said quietly. "You're home. You're safe. We're together. We have the children. This is what we spent three years waiting for. At least I did."

He rubbed his eyes with his thumb and forefinger. "But I never thought it would be like this."

She went and sat on the arm of his chair. He didn't look at her. She put her hand on the back of his neck. She lay her head against his. God, how she'd missed that aroma.

"I don't know if I can explain this to you, Michael. Before you went away, I was afraid of you." She felt his body stiffen. "Not that you'd hit me or do anything cruel. You were much too good for that. Even your tempers never lasted. But I was afraid of you. Of displeasing you. As if I were a child and you were the father." He started to speak, but she put her fingers over his mouth. "Wait, let me finish. When you went away, I was miserable and terrified. Like a little girl who'd been abandoned. Well, I grew up during the war. I had to. You're right, I can take care of myself and I can take care of the children. And I'm not afraid of you anymore. But that's the strangest part of it. Now that I'm not afraid, I love you more than ever. I love the kindness and generosity that make you want to take care of me even if I don't need taking care of. I love your gentleness with Ted and Nina. I love the fact that you're the kind of man who thought you had to enlist, even if I was furious at the time, and that you want to help people, even if you keep telling me you're not a do-gooder, and that you can make me laugh. I love the way you look and the way you stand with your hands in your pockets and your weight on one foot and the way we make love."

He pulled her down into his lap. Her dress was still open in back, and his hands were warm against her skin. "I'm sorry, Eliza. For ruining tonight for you."

She put her arms around his neck. "You didn't ruin tonight for me. Without you it wouldn't have been much of a night."

"I don't believe that. All those accolades. All that admiration."

"You saw Isabel. She's had more accolades and admiration than I ever will. She's a bigger success than I'll ever be. Did she look happy to you?"

He slid the dress down her arms and kissed her shoulder. "Is it too late"—his mouth traced a line to her breast—"to add my congratulations to the crowd's?"

She began to undo the studs of his evening shirt. "It's what I've been waiting for all night."

Eliza lay in the darkness listening to Michael's breathing and feeling it against her shoulder. His arm pinned her to the bed. She disengaged herself gently. His protest was half unconscious. "I thought I heard Nina," she whispered. He sank back into sleep.

Her bare feet made no noise on the parquet floor of the hall. The apartment slept in silence. Nina had made no sound in the night. Eliza had simply felt the need to see her.

The baby lay sleeping, a tiny fist drawn up against her mouth. Eliza smoothed the pink and white patchwork quilt Michael had insisted they buy on that weekend in New England. Until then Nina had slept under the old blue blanket that Teddy had worn to softness. On the shelves over the crib half a dozen new stuffed animals kept watch. Michael had said he was going to spoil her, and he wasn't wasting any time. Eliza looked down at the baby. She'd let Michael spoil her, but she wouldn't let him ruin her. Eliza had learned her lesson. She was going to pass it on to her daughter.

Crowley followed Lily into her suite at the Waldorf. She'd left the house on Sixty-seventh Street right after V-J Day, but she'd refuse to take an apartment until the play opened. Besides, the Waldorf was where Jerry stayed when he came to town. This way they could have propriety in the public eye and each other as well.

The maid had left a telegram on the hall table. He picked it up and handed it to her. "News travels fast."

"Probably just a late break-a-leg wish."

"I have a feeling not. Open it."

She tore open the envelope. "You're right. News travels fast. 'Congratulations on your triumph. Await your return with open arms. Love, A.Z.' " She laughed. "The bastard."

He sat across from her and pulled open his black tie. "What are you going to do?"

"I have a six-month contract with the play."

"After that. Tell him to go to hell?"

She picked up the telegram and read it again. "I don't think so. I like World. A.Z.'s a bastard, but other people there have been good to me. Fred. Even Gus in his way. I'll go back to World, but I'm going to hold up the great Alec Zeal. Absolute highway robbery."

"More money?"

"More money. Script approval. I'm not a piece of meat anymore." She looked up from the telegram she'd been studying and saw him staring at her. "You think I'm a bitch?"

"I think you're smart."

"Not where it counts."

"What do you mean?"

She stood and crossed the sitting room to the bedroom. "Nothing. I didn't mean to say that."

He followed her into the bedroom. "Maybe you didn't intend to, but you did. What did you mean?"

"I meant I'm not smart about men."

The scar that bisected his eyebrow had turned white. "Thanks a lot."

She turned away from him and began taking off her bracelets. "Look, Jerry, you know how I feel about you."

He put himself between her and the dresser. "As a matter of fact, I don't."

"The last couple of months have been wonderful. . . ."

"Oh, I get it. 'The last couple of months have been wonderful, Jerry, but now it's over.' Lily's back on top. Well, I just hope this time you do better than that washed-out Polish count or that sadistic middle European director."

She took a step back. "Not to mention a smooth-talking Irishman who made it all the way to the White House fighting for the little guy. Who's so busy fighting for the little guy he hasn't got time for anyone else—conveniently."

"What the hell is that supposed to mean?"

"It means I was stupid. Again. That line about liking to wake up with Lily Hartarski."

"I meant it. I love waking up with you."

"People who like waking up together usually do something about it. Something permanent."

He sat back on the edge of the dresser. "You mean marriage."

She turned away and went and stood in the window. She still hadn't got used to the dazzle of the city without the blackout. Usually it made her hope rise like a comet but not tonight. "Forgive me for using a dirty word."

Behind her the silence was growing, crowding up against her, pushing her out of the warm intimacy of the room into the night beyond. Well, that was all right. She didn't need marriage to Jerry

Crowley. She had all those good reviews and the telegram from A.Z. She had a future again. And there'd always be men in that future.

"Do you mean you want to marry me, Lily?"

"I already apologized for bringing it up. Bad taste."

"You know what you'd be getting yourself into. I wouldn't be around much."

She didn't say anything.

"I'm not rich, Lily. I've got more money than I've ever had, but I'm not rich. Not like those other guys. Not like you, for that matter."

She was still silent.

He crossed the room and stood behind her. "And I'm not a hero like Tom."

"Would you just let it go," she said quietly. "You don't have to make excuses."

"I'm not making excuses. I just never thought of marriage. Especially marriage to you."

"In other words you had a nice girl in mind. Not someone who's slept around Hollywood and the ETO. To think I thought you were different—"

He pulled her around to face him. The gesture wasn't gentle. "I meant I didn't think you'd want to marry me. You're a star, bigger than ever now. I'm still pretty small potatoes."

"I have to hand it to you, Jerry. I've had a lot of lines used on me, but I've never been told I was too good for anyone before."

"Boy, do you go to extremes. All those years you believed every guy who came along. Dressler, that two-bit one-star general—"

"Don't stop now. Throw them all back in my face."

"I'm not throwing anything in your face. I'm trying to talk to you, but these days you're too smart and tough to listen to anyone."

"Oh, I'm listening. And I get the message. If this were a musical, it would be your cue to break into 'It Was Just One of Those Things.'"

"In other words, I'm being banished for the sin of telling the great Lily Hart she's not perfect. Fine, terrific, I'm on my way. I never did like hanging around where I wasn't welcome."

"That's not the way I heard the story," she called after him. "All those heroic beatings you took for getting your foot in the door of those nonunion factories. All that fearless—"

The door slammed on her sentence. She didn't bother to finish it. There was no point now.

Isabel let herself into the house on East Sixty-seventh Street. It was quiet but not empty. A few weeks after the end of the war, her mother had brought her father home from Palm Beach, where he'd been taking it easy ever since his heart attack.

Isabel closed the door behind her. It made a heavy, solid sound. Her high heels clicked quietly across the foyer floor. She imagined she heard an echo. She thought of the way Eliza used to arrive home from work and stand at the door calling to Teddy, who'd come hurling into her arms. She remembered Lily arriving from Hollywood or a USO tour with gossip and presents and reports of a new affair. She tried to recall the dozens of servicemen who'd come for a drink or a meal or a much-needed bed; John Whelan, who'd always seemed to be at a tilt, partly because of his leg, but mostly because Eliza had knocked him for such a loop; Sam, who used to arrive like a party, bearing black market scotch and high spirits; Andy, who, the few times he'd been there, had had the aura of a man just passing through. They crowded around her in the dark foyer, whispering old jokes, echoing laughter that had atrophied long ago. Isabel sat on the bottom step and stared into the darkness. Gradually the tears began to run down her cheeks. Those times would never come again.

43

THE MORNING after the opening of Eliza's play Jerry Crowley took the Congressional Limited back to Washington. He didn't call Lily before he left. Once he reached his office he was too busy. By the time he got home that night she'd already left for the theater, or so he reasoned.

Ten days later he boarded the Congressional Limited for New York. When he checked into his usual suite at the Waldorf, he actually picked up the phone to call her. The receiver felt cold in his hand. He stared at the photograph of her in one of the tabloids he'd bought at the newsstand downstairs. She was with some guy who'd made a bundle on the Norden bomb site, the capitalist son of a bitch. He replaced the receiver in its cradle.

Two days and a dozen meetings later he was checking out of the hotel when he looked up from the desk and saw her. She'd been watching him, but now she turned away quickly. He put his billfold back in his pocket and crossed the lobby to where she was standing in front of the elevators. He came up behind her, standing so close he could smell her perfume. "Hello, Lily."

She turned and rearranged her features in the phoniest imitation of surprise he'd ever seen.

"Come on, Lily, you're not that good an actress." He tried to laugh. The sound was as artificial as her expression.

She smiled. Her mouth tugged down at the corners. It took his heart with it. "You're right. I saw you, but I didn't think you wanted to see me."

He went on staring at her. He was a good negotiator because he always knew when to yield. "That's all I've wanted to do for the past two weeks. I missed you like hell."

"I missed you too."

"It didn't look that way from that picture of you in the *Daily News* a couple of days ago."

She smiled again, and this time there was no tragedy to it. "I went out with him on purpose. I know how you feel about 'capitalist sons of bitches.' "

He took his suitcase from the bellboy, who'd been lingering a few feet away, and steered her into the elevator with his free hand. "I have to warn you about one thing though, Lily."

Her small, even teeth worried her lower lip. She'd always known she was different. Other women were wives and mothers. She was America's mistress. America's and Jerry Crowley's. It wasn't everything, but it was a lot. It was certainly more than she would have had if it hadn't been for the war. She put her arm through his. "You don't have to say it again. I know. You're not the marrying kind."

He folded his hand over hers. "You still aren't listening, Lily. I was going to say that I'm not a violent man, but I'm going to flatten the first person, man or woman, who calls me Mr. Hart."

"Bring the boys home for Christmas!" America demanded, and some of them actually made it in time. There were husbands and sons and brothers around the tree again along with the first bright consumer goods coming off the assembly lines in this brave new postwar world. Suddenly there were things to buy, but suddenly there was less money to buy them. Six and a half million war workers waited apprehensively for a pink slip in the paycheck. Twelve million returning servicemen needed a job. Jerry Crowley had his work cut out for him.

Women, of course, were the first to go. They'd been hired with the warning that they were doing a man's job only until he could return to do it himself. Now newsreels and newspapers and magazines vied to tell them how fortunate they were to return to the home. A woman physician warned against working women who neglected their husbands, deprived their children, and frustrated their own natures, and miraculously, no one suggested that the physician heal herself. Magazines that had spent four years dreaming up quick meals for Rosie the Riveter to feed her family, though never once suggesting that Walter the Welder pitch in and help, now began featuring recipes that were whole afternoons in the making. After all, that was what the returning boys wanted, what they'd fought for, what they were entitled to. A decent job, a little house in the suburbs, a couple of kids, and a wife to manage the last two. It was, women were assured, what they wanted too. When Isabel broadcast the findings of a study revealing that 75 percent of the women who'd taken jobs during the war wanted to keep them, word came down from upstairs to delete the item from the next newscast. She was exacerbating the unemployment problem.

Isabel had problems of her own. The world was entering the postwar era as if it were Noah's Ark. Everyone was in twos. Eliza had Michael again, Lily had Jerry, even her mother had her father, and Spence was waiting for the arrival of his French warbride. Only Isabel was alone.

To be sure, there were plenty of men in her life. They worked beside her, took her to drinks and dinner, the theater and parties. Most of them tried to take her to bed as well, but Isabel wasn't interested. Word got around that Isabel Childs was married to her work. One rejected newsman who had a big but particularly fragile ego insisted she was a lesbian.

Isabel, however, had no doubt about the nature of her desires, and they were beginning to make themselves felt again. She missed Sam. She'd stopped waiting for Andy. And she knew she wasn't going to be true to their memories. As that first postwar Christmas approached, she knew she was shopping for an affair.

Matthew Gardner knew it too, but then Gardner had been watching Isabel for a long time. He thought she'd improved with age. She was more attractive, more confident, and, a consideration for a married man, a little harder.

He complimented her on the first two traits one evening at a noisy cocktail party honoring a returning correspondent. They were standing in a window far above Rockefeller Center, and around and below them New York sparkled in holiday brilliance for the first time in years. The view and the alcohol and the season conspired to bring Gardner a step closer and make Isabel smile up at him. She took a sip of her drink and studied him over the rim of the glass. He was handsome in a dry, impeccable kind of way. He was married. And he didn't give a damn about Isabel. All he wanted from her were good Crossley ratings and an affair.

That was fine with her. She, too, was interested in good Crossley ratings and an affair. Anything more was too dangerous. It left scars.

Gardner suggested they get out of this madhouse and have a quiet dinner. Isabel agreed. Neither of them had any sensation of falling as the elevator descended.

Gardner mentioned the Stork. He'd learned early in life that if he could get a woman on the dance floor, he stood a better chance of getting her into bed. Isabel said the Stork would be fine.

The maitre d' knew them. The waiters fawned on them. The wine was good, the steaks excellent, the music helpful. Isabel began to wonder if Gardner—she'd been calling him Matt all night, but she still thought of him as Gardner—kept a *pied-à-terre* in town. She wasn't quite up to that sofa in his office.

That was when he turned up. He stood there looming over their table and looking down at her.

She'd seen Andy Barnes out of uniform but never in civilian clothes. The dark pin-striped suit—off the rack at Brooks, Isabel guessed—did little for him. He looked young and raw beside Gardner. It would have been better if he hadn't. Isabel's heart went out to him.

She introduced the two men. Andy asked her to dance. Gardner was gracious about it.

She moved into Andy's arms. She couldn't have taken her heart back if she wanted to. His hand exerted a gentle pressure at the small of her back until she closed the distance between them. "That's better," he said, as he had the first time they'd danced.

"How does it feel to be back?" she asked because he'd shown no need for conversation.

"Strange."

There was another silence.

"Have you gone home yet?"

"You mean Connecticut? I lasted for less than a week."

She looked up at him. "Too dull? Too much security?"

"Just too strange," he said again.

"I can't believe Captain Barnes is having trouble readjusting." She was still looking up at him, and something in his face made her regret the words.

"Nothing's the way I expected it to be. Or even the way I remembered it."

The music ended, and he returned her to her table and disappeared into the crowd.

Gardner looked at Isabel and knew he'd been wrong about the dance floor. Or rather he'd been right about its effect, but wrong about the characters. If anyone was going to get her into bed, it would be that ex-flyboy. He signaled for the check and wondered if he ought to drive out to Darien after all and surprise his wife.

Isabel told herself he wouldn't call. She was right. The war was no longer an excuse. Andy Barnes didn't need an excuse. Any more than he needed or wanted ties. Years ago Spence had said if ever a man was made for this war it was Andy Barnes. Now Isabel knew that if ever a war had been made for a man it was Andy Barnes.

She tried to work up some interest in Matthew Gardner, but that was a losing battle. Besides, it was the holiday season, not exactly an auspicious time for an affair with a married man. Everyone was with families and loved ones. Isabel was alone in the sitting room that Sunday evening when Spence stopped on his way out. He was meeting some friends for the first of what would become an annual postwar event, the lighting of the trees along Park Avenue in memory of dead servicemen. "We're going back to Jack Livingston's for supper afterward," Spence said. "He gave me orders to bring you along."

The ceremony was in memory of dead boys, but that night Park Avenue was alive with children. Small girls in velvet-collared coats and leggings and boys with leather hats, the earflaps buttoned down against the winter air, swung excitedly from their parents' hands. A crowd spilled down the steps of the Brick Church and across Park

Avenue, closing it off to traffic. Isabel looked up into the icy night. The church spire pierced an unforgiving black sky. Squares of amber light glowed in the somber apartment houses, silhouetting groups of people who stood looking down at the holiday celebration.

Spence took Isabel's arm and steered her through the mob to a group of half-familiar faces. They belonged to the boys she'd grown up with who were men now, faces carved by experience and punctuated by eyes that had seen too much. The left sleeve of Paul Livingston's coat hung empty from his shoulder. His brother Jack held the hand of a small boy with fat red cheeks. Jack introduced Isabel to his wife, a pretty woman in a mink coat who spoke with the easy cadences of the West Coast. Jack had been stationed in San Francisco for most of the war.

The carol singing began. They worked their way through "Hark, the Herald Angels Sing," "O Little Town of Bethlehem," and "Silent Night." Then the minister standing at the top of the church stairs led them in prayer in memory of those who'd died in the war. Mothers hushed overexcited children, and men stood with bare heads bowed. A soldier stepped forward from the choir and played taps. The notes floated achingly thin and lonely over the silent crowd and disappeared into the cold night. An older woman beside Isabel took a handkerchief from the pocket of her fur coat. The man beside her bit his lip. Isabel felt the tears welling up. Sam should be here, making his silly jokes and singing his heart out because he loved lights and people and life. Sam, who, as he'd put it when they'd first met, had had an absurd but sincere desire to see the end of the war.

She felt Spence's hand on her shoulder and covered it with her own. Only then did she realize it wasn't Spence. She turned. Andy Barnes was standing behind her.

Taps ended. His hand remained on her shoulder. From the steps of the church the minister cried, "Let there be light," and all the way down the avenue trees glittered to life. The choir broke into "Joy to the World," and the crowd joined in. All except Isabel and Andy. He stood there looking down at her. "I heard about your friend, Wicker," he said finally. "I didn't know last time I saw you. I'm sorry."

She remembered the time in England when his nightmare had

awakened her, and she'd said she was sorry. He hadn't wanted her sympathy then, and she didn't want his now. "The war," she said, and shrugged. His hand fell from her shoulder.

"The war's over."

"The war's over," she repeated, "but you're not the only one who's having a hard time getting over the war."

She took her hand from her pocket and held it out to him. "Merry Christmas," she said. The words sounded like goodbye. She turned and began walking down Park Avenue. Behind her the crowd had reached "Deck the Hall." Husbands and wives, parents and children raised jubilant voices to the winter night. "Fa la la la la." The sound followed Isabel down the street like a jeering crowd.

She quickened her step. Park Avenue stretched before her, a black canyon leading to the cold heart of the city, the scene of her life, her work, her success. On the trees, lights glistened like ice. The wind whipped at her hair. She turned her coat collar up and jammed her hands back in her pockets.

She felt his presence beside her before she saw him. He matched his step to hers, his own hands jammed into the pockets of his coat. They took several blocks in silence. Their strides were disparate, and every now and then they fell out of step with each other. Then one of them caught up. Isabel had a feeling that was the way it would always be.